Melody

A Novel

ALSO BY STACY-DEANNE
Everlasting

Melody

A Novel

STACY-DEANNE

STREBOR BOOKS

NEW YORK LONDON TORONTO SYDNEY

SBI

Strebor Books
P.O. Box 6505
Largo, MD 20792
http://www.streborbooks.com

ISBN 978-1-59309-204-7
ISBN 978-1-4165-7887-1 (e-book)
LCCN 2008925332

First Strebor Books trade paperback edition June 2008

Cover design: www.mariondesigns.com
Cover photograph: © Keith Saunders/Marion Designs

10 9 8 7 6 5 4 3 2 1

Manufactured in the United States of America

For information regarding special discounts for bulk purchases,
please contact Simon & Schuster Special Sales at 1-866-506-1949
or business@simonandschuster.com

The Simon & Schuster Speakers Bureau can bring authors to your
live event. For more information or to book an event, contact the
Simon & Schuster Speakers Bureau at 1-866-248-3049 or visit our
website at www.simonspeakers.com.

To my mother, Elva,
You were my mother, sister and best friend.
There is not a moment that goes by that I do not miss you.
You went through all of my journeys with me and
creating Melody was one of them. Melody is the
most favorite story I've ever written so it's only fitting
to dedicate it to you. I love you endlessly.
We will be together again some day.
I hope I continue to make you proud.
Elva N. Reed (RIP)
(1946-2006)

Acknowledgments

I would like to send out a special thanks to everyone at Strebor and Simon & Schuster. Thanks for making writers' dreams come true. Special thanks to Zane, you are a phenomenal woman and you've used your expertise and knowledge to bring other writers to the forefront. It means a lot that you appreciate my work. It's been a pleasure working with you.

To Charmaine Parker, thanks for being a shining light for us authors while we go through publication, editing and just plain waiting. I've had a lot of questions and you never hesitated to help me along. Thanks for always being cheerful, positive and for the time you spend helping authors' books to reach their final stage. I know the job of helping us all can't be easy, and it is not taken for granted.

Last, but not least, thanks to the readers for picking up this book. I hope you enjoy it. I wrote it for all of you.

Chapter One

Melody Cruz hated to make assumptions. Yet what else could she think? She smelled his overpowering cologne, still she didn't turn around. She could feel Keith's presence as he entered her bedroom. Already this had been *too* much.

"What are you doing in my room?" She cuddled her bare bosom. "Answer me, Keith!" He didn't. "What's your problem?" What *was* his problem? Here she stood half-naked while his eyes fondled every part of her body. "Just go away, please." She shook. "Please go back into the living room."

She had no idea what to make of this. He'd been one of the most attractive men she'd ever seen. His alluring green eyes rested within his creamy tanned skin. His magnificent dark hair completed the picture of perfection. Yet something about Keith Taylor seemed off. Even his good looks weren't enough to keep Melody's mind off his latest action.

She sensed that her being frightened turned him on. He took deep, hollowed breaths. She imagined him smirking. His handsome face flushed with demented delight.

How could she feel this way about a man she'd just met? What did he want? Something about him brought out fear that she couldn't explain. Already she felt his mind controlling her emotions.

She still refused to look at him. Even at twenty-three years old Melody felt uncomfortable about being naked in front of men. A familiar self-consciousness awoke inside of her. Her body shut down beyond her control.

Keith panted loudly through deep grunts. Melody's knees knocked, her fingers sweat and her body ached from anxiety.

"Mmm...*beautiful*," he whispered. She heard him crack his knuckles, while she envisioned cracking his *neck*. Suddenly the breathing sound disappeared. His cologne drifted from the room. She took a deep breath, realizing he'd left. She retrieved her blouse and went to the hall. She wanted to glance down the stairs before locking her bedroom door. "Oh my God," she sighed. Talk about a lasting first impression.

Her sister, Sarah, always managed to attract the oddest men on the planet. Melody wasn't surprised that Keith Taylor made Sarah's list of latest lovers. Melody picked up on Keith's disturbed nature the first time she laid eyes on him. She wouldn't dare leave her room until Sarah arrived. Luckily she didn't have to wait. She heard Sarah rushing upstairs.

"Hey, Mel, you in there?" Sarah knocked.

"Uh, just a minute." Did she sound nervous? She didn't

want to sound nervous. She ran to the door and the thought of their parents entered her mind. Melody never could understand why they forced their way into her head at the oddest times. Maybe it was a sign. She always had the feeling they looked over her and Sarah from heaven. She needed that comfort right now. If not now then when?

She barely remembered their parents. They'd died in a car crash when Melody was three and Sarah was six. They were the result of a biracial romance; a Latino mother and a white father. That may have explained Sarah's undying interest in white lovers. Melody couldn't remember Sarah ever dating a Latino guy. They were so different that Melody often had to convince herself that they were sisters.

Sarah had blonde hair and shimmering green eyes. She didn't have a single Latino feature. Melody, on the other hand, couldn't have looked white if you doused her in flour. She had dark skin, long dark hair, dark brown eyes and thick luscious lips to match. Melody had been graced with height. Her father had been very tall as well. Sarah took her height from their mother, who had to stand on boxes to grab cans from the kitchen cabinet.

Melody equated her parents' differences with the differences between her and her older sister. They were equally beautiful in different ways. Melody kept their mother's maiden name, Cruz. Sarah went by their father's name,

Johnson. Melody was the sensitive, self-conscious one. Sarah was the strong, confident, successful one. They both had big hearts but wanted different things out of life.

Melody just wanted to be happy. She didn't care about materialistic things or money. She could live in a shoe if she had someone truly special to share it with. Sarah's idea of love relied on a man's looks, money and status. She was independent, make no mistake. But Sarah *lived* for men. She based her entire existence on what men thought of her. She didn't seem to feel complete without some man's attention.

The sisters were separated after their parents died. Their uncle only wanted Sarah, claiming he couldn't afford to take care of two small girls. Melody had long ago dismissed his excuse. How much more could it have cost to take care of a three-year-old, anyway? Melody got stuck being raised by Aunt Lucia who had never been able to take hold of her bills, let alone her devastating mental problems. If Lucia's mental state ran in the family, Melody wondered if she'd snap, too, one day. Sometimes she felt insanity would be an improvement.

Sarah acquired the best of everything. She dated the best-looking men and wore the best-looking clothes. She got *all* the attention, always. A gorgeous blonde beauty? Melody couldn't compete. She didn't want to, and she didn't try. She loved Sarah deeply, and they were extremely close. Sarah had always been there for her. Melody would have done anything for her. She just couldn't understand Sarah's obsession for pleasing the men in her life.

Melody opened the door and fell into Sarah's arms. Sarah rocked her back and forth. Keith had given her the fright of her life. No need in wasting time. Melody would have to tell Sarah about Keith before Sarah fell in love with him.

"Sarah...uh..." Melody panted.

"Hey, baby sis, what's wrong?" Sarah squinted. She playfully wrapped a chunk of Melody's hair around her finger. "I love to be hugged but this doesn't feel right, Mel."

Melody struggled to force out the words. She couldn't imagine how silly she would sound. "Sarah, Keith...he..."

"Oh yes! Let me tell you about Keith." Sarah giggled. "He is the absolute greatest guy in the world!"

"No Sarah, listen to me..."

"Oh he's made me the happiest woman in the world. Sit down Mel, and let me tell you what he did for me." *Let me tell you what he did* to *me, Melody thought.*

"Sarah, please listen, okay? Look, Keith..."

"He heard about me not being able to take those college courses and guess what?" Sarah rubbed Melody's arm, which irritated her newfound goose bumps.

"What?" Melody moaned. She hoped her attitude would signal some hint to Sarah. She gave up interrupting her big sister. No one could stop Sarah when she gloated about yet another one of her "new men."

"He's paying for my courses, Mel. Isn't that wonderful?"

"How?" Melody glanced around the room. "Those courses are running from fourteen thousand and up."

"I know but he had money saved up from a trust fund. And he gave it to me." Sarah leaned over in a flirtatious pose. "Wasn't that just the sweetest most considerate thing you've ever heard? I love him, Mel." Melody now had cause to worry. If Sarah had fallen in love with Keith she couldn't burst her bubble by telling her what had just happened. But what could she do? Let Sarah believe that this obvious prick could be the man of her dreams?

Melody took a deep breath. Once again her obligation to Sarah's feelings would win over common sense. She couldn't hurt her. The only thing she could do would be to stay away from Keith. She wouldn't give him the opportunity to be a jerk again.

"What were you going to tell me?" Sarah ran her fingers through her long, thick blonde crinkles. Melody looked at her own hair in the mirror. She'd have died for an ounce of the features Sarah had.

She found herself attractive, but Sarah had been blessed with the looks of a medieval goddess. She had always been the prettiest sister no matter what Melody did. Melody found it funny that she'd never been jealous of the attention Sarah got from men. Or maybe she had been and didn't give into it. She thought of Keith. Had she temporarily given into his twisted perversion? She abruptly dismissed the thought.

Funny how Keith had Sarah yet he had come into Melody's bedroom to get a glimpse of her naked. He knew she'd come up here to change. He probably had it in his mind to follow her the minute she walked in the door. Could this be the first time in their lives that a man preferred her to Sarah? If she hadn't been so afraid of Keith, she would've tempted the situation.

Of course she couldn't hurt Sarah by banging her new boyfriend. But it would have been interesting to see what a man saw in her and not in Sarah. She shook away the thoughts. Sarah rambled on about things Melody could not care less about. What had she been thinking? Sarah had always looked out for her. For that, she'd protect Sarah from knowing what Keith had done.

"Oh Mel, I'm so happy." Sarah sashayed to the mirror. "You think I'm gaining weight?" She turned around to check out her figure. Sarah had such a beautiful shape that a little more weight wouldn't hurt her. On the other hand, Melody looked like a stick with legs. She smiled. At least God blessed her with a full bosom. That had been something Sarah had always missed. "Okay, what were you going to tell me when you practically attacked me a while ago?" Sarah grinned.

"Uh, is Keith still downstairs?" Melody walked to the dresser.

Sarah held her hair in a pile on top of her head. "No, he left. So you never told me."

Melody stared into the hallway. "Told you what?" she mumbled.

"Jesus, snap out of it, Mel!" Sarah shook her. "What do you think of Keith, dummy? He's hot, isn't he?" Sarah rubbed her breasts.

"Who has time to think? You have so many guys I can't keep up."

Sarah grimaced. "Funny, Miss Thang. But seriously, I need to know your opinion, Mel."

"Believe me, you don't want my true opinion, Sarah."

She stared at her. "And what the hell does that mean? You got a problem with Keith?"

She wanted to tell her what a pervert he seemed to be. He reminded Melody of some horny yuppie, college-educated moron with a flashy bank account. She still couldn't bring herself to hurt Sarah's feelings. Sarah and Aunt Lucia had been the only family Melody truly had. She wished she could tell her the truth, though. She became nauseated seeing Sarah drool about Keith. Yep, she'd definitely stay away from him from now on.

She thought of those prime-time cop shows. Why bother mentioning what had happened if it didn't mean anything? Keith hadn't touched her. He hadn't really done anything except spy. What man wouldn't spy on a young woman? Maybe she had *assumed* he'd come up there for that. Maybe he thought her room had been the bathroom. She bit her tongue. She couldn't even sell the idea to herself.

If it hadn't been strange, how come she felt so violated? How come she got the feeling he'd followed her on purpose? Melody wasn't used to feeling this helpless. She looked at her sister. She'd never seen Sarah glow when she spoke of any man like she did today. Keith could be in Sarah's life forever. And Melody didn't have the will to stop it.

She'd never been so confused. She wouldn't dwell on what had happened any longer. It would be worthless to tell if he hadn't really done anything. Besides, Sarah seemed to think Keith walked on water.

"Baby girl, you're still shaking." Sarah rubbed her shoulders.

"Yeah, yeah, I, uh...I just had a small fright. It's nothing now."

"You sure?" Sarah's angelic eyes studied Melody's face.

"Yeah, I'm sure." Melody smiled. "So, tell me more about Keith."

❀❀❀

Melody had to talk to someone. She couldn't get the Keith episode out of her head to save her life. Luckily, she had two best friends in the wings. Her homegirl Aileen had been the first choice. Since Aileen had her own problems to deal with right now, Melody decided not to burden her. She also got the feeling that a male friend would be the better choice. She secretly called Craig over after Sarah went to take a nap.

Craig could give her insight on why a guy would act

the way Keith had. He'd help Melody decide if she *had* overreacted, or if Keith could be the biggest creep of the century. No matter what he would say, it couldn't wait. She laid out a spread of donuts and coffee. He might have been a twenty-four-year-old artist but Craig Banks had the appetite of a fifty-year-old cop.

Craig and Melody were close as two friends of the opposite sex could be. So she knew she could trust his opinions. He arrived a few minutes after she set up the food. She opened the front door to Craig swatting flies from around the porch light. He wore that tan shirt she loved. The porch light sparkled against his blond hair. This had to be the strangest day in the world, she thought.

Melody checked to see if she saw a full moon as she opened the door. First, she'd endured Keith's craziness. Now she found herself looking at Craig in a way she hadn't in years. They'd dated a little in school, then agreed that being friends was better for the both of them. It had been times like these that made Melody rethink their decision. She just couldn't stop staring at him.

He looked so inviting. Those baby-blue eyes silently seduced her. A small breeze floated between them. She enjoyed the calmness of the moment. She loved life in Albany, New York. May's weather enhanced her appreciation for the laid-back city.

"Hey, come on in." She hoped she didn't look too much like a flake.

He yawned. "Mel, is this uh…" He grinned. "One of your 'Craig' moments?"

He rubbed his chin.

She grinned. "'Craig moments'? I have no idea what you mean."

"You know exactly what I mean." He smirked. "One of those moments when you expect me to save your sanity or at least your life?" He touched her chin. "You know I'm always here when you need me, Mel. But I gotta tell you that your phone call almost made me shit my pants. Thought I'd come here to find you swimming in a pool of blood."

"Craig, could you for once let someone tell you what they want before thinking you know all the answers?" She walled her eyes. "I can't tell you how annoying that is."

"Well, I've been doing it for years, so you should be used to it by now." He grinned.

"Silly ass, no." She sighed. She'd forgotten that Craig could be a top-notch asshole at times, too.

"Ah!" He laughed. "You called me a 'silly ass' in Spanish? You *must* be pissed if you're speaking words of your motherland," he teased.

She laughed. "Would you shut up and stop being such an asshole? God I don't know why I care about you so much."

"Well, I…shit doughnuts." He ran to the snacks. "I'm here for you as long as the doughnuts and coffee is." He bit into the glazed chocolate-filled one. "Mmm, this is my favorite. So what's up?" She sat beside him.

"Remember this morning when I said I met Keith, Sarah's boyfriend, at Caper Enterprises?" Craig nodded.

"I told you I didn't like his attitude and thought something may have been off with him. You remember that?"

He licked his lips. "Of course, I remember, it was just this morning. What am I, eighty years old? I don't have Alzheimer's yet, Mel." He mumbled while chewing.

"Well, you said I wasn't giving him a fair chance. And that I always judge Sarah's boyfriends before getting to know them." Melody twiddled her fingers.

He wiped crumbs on the thighs of his jeans. "Here we go. Did I say you always did this or didn't I say it? Mel, don't start with all of this again. You need to get yourself some help. You don't want to share Sarah with anyone, do you? Give the guy a break. Maybe he's just an asshole. She'll figure it out."

"Craig, this is not like those other times. Okay, I have never liked Sarah's boyfriends but I had cause." He walled his eyes. "All of them have been jerks, I'm telling you! I don't know where she meets these guys, *Creeps R Us*?" Craig grinned.

"But none of them hold a candle to Keith Taylor. Something, uh…happened."

Craig grabbed another doughnut. "What happened, Mel?"

She exhaled. "Craig, he saw me…*naked*." He dropped the doughnut on Sarah's pristine carpet. "Watch it, Craig!" Melody rushed to clean it up. "Sarah turns into Kathy Bates in *Misery* if she sees one crumb on this floor."

"Fuck the doughnut, okay?" He gasped. "How the

fuck did he see you naked? Even when we went out, *I* didn't."

She sighed. "Craig it was the most frightening thing I have ever experienced. He didn't touch me but it was just like he had. I have never been that afraid. The minute I knew he was there I just got this fear that I couldn't control. It overtook my entire body. I shut down, Craig! I couldn't even move and my words shook. I didn't think people could have that kind of power over someone until I met Keith Taylor."

He stared in midair. "What exactly happened?"

"Keith had been waiting here when I got home. He said Sarah had given him a key and told him to come by. So, of course you can imagine how pissed I was to find a man I'd just met this morning sitting in my own living room. I went in my room to change and the next thing I knew he was up there too. I didn't know what to think."

"What kind of shit is that?" Craig grimaced. "Did you tell Sarah?"

"I couldn't." She twiddled her fingers to subdue the tension of rehashing the Keith episode. It didn't work. Nothing seemed to get her mind off that moment.

"You have to tell her, Mel! Who knows what could have happened!"

"I just couldn't, Craig. She's too into him already and it seems pathetic. Look, Sarah isn't happy that often and I can't take that away. Especially when I don't know what the hell exactly happened!"

He shook his head. "It makes no difference, Mel. She needs to know what kind of guy he is. This man is a creep. If I can tell just by what you say, then I know he's up to no good. What kind of man goes into a woman's bedroom like that? I can only think of one kind and most of them end up behind bars, Melody."

She chewed her thumb. "Maybe I misunderstood his actions. Maybe he was just looking for the bathroom."

"Oh yeah." Craig sniggered. "And he just happened to stop into your bedroom along the way, huh? Believe me, Mel. If a man goes into a woman's bedroom you can believe he intended to." So far Craig's theory hadn't comforted her the way she hoped. Why couldn't she stop thinking about it? It seemed like Keith continued to violate her privacy as the day went on. "Melody, don't go thinking like this is your fault, all right?

It's just not normal, baby. You didn't need me to tell you that."

"I suppose not," she sighed.

"So, what's the deal? You gotta tell Sarah before it's too late. I got a feeling that Keith is someone who needs to be out of the picture, as soon as possible."

"Craig, I'm gonna let it go." She shrugged. "I mean, I can't hurt Sarah over one incident."

He scoffed. "You still trying to make yourself believe that what happened wasn't what you think happened?" He shook his head. "Mel, we've known each other for years, and I've never seen someone stop you from doing what's right." She ignored his gaze.

"Go tell Sarah right now. You know that's the only choice you have. If the tables were turned and your boyfriend looked at Sarah…"

She scoffed. "My boyfriends *do* look at Sarah. That's why they don't stay my boyfriends for long."

"Do I look like I am kidding, Mel? This shit is serious. No telling how far this guy will go next time. Okay today, he watched you undress. What's next, he puts his hands on you?"

"Oh no, he wouldn't do that."

"How the hell do you know?" Craig grinned. "Did you know he'd come up to your room today, too? I know you're scared. If not, you wouldn't have begged me to come over here. You know what needs to be done so do it, Melody. If not, then don't mention this ever again. Damn, I'd love to meet this guy and give him a piece of my mind."

She looked at him. "Is it because you care? Or because you're *jealous*?"

He unconvincingly scoffed and tugged on his earring. "Of course, I care. I may even be a *little* jealous."

"I knew it!" She laughed. She valued Craig's friendship like nothing else. Yet, she missed those times when they did more than talk.

"Melody, this is serious." He sighed. "Are you okay?"

She smiled. "Yeah."

"You sure he didn't touch you? You can tell me if he did."

"No, I'm fine, thanks."

A noise interrupted them from upstairs. Sarah walked into the den. She had endured a very hard week working and going to school. She did her best to provide Melody with decent support as well as a suitable place to live. Most sisters couldn't be in the same room with each other for a minute—let alone live together. Melody felt blessed to share such a friendship with Sarah. No matter what else happened they could always count on each other.

"Hey," Sarah said as she stretched. She flinched until her eyes adjusted to the light. She looked great even after a hard nap. Craig shook his head. Melody didn't have to guess. Sarah and Craig were already on their way to another one of their famous confrontations. Sarah hadn't forgiven Craig for dumping Melody in high school. Melody hated seeing them fuss like children, yet it brought a certain spark to their relationship.

She wondered if the tension could be mistaken for sexual chemistry. She chuckled. It would have been interesting to see Craig and Sarah succumb to such a fantasy. Melody wouldn't have been surprised if Craig found Sarah attractive. He'd be the only man in the free world who didn't.

"Craig," Sarah sighed. "What a lovely surprise." She acted as if the statement would eventually choke her. "You're here and eating our food…like always." She walled her eyes.

"Nice to see you, too, Sarah." He stood. "Don't worry. I was just leaving, baby."

Melody definitely saw chemistry between them. She wondered why she paid so much attention to Craig these days. Could she still be in love with him after all this time? Had her friendship with him been just an excuse to hang on? Craig slapped Melody's back. She juggled from her thoughts.

"I swear, no one daydreams like you, Mel." Craig kissed her cheek and smiled at Sarah. "So did Your Highness enjoy her royal nap?"

Sarah faked a smile. "I'm not in the mood to get into anything with you, Craig."

He shrugged. "No, you're never in the mood for me are you, Sarah?" He went to the door. "Bye, lovelies. Mel, you know what you need to do." She waved.

"Bye, Craig." Sarah waved. "And thanks for stopping by unannounced, like you always do." He left. "He's such an asshole." Sarah noticed crumbs on the carpet.

"Mel, I swear I could get a Saint Bernard who'd keep things cleaner than you do."

Melody cleaned the spot she'd missed. "How was your nap?"

"Restless." She sighed. "I kept waking up before Keith kissed me." She grinned.

Melody walled her eyes. "I'm sure you'll dream about him again. Sarah, I really need to uh…talk to you."

"Mel, how can you be friends with Craig after what he did?"

"I admit, he might not have been the right boyfriend for me but he is the right friend."

"Please." Sarah took a doughnut. "Stop kidding yourself. He's only your friend because he doesn't want to cut the strings completely. He's scared to really let you go."

"And what's wrong with not wanting to let someone go?" Sarah looked at her.

"We all hold onto some things, Sarah." Sarah licked powdered sugar from her thumb.

Melody thought of Keith. "You understand what I mean, Sarah? We all hold onto things even if we don't need to."

"Melody, why the hell are you talking in riddles today? What's your problem? I mean you've been acting like a nutcase since this evening. If something is on your mind, I wish you'd be woman enough to tell me about it."

"It's just so hard to say this. Sarah, I don't want you to think that I'm trying to run your life. I truly want you to be happy and..."

She slapped Melody's lap. "I think I know why you're acting so weird today, baby girl."

"Uh, why?" Melody stared.

"Lucas Lawson." Sarah winked.

Melody grinned coyly. "Lucas Lawson? Where did that come from?"

"Well, Keith works at Caper Enterprises under Lucas' father."

"So?"

"Well, when you went up there did you see Lucas himself?" Sarah chuckled.

Melody grinned. "Maybe. Okay, it was sort of like fate. Imagine seeing someone you've really missed after all this time, Sarah." She smiled. "Can you believe he's even more handsome now than he was back then? Maybe it's time we got together again. We were so close growing up. Well, until I dropped out of school."

Sarah nodded. "I have to admit, Lucas Lawson was the cutest guy you hung with."

"And not to mention him being the son of very wealthy parents never hurt anything either." Sarah laughed. Melody hit her head. "Wait, now I'm sounding like the gold digger you are."

"Hey!" Sarah laughed. "I'm not a gold digger, okay. I support myself and there is nothing wrong with wanting a guy to spend money on you. Melody, you should really give Lucas a chance. I mean, not many women have a man like Lucas after them."

"Oh please, that was a long time ago, Sarah. We were in high school. Before it used to be the four of us— Lucas, Craig, Aileen and me. Sure, Lucas and I flirted with the idea of getting together but if it was meant to be we would have, right?"

"Look, you were a teenager then and you were with Craig." Sarah walled her eyes. "For what, I don't know. Everything's different now. You're a woman and Lucas is a man." She laughed.

"Thanks for clearing that up for me, Sarah." Melody grinned.

"Seriously, if fate threw you two back together, he could truly be the one, Mel."

"Somehow I'm not convinced."

"You'd be a fool not to be. The man is prime-A material, Melody. And I got the feeling many women want him. If he wants you, I wouldn't fuck things up by being too damn slow. A man like Lucas won't wait forever."

"Which proves my point. If he can't wait for me, then he isn't the one for me." Melody stuck her head into the air.

Sarah chuckled. "You know, you got this goody two-shoes thing happening, and it really gets on my nerves."

Melody laughed. "He's just not my type, okay? Let's drop it."

"And what is? A starving fair-haired artist who dumped you?"

Melody sighed. "What happened between Craig and me is none of your business."

"Really? You didn't say that when I dried your tears after he stepped all over your heart, back then."

"And as a matter of fact, if Lucas and I do get together it will be none of your business, either! I don't say anything about the dicks you bring home so don't say anything to me!" Melody rushed to the stairs. Sarah ran after her.

"Wait!" Sarah pulled her back. "If you'd come back to reality, you can see I only said what I did because I love you, Mel." Melody jerked away from her. "Mel, what's going on? What happened to you today? Why are you acting like this?"

"No…nothing happened, Sarah."

"Bullshit, you've been shaking since I got home this evening. What did Craig mean when he said '*you know what you need to do*'? Mel, you know we don't need to keep secrets from one another."

"Sarah, this has just been a very hectic day. And I…"

Sarah hugged her. "Look I'm sorry, okay? You've obviously got something on your mind today, and all I've done is teased you." She pushed Melody's hair behind her ears. "*Todo será de todos los derechos*, sis. You need to loosen up, Mel. I think I got the perfect thing for you. It's part of the reason I wanted to know how you felt about Lucas." She beamed.

"What's going on?"

"I forgot to tell you that I'm going out with Keith and Lucas tonight." Sarah shrugged. "I told them that you'd be joining us."

"What? Oh hell no! Forget it, Sarah. You had no right to do that without asking me. How many times do I have to tell you that I don't need you to construct a social life for me? If I want to go out on dates, I'll set them up myself."

"Melody, any other day I would've let it slide, but you need to get out of the house! You're so wound up you can't even breathe!"

"Sarah, I don't have time for this. I've been looking for a job for a week straight. I'm so tired I could sleep for months." Melody wondered if Sarah had been born this blind? Couldn't she see that Keith made Melody uncomfortable? Couldn't she see that everything had been fine before she brought her new boyfriend from hell into the picture? Melody would have to tell her what happened *now*. She wouldn't be able to stay composed through dinner. She sure as hell couldn't go. "Sarah, we need to talk about Keith once and for all."

"What about him?"

"I think he's kind of strange to be honest."

"Okay, I know he's a little weird but that's just his way. He's a very nice guy once you get to know him."

"To be honest, Sarah, I don't *want* to get to know him."

"And why not?" Sarah scoffed. Melody readied herself for another argument.

"For one reason, he's flirty and sneaky."

"Oh!" Sarah laughed. "He winked at you or something, right? He does that with everyone, Mel. He's just that kind of guy. He's very handsome, so whatever he does, women take it the wrong way."

"Once again your mouth is moving when you need to be listening, Sarah. Do you know what you are getting into? How much do you really know about Keith Taylor?"

"Damn it, Mel, you always do this shit!"

"Look, you asked me what I thought of Keith and I'm finally telling you! I asked a simple question, and if you can't answer it, then that says a lot about how much you probably don't even know about him!"

She looked at her long, manicured fingernails. "Why should I be surprised at this coming from you, Mel?

You've never liked any of my men so why would you like Keith?"

"Oh, would you stop being so damn melodramatic, Sarah? You can't see the signs but I do! Something is wrong with him. You may think he's the man of your dreams but I see something you should be aware of."

"And you're an expert on men because…" Melody walled her eyes. "Tell me Melody, when's the last time you had a boyfriend?"

"Just because I don't have a different guy every week doesn't mean I never had a boyfriend, does it? I, unlike you, wait to let relationships grow. I don't sign myself off to the first man who gives me head!"

"Oh, take that back!"

"I won't! If you didn't want to know how I felt about Keith then you shouldn't have asked. I don't like him and I probably never will!" Melody stood from the stairs. "I don't want him in this house ever again."

"Let me fill you in on something in case you've forgotten. I took you in when Aunt Lucia went bonkers, Mel. I've been supporting you all this time. Don't you think I deserve a little respect? The least you could be is happy for me. "

"This isn't about respect, Sarah! Baby, something is off with him. Keith is a creep!"

"Oh yeah, like, Tom was a creep? And Mitch was a creep? And Benjamin was a real creep?"

Melody sighed. "Sarah, listen to me. I'd never say something just to hurt you but I got a feeling about him that's not going away."

"Well, let me tell you what to do about your feelings, sis. You can sit on them because they don't matter when they come to Keith, okay? So just mind your damn business, and stop trying to make my life as lonely and pathetic as yours!" She ran upstairs to her room. Melody stomped in a second later.

"You won't listen because you know I'm right, Sarah! I know you've seen some signs but you won't admit it!"

Sarah got on her knees in the closet. "Pass me my black heels."

"Sarah, I..."

"Pass me my shoes."

Melody threw them at her. "Sarah, I don't think I said anything wrong. It's not my fault you can't take an opinion different from yours. Why are you being such a bitch about all this?"

"Maybe I've had it up to here with your disapproval! If I like a guy, it shouldn't be up to you. You don't even know Keith. How can you judge him like this? What could he have said or done already that makes you dislike him?" Sarah held her hips. Melody knew from that moment on it didn't matter what she said. Sarah's mind wouldn't budge when it came to Keith.

"Fine Sarah, fuck it, okay." She gaped. "It's your life, isn't it? And you're right. It shouldn't be up to me to choose the men in your life." Sarah nodded. "But don't say I didn't warn you."

"Melody, what in the hell are you talking about?" Sarah squinted.

She shrugged. "What does it matter, huh? I'm through with it. I just want you to be happy."

"If that were true, you'd lay off and understand how much he means to me, Mel." She exhaled. "I'm not trying to be bitchy. I just want you to understand that Keith's different from the others, Mel. Please give him a chance. I feel he could be the one. I've never felt like this before. Please don't take this away from me now."

"Like I said, I'd never hurt you, Sarah." Melody sighed.

"Please come to dinner with me, Melody. Let Keith prove to you how wrong you are about him." Melody looked at her. "I know you just got the wrong impression. First impressions are a bitch." Sarah chuckled. "Once you get to know him, you'll love him just as much as I do. Mel, you're twenty-three. Don't you want to see what life has to offer you with Lucas?"

She knew Sarah told the truth. Melody had to start living a life of excitement before it was too late. Maybe Lucas would be the key. She'd endure one night with Keith just to see where things would lead with Lucas Lawson. They'd always been close, even though Melody felt she hadn't been in his league. Lucas had been the richest boy in school. Hell, he'd been the richest person she'd ever known. He came from a long line of successful people. She had nothing to offer Lucas.

She wasn't the greatest catch. Melody had dealt with deep problems in her life. She even thought of herself as crazy sometimes. She amazed herself at how she could live with the mental setbacks she'd had in the past. She'd always been known for taking the easy way out when things got hard. She'd dropped out of school without a second thought because it had been difficult juggling schooling while combating the hassles of teen life. She'd never been one to deal with trauma. Sometimes she ended up paying for the consequences. What would the fabulous Lucas Lawson think about that?

Sarah shook her. "Earth to Mel." She laughed. "Boy, you got this daydreaming down to a T, don't you? Anyway, Lucas told me that he wants you to see his father about a job at Caper Enterprises."

"No, Sarah."

"I told him you'd definitely consider it."

"Damn it, I don't need you to keep running my life, Sarah!"

"You aren't in a position to say no since you haven't had a job in I can't tell when. I can't continue to pay for everything on my own, Melody. You aren't getting any answers from the jobs you've applied to, so I took the initiative. As long as this is my home, I think I have the right to ask you to contribute the best way you can."

"Bullshit, Sarah. You just want me to start seeing Lucas. This also means I'll be working with Keith if I get the job. So I suppose you think it would help my opinion of him? Fat chance. I've seen what I need to see, and my opinion will never change."

She slipped into her black silk dress. Melody had always been obsessed with that dress. Sarah always pointed out Melody's lanky, long frame to discourage her from borrowing it. "You're just afraid you won't be able to contain yourself when you're working with Lucas. How would it look if his father walked in and caught you two doing it on Lucas's desk?"

"Sarah, you must have forgotten that you're the fast one and not me."

Sarah laughed. "Funny, but you know what he told me when I saw him the other day, Mel? He said he's looking for someone to 'share' his future with. You know, like a wife? Could be you." Melody turned away. "Please, little sis, come with me. You and Lucas can discuss the job and you can get to know him, again. I bet he hasn't changed."

Sarah flipped her hair off her shoulders. "You're going."

Melody chuckled. "Excuse me? Since when do you tell me what to do?"

"I'm ordering you to come with us *and* accept that job. That's final."

Melody sighed. "I don't believe I'm doing this."

"Believe it." Sarah winked.

Chapter Two

The guys picked them up right on time. Thank goodness Albany's nighttime traffic took pity on them. Melody discovered some interesting qualities about Lucas on the way to Jayson's restaurant. He'd grown from an interesting teenager to a very charming young man with a strong head for business. They spent the ride catching up on his life. He looked dashing in his black shirt and slacks. They reached the restaurant too early in Melody's opinion.

She couldn't fathom anything being more interesting than talking to Lucas. The way he looked at her told her he felt the same way. Maybe Sarah had been right. Maybe them meeting up again had been fate. Melody couldn't figure out how she could feel so close to someone she hadn't been around in years. It seemed only yesterday that they were teenagers running through the school courtyard.

Now they were adults making lifelong decisions. Melody anticipated where the night might lead. She'd let down her guard and enjoy the night with no further worries. She'd also do her best to ignore Sarah's new boyfriend along the way.

"You ladies look as scrumptious as the food." Keith kissed Sarah's hand. He seemed to hold it too tight, Melody thought. She tried to figure out if they were sleeping together or not. If they weren't, something told her it wouldn't be long. Melody faked a smile for Lucas despite being disgusted by Keith. Keith flashed Melody that gorgeous smile. Charming or not, she wouldn't give him the benefit of the doubt about today's incident.

"Melody, you look so beautiful. Man, I can't believe we're sitting here like this after all this time." Lucas smiled through perfect teeth.

He hadn't changed a bit unless you count the fact that he'd grown more gorgeous. He ran his hands through his dark hair. Those magnificent half-Italian features ran rampant to anyone he passed. He reminded Melody of those suave men from classic films. She loved to curl up in front of a Cary Grant film every now and then. She wondered what tickled Lucas's fancy when it came to relaxation.

Melody smiled at Lucas's compliment. "Thank you, Lucas. It took me a while to figure out what to wear, seeing how I didn't know I was even going out tonight." She glanced at Sarah. Sarah obviously caught the hint in Melody's voice. Melody ignored Keith's cunning glance. Already she had the capacity to hate this man beyond belief.

"Luke, I believe we got the two most beautiful women in the restaurant." Keith laid his arm on the back of Sarah's chair. "What more could a man want, huh?"

Lucas shrugged. "I can't see anything else better than this, Keith." He looked at Melody. "So Melody, how's life living with Sarah?"

She giggled. "Has its ups and downs. It's pretty cool. I really am glad for this little arrangement."

"And a fine arrangement you two have." Keith smirked. Melody ignored him.

Lucas took her hand. "Melody, I think working at Caper will surprise you. Believe me, my father will want to take you on. Sarah told me how depressed you've been lately and..."

"*What*? I haven't been depressed!" Melody sighed. "I've been stressed out lately, that's all." Keith grinned. "Look, why is everyone so wrapped up in what I do?"

"Mel, calm down, okay?" Lucas looked at Sarah. "Did I say the wrong thing?"

"No, Lucas." Sarah sipped wine. "Mel's just having one of those days. You gotta excuse her. Nuns know how to have more fun than she does."

"Mel, we should get the ball rolling. Sarah told me how you've searched for a job for months and haven't come up with anything. I remember how smart and resourceful you were. You had a great mind for technology and bookkeeping. I'm sure that a job at Caper could..."

"Lucas, not now, okay?" Melody sipped wine.

"I want you to talk to my dad as soon as you can." He sighed. "Sorry if I pushed."

"Oh, you gotta push Mel or else she won't do a damn thing." Sarah walled her eyes.

Melody set her glass on the table. "I know something I want to do right about now. It involves my foot and your ass."

"Ladies, it's okay." Lucas grunted. "Didn't expect the job to offend you, Mel."

"Lucas, I'm not offended." She took his hand.

"So, I've been catching the latest news reports." Keith sipped. "On that rapist."

"Oh God," Sarah moaned. "They talk about it enough on television that I'm sick to death of it."

"It needs to be talked about in order to catch him, Sarah." Melody sighed. "It's amazing how someone can terrorize an entire city, yet the police don't have any clues."

Lucas chewed. "I bet they would work a little harder if the victims weren't black women. You know how the police are."

"Tell me about it." Sarah smirked. "If they were white women they'd have the fuckin' National Guard down here looking for the guy."

"All the women have been black?" Keith raised an eyebrow.

"Yeah." Melody thought of Aileen. Being black, beautiful and alone most of the time made Aileen Andrews a perfect candidate for the sadistic violator.

"So, is it a black guy or…" Keith gaped.

"No, they say it's a white guy with some strange obsession for black girls." Sarah walled her eyes. "And you'd think the police could come up with something, right?"

"You think it's racially motivated?" Lucas wiped his mouth. "I mean, like, the man is really racist or something and this is how he takes out his frustration on black women?"

"I don't care what his reasons are. He needs to be locked up, that's for sure. Before he hurts someone else." Sarah sipped.

"Uh, let's not talk about rapists, okay?" Melody sighed. "I'm jumpy enough as it is."

"They already nicknamed him." Keith chewed. "They call him the 'Albany Predator'."

"Keith, I said I didn't want to talk about this anymore." Melody sighed.

He nodded. "Point taken. So Melody, are you interested in working at Caper? I find that a great idea. Don't you, babe?" Keith leaned against Sarah.

Sarah scratched her back with her fork. "Oooh," she moaned.

"Are you okay?" Lucas grimaced. She nodded unconvincingly. Lucas continued, "Keith, Sarah and I figured working at Caper would be good for Melody, you know?"

Keith smirked. "Oh really?" He stared at Melody while he caressed Sarah's lap.

"As in, work with *us*?" He raised an eyebrow.

"Yes." Lucas looked at her. "But I see me mentioning it only spoils the mood, so I won't mention it again."

"I just need to think about it, that's all, Lucas." Melody smiled. She watched a waiter sit an attractive couple at the table next to theirs.

"Goddamn it!" Sarah slammed the fork on the table. People momentarily looked up from their meals. Two waiters shrugged at each other.

"Sis, what's the problem, huh?" Melody grinned.

"Shit, my bra's practically eating me alive. I'll be right back, gentlemen." She gestured to the ladies' room. "Mel, could you come with me, please?" Melody followed, grinning.

Lucas shook his head. "Sarah's something else, isn't she?"

"Yeah." Keith stared at Melody. "So, tell me how well you and Mel know each other again, Luke." Keith smirked.

❊❊❊

Sarah high-tailed it to the mirror. She nearly ripped her dress off to get to her bra snaps. Melody strolled in grinning.

"Well, it's not such a perfect night for you after all is it, Miss Sarah?"

"Mel, this is no time to be funny." Sarah exhaled. "This damn bra is killing me, I swear!"

"Hold on, let me help." Melody noticed red marks underneath Sarah's straps.

"Whoa." She rubbed the marks. Sarah flinched. "God, your bra's so tight I'm surprised you could breathe."

"I just bought this damn thing for ninety dollars."

"Ninety dollars for one bra?" Melody shook her head. "Just like you, sis, living above your means and everyone else's."

Sarah smirked. "Won't have to for long with Keith in the picture. He's fantastic, isn't he, Melody? And he's so nice to you. Wonder how he'd feel to know you been dogging him behind his back. Maybe I should tell him."

Melody shrugged. "Tell him. Maybe it'll be a surefire chance of getting rid of the son-of-a-bitch. You sure you got the right size bra?"

"Yes, I got the right size!" Sarah looked in the mirror.

"Oh, is someone touchy? Is someone perhaps gaining weight?" Melody grinned.

"This has nothing to do with weight, believe me." Sarah rinsed crumbs from her mouth. "Okay, let's go."

Melody blocked her. "Wait, I need to talk to you."

"Later, Keith's waiting."

"Is that all you care about? Keith?"

Sarah sighed. "What do you want to talk about now, Melody?"

She squinted. "I've been trying to figure out why it took you so long to bring him around. You've been seeing him for a while."

"Hell, I don't know. Uh, I guess I didn't want you to meet him until I was sure of him myself, that's all. Please don't read anything extra into this, Mel, like you always do. Keith and I are taking it slow." Sarah waved her purse.

"Hmm, doesn't seem too slow to me by the way he was fondling you. Sarah, he practically gave you a finger job in the car."

"Oh, Mel, you're disgusting and I don't have time for this." She tried to leave. Melody held her ground.

"Do you know enough about him? The kind of guy he is?"

"For the last damn time, I'm not about to get into this with you." Two ladies walked into the restroom. "Can we please just go back and have a nice dinner? If you got something to say about Keith, it can wait until we get home."

"Sarah, Keith is a jerk, and the more I spend time with him, the more I know it's the truth."

"I am getting sick of this shit, Mel. Now I'm always there for you, so now you need to be there for me. You're just jealous because once again, you see Keith as someone who will eventually take your place and that's not the case!"

The ladies watched curiously from the other mirror.

"No, believe me, I am the only damn one in here who knows the real deal, Sarah! This isn't about me. This is about Keith, and you not seeing the obvious signs!"

"Damn it, Mel!" Sarah slammed her purse on the sink. "If you got something to say, then say it in plain English this time! You've been barking about Keith all day, yet you haven't mentioned shit as to why! Give me a genuine reason and maybe I'll consider taking you seriously!" She moved her hair from her mouth.

"Sarah, one thing I can do is read people. I do it damn well even if you don't like that quality. And many times I am right. He…he is too controlling with you."

"Controlling?" Sarah laughed. "Oh, and you can tell this because…"

"The signs are right there, Sarah." Melody counted on her fingers. "He finishes your sentences. He orders for you. He tells you how to dress."

"He does not!"

"Bull, you wore this sleazy dress to impress him!"

The ladies grinned.

"Because he's my boyfriend, not because he's controlling, Mel! Like I'd let a guy control me." Sarah looked at the ladies. "You believe this?" They shrugged.

"He controls you and it's only going to get worse. Sarah, you act like you're in a damn daze when Keith's in the room. You hang on to his every word and you act like it's against the law to disagree with him!"

"I don't have to listen to this shit, Melody!" Sarah shoved her out the way.

"Sarah, wait." Sarah stopped at the entrance door. "Look how he acts when other guys give you attention. Most of the men have been staring at you since we got here, and Keith looks like he's about to shoot up the place."

Sarah turned around. "Looks to me like you're so wrapped up in my life you don't even have time for one of your own, Melody."

The other ladies looked at each other.

"You can insult me all you want, but it doesn't change the fact that you are way over your head this time, Sarah. Something is wrong with Keith. I wouldn't be saying that if it weren't true!"

"Go to hell, Melody!" Sarah stomped out the restroom.

The men stood in respect when the ladies made it back to the table. Keith helped Sarah into her chair. Melody decided to let things run their course. If Sarah wanted to be bullheaded about her warnings, she wouldn't entertain the trouble. Lucas kissed Melody's hand. He helped her into her chair. Fortunately she had other things to think about tonight besides Sarah and Keith. Lucas's undying attention made her feel like the only woman in the world.

"Melody, I hope I didn't upset you earlier." Lucas rubbed her hand. "That was never my intention. I guess I'm not as smooth as I seem." He grinned.

"Oh, believe me, you are as smooth as you need to be." Melody winked. She noticed Keith watching her again. She ignored him. He kissed Sarah's neck.

"Well, to make it up to you, could I have this dance?" Lucas stood.

"Uh…" Melody grinned. She hadn't slow danced in so long she wondered if she remembered how. Yet the way Lucas gazed at her made her want to try anything. She also couldn't wait to get away from Sarah and Keith's necking display.

Lucas took her hand, and they found a perfect spot on the dance floor in between two couples. Everything screamed *perfection*. Lucas's attention, the low, seductive lights and the fantastic dinner. He pulled Melody close before she realized it. It had been so long since she'd been this close to any man. Sometimes she had to remind herself that having fun at her age was allowed. She chuckled at the thought.

"What's so funny?" Lucas whispered. His breath hit a spot on Melody's top lip that seemed to warm her entire body.

"Nothing." She chuckled again.

"Something's making you laugh." His powerful dark eyes shimmered with the lights above them as they enjoyed a charismatic slow dance. Lucas's moves were so graceful that Melody wondered if he'd taken lessons. His black hair appeared blue underneath the luminous lights. The more Melody spent time with Lucas, the more she remembered the good old days.

She laughed. The couples next to them glanced at her. They eventually went back to their own charismatic moments.

"Now what's so funny?" Lucas laughed. "I don't think it's a good sign when a woman laughs while we're dancing. What, do I have a piece of bread or something in my teeth?"

She laughed. "No!"

"What then?" Lucas grinned. "Is something hanging out of my nose?"

"Oh man, that's gross." Melody guffawed. "I was just thinking, that's all. Isn't that what you're supposed to do while dancing. Let the mood take you away?"

He smirked. "I suppose so. So that's all, huh? You sure you weren't laughing at me?"

She nodded. "Since we're dancing, I might as well ask you something. Do you have a girlfriend, Lucas?"

"Come on, Mel, you know me and girls. I haven't changed that much." He walled his eyes.

"And what does that mean?"

"You know how picky I am with women. I can't help it. I'm picky with everything." She grinned. "I can't even decide on what pair of socks to wear in the mornings without regretting the decision. You think I could be fulfilled with one girlfriend?"

"Ahh, I see." She raised an eyebrow. "So, it's not that you can't find one; it's just that you have so many." She laughed.

"I date, yes." He shrugged. "We *are* in our twenties, Mel. This is the age to have fun. I haven't been with a lot of women if that's what you're thinking. But if you want to know if there is someone special in my life, then the answer is no." Melody smiled.

"Do you have a boyfriend?"

"No, I'm not too good when it comes to relationships. I kind of got other things on my mind."

Lucas grinned. "I remember how you and Craig used to break up and get back together, like what, every damn weekend back in high school."

"You remember all that?"

"Of course." He winked. "I probably kept up with your relationship better than you guys did." He grinned. "I always thought about you, Melody. And it wasn't just about friendship."

She stopped dancing. "Lucas, did you have a crush on me back then?"

"Well kind of, yeah." He twirled her around. "Are you surprised?"

"Of course! I mean the most handsome and wealthiest boy in the school liked me?" She laughed. "I wish those bitches who used to give me trouble back then knew this. Why didn't you tell me before?"

"Duh, because you were with Craig. Then by the time it was all over, school was over and we'd all split ways. Anyway, I knew you didn't feel the same about me so..."

"Unbelievable." She sighed. "Lucas, I wish you'd said something back then!"

"Why?" He laughed. "Would you have dumped Craig or something?"

"No, but it would have been nice to know. I mean, that was my awkward stage. That's definitely the time to tell a girl you're interested in her."

He laughed. "You're something else, Mel. And I've missed you constantly all this time. It seems like fate just being here like this, doesn't it?"

"Yeah." Melody glanced at the table. Sarah sat in Keith's lap while he fondled her backside. She wondered how far they'd go in public.

Lucas exhaled. "May I ask why you left school? I never had the courage to back then."

She ran her hand down his arm. "So much was happening. I had too many problems. I couldn't deal with Aunt Lucia going crazy by the second. I missed being apart from Sarah all those years. No one in the school seemed to be able to stand me but you, Craig and Aileen. I felt so alone. I wanted to cut out everything that made me unhappy. School just made everything more difficult. I couldn't handle it. I just needed space."

"Yeah, I remember your Aunt Lucia. The one who took care of you. I keep forgetting you and Sarah were raised apart after your parents died. She went with an uncle, right?" Melody nodded. "Your aunt had mental problems or something, didn't she? I think Aileen said that back then."

"Yes. Seems like Sarah got the best end of all the deals. She got the decent upbringing while I was stuck in that hole with Aunt Lucia. She got the ability to get any man's attention. She got the looks. She had and still has...*everything*." She looked at Lucas. "I know that sounds spiteful but, it's the truth, isn't it? Lucas, I love her more than anything, but at times I can't help feeling inferior when it comes to her."

"What?" Lucas grinned. "Mel, you gotta be kidding me. Sarah's beautiful but she doesn't hold a candle to you."

She scoffed. "Come on, Lucas, you don't have to be polite."

He pulled her away. He looked her in the eyes. "Melody, you're one of the most beautiful women I've ever seen. I mean that." She knew he did. Something about Lucas told her he never lied. "Stop comparing yourself to Sarah."

She scoffed. "It's not easy, believe me."

"Sarah loves you a lot, you know?" She nodded. "She just wants you to be happy. That's why we were talking about the job at Caper. We weren't doing it to hurt you, Mel."

"I know. It's just that…" Lucas moved away again. Her arms glided from his body. "What?" She chuckled. He wrapped his hand underneath her hair, pulled her close and passionately kissed her. Normally public displays of affection embarrassed Melody. But tonight, she'd have it no other way. She pushed him away out of reflex. She enjoyed his kiss a little too much. It had been way too soon.

Lucas wiped lipstick from his mouth. "What, you didn't want that, Mel?" he whispered almost as if he were begging for more.

"I wanted it too much, Lucas. That's the problem. I told you I'm not good in relationships and I meant it."

He nodded. "I forgot how fragile you always were. I need to take my time."

"I don't like how you said, 'fragile,' Lucas. I'm not some vase that's about to tip over and break. And I don't like how people think they gotta protect me all the time. I get enough of that from Sarah. I don't need it from you."

"I…" He sighed. "I didn't mean to offend you, Melody. God, I mean, I don't know if you're going through something, but look, I'm on your side." He took her hand. "Don't think that everything I say is some knock against the person you are."

"I'm sorry." She rubbed her face. "I don't know what's wrong with me."

"A lot of people care about you, Melody." He stepped back. "You just need to let them, okay?" He kissed her cheek.

"I'm sorry." She sobbed against his chest.

"It's...Jesus, Melody, are you okay?"

She shrugged. "I don't know what's wrong. My emotions are just high today." She looked at the table. Sarah had gone somewhere, probably the ladies room. Keith gazed at Melody. She had the feeling he'd been watching the entire time. He held up his glass in a salute before taking a final sip.

"What's wrong, Mel?" Lucas looked at Keith. "Melody, are you sure you're okay? Did something happen to you today? I know we haven't been around each other in years, but you could talk to me then, and you can now." She looked at him. "Whenever you need a friend, I'm here for you. But I gotta tell you, I want to be much more than that already."

"I just need things to be taken slowly, Lucas. Okay?" she whispered.

"I understand." He pulled her close. They began to dance.again "I'd never pressure you, Melody. Just remember that I want you to lean on me. Lean on me any time you need to."

She pulled him closer. "If it will always feel like this then I'm willing."

Lucas smiled.

❁❁❁

Melody and Sarah were home before they knew it. Melody enjoyed the night ride. She thought of his kiss every time she looked at Lucas. He grinned whenever he caught her stare, proving he'd been thinking about it, too. Melody wondered if she were crazy giving up on passion so easily. Sarah and Keith cuddled on the way to the front porch. Melody couldn't believe she'd hidden her distaste for Keith.

"I have never been so happy to see a porch light in my life!" Sarah leaned against the door. Keith pulled her close. Melody couldn't believe they weren't raw from all the kissing they'd done. Sarah moaned as Keith ran his hand under her dress. Once again Lucas took her attention from the moment.

"Luke, you and Melody want some time alone?" Keith looked at them. "I know we sure as hell could use some." He grinned.

"Keith, I need to speak to you for a minute." Sarah unlocked the door. Keith followed her inside the house.

"So, still tense?" Lucas held Melody close. The wind slightly blew his hair out of place. He easily fixed it with a gentle sweep of the hand. He had the most beautiful hair Melody had ever seen. She hadn't forgotten that in all these years.

They heard Sarah and Keith bumping against the door. It hadn't been difficult to imagine what they were doing. "I had a very nice time, Lucas. I'm glad I decided to take Sarah up on the offer."

He felt her hair. "I meant what I said, Mel. Whenever you need anything, I'm just a phone call away."

She smiled. "And I got the number."

"Use it." He kissed her cheek, and she wondered why he stopped there. Funny how she wanted more now opposed to when they were in the restaurant. "Uh, I couldn't help sensing something, Mel." He shifted. "You don't like Keith, do you?"

She turned away. "Why would you say that? I hardly know the guy."

"Keith, stop!' Sarah laughed from inside.

Melody walled her eyes. "Lucas, has Keith mentioned Sarah to you a lot? I mean, at work do you two talk?"

He scratched his forehead. "Keith's a good friend of mine. But he's very private. He doesn't let people get too close to him."

"Do you know why?"

Lucas moved back. "How come I get the feeling you're doing a little detective work on my man in there?"

"I was just wondering. A girl has the right to know about her sister's boyfriend, doesn't she?" She swung her purse around. He pulled her close once more.

"You are so beautiful, Melody." Lucas gently pushed her against the door. Melody eagerly awaited the kiss. Keith opened the door before they got the chance to enjoy it. Lucas rubbed Melody's cheek. She nuzzled against him.

Keith stared at them. "Well, I guess Sarah and I aren't the only ones falling prey to passion tonight." He dug in his pockets. Just looking at Keith infuriated Melody.

"Well, I guess we'd better go then, huh?" Lucas whispered.

"Are you talking to me?" Keith grinned. "You're looking at her but are you talking to me? Come on, let's go, man. I think we both need to let the ladies have a little rest and relaxation."

Melody didn't know what the hell Keith meant by that line, but she'd do her best to ignore him.

Lucas held her. "If you want to do this, we can take it slow, okay?" Melody nodded. "I don't want this to end, okay? I really want us to spend time together like we used to."

"I know." Melody kissed him. The action seemed to surprise Lucas *and* Keith.

"Thanks again for the lovely evening, Lucas."

"Shh." He held his finger to her lips. "Don't ever thank me for allowing me to spend time with you. Besides, the loveliest thing about this evening was you." He looked back as he stepped off the porch. "Good night, Melody."

"Good night, Lucas."

Keith grinned and followed Lucas to the car.

Melody leaned against the door when she got inside. She couldn't explain the hold Lucas had on her already. She couldn't wait to see him again. She'd find any excuse just to get another sample of the excitement they shared tonight.

Sarah guffawed. "Oh yeah, baby!" she teased.

"Oh yeah, what?" Melody ripped off her shoes.

"You know what!" Sarah laughed. "Now tell me I was right! Tell me you had a wonderful time tonight."

She shrugged. "Okay you were right. Lucas is even more terrific."

"Told you." Sarah headed to the kitchen. "You want a snack? I'm dying for an ice cream float."

"Sarah, we just had a five-course meal and you're still hungry? I'm beginning to wonder." Melody rested on the arm of the couch to rub her feet.

"Wonder what?"

"Well, with the signs I'm seeing…are you pregnant?" Melody laughed.

Sarah popped into the room. "Girl, don't even play like that. If I was pregnant, it was because a pig flew somewhere around here."

Melody laughed. "What should I think? Your clothes are tight. You're eating even more than usual. You're complaining about weight gain. Maybe you should take a test to be…"

"I'm not pregnant!" Sarah guffawed from the kitchen.

"Besides, this night was about you and Lucas. Don't try to change the subject."

"Oh Sarah, it was amazing. He kissed me. And it was like a kiss, a kiss you couldn't even invent. I swear my hair almost melted!" Melody fiddled with her hair.

"And he's so gorgeous. He looks even better than he did in school." She kicked her feet playfully. "And another thing that makes him really great!"

"What?" Sarah walked in with an overlapping mug of vanilla ice cream. Root beer slithered from the sides of the glass.

"He thinks I'm prettier than you." Melody laughed. "Na, na, na, na, na!"

"Like I give two shits what Lucas Lawson thinks." Sarah chuckled. "So, is he a good kisser?"

Melody sighed. "I can't even describe what it did to me. And you know I needed something, seeing how I haven't had sex in what… Shit, I can't even remember."

Sarah laughed. "I don't know how you do it, girl. I go three days without sex and I'm practically climbing the walls." She slurped some of the float. "I mean, getting dick on a regular basis keeps you grounded. You should try it, Mel."

Melody threw a pillow from the couch. "Fuck you." They laughed. "But I tell you, when Lucas kissed me, I felt like getting on my knees right then and there. That's how horny he made me."

Sarah laughed. "I bet that would have been a sight.

You going down on Lucas on the dance floor." She squinted. "*Would* you go down on him?"

"Sarah, such personal questions." Melody pretended to be offended. She laughed. "Maybe." She slipped off her stockings. "Would you go down on Keith?"

Sarah contemplated the question. "Well, you gotta understand how Keith works. With him, it's not like sex is anything ordinary, you know?" She sat on the edge of the sofa.

"What do you mean?"

"Keith is into a lot of things, sexually. I mean, he's a freak, to say the least."

"Well, you always loved the freaky white boys."

Sarah grinned. "You say that like it's a bad thing. Seriously, Keith brings out something in me I didn't know I had. The sex is incredible, and the things he can do with that tongue…"

"Sarah, please." Melody held her stomach. "That's a little too much information, okay? I just wanted an answer, not a visual."

"I'm sorry if talking about that rapist ruined dinner for you, Mel. You're worried about Aileen, right? I'm sure she'll be okay."

"How can we be so sure, Sarah? I mean, she fits what he looks for and the police haven't come up with squat. I wonder if they're even trying."

"Well, the mayor did put the city on curfew a few weeks ago hoping that helps. Hey, I feel sorry for the women who are raped out of bad luck, but I can't feel sorry for the ones who aren't being careful."

Melody scoffed. "You mean by going off at night or going off to work alone?" Sarah shrugged. "Sarah, a woman has the right to do what she wants. No creep has the right to take that away. Is a woman supposed to stop living her life because this man is terrorizing people?"

"Yes, if they don't want to end up on the evening news as one of his victims. I know you don't agree with this curfew, but it's a guaranteed way to keep women safe."

"No, it's not. Sarah, a lot of the victims were raped at home. How the hell is a curfew going to help them? It's not like the man is just picking women out on the street! I mean, you think it's fair that the mayor set rules for the women like it's their fault that this man is raping people? Come on, Sarah."

"Look, it may not be the best solution, but it will keep at least a fraction of women safe. That's better than nothing, Mel." Sarah finished her float. "If a woman expects to stay safe, sometimes she has to play by someone else's rules." She left the room.

Melody sighed. "Spoken like someone who's never been a victim."

Chapter Three

Melody awoke to Sarah scrounging in her bedroom during the night. Seconds later the hall light popped on. Melody peeked from her room. She straightened the long T-shirt she wore as a gown. "Sarah, are you okay?"

"Ah shit!" Sarah yelled down the hall. Melody rushed toward her.

"Sarah, are you okay?"

"Yeah, I just stubbed my toe!" She shoved the chair out the way. "How many times I gotta tell you not to leave chairs in the hallway? It's too damn narrow as it is."

"I had to change the hall light. It's your damn fault since it was your turn to change it, anyway. Why are you up?"

"I heard something downstairs. I thought it was you." Sarah edged to the stairs. They heard a thunderous bump against the front door. "Shit, what was that?"

"I don't know." Melody shook. "Sounds like someone's trying to break in or something." Sarah ran downstairs. Melody tipped into the dark living room behind her.

Sarah listened at the door. They heard the sound again. She turned the doorknob.

"Sarah, what in the hell are you doing?" Melody grabbed a book. "Don't open that door! You, idiot we could both end up on the news tomorrow! It could be that rapist."

The doorbell rang.

Sarah glared at her sister. "A rapist who rings the doorbell, Mel?" Melody lowered the book. She still wasn't convinced, and she didn't care how stupid she seemed. They weren't accustomed to late-night visits. These days a woman couldn't be too careful whether she fit a rapist's victim profile or not.

"Sarah, don't open it!"

She laughed. "Just keep the book high and hit him when I let him in."

"You think it's funny, but I'm practically pissing here." Sarah opened the door.

Keith waved, drawing attention to his elaborate Cartier watch. Melody would have *rather* it been the rapist. "Fuck," she whispered. She still wanted to hit him.

"Hey, babe." He stared at Sarah's flimsy nightgown.

"Keith." She brushed her hair down. "What's going on?"

"I'm sorry." He looked at Melody. "I must have scared the shit out of you both, huh? Well, you won't believe the luck I'm having tonight. I had this killer migraine so I went to the corner store. Well, when I got home, I couldn't find my house key anywhere."

"Oh no," Sarah sighed.

"Yeah, so I am locked out of my house, and I still got this headache." He rubbed his forehead. "There was no way I was calling a locksmith or something at this hour so…" He looked at Melody. "What's with the book, Mel?" He grinned.

"Melody, put it down." Sarah walled her eyes.

"Maybe I don't want to."

"So your brother wasn't home either, Keith?" Sarah rubbed Keith's forehead.

"You have a brother?" Melody grimaced. She wondered if *he* liked to spy on naked women too.

"No, he had plans. I tried to call him but my damn cell phone isn't working."

Melody crossed her arms. "How convenient." Sarah glared at her. "I recall your phone working this evening at the restaurant."

"Well, it's not working now." Keith smirked. He took Sarah's hand. "Baby, I didn't mean to wake you but I had no choice but to come here."

"Well, it's late. Why don't you stay?" Sarah smiled.

"Uh, Sarah, are you on crack or just crazy?" Melody walked toward them.

"He's staying, Mel." Sarah gritted her teeth. "This is my house, remember?"

"It's my home, too, since I live here! You can't just invite people to stay here, Sarah! Especially a strange guy."

"He's my boyfriend, Melody!" Melody shook her head in disapproval. "Why don't you just grow up, huh?"

"Why don't you get a fuckin' clue, Sarah? Can't you see he's lying?"

"Shut up! You have no right to say that about Keith! He's having a bad time. Can't you understand that? We have to help him!"

"I don't have to do shit when it comes to this...this..."

"Watch your mouth, Melody." Sarah made a fist.

"Whoa, whoa, whoa!" Keith waved his hands. "Ladies, please! Now I didn't mean to cause any problems."

"Ha! The moment you've been involved there have been nothing but problems, Keith."

"You have some sort of score to settle with me, Melody?" He put his hands in his pockets. "I don't see what the hell your problem is."

She looked at Sarah. "I don't think you want me to mention it in front of Sarah now do you?"

He walked toward her. "I wouldn't have asked if I didn't want to know."

"Go on, Melody." Sarah smirked. "You got a problem with Keith, then tell him." Melody turned away. "Keith, you can stay here. It's not a problem, believe me."

"I don't want to make Melody uncomfortable."

"Oh bullshit! Your *existence* makes me uncomfortable, Keith!"

"Melody, stop it!" Sarah shoved her. "He is staying tonight and that's the end of it! I'll go get some blankets, Keith. You can sleep on the couch." She left the room.

"Who do you think you are, Keith? Sarah may be

blinded by your fancy suits, good looks and Cartier watches, but I'm not."

"Oh really?" He smirked. "Maybe I should have worn my Omega then."

"And you're not at all funny." She shuffled toward the couch.

"Look, we all seem stressed out tonight. Maybe it's a full moon or something I don't know. I'm sorry if you have a problem with me, Melody."

She raised her hands. "How come everything you say seems...I don't know, rehearsed?"

He shrugged. "I guess that's how you're seeing me. I realize you need time to get to know me. It'll take time."

"I don't want to get to know you, Keith."

He shrugged. "Well, I want to get to know anyone who is important to Sarah. I really care about her." Melody walled her eyes. "Did you have a nice time tonight? I hope you did."

"Do you?" She shook her head.

"Sure. Didn't Sarah look beautiful?"

"Sarah always looks beautiful."

"You did, too, Melody. I get the feeling you always compare yourself to her. You shouldn't."

"I don't need to be analyzed by someone I just met, Keith."

He grinned. "Lucas was right. You're something else."

"So you've been discussing me with Lucas, is that it? What did he say?"

"Nothing I didn't already know. He thinks you're fantastic. Melody, I'm taking the chance to know you more. Could you be fair and do the same with me?"

"What kind of game are you playing, Keith?"

He smirked. "Let's just be honest, shall we? I figure you got a big problem with me. What is it?"

"My problem is that little stunt you pulled this evening, Keith."

"What stunt?" He licked his lips. Melody swore he was checking her out yet couldn't be sure.

She held the end of her T-shirt. "You know exactly what I'm talking about, Keith. When you came into my bedroom this evening and didn't leave."

"Oh, that?" He grinned. "Mel, it was just a misunderstanding. You didn't tell your sister, did you?"

"No."

"And you don't need to. It was nothing. I just got lost."

"*Lost*? Keith, is 'stupid' plastered on my forehead?"

He glared at her creamy thighs. She held her T-shirt tighter against them. "We all get lost sometimes, don't we, Mel?"

She backed away. "Okay, forget that. What about when we all went out tonight? Why were you constantly staring at me?"

He glanced around the den. "I wasn't staring at you."

"Keith!" She laughed. "I can't believe you're standing here lying. Every time I noticed you looking at me, you'd wink or smirk. Am I supposed to believe that's just a coincidence? You can lie your way out of what happened in my room, but you can't deny that you were staring at me all night."

"Nice T-shirt." He groaned. "You have such a beautiful body, Mel. I can't see why you continue to cover it up the way you do."

She exhaled. "Keith, what in the hell are you up to?"

"Games, Mel. Don't you like to play games?"

"No." Her voice shook.

"Something tells me you do." He moved his mouth to hers. She jumped back.

Sarah walked in with Melody's old pillow and some blankets.

"Sorry it took so long. The things tumbled out of the linen closet." She passed Keith the items.

"I appreciate this, babe." He kissed her. Keith made up the couch.

"Come on, let's go to bed, Mel." Sarah took her hand.

"And I'll make sure to lock my door." She looked at Keith.

Melody awoke to the sounds of lovemaking coming from Sarah's room the next morning. She wasn't surprised. She knew Keith would finagle his way into Sarah's bed. She screeched like a cat in heat. Keith delivered a couple of "bear" grunts of his own. He *must* have been something in bed. The sounds were so exhausting Melody lit a cigarette to take her mind off of what she *wasn't* getting.

Of course, Melody should have been used to her sister

sexing men early in the morning. But none of those guys had been Keith Taylor. Melody vowed to learn his angle by the end of breakfast. She got a headache whenever she thought of Keith. She wished she could just take the day in bed. She figured Sarah and Keith hoped the same thing by the sounds coming from that room.

Melody yawned in her huge bedroom mirror before she began to brush her teeth. She decided she'd shower some time later. She wasted no time lighting another cigarette when she finished. Sarah and Keith were still going strong. Melody took a long puff from the little white rod. She couldn't help thinking of Lucas during moments like these. Her stomach tingled. And oh yes, she knew why.

She wanted Lucas already. So why had she put the brakes on? Why couldn't she be more like Sarah? Why did she have to take things so slow? Could she be in love with Lucas? Maybe she had been since they were teenagers. She hadn't met anyone who made her feel like this. She thought of her last lover, Enrique. Hands down, he'd been the best lover. They'd met at a coffee shop close to Sarah's job.

From the moment Melody and Enrique locked eyes, they'd felt the heat. That quickly fizzled. Enrique had been great to fuck and go to lunch with, yet love never entered the picture for Melody. Sarah always said she couldn't understand why Melody didn't allow herself to be happy. Melody tiptoed downstairs, and wondered the same thing.

Enrique didn't stir half the emotions in Melody that Lucas did. She'd definitely go after that job. She already knew Lucas well. Now she craved to know him *more*.

She dug around the kitchen for something quick to fix. They were out of pancake mix. She wasn't about to struggle through a scratch recipe. That wasn't Melody's style. She liked things quick and fast. She heard Sarah moaning upstairs. Well, there were *some* things Melody liked to take her time with. She remembered the instant waffles in the freezer. Laziness discouraged her from fixing the waffles.

She opted for chocolate chip ice cream instead. People wondered how Melody kept her trim figure. A regular meal to her consisted of a Big Mac with extra cheese. She slid on the tall countertop. She inched her spoon into the cool treat. It reminded her of the days when she didn't think of growing up. She'd been amazed at how things had changed.

Keith walked in wearing silk boxers. He ran his hand down his muscular chest. He flashed that smirk that she'd already begun to hate.

"Morning, Melody." He looked at her thighs. She crossed her legs at the ankles.

"Good morning," she mumbled.

He leaned his arm against the wall. "Well, did you sleep well?"

She licked the spoon. "Not as good as you did, apparently."

"Oh yeah." He rubbed his hair. She figured he'd pretend to be shy for her benefit, but he didn't. She'd heard every disgusting grunt. "Well, I'm sorry if we woke you."

He stared at her. "Ice cream for breakfast? That's not very healthy."

She walled her eyes. "Yeah, well it's all I felt like dealing with."

"Mind if I grab a spoon and join in?"

She glared at him. "Thought you just said this was unhealthy."

"It is, but I love chocolate chip ice cream like the next guy." He grabbed a spoon from the drawer, and slid on the countertop next to her. She scooted beside the refrigerator. He swallowed a runny chunk of ice cream. She passed him the carton.

"Uh, you sure?"

"Go on and take it." She crossed her arms. Keith took the treat. She didn't know how long she could stand being alone with him. She decided to do some digging to pass the time. "So you gonna call your brother?"

"Uh…" He nodded. His hesitation had been a big hint. Melody watched enough police shows to know how easily you could throw a suspect off base when they lied. Keith glanced around the kitchen.

"Your brother, Keith? You know, you said you needed to call him to get into your house."

He smirked. "Well, I can see nothing gets past you, Mel." He slurped the ice cream. "I haven't had a chance to call him yet." He scraped his spoon against the carton. Melody hated that.

"Why do you speak as if you've known me for years, Keith?"

"Feel like I do. Sarah and I talk about you all the time. I know about how you grew up apart. I know how different you are from each other." He looked at her thighs again. "I know how you're both the same."

She moved from the countertop. "Why do you keep staring at me?" she whispered.

He licked his spoon. "I bet you wish I was Lucas, huh?"

"Excuse me?" She frowned.

"I said you probably wish I was Lucas, right?"

"No, I wasn't thinking about him." She glanced out the window behind his head.

"Bull, Melody. I can see it in your eyes. I know enough about you already to know when you're lying."

"Really?" She smirked. "So you must have known I couldn't stand you from the moment we met."

He shrugged. "I kind of picked up on that. But there's nothing I enjoy more than changing a beautiful woman's mind." He set the ice cream beside him. "You think that this with Sarah is just a fling, don't you?"

"Maybe." She waved her hands. "I have no cause to think otherwise."

He stood. "Are you always like this, Melody? Do you always think that your word is law? That what you think is the only thing that matters?"

"I don't have to listen to this garbage." She turned to leave. He blocked her. Funny, she expected him to. "Move, Keith."

He smirked. "I want us to clear the air, once and for all."

"Where's Sarah?" she exhaled.

"Why do I get the feeling that you're um…" He stared at her neck. "Are you trying to change the subject right now?"

"There is no subject where we're concerned, Keith."

"You can't see how much Sarah and I care for each other? I'm not going away, Melody." He rubbed her hair. She shoved his hands away. "So you can get that thought out of your head. Try any little tricks to…"

She grinned. "Believe me, I won't have to. If you're anything like the other men she's been with, you'll be gone by the end of the month."

"But I'm not like anyone she's been with, Melody."

"Oh believe me, you don't have to tell me twice!" She tried to leave again. He pulled her back. He wrapped his hands around her waist. "Let go of me, Keith!"

"This is a different feeling for you isn't it, Mel?" She struggled in his arms. He forced her back inside the kitchen. "We both know how much you like to be in control."

"Let me go, you bastard!" She struggled, and he smiled.

"You see…I'm the same way." He held her tighter. "We both want control, Mel. We want to keep control, don't we?" He pressed her against the refrigerator.

"If you don't let me go right now, I'll…"

"What, huh?" He grinned. "What will you do, Mel? You can't stop me from being with Sarah. I think I need to make that clear." She whimpered. "I think this could be a great experience for all three of us."

She broke free. "Fuck you, all right! Who do you think you are coming in my home and manhandling me?"

"I just wanted to get things out in the open, Melody. I really meant no harm." He laid the ice cream in the sink. "Did I scare you?"

"Don't you ever touch me again, Keith." She slapped her hair from her eyes. "Ever!" She stomped out of the kitchen. He followed.

"Melody?" She stopped by the stairs. "For what it's worth...I did come to your room on purpose yesterday." She shook. "And I can do it again, any time I want." He stood directly behind her. "You want to play the game with me, then we'll play it." She gaped. "And baby, I play it like no other." He went upstairs.

Sarah came downstairs fully dressed. Melody struggled to gather her senses. She knew the feat would be useless. Sarah wore a dark pants suit that put most supermodels to shame. Melody rarely complimented her these days. Why remind the angel that she had wings?

"Morning, sis." Sarah kissed her cheek. Melody held her trembling hands behind her back. "Listen, I want to apologize, all right?" Sarah slipped her purse on her arm. "We just have to meet some common ground about Keith, Mel. I really don't want this to get out of hand."

"Keith?" Melody shook. Just thinking of his name petrified her. He wanted something. She assumed that had been Sarah. She remembered how he just held *her* in the kitchen. Now, Melody wasn't so sure. A man had never been so forceful with her before.

"Mel!" Sarah shook her. "Jesus Christ, this daydreaming you do, sis." Sarah sighed. "Are you sure you're okay? You look flushed."

"I'm fine, Sarah."

"And you're shaking. How come you're still in your pajamas?"

"Sarah, something uh…in the kitchen…Keith…"

Sarah hugged her. "I love you, and I hate it when we fight." She kissed Melody's lips. "Can you forgive me?"

"There is uh, nothing to forgive." Melody wobbled.

"Melody, are you sure you're okay?"

"Fine, Sarah." She glanced upstairs. "I don't know why I'm so on edge these days. Maybe it's getting close to my period."

Sarah walled her eyes. "Tell me about it. Thank goodness, I'm done for the month. I don't envy you, sis." Sarah chuckled. "I know the kitchen's kind of bare so why don't we go out to breakfast? Let me make it up to you about the fight last night."

Melody noticed Keith's shadow in the upstairs hallway. She made sure not to speak until he walked on. "I'd love to Sarah but I got other plans." She heard Keith brushing his teeth in the bathroom. "I planned to go talk to Aileen today. I've missed her lately, and I've been kind of worried. With that rapist around, I get scared when I haven't heard from her in a few days, you know?"

Sarah tilted her head to the side. She glared at Melody. "Are you sure that you're okay?"

"Of course." She chuckled. "Why wouldn't I be okay? Oh good news, sis. Uh, I'm going to go after the job at Caper, after all."

"Oh Mel, that's great! I know things'll fall into place for you now. It's not healthy the way you hang around the house letting life pass you by. At least with a job you'll feel like you got a purpose." Sarah checked her watch. "Well, I'd better get out of here. I'm just waiting for Keith to finish up. Can you believe it? I'm only twenty-six and already looking forward to retirement? Hey, I got a great idea."

"What?" Melody smiled.

"Why don't you let Keith drop you off at Caper? Then you could get to know him better."

Melody no longer cared about getting to know Keith better. She'd stay away from him like her life depended on it. "Sarah, I have a jeep, remember?"

"Yeah, but you're always harping about how much gas that thing guzzles, and we need to be extra tight around here for a while."

"It's fine Sarah, really. Me riding with Keith is not a good idea. I hope you have a good day at work."

Sarah straightened her collar. "Oh, I have a feeling I will. I'm gonna see if Keith's almost ready." She went back upstairs.

She always boasted about the prestige of being Mr. Pepskin's head assistant. Melody found Mr. Pepskin to be a big jerk. He never showed Sarah an inch of respect, yet she'd obviously swallow cut glass for him. How could Melody judge? At least Sarah had a job. Melody would drown if she didn't find something soon. She felt terrible having Sarah foot the bills for so long.

❁❁❁

Caper Enterprises had easily become one of Albany's most successful advertising firms. The huge skyscraper stood in the middle of the downtown area. It couldn't be missed. Melody had always been amazed at how hectic this area could be in the mornings. Crowds of people waited at the bus stops. People ran across the intersections with cups of coffee.

Women fought the wind under overpasses to keep their skirts from flying over their heads. Groups of men in suits chatted by traffic signs. Streams of cars flowed in millions of directions. Little kids rushed to catch the city bus for school. The continuous horn honking resembled an orchestra. People scrambled to diners and doughnut shops while heading to work.

Melody felt alive just seeing everyday people carry on their normal daily routines. It beat sitting in front of the television all day. It beat lying on the couch, wondering why the last job she contacted didn't called. She didn't feel self-conscious today. Usually she did. No, she felt confident. Something told her that this would be the beginning of a new life for her. Sarah had been right. She needed to start living before it became too late.

She arrived at the twenty-three-story building twenty minutes later. She would have arrived sooner if it hadn't been for downtown traffic. She gazed at the gigantic building. A wave of dizziness hit her the moment she stepped from her jeep. Something about big buildings had always frightened her. Crowds of people scattered up the walkways.

They scurried into the building as if they belonged there. Melody felt like some caged animal. She hoped her confidence wouldn't abandon her. You couldn't impress people if you weren't sure of yourself.

Four other businesses shared the skyscraper. The law firm for Caper Enterprises sat on one floor. A small cancer center took up a group of floors. A gynecologist held his practice in the building. Even a local television station shared the space. Melody entered the illuminated building. She wondered how others handled such numbing, long aisles. Or maybe they only felt like that if you didn't know where you were going.

A large sign with directions stood at the first corner. She hoped for a shortcut to Caper's floor. She held her breath on the elevator. She'd always been afraid of the elevator dropping to an unknown destination. Instead, the elevator stopped on the desired floor. A young man waited until she got off before he got on. He smiled, and she wondered if many of the people here were friendly.

Men in white dress shirts and dark slacks smiled while she passed. She turned to see a few of them checking her out from behind. She enjoyed the attention. Sarah had always insisted Melody to use her feminine wiles. She didn't think she had any, until now.

She made it into the cozy waiting room a minute later. She wasn't surprised to see it full of men. You couldn't expect many women in the corporate world. Melody spoke to the secretary. She instructed Melody to take a seat for a moment. Melody scanned the waiting room's occupants. All the men seemed under thirty-five. They were all white.

They all looked like they'd been born with silver spoons in their mouths. Melody crossed her legs. She imagined they had run up their trust funds, or totaled one of their many cars. They sure as hell didn't look like they needed to work. White-bread city. Melody swore their socks cost more than her entire outfit. They all wore Rolexes. They all wore the hottest suits for today's male fashion.

Melody couldn't imagine ever fitting in here. Yet, Sarah and Lucas seemed convinced that she did. She wondered if Lucas's dad would remember her.

The secretary pulled off her bifocals. "Miss Cruz, Mr. Lawson will see you now."

Melody checked her face one last time. She took a deep breath. She entered Dave Lawson's office. The door automatically closed behind her. Dave chatted on the phone. He smiled. Now she remembered him. Dave had always been kind back then. He had all the money he could need, yet you wouldn't know it from his attitude. He'd always been a generous and fair man.

Lucas had received the best of both worlds. He'd gotten Dave's looks as well as his business sense. What more could a young man in today's world need?

Dave waved. "Be with you in just a moment, Miss Cruz. Feel free to look around the office." Melody nodded. She didn't get these corporate types. Since Dave was Lucas's father she wouldn't be too hard on him.

She walked around the posh office. Dave sat behind a cluttered desk equipped with a fancy computer and deluxe phone system. Behind his desk stood a giant window where he could probably see the entire city. Melody figured he stared out that window a hundred times a day. She knew she would. If she would be lucky to get her own office, she would definitely spring for one with a window.

Two big, silver file cabinets sat in the corner beside boxes of files and loose papers. Plants hung from every corner of the room. That explained the organic fragrance Melody noticed when she walked in. Dave rattled off about some rival company. He smiled at Melody, then turned the other way. He needn't be worried. The last thing she cared about was his business deals.

She'd come to start anew. She hoped this job would

help her accomplish her goal. She paced around the shelf of tumbling books. Wrinkled papers fell from the books' creases. Obviously being rich didn't mean you were neat. Dave's office had been the sloppiest workplace she'd seen.

A vibrant family portrait of Dave, Lucas and Lucas's mother sat on the tiny endtable beside the door. She'd never seen such a perfect-looking family.

Melody hadn't necessarily hated being raised by Aunt Lucia. Still, she'd missed having parents more than anything. It had been hard to grow up the product of people you didn't remember. She questioned everything about herself, wondering if she resembled at least one of her parents in any way. She imagined that Sarah embodied all that they represented. Melody often wondered how two sisters could be so different.

She did a double-take when she saw Lucas's mother. She'd forgotten that the lady had been some Italian model back in the day. She wasn't famous but Melody remembered Lucas mentioning every aspect of his mother's exciting modeling career. She glanced at Dave. He waved his hands furiously. He shouted between rapid breaths. She wondered how the Lawsons first got together.

What exactly had Dave done to pull such a fascinating creature like Lucas's mother? Or had *he* been the fascinating one?

He hung up. Melody wondered if he remembered that she'd been in the room.

"Sorry about that, Miss Cruz." He smiled. "You know it's hard to be the boss." Melody smiled. "You want respect but you don't want to seem like some tyrant. Sometimes, it's hard to get people to do things while trying to be so understanding."

She put the picture down. "I can imagine the hard work you do, Mr. Lawson. You should be very proud for what you've accomplished. It must feel great to know that you became such a success all on your own."

He blushed as he touched his scattered goatee. "Well, aren't you the charming one? I do remember you well, you know? Lucas never really stopped talking about his old friends. When he spoke about you, though, he always acted as though something was missing." Melody looked at him. "Like, a part of himself, you know? Since last night he's been dancing on air."

Melody grinned. "Dancing on air, huh?"

"Yep. Whatever happened between you two last night made him very happy. Anyone who makes my son happy is all right with me. Especially when she's so attractive and witty."

She squinted. "Do you really remember me or are you just being polite?"

"Oh no, I remember you, Melody. I never forget any-one. Please sit down."

She sat in one of the cushioned chairs in front of his desk.

"Your office is amazing, Mr. Lawson. Well, the entire

building is. I hope I can find my way through here each day." She caught herself. "I mean, uh, if I get the job."

"Would you like some coffee, Melody?" She declined. "Yeah, this is a big building, isn't it? But don't let it intimidate you, Melody. If you do get the job, I'm sure you'll get used to things quickly. Anyway, you can always ask someone for help and that includes me." He straightened his red tie.

"I appreciate that, Mr. Lawson."

"I helped make the plans for this building, you know? I have a degree in architecture." He smiled.

"So I guess you have a hand in everything that goes on around here. I can see why you probably get overwhelmed with your job."

He clasped his hands. "No need to be nervous, Melody. Just act like we're old friends." She smiled. "I looked at your résumé this morning." She nodded. "It's very impressive, and you made sure to detail how well you are with computers and bookkeeping. You have any experience in accounting?"

"Yes, I took a few courses in accounting at community college right after I got my GED."

"Mind if I ask why you dropped out of school?"

"Uh…" She shifted in the seat. "Well, my aunt started having mental problems. She just snapped. I don't know why or how but she just went downhill all of a sudden. I think she had some kind of breakdown or something. Her doctor couldn't explain it either and after she'd been put on medication, she got even worse." Mr. Lawson nodded. Melody continued.

"She couldn't take care of things on her own. She'd gotten so bad that she couldn't afford to take care of the house or the bills. I took a little job long enough to get money for things. It wasn't a lot but it helped. Anyway, I was so embarrassed about how things had gotten that I began to blame myself."

"Why would you blame yourself for something you had no control over, Melody?"

She shrugged. "I guess I always blame myself for everything. I've always taken things on my shoulders even when I couldn't handle things on my own. Anyway, I'd been having problems in school. Craig, Aileen and Lucas were the only friends I had." She chuckled. "I wasn't popular and I just felt so alone. Most of the other kids couldn't stand me for some reason. I can't tell you why. I guess because I am a bit of a loner and didn't participate in the so-called cool social activities they were all in." She walled her eyes. "Add the embarrassment of my private life and then my teachers began to find out things so I just left." She shrugged. "Mr. Lawson, I'm capable of doing a good job, no matter what it is. I'm trained in working with computers, and I have certificates and…"

"Melody, I wasn't putting you on trial, dear." He laughed. "I just wanted to know a little more about you. Believe me, it has no bearing on my decision as long as you're qualified for what I want you to do." He scanned her résumé. He asked the basic questions. She did her best to give the most impressive answers. "So…" He leaned back in his chair after the grilling.

"So…" Melody chuckled.

"Are there any concerns you have about working here, Melody? Anything I should take into account before making my decision?"

"Well, are there any women working here?" She pointed to the door. "I mean besides the secretary?"

He chuckled. "Look, I'm not one of those bigoted or sexist corporate types. I was raised to believe that women can do anything men can. And sometimes even better." Melody grinned. "Honestly, the women we've encountered couldn't rise to the needed expectations, and that is the truth. Some just didn't seem to be in it for the long haul. I guess they found something better along the way. Most of the women that do work here do not work on this floor so…" He shrugged.

"Well, I appreciate the honest answer. If I do work here, I wanted to make sure this will be a decent environment for a woman."

"Melody, we have a very strict code of conduct here. We're very strict against things like sexual harassment and of course, other things that could erupt between co-workers. We discourage employees from dating, but it's not a policy etched in stone. We allow it, if the employee's work is not compromised by their outside relationship. Other than that, there's no need to worry. Anything else?"

"Mr. Lawson, I want you to know that I didn't go to Lucas for this job. I'm not using him in any way. He offered the chance to me. I work hard, and I don't expect handouts. I've gotten the shorter end of the stick all my life. Believe me, I know how to prove myself. I really like Lucas. I would never use him."

He grinned. "Lucas isn't even the type to let himself be used. Melody, I know my son does nothing unless he wants to. No one thinks you're taking anyone for granted. I know, he set this up himself. There's no harm done." He leaned back again. "From what I've seen, I think you will fit in well here. Better than some of those spoiled young bucks out there in the waiting room."

"What about all those fancy degrees and majors they have?" She grinned.

"What makes you think they have those things?" He leaned up. "Just because someone has money doesn't mean they have a decent education, Melody. Some of them may have the smarts, but most of them just dress up and play the part. There are a lot of people working here who have no business being here. It's how they handle themselves and push themselves that makes the difference. And you need that no matter who you are or how much money you have."

She grinned. "You remind me so much of Lucas."

He smiled. "I'm very impressed by you, Melody. We do have some young men who stand above the rest. Michael Grant and Keith Taylor are excellent employees here. They've built a model of leadership for others here to learn by. Michael has a BA. Keith has an MBA. Highly qualified young men. Of course, you already know Keith."

"Yes, but I had no idea he was so qualified."

"Keith is a genius when it comes to this business. It's all about how he thinks, you know? He has that spark that will surely send him far. You know if Keith plays his cards right, he could be sitting right here in *this* office as CEO one day. I've never felt that way about anyone else. He has what it takes to go straight to the top."

She faked a smile. "So you think very highly of Keith?"

He nodded. "He's definitely someone I have high hopes for. He's an amazing young man. But you've met him. I'm sure you think so, too. I mean, everyone who's met him does. Sure you don't want any coffee?"

"No thank you, sir. So I guess Keith's a big man around here, huh? Probably nothing he couldn't do to get on your bad side."

Dave guffawed. "Well, so far it's been a pleasure having him on the team. I'm sure he wouldn't mind showing you the ropes."

She walled her eyes. "Well, I'm glad you have someone you truly value. I can imagine how hard it is to find good workers fresh out of college. So, what exactly will my position be at Caper?"

"Good question." He looked at her résumé. "Well, I think you have the qualifications to start off as office assistant. You'll have your own office. Uh, basically you'll do the odds and ends that need to be done for the executives and higher employees. You'll be in charge of files and making sure they get where they need to be on time. You'll proofread memos, transport documents to computer databases, record keeping and maybe even some minor accounting."

"Wow." She grinned. "Uh, I had no idea I'd start off doing such an important job. I figured I'd be answering the phone or making coffee."

"Melody, don't sell yourself short. You have the qualifications, and with more experience, you could have the makings of an executive."

"Me, an executive?" She guffawed. "I can't believe this! All this time I've been searching for any old job, setting my standards high and low and now a great job falls into my lap like this."

"I am glad you're excited. Be warned, though, the pay starts at a little over minimum wage."

She smiled. "Mr. Lawson anything would be better than not having a job at *all*."

He nodded, chuckling.

Chapter Four

Melody arrived home an hour later. She got the groceries from the backseat of her jeep. She wondered if this day had been too good to be true. Keith's fancy car sat on the street. She took a deep breath. He wasn't in the car, which meant he'd taken it upon himself to go inside. She did her best not to cause a scene by shouting in the front yard. She'd never been so enraged.

She didn't know how much more of these little surprises she could take. She literally shook at the front door. Her hands trembled until it became impossible to get her key. She tried to shake this morning's episode out of her mind. Keith assaulted her. At least she'd taken it that way. He'd acted so maliciously. She hadn't confronted him because Sarah had still been around.

Now they were alone again. Melody had every right to throw him out of the house. She unlocked the door as she cradled the groceries under one arm. Why did Keith frighten her? What if he touched her again? What if she confronted him and he turned out to be a bigger jerk than she realized?

She stepped inside. Keith wasn't anywhere to be seen. The radio lightly played from the kitchen. Melody recognized the song immediately. She and Lucas had danced to it at Jayson's last night. She set the groceries on the table in the den. What the hell was going on here?

"Keith?" She touched her lips. She hadn't expected her voice to tremble. Keith scared her to death. Unlike Sarah, Melody found it smart to listen to women's intuition. Besides, it hadn't steered her wrong before. She wouldn't entertain Sarah's "benefit of the doubt" attitude any longer. Keith had a serious problem. And it went way beyond the subject of control.

She went toward the kitchen. Keith walked out with a dishrag. She'd had nightmares about that famous smirk.

"Hello, Melody." His eyes scanned her entire body.

"Keith," she exhaled. "What...what the hell are you doing here?"

He shrugged. "Just look, relax and don't run off screaming." He grinned. "Sarah hadn't realized I had the day off. She said I could come by when I wanted so I wanted to make dinner for her. You know, as a surprise."

Melody figured something had to be wrong with her hearing. Could someone be so bold as to come into someone's house when they weren't home? She looked at Keith as he stood there as if he owned the place.

"I thought I heard a car door," he continued. "A moment later, I knew it was *you*."

"Oh yeah, why?" She shook from anger.

"I smelled you." He crossed his arms.

"What the hell are you talking about?"

"That perfume. It's not easy to ignore, you know." He tilted his head. "You seem flustered, Mel. Is something wrong?"

She chuckled. "Is some…of course, something's wrong, Keith! What in the hell do you think you're doing coming in here like you own the place? This is our home, it's not yours! Who do you think you are? I want you out of here!"

He sighed. "I thought we were finally starting to accept each other, Melody."

"Look, I want you to get the fuck out of here right now! You have no right to come in here and I never want you here again."

"I have every right because Sarah gave me a key. She told me I could come by whenever I want and I plan to do just that. I don't know why the hell you're so angry." He scoffed. "Jealous because I said I was cooking for Sarah? You can have some of the damn steak, too, if you want, Melody." He headed for the kitchen.

"Don't walk away from me, Keith!" He stopped. "I want you out and there are gonna be no negotiations!"

"Sarah does so much for you. Can't you at least be civil and let me surprise her? I only came here because I care about her. I didn't even know you'd be here."

"Oh!" She laughed. "Well, I live here, Keith! I have a reason to be here."

He sighed. "Can we please just start over, Melody? This is becoming exhausting, to say the least." She shook her head. "I didn't mean to cause any problems, I swear. I was only gonna make dinner, then leave. I didn't think you'd be here. Sarah told me you had errands to run."

She rubbed her forehead. "This isn't right. I have a big feeling that this isn't right, Keith."

He shrugged. "I don't know what to say. All I can tell you is why I'm here. I know we got off on the wrong foot. Why can't you just give me a chance, Melody? We both love Sarah. You have no idea how much I care about her."

"Do I look like I want to hear this?" She pointed to the door.

"At least let me finish the steak before I go. You can finish everything else. I've got wine chilling in the refrigerator." He stared at her. "You look tired."

She rubbed her forehead. "I went to see Lucas's father about the job." She didn't know why the hell she felt like explaining that to him.

"Did you get it?" He grinned.

She watched him. "Yes."

"That's wonderful, Melody! You should be proud of yourself."

"You seem more excited about it than I do."

He shrugged. "I can't help thinking how wonderful it would be having you there, Melody." His eyes went to her breasts, then back to her face. She crossed her arms to divert his attention. "You know, I could show you the ropes." He walked toward her. She moved to the couch.

"Yeah. Mr. Lawson told me how impressed he is with you. I had no idea you were so qualified." She walled her eyes. "I guess people think you're God on earth, huh?"

"Usually, most people do." He grinned. "Does that threaten you, Mel?"

She sighed. "Does what threaten me?" She moved her hair from her face.

"Well, how people react to me? That people appreciate me. Does that threaten you?"

"Why in hell would it threaten me? I could not care less." She looked at the fresh tan carpet they'd put in last month. Sarah said it would accent the room perfectly. She'd been right.

"Would you uh, like to try my steak?"

"No. Keith, I just want you to leave."

"Come on, Melody. Try, damn it!" He laughed. "I'm not that bad of a guy once you get to know me. Sarah likes me. Doesn't that say something?" She walked to the television. "We shouldn't have to go through this song and dance every time we meet."

"You mean that, Keith? You really want us to become friends?"

"Yes."

"Then why did you threaten me this morning and nearly scare the shit out of me?"

"I don't remember this. When did I uh, threaten you?"

She couldn't even raise her voice for being so appalled. "I'm sick and tired of this game, Keith. You know damn well what I'm talking about. You grabbed me in the kitchen this morning and told me how much you liked being in control." She panted. "That was when I knew I didn't want you anywhere near my sister or me."

"I see." He sucked his bottom lip. "I got angry, Melody. You were questioning me and you practically insulted my relationship with Sarah."

"Oh, you didn't seem insulted, you seemed...you seemed..."

"What?" He walked toward her. "Seemed what?"

She exhaled. "Aroused." She nearly fainted from her own admittance. Yet it had been true. Keith seemed to enjoy that strange moment in the kitchen. She wondered if he could adequately deny that, too.

"Maybe I *was* aroused." He ran his hands through his hair. "It's natural to be, you know? You are a very attractive woman, Melody. And I had my hands on you."

She moved away. "And you had no right! I won't put up with this anymore, Keith! I don't care what your motives are; we're not doing this!"

"Doing what?"

She shook her head. "Stop fucking with me! You know what I mean. I want you to stop all of this now! I don't think it's cute and I don't think it's funny!"

"Jesus." He backed away. "Am I...scaring you, Melody?" He pointed toward the kitchen. "That's the song from

Jayson's. The one you danced to with Lucas. You remember? I love this song. Does me playing it bother you?" She sniffled. He rubbed her shoulder.

"For some reason, I think you like scaring me, Keith. Why can't you just leave Sarah alone? Believe me, you're not the one for her." She moved away.

"I can't do that, Melody. I'm with Sarah now and you have to accept that." He swayed to a different slow song. "Come on and let's start things over right now." He took her hand. "Let's dance. We can have a polite and friendly dance."

"No, I don't think that's a good idea."

He smiled. "I'm trying to be nice, Melody. You could at least see me halfway."

He pulled her close before she could object. She didn't understand a thing, anymore. Keith flipped her entire world upside down. She hated how he could talk his way out of everything. She hated that he'd been so good-looking and charming. He made her feel stupid, childish. He had gained control of Sarah's heart. Melody would do her best to keep him from gaining control over her own mind.

"What are you thinking?" He lightly twirled her around.

"I've never met anyone like you before, Keith."

"Oh? Should I take that as a compliment?"

"No, I didn't mean it as one."

He laughed. "God, you're a hard piece of stone to

crack, Mel. What do I have to do, huh?" They swayed angelically. "Is there anything I can do to win you over?"

"No." She remained rigid.

"God, it amazes me how different you and Sarah are. Yet, you're also very alike in so many ways."

"How?" She looked him in the eyes. He had beautiful eyes. Yet that didn't change her opinion of him.

"I bet people nearly fall out when they see that you're sisters." He grinned. "I know I nearly fainted when Sarah told me she was half-Latino. I mean, I had no idea. There weren't any signs. You're also different when it comes to your tastes." Melody walled her eyes. "You're both gorgeous, but Sarah's beauty is more apparent."

"Oh, thanks a lot." She sighed.

He smiled. "Wait and let me finish here." He twirled her around. "Yours is apparent, too, but it goes deeper than that. I mean, with Sarah, you see her and you go crazy. What man wouldn't? She's beautiful and we all know this. But you're like a fine painting. You know how some paintings may not strike you as much at first, but when you keep looking at them..." He stopped. "You realize more and more how fantastic and lovely they really are."

She tried to move. "Keith…"

"You understand, Melody?" He placed his hands on her face. She tried to pull away. He firmly held her like he had this morning. She'd only known Keith a short while, but long enough to know he manipulated everyone around him. She refused to be taken in. Something told her that his bite wasn't only misleading but potentially dangerous.

"Keith, I want you to leave now, okay?"

"Really?"

"Yes really." She struggled in his arms. "Now, let me go."

"I will if you say it like you mean it." He squinted. "Convince me, Melody."

She pushed him away. "Get out right now, Keith!"

He got on his knees. He pretended to hold a camera. "That's good, Melody. Now, look into the camera, darling. Oh yeah, that's it. Now take it from the top! Come on, say the line, Melody."

"I won't take this shit from you anymore." She opened the front door. "Get the hell out, right now! If you don't leave right now, I swear I'll call the police, Keith. I don't want to ever see you here again. Do you understand me?"

He stood. He got his car keys from the table. He stopped beside her once he reached the door. "I can't read you for the life of me. But something tells me it's going to be fun to try."

She held the door. "Get out, Keith." He pulled her close. He held the back of her neck until she settled in his arms. Melody desperately tried to move. Keith plunged his lips over hers. "Mmm!" She felt she'd die from the strangling kiss. She managed to snatch her head away.

"Stop!" She pushed him away. "Get out! I will call the police, I swear to God, Keith!"

He wasn't laughing. He wasn't speaking. He wasn't *moving*. His stare never left her face.

"Get out!" she shouted out the door in case she needed immediate help. He left without a word.

Melody watched until he drove away. She *had* to make Sarah believe her now. Each moment Melody spent with Keith pushed her closer to lunacy. She didn't know the hold he had on her. She just knew she had to get him out of their lives before it became too late. She exhaled against the door and wondered if it was already too late.

❊❊❊

"We need you! We can't do this on our own!" Detective Steven Kemp paced around the dusty interrogation room. He'd made detective at a younger age than many for his skill at cracking cases. His temper had been his downfall. He never realized that patience could get you farther than frightening someone to death.

He sighed at the shaken young black woman sitting in the middle of the room. Steven ran his hands through his flaxen hair. His gorgeous face was torn with frustration. He penetrated everyone with those killer blue eyes. Detective Brianna Morris leaned over the table doing her best to talk some sense into her partner and ex-lover. Being a black woman, she had her own natural fears about the rapist. She could easily have been on his list. Being a cop didn't matter.

She wasn't only lovely, but a challenge as well. She'd been working the sex crimes unit long enough to know that most rapists loved challenges. She wanted to catch the guy the same as Steven. But she wouldn't resort to scaring the victims in order to do it.

"Steven," Brianna sighed. "I want to catch this bastard just as much as you do, but this is not the way. We can't interrogate the victims like they've done something wrong!"

He looked at the woman in between them. "Look, I'm sorry if I frightened you." He knelt beside her. "But you may be our only hope, right now. The man who tried to rape you last night could have been the Albany Predator." Steven glared at Brianna. She sighed. "You gotta tell us all you remember."

"You don't understand." The young lady shook. Her puffy ponytail resembled a black cotton ball. She looked lovely even in tears. The cops imagined she could be an even bigger heartbreaker otherwise. "Detective Kemp, you can't know how this feels." She sniffled. "You think that just because I got away that I shouldn't be afraid? I'm afraid, okay. I don't even think I can go back to my own damn home!"

He touched her knee. She jerked. "Look, I'm sorry, okay? I guess me being a man, I can't understand. But you were lucky, okay? You weren't raped, and what you tell us could help."

"Why badger me when this man has raped nearly half the black population in Albany? There's a new victim in the paper every day!" Steven and Brianna exchanged glances. "Oh, I get it. The victims aren't talking? So you want me to do their dirty work?"

"Monica?" Brianna stood in front of her. "You got away, true. But don't believe that you're safe now. He is still out there and something tells me that he hates it when he doesn't get his way." Monica held her head. Brianna got on her knees. "I know how frightened you are. I'm a black woman myself, and I've been crazy since this started happening. I want to catch him more than anything, believe me."

"Detective Morris, you're also a cop with a gun and a police force to protect you. I think that's the difference between me and you. This isn't fair. You can't expect me to give you all the answers."

"Monica, we need you, damn it!" Steven hit the table. "Think about what you felt last night! Think about the fear you still feel! Now do you want another woman to feel this way? He may not stop if we don't get him. He could even move on to another place! And we don't know if he will stop at rape."

Monica sucked her fingertip. "What do you mean?"

Brianna shrugged. "We don't know how far he could go or has gone. We only know of the women who've come forward. We're sure that many were too afraid to. Monica, you may have been the only one who's fought him and lived."

"Oh God. You mean he may even be…a killer?"

"You tell us." Steven sighed. "Monica, I'm sorry for how I came down on you. But we need you right now. We need everyone who's come close to this asshole to help us. We can't bust him alone. Every time we think we have a pattern, he switches on us. He lays low for days, then he rapes like crazy for weeks. All we know is he's white and…attractive."

"He's gorgeous," Monica whimpered. "He wore a mask but I could tell by his mouth and eyes. You would think a man like that wouldn't have to rape anyone. I've never come across someone so…so violent. I can't get it out of my head how he shoved me down on the couch and…his hands…his lips were so…so hard. I never knew you could kiss someone so roughly. I kept begging for him to leave me alone. I couldn't believe he'd been in my house all that time, almost the entire night, and I didn't know it."

"Don't blame yourself." Brianna took her hand.

"The mayor thinks a curfew is gonna stop this guy? Oh no, you have no idea who you're dealing with!" Monica shook. "He is a monster, I swear to you! He doesn't care who he hurts. He likes to hurt he…he's so sick…he's…oh God!" she sobbed. "I can't get it out of my head! He had me on the couch and I…I don't know where I got the strength, but I kicked him. I kicked him and I ran. I ran as fast as I could!"

Brianna held her. "Shh it's okay, Monica. It's gonna be all right. You don't have to tell us anything right now." Steven walled his eyes. "But, we do want you to talk to the officer downstairs to go over your report, okay?"

Monica stood. "Thank you. If I can get myself together, I will talk to you. I'm not trying to protect him, but I'm just so scared."

"We understand." Steven nodded. "Your well-being is what's most important here."

"May I go now?"

Brianna nodded. "You have our number. Please use it. You can call us day and night."

"Thanks." She left.

"Fuck!" Steven kicked the chair.

"Steven, please, calm down, all right?" Brianna rubbed her temples. "Look, this has been a very grueling case and we need to regroup and…"

"What? Start from scratch?" He chuckled. "News flash, Bree, we're sitting right smack in the middle of scratch because we haven't found one fucking thing to bring us close to that maniac!"

"Don't you think I feel the same way? Steven, I'm a woman myself! Do you think I like having other women terrorized by this man? If I had him now, I'd probably hang him by his balls, but that is not the way to handle things." Steven shook his head.

"We're cops, Steven. We are allowed to be afraid, but we're not allowed to lose control."

"Seems to me you need to start losing control before it gets too late, Bree."

She ran her hands through her curly black hair. Her almond-brown eyes fluttered at the remark. "Is this personal, Steven?"

"Come on, Bree." He sighed.

"No, I'm just wondering because you've been shooting remarks at me for weeks. Do you blame me for us not finding this guy? I'm only one woman in the department, Steve."

"I know that, Bree. Look, I still care about you, even if you don't want me to." She looked away. "I know it's been a long time but my feelings never died. I will always have this need to protect you."

"So why do I feel like you're blaming me for what this guy is doing?"

"Look, I just get sick of you questioning my methods all the damn time. This shit is hard for me, too, Bree. I mean, lately all I think about is that bastard and trying to catch him. And it's not easy with a bitchy female captain breathing down my throat."

Brianna grinned, thinking of her rough superior. "Well, that's her way."

"I went off on Monica because I can't see how she can sit there and not want to help."

"Then you truly don't understand what it's like to be

afraid. You were right when you said you couldn't understand her fear being a man, Steven. Think about that. Remember her words when you come down on another victim like it's her fault."

He rubbed his chin. "Jesus, is that what I was doing?" She nodded. He sat down. "Brianna, I'm so worried."

She touched his shoulder. "We'll catch him, Steven."

"No." He laid his hand on hers. He looked her in the eyes. "Bree can't you see why this case winds me up more than any other we've dealt with? We've probably gone after what, millions of rapists? But can you see why this bothers me? It hits a little close to home, sweetie."

"Steven." She knelt beside him. "You're talking about me, aren't you? Oh Jesus, that's why you've been acting so crazy. You're worried about me. Steven, I'll be fine." She smiled. "We'll get this asshole like we've gotten all the others."

He exhaled into his hands. "If anything ever happened to you, I don't know what I'd do." She walked to the other side of the room. "I never stopped caring for you, Bree."

"Steven, please." She leaned against the wall. She rested her hand on her gun. "We can't keep going on like this."

"Bree, I have tried to get over you, but…" He chuckled. "You're too amazing for me to do that."

"Steven, we can't go back."

"What, because we're cops?" She turned away. "Bree, I didn't fall for that flimsy excuse when you dumped me, and I sure as hell won't now."

"This is not the time, Steven. We have to think about this case. Now, you know you are my friend and partner. I care about you deeply, but as far as what we used to be, it's…it's out of the question."

He shrugged. "Everything seems to be 'out of the question' with you these days, huh?"

"Stop it, Steven! Damn it, look at the big picture! We have a man terrorizing people! The last thing we need to talk about is some love affair that we couldn't even hold on to."

"That you didn't *want* to hold on to." He held his waist. "I guess being with me was exciting at first. Then when you found me to be your career competition, you lost the fire, huh?"

"Steven, you know why I broke it off." She leered at him. "You *know* and I don't want to discuss this right now."

"Are you prepared if this guy comes after you, Bree? Can you honestly handle that? I think about that every day. I hope you're scared because you need to be."

"I don't need you to tell me how to be, Steven. Unlike you, I don't need to be led around by the nose to get things done," she scoffed. "Let's just stick to the job and let all this other shit go. Agreed?"

He sucked his lip. "Agreed. After all, you're the better cop, aren't you?"

She sighed.

Captain Jersey flounced into the room. The middle-aged woman overlooked her officers with gravity. She held a clipboard against her chest. Her green eyes shimmered through her red-rimmed glasses. She straightened the lapel of her gray suit.

"Kemp, Morris, I've been looking all over for you. What happened with the girl?"

"Monica?" Brianna shrugged. "Nothing much."

"And why not?" Jersey walked up. "She was almost raped. We know it was the predator, and she sure as hell knows. Why isn't she still here helping us find this guy?"

Steven gulped. "Captain, she was too frightened to be of any real help. She was shaking so badly she could hardly talk. We told her to call us when she got herself together, and she agreed she would." Jersey looked at the chalkboard in the back of the room. "I see. You are supposed to be the best in the sex crimes unit. Am I wrong? Yet each day you come up with nothing."

"Captain, it takes time."

"We don't have time, Morris! This man is dangerous. The rapes are happening closer and they get more and more violent each time. We gotta get his ass off the street before he kills someone!"

"So you get that feeling too, huh?" Steven sighed. "Captain, we're doing what we always do, our best. We feel that the victims are opening up more and more. We can't make them talk." He looked at Brianna. "We'll go over the victims' statements and see if there are any leads. But we've talked to everyone we felt may have known or seen some man at one point who fits the description, and we get shit each time."

"I don't like badgering victims, but at this point we have no choice." Jersey tapped her foot. "I want you to start arresting the victims if they refuse to cooperate."

Brianna jumped. "Oh, Captain, that's not a good idea. I mean these ladies are already over the top. If we treated them like they did something wrong, it could damage them for life! Captain, we just can't do it like that."

"We have no choice, Morris. The victims are the only ones that can tie things together for us, and if they're holding out it's going against the investigation. We can't let that slide. We'll just have to bring them in."

"This is sick, Captain." Brianna sighed. "We can't force them to do this. Look at what they've been through."

"I am, Brianna. I don't want anyone else to go through this either. So we'll do it my way. Until you can find something else solid that gets us closer to the rapist, we'll sweat it out of the victims." She went to the door. "And if they don't cooperate, they'll spend time here with us…in jail." She left.

"What the fuck was that?" Steven shook his head.

"Fear." Brianna went to the door. "Don't you recognize it by now?" She left.

❁❁❁

Melody decided to take that spin by Aileen's after all, later that day. She never needed her girlfriend so much. She hadn't gotten any relaxation at home. She couldn't stop thinking about Keith's kiss. She kept her eyes focused on the car in front of her. Driving always took her mind off weird situations. The perfect time to think things out. Course the situation had been more than weird.

She didn't care to figure out the "why" when it came to Keith anymore. She just wanted him gone.

Melody and Aileen were closer than friends could be. Entering adulthood hadn't affected their relationship, either. At times Melody considered Aileen her sister. After all, she shared things with her that she hadn't told Sarah. Melody knew Aileen could help her come to terms with Sarah's intimidating new boyfriend.

Melody and Aileen had tons of things in common. They both loved the same music. They loved the same types of food. They even dressed similarly. They were both tall. They both loathed beauty regimes like doing hair and nails. They were quite creative. They were both hopeless romantics. They both loved to read but hated to be called "bookworms."

Melody loved Agatha Christie. Aileen had always been obsessed with Sidney Sheldon. Neither had missed a book by their favorite authors.

Melody respected Aileen for being a leader instead of a follower. Aileen never cared what others thought. She didn't care if an entire city disagreed with her. Nothing dissuaded Aileen's opinions, if she truly believed she was right. Such bravery wasn't easy to find in people under thirty. Her strength had been the reason everyone looked up to Aileen in high school. They came to her for advice. She always seemed to make the worst problems easier to handle.

Melody turned toward Aileen's street. She remembered when Aileen had been voted "Most Beautiful Senior," yet hadn't made prom queen that last year. Of course she didn't care. Aileen didn't succumb to society's traditions. She'd been more interested in creating her own. She had been one of few blacks at their high school.

Melody wasn't even sure if there had been another black girl there at the time. Melody had been the only Hispanic at Cleveland High herself. Hands down, Aileen had been slapped into the "pretty" group. She'd gained popularity at Cleveland without even trying. Melody had been the complete opposite. Yet they fit together, then as they did now.

A friendship couldn't get any better than this. Melody grinned when she thought of Aileen's wedding to Jonovan. Aileen had gotten married straight out of high school. Melody had been the maid of honor. She remembered tripping at the reception and dousing Aileen's beautiful dress with grape soda. Anyone else would have banned Melody from their life for embarrassing them on such a perfect day.

Aileen hadn't batted an eye. She simply took Melody by the hand and playfully danced with her. In fact, Melody couldn't *remember* a time when they argued. She wondered how she could be so connected to Aileen yet struggled to feel closer to her own sister. She wiped a tear. She hadn't meant to cry, but it sometimes happened while strolling down memory lane.

Her fondest "Aileen" moment had been when Aileen had her daughter, Danielle. Melody had taken her to the hospital on a rainy afternoon. Jonovan drove big rigs from state to state for a living, so he'd been out of town again that week. Aileen didn't hesitate to call Melody when her water broke. In her own words, Aileen had refused to ride in some "tacky" cab to go to the hospital. Even in labor, Aileen could be a hoot.

Melody had also been the first, besides Aileen, to hold Danielle. In return, she'd been named Danielle's godmother. Melody cherished the title, and she hoped she could live up to it, if need be.

Melody reached the driveway. She stared at Aileen's white two-story house. The front door was open. All of the homes in this neighborhood looked the same. To make matters worse, the residents' addresses weren't visible on the curbs. Melody always looked for Aileen's immaculate little garden to make sure she had the right home. A tin watering pail sat lopsided on the porch.

Water dribbled from the garden hose in the yard. Melody didn't like this scene. Aileen never left the door open, and she never left the garden hose out. She never left her pail on the porch. Aileen always kept everything in order. She always reprimanded Melody for leaving things in disarray. No, something definitely wasn't right.

Melody eased from her jeep as she looked next door.

Even Aileen's nosy old neighbor wasn't outside. Melody couldn't remember a day when the elderly lady hadn't been on her porch. She crept to Aileen's door. She felt a chill when she walked inside. She saw the light from the kitchen.

She heard a noise in the back hallway leading toward the bedrooms. Melody took a deep breath. She called out Aileen's name, yet didn't receive an answer. She shouted at the top of her lungs. She checked the kitchen, den, living room and master bedroom. She ran to the phone in the den. Before she could dial 911, someone touched her from behind.

"Ahhhhhh!" Melody fell on top of the small desk. Aileen tumbled over her. "Ahhhh!" Melody waved her arms for dear life.

"Mel!" Aileen hollered. Melody's eyes settled on Aileen's brown pupils. Aileen shook her head. "I won't even ask." She stood. She brushed dust from her denim shorts. Her thin T-shirt fell damply against her dark skin. Her hands were covered in yellow gardening gloves.

"Oh God," Melody panted. "Oh, Leen." She stood. "I thought… I thought you…oh God, I'm glad you're okay." She hugged her.

"I know what you thought." Aileen shook her head.

"Oh, Leen, I was so scared! Do you know how I felt coming here and seeing the door open like that? I yelled for you and you didn't say anything! I was about to call 9-1-1."

Aileen walled her eyes. "Yeah, well, I don't think they'll find a black woman gardening at home that serious, Mel."

Melody sighed. "Leen, I thought maybe the rapist had…" She looked at the walls. "What's wrong with me? Why am I so damn scared all the time?"

"Mel, I was in the closet getting some shears." Aileen pointed to the tools on the floor. "I didn't answer because I had my headphones on and I didn't hear you at first. When I heard someone walking around in my house, I ran out to see what the hell was going on." Aileen's fluffy ponytail bobbed. "Well, I could use some explanation, Mel."

"Aileen, how could you leave your door opened like that with that rapist out there?"

"Here we go." She went into the kitchen. Melody traipsed in behind her. Aileen grabbed a can of grape soda from the refrigerator. "Melody, I don't want to hear one word about that rapist."

"But Leen, I…" Melody sat at the table.

"Not one word, Mel. I can't live like this. If it's not Jonovan on my back about being careful, it's my mother, or you. I'm fine. You're the one who looked like she had a meeting with a train wreck."

"I just got so scared. Leen, you gotta be more careful. This man is a monster. Did you see what he did to that last lady he raped? He beat her in the eye with a lamp, Leen. You saw her on the news! He practically caved in her eye. This man is not only a rapist, but he's a sadistic torturer who has some vendetta against black women."

"I know that, Mel." Aileen grinned. "I see it on the news. I see it in the paper and I am sick to death of it."

"Let's see how sick to death of it you'd be if it happened to you." Melody squinted. "Aileen, you got to take this seriously. If I were you I'd be shitting bricks."

"Melody, I'm not gonna live in a box because of some creep! I have to live my life. And what's the big deal here? There have always been rapists and killers running around this city! What makes this one so different?"

"Because he's targeting black women, Leen!" Melody hit the table.

"Rapists target all women every day, Melody. You think he's the only one out there?"

"No, but he's the only one beating women to a pulp, raping them and leaving them for dead." Aileen turned toward the sink. "And all of the victims sounded just like you, Leen, thinking he wasn't gonna get them. Aileen, you're too smart to be so careless right now. How could you leave your door open like that? Daytime or not, it's still a bad idea."

"And I paid the price since you're here lecturing me." She sipped soda. Melody rubbed her forehead. "I'm sorry, Melody. I'm just so sick of people staring at me like I'm about to be on the six o'clock news. Just because I meet this asshole's requirements, it doesn't mean I'm on his list. He can't rape everyone, Mel."

She scoffed. "Is that supposed to be comforting?"

"I really don't want to talk about this again. Jonovan and I had a big fight over it this morning, and I don't want to repeat the same scenario with you." She passed Melody a Sprite. Melody loved Sprite like mice loved cheese. They sat down. "Oh, Mel, this marriage thing sure is tough sometimes."

"What's up, Leen?"

"Jonovan got on me about going to the store by myself last night. I'm always cautious, but he wasn't hearing it. Today, he wanted to call his boss and tell him he wasn't going to do his delivery in Dallas because he didn't want to leave me here alone." She sighed. "Well, we got into a big argument about it and he ended up going off to Dallas angry, anyway."

"Well, how long will he be gone?"

She walled her eyes. "A couple of weeks or more. He has other deliveries to do around Texas, too. Damn, Mel, I tell you that this is not like I thought it would be."

"Marriage?"

"Yeah. I mean, I know Jonovan needs this job to support us, but I don't know if I can deal with him being gone all the time for much longer. I knew being a truck driver would cause him to be gone a lot but I had no idea." She stretched. "Seems like he's gone way more than he's here and it's getting hard for me. I need him, too, Mel."

"Aileen, you know he's doing this to better himself.

He's saving up so he can go to college and get a business degree. Leen, everything will fall into place. Once he gets his degree he can quit driving trucks, and with his business mind, he'll be moving up in the corporate world in no time." She slapped Aileen's wrist. "I know you miss him now, but it's worth it, Leen. Just don't give up on that."

"Melody, you're talking about dealing with things *then* and I don't know if I can deal with things *now*. I love Jonovan for being a hard worker and he does a damn good job of supporting me and Danielle, but that doesn't make up for him not being here. We started off talking about this and now we're arguing about it. Seems like everything's an argument these days."

Melody took Aileen's hand. She felt guilty. She'd run to Aileen's to sort out her problems, not having any idea what she was going through. It couldn't be easy raising a child with an almost nonexistent husband. Melody made up her mind not to burden Aileen with her problems, unless Aileen brought them up.

Chapter Five

"So, enough about me. How are you, girl?" Aileen grinned. "You haven't been coming by as much. I miss my girl. Lately, I've been thinking of all the crazy shit we used to do. Remember that time we skipped school with Craig and Lucas?" They laughed. "We played chicken on that train, remember?"

Melody grinned. "How could I forget. I can't believe we did something so stupid and dangerous!"

"Hell, we were teenagers. What do you expect?"

"And I can't believe you of all people went along with it, Leen. You always seemed to be the one telling us not to do things, like you were our mother or something. What got into you on that day I wouldn't know." Melody cackled.

"Remember Lucas slipped and almost fell off?" Aileen shook her head. "Man, it was scary as hell back then, but it's funny now!"

"Yeah." Melody sat back. "We've been through a lot, Leen. It's amazing that after all this time, we're still friends."

Aileen's laughter settled into a calm smile. "And we

always will be. You're my sister, Melody. I love you so much."

"Oh Leen, I love you, too." They hugged. "That's why I'm so worried." Melody moved away. "I know I nag you, but I want you to be safe."

"And I will be." Aileen pushed Melody's hair behind her ears. "So how are you, Mel? I sensed the strange mood the minute we started talking. What's the deal?"

She chewed her tongue. "I'll be working at Caper Enterprises." She braced herself for Aileen's excitement.

"Caper Enterprises? You'll be working for Lucas's father?"

Melody nodded.

"Oh my God! Melody, Caper is one of the most successful advertising firms in the nation! How did you go from not having a job to all this?"

She shrugged. "Sarah and Lucas had been talking about it behind my back, and Lucas presented the idea to me. I need a job and his dad said I was qualified to work as an assistant, so there."

Aileen grinned. "Uh-huh. So you'll be working with Lucas, huh? Now that's gotta cheer you up."

Melody grinned. "Why do you say that?"

"Come on, Mel. You were in love with Lucas back then, and you're in love with him now."

"I am not!" She chuckled. "How can you be in love with someone you haven't seen in years?"

"You tell me." Aileen winked. "Be honest, girlfriend.

Doesn't working with Lucas, and the thought of being around him every day excite you?"

Aileen didn't know the half of it. Lucas had to be the main reason Melody entertained the thought for a second. She must have been in love with him if she were willing to put up with being around Keith Taylor every day. She shivered. Aileen gaped. Melody gripped the table and she took a deep breath.

"Oh goodness, it's okay, Mel." Aileen held her. "Panic attack?" Melody nodded. She heaved for a moment, then her breathing returned to normal. "I thought you said you didn't have these anymore." Aileen rocked her.

"Well, I haven't...for a while." She exhaled. She touched her chest. "Just...when I get...frightened."

"Mel, what's the matter?" Aileen pleaded. "You're shaking like a leaf. You're splitting in two before my eyes. Look at me, honey." Melody did. "What's going on? You know, you can tell me anything. Did something happen to you?"

"Where's...Dan...Danielle?" Melody wheezed. She glanced around for the adorable two-year-old.

"She's sleeping." Aileen got a glass of water. "Here drink this, Mel. Take your time, honey." Melody sipped the water. She leaned back in the chair. "You're sweating a river, Mel. You're burning up." Aileen felt her forehead. "Maybe you should go to the doctor."

"No, I'm all right, Leen. It's just a panic attack." She sipped more water. "I'm doing fine, now." At least she thought so before she began thinking of Keith again. "Just so much on my mind, you know?"

"This stuff on your mind…it's the reason you rushed down here in the middle of the day, isn't it?"

Melody scoffed. "I didn't rush." She finished the water.

"Mel. Talk to me." Aileen took her hand.

"You're gonna think it's silly if you're anything like Sarah."

Aileen grimaced. "Please don't compare me to Sarah." They grinned. "Seriously, tell me what's going on. You know you can talk to me, if no one else."

"Well, Sarah has a new boyfriend and…"

Aileen gaped. "Wait a minute." She sat up in the chair. "Sarah has *another* boyfriend? Was she born with some radar that attracts every Tom, Dick and Harry in New York?"

"No, but it sure seems like it. Anyway, his name is Keith and he works at Caper. Oh, Leen." Melody shook her head. "Girl, something is really wrong with this guy. He's not right in the head and I seem to be the only person who sees it."

"Well, what's going on, Mel?" Aileen propped her feet on the table.

"You should see him. The dude looks like he stepped off *Jet Set* magazine or some shit. He wears these posh suits and he drives this fancy car. He looks like he has money coming out of his ass. Worst of all, he acts like he's God's gift to women. He's obnoxious beyond belief."

"Is he fine?"

Melody shrugged. "I guess, if you like that Wall Street-yuppie look."

Aileen grinned. "Come on and give it up. He's got it going on, huh?"

"Okay, he's one of the most attractive men I've ever seen. But I am not attracted to him at all, Leen. I can't stand him." Melody walked around the kitchen. "On the surface he seems like the perfect guy. I can see why Sarah would fall for him. I mean, she has no idea how he acts when she's not around."

"And..." Aileen turned in her chair to face Melody. "How does he act?"

"He acts one way with her, and another with me." Melody filled her glass with ice and water. "He just does the craziest things."

"Like what?" Aileen's bottom lip hung open.

Melody looked at her. "Like sneaking up to my room to see me undress."

"Say what?" Aileen grimaced.

"Yeah, and he grabbed me this morning in the kitchen. Sarah was right upstairs getting dressed."

"Define "grabbed.'"

"He put his hands around my waist, and he wouldn't let me go."

"Well, did you tell him to stop?"

"Yeah, I screamed for him to get the hell away from me. He didn't seem to care what I said, as long as he could get his point across."

"Uh, uh, uh, uh, uh." Aileen shook her head. "What kind of shit is he pulling?"

"I don't know. All I know is that I have never felt this way around someone before. You ever have that feeling that something is out of place, but you don't have the power to fix it? Like a recurring dream when you're drowning, and the only person who can throw you a life preserver...*won't*. Get me?"

"Uh, no. But keep talking." Aileen cradled her knees to her chest.

"He's gone way out of bounds with me in more ways than one. But that's not the most important thing here." She bit her lip. "Leen, Keith Taylor is no good. He's hiding something, I can feel it. You should see how he acts with Sarah, too. It's so sickening, how she coos over him when he seems to think of her as just some object. Every little thing she does now is to suit him."

"Well, you know Sarah's one of 'those' women who drops everyone else in their lives when they get a new man." Aileen finished her grape soda. "Unfortunately, she seems to have a new man every week. Can you say, 'skank'?" She chuckled.

"Hey, watch it." Melody grinned. "That 'skank' is my sister." They laughed. "Seriously, Sarah is not a skank; she's just looking for love in all the wrong places. See, Sarah looks at a guy's material worth and shit like that. She doesn't know a damn thing about a man's heart."

"And you do?" Aileen grinned.

"I know more than she does. If she wasn't blinded by Keith's persona, she'd see the kind of man he is."

"And what kind of man is that?"

"A *dangerous* one." Melody sighed.

"Have you discussed this with Sarah?"

"If she listened, would I be discussing it with you? Besides, with the way Keith's acting I'm beyond convincing Sarah. I have a feeling that this is going to really get out of control. It's just the way he makes me feel. You know how some people make you feel frightened?" Aileen nodded. "And when you feel that way, then something is really wrong."

Aileen stood. "If Sarah won't listen, you gotta just handle things yourself. If Keith continues to act this way with you, you gotta be firm, Mel. Let the fucker know that you're not taking his bullshit. See, he's doing this because he knows you're taking it." Melody nodded. "Seems to me he's a manipulator, Mel. I bet he's pulled this shit with tons of people, except they fall for it. But you don't."

"That's right. I think that's the main reason he's fucking with me. He knows I can't stand his ass, and he wants to control me like he does Sarah." She set her glass in the sink. "I forgot to tell you another thing. This evening, he kissed me." Aileen gasped. "That's why I came over here. I really need some advice."

"So he's attracted to you?" Melody shrugged. "What did you do when he kissed you?"

"I told him to get the hell out of my house."

"Didn't Sarah hear?"

"No, Sarah was at work. Keith had the day off and he was in our house when I got home. Sarah gave him a key."

"Oh wait, wait, wait, wait, wait." Aileen rubbed her face. "You mean this guy, with the way he's acting has the opportunity to go in and out of your house, at will? How long has Sarah known this guy?"

"Probably a couple of months, if that."

"Oh no, this isn't right, Melody. There's no way in hell he should have a key. He shouldn't be able to just waltz into your home like that. Melody, you gotta take care of this, even if Sarah won't. Keith is taking control of Sarah's life, little by little. If you don't put an end to what he's doing now, he'll take control of yours, too. You gotta stand up to him, Melody."

"And if that doesn't work?"

"Then go to the police the next time he lays a finger on you."

❊❊❊

Brianna couldn't believe she loved being a police-woman. She'd started on the police force at twenty-two. She'd outranked many of the officers in the academy. She made detective at thirty. Now, at thirty-five, she felt at ease. She'd had her share of frantic and tragic moments over the last fourteen years. But that hadn't outweighed her love for the job. In fact, she'd grown more respect because of the danger she'd encountered.

She couldn't see herself doing anything else on this earth. People were always shocked to find out that she was a detective. She scanned her latest report about the Albany Predator. Maybe people were right. She could have picked a more glamorous lifestyle. She was beautiful, but she liked to think she was sexy. She was inquisitive with tons of potential. Yet catching sexual predators had been the only thing on her mind.

She struggled to block out the sounds of the noisy police station. Despite all of its faults, she wouldn't have given up her career for anything in the world.

Especially *now*. She flipped through the sketch artist's drawings of the supposed Albany Predator. Brianna hadn't wanted to nail someone so much. It hit too close to home. Her desire grew from a place she couldn't recognize. Even if she hadn't been black, she'd want the bastard. Steven laughed from across their adjoining desks. Detective Pete Cunningham once again entertained Steven with his regular pastime of telling dirty jokes when he should have been getting the damn phone.

"Cunningham!" A detective waved from eight desks down. "Get your damn phone!"

"Huh?" Cunningham struggled to hear beyond a sea of over fifty detectives walking to and fro. Their chattering voices resembled the sound of a thousand typewriters. Brianna shook her head. How she'd gotten used to this, she'd never know.

"I said answer your phone!" the guy hollered.

"Huh?"

"Answer the fuckin' phone!" A detective sitting next to Cunningham left for the soda machine. Cunningham scoffed. He took his time answering it. Steven leaned back in his chair, grinning. He noticed the gravity of Brianna's lovely face.

"Really been working there, huh?" He leaned to see the sketches. "Too bad he looks like your average soap actor. Sure as hell would help us if he didn't look like he walked off a poster."

Brianna chuckled. "Yeah, he looks just like you." She held up the picture.

"Say for real!" Cunningham got off the phone. Another detective stopped to see the sketch. A group began to tease Steven within minutes. "Morris is right, he does look a little like you, Kemp!" Cunningham guffawed.

"He sure does!" A fat middle-aged detective grabbed one of the sketches. "Hey, maybe that's why you can't find him!" They laughed. "Been holding out on purpose, huh, Steve?"

"Funny." Steven looked at Brianna. "See what you started, huh?"

"Shit, it's not Bree's fault. Damn." Cunningham squinted at one of the sketches. "No joke, he looks just like you, Kemp. Where were you last Friday?" They laughed.

"Okay, enough with the teasing, huh? Don't you guys got something to do?" Steven chuckled. The cops slowly milled back to their desks.

"Good eye, Morris." Cunningham walked off.

Brianna grinned. "They're just playing, Steve."

"Well, it's not that funny to me. I don't want to be compared to that asshole." He rocked in his chair. "Going over the victims' statements again?" She nodded. "I've been over them about twenty times and can't pick up a damn thing. I think I'll contact Monica again."

"Just give her time, Steven. She'll contact us if she knows anything. I believe that. I don't think she'll want this man walking around if she can help put him away."

"But we got sketches, statements, even some witnesses who have seen this guy, yet we still come up with shit." He sighed. "He's a smart son of a bitch, I tell you. He s going from neighborhood to neighborhood, and we don't have a clue where he'll strike next."

"I've been thinking." Brianna twirled her pencil. "We know his pattern, right? He rapes and rapes for days straight, then he stops for like weeks." She shrugged. "We can't get a handle on anyone who looks like him." Steven nodded. "I'm thinking he's coming from somewhere else."

"What, you mean you think he doesn't live in the city, but is coming to Albany to rape? That wouldn't make sense. He knows too much about the city's navigation. He's obviously staking out his victims, Bree. You have to live in a city to have that kind of time. Anyway, I don't know if anyone would start raping long distance."

She shrugged. "Just a thought, even though it does seem pretty farfetched." She straightened her papers.

"What's farfetched?" Cunningham returned to his desk with a cinnamon roll.

"I was talking to *him*." She gestured to Steven.

"Oh, excuse me, Madam." Cunningham pretended to be offended. Brianna chuckled. "I'm going to relieve my bowels."

"Ugh." Steven crossed his arms. "A little too much information, man."

"Really." Brianna gathered her things.

"Kemp, do me a favor and answer my phone for me, okay? If it's my girlfriend, put her on hold."

"And if it's your wife?" Steven grinned.

"If it's my wife, hang up." Cunningham left the room. They laughed.

"He's some piece of work, isn't he?" Steven yawned. Brianna stood. She scooted her chair underneath the desk. She turned off the tiny lamp.

"Good night, Steven." She slipped her purse on her shoulder.

"I was gonna stay here and work a little longer. I thought you might…"

"No, I've had as much of this case as I can take today." She grabbed her Thermos. "I just want to go home and go to bed."

He looked at his watch. "It's only seven, Bree."

"Good night, Steven."

"Bree?" She turned around. "We'll get him, baby. Don't worry too much about it, all right?"

She smiled. "See you tomorrow." She left.

"Shit." Steven clasped his hands. A tall black detective walked up.

"Kemp, you still hitting that?" He laughed.

"Fuck off, Simpson."

Simpson sat in Brianna's chair. "Just saying, that's some piece of ass you probably don't want to just let go. I thought you said this break up was temporary."

"What business is it of yours?"

Simpson laughed. "It's not, but boy, do I love rubbing it in." He walked off.

Steven faked a laugh. "Fuckin' cops." He left his desk.

Brianna wished she never had to leave home again. If the nights in Albany seemed long to the general public these days, they appeared more daunting for Brianna. She'd never been at such a standstill with an investigation before. She'd dealt with rapists for years. She knew how to study their patterns. The key had always been to get them where they'd strike next.

The problem with the Predator had been that no one had a clue about his motives. By this time, Brianna usually had a list of motives for a roaming rapist. The motives were what allowed the cops to be a step ahead. She couldn't figure out the Albany Predator if her life depended on it. She couldn't tell if his actions were racially motivated, or if he hated or *fantasized* about black women.

The victims hadn't been much help. Most of them

chose to clam up. The ones who hadn't tended to forget the most important factor of their encounters with him. Steven seemed so sure they'd catch him. She wished she had his confidence. She walked around her cozy, two-story home. She lived in a beautiful neighborhood. The people loved having a cop within their grasp. They thought it ensured safety.

Brianna knew better. In fact, most crime-ridden neighborhoods had cops at their disposal. The general public had no idea how determined a criminal could be. Killers were dangerous. Kidnappers were relentless. Yet rapists stirred up awareness in a community that could not be denied. They were the lowest of the low. They were the uptime of anything sinful and horrid, and the Albany Predator seemed the worst yet.

Brianna finished a cup of cinnamon tea. She thought about the Predator's recent rapes. She'd never felt so desperate. Maybe Captain Jersey's way would be the answer. Brianna didn't like the idea of arresting victims, but if it kept others safe, she'd open up to it. She heard Davis purring in the distance. She headed upstairs to bed. It hadn't even reached nine o'clock. She hadn't been to bed before ten in years.

She headed for her closet and laid out her clothes for the next day. Davis slithered into the room. The tan-and-white feline found his favorite spot in the corner. He licked his paws and buried his head into the thick carpet. Brianna rushed to pet him. Davis purred, letting her know he enjoyed the attention. He rolled over on his back as she caressed his furry belly. He licked his tongue out in avid appreciation.

She grinned. "You like that, huh?" He purred. She figured he deserved a snack before heading to bed. They went downstairs. Davis took off toward the dark den before Brianna reached the kitchen. She opened a can of cat food and poured it into Davis's little red dish. "Davis, come here!" She made a high-pitched sucking sound through her teeth. "Come on, I'm tired. Momma's gotta go to bed, okay?"

She heard clicking in the den. She imagined Davis pulling on the snaps of the curtains like he always did. She peeked inside. The soft carpet felt like heaven against her naked feet. Davis wasn't there. She felt a chill. Something wasn't right. She wasn't like those stupid women on television who went searching their house without means of protection.

She was a cop, damn it. She knew how to handle herself. She knew what to do. She thought of her gun in her bedroom first thing. She was rushing toward the stairs when she heard a low growl. "Davis?" She turned from the stairs and propped against the wall. She heard a crash in the kitchen. Dishes tumbled in the sink. She ran to the living room and grabbed her pepper spray from the little desk in the corner.

She turned off the hallway light. Someone had it in mind to surprise her, but she'd do the honors first. She waited in the darkness.

"Meow." It came from the den. Brianna stood inches

away. She took measured steps. She heard the low meow again. It didn't sound anything like Davis. In fact, it sounded almost…like a *human*.

She tried to ignore her pounding heart. She put her faith in that top-notch police training that she'd grown so fond of. She held the pepper spray behind her back. If only she could get to her gun; she had no time now. She entered the den. She swore she could taste the body heat. That's how close she'd come. Or more importantly, how close the intruder may have been.

She held her chest. "I've got a gun here," she lied. "I'm a police officer! I want you to show yourself right now, or I will fire!" She exhaled. "Do you hear me? I know you're in here. Do the smart thing and come out right now! I don't want to hurt you, but if I have to, I will." She stood back. The intruder could have been closer than she thought. "Did you hear me? I want you to step out slowly with your hands up. I *will* fire!"

She flicked on the lights. She scanned the room. She saw her computer, phone, television and fax machine all in place. She checked to see if someone hid behind the couch. She heard footsteps in the other room. She ran into the hallway. She ran to the stairs. Damn it, she needed that gun. She stared upstairs at her bedroom. A bead of sweat fell down the bridge of her nose.

"Ahhh!" she screamed.

Someone whipped her around so fast she nearly tumbled over. Her arms were locked behind her back.

She felt the softness of leather gloves against her skin. A strong man in black clothes and black boots held her close. He rubbed his face against her ear.

Brianna felt the fabric of a soft knit cap. "Drop the pepper spray, now," he ordered calmly. He held her arms tightly against him. One arm squeezed her waist. "I said…drop it."

She exhaled and followed the order. "Okay, just take it easy." He jerked her hair until her head rested on his shoulder. "Take it easy, all right."

"Yeah," he chuckled. "I'll 'take' it easy; don't worry about that, baby." He ran his hands down her flimsy T-shirt. She always wore a T-shirt and panties to bed. This had been one night she wished she hadn't.

"You're him aren't you?" She breathed. "The Albany Predator."

"What do you think?" He rubbed her nipple with his free hand. "Now, I don't want you to move, honey. I don't want you to move, or think. I don't want you to do anything. You understand me?"

"Yes." She shut her eyes.

He cackled lightly. "You know me? Huh, you know me?" He rubbed her soft brown neck. "Well, I know you, too, Brianna. I know all about you. You think just because you're a cop it makes a difference? It doesn't. In fact, this makes it more worthwhile. Know why?" He jerked her hair. "Because you're a challenge. And I'm no amateur."

"I...I know you're not." She kept her voice leveled despite her fright. "We can talk, you know? We can just talk."

"I didn't come here to talk. How does it feel to be so close to something you've wanted for so long? You've been hunting me..." He ran his finger across her belly button. "I've been hunting *you*. Oh God, do you know how good this feels?" He leaned against her. "Answer me."

"I..." A tear ran down her face. She refused to be his victim. She wondered if she truly had a choice.

"I want you." He caressed her neck. "And I'm gonna have you. Do you understand that? As long as you understand that, this can be painless and smooth." He slipped his hand down the front of her panties. She struggled. "Shh, be still, okay. We don't have to do this the hard way, do we, Brianna? I just wanna see it, okay? I just want to see your twat, okay?"

She shivered. "Look, you don't want to do this, okay? You are not going to get away with this. You're fucking with a cop and that's not a good idea, believe me."

He turned her around. He stared her in the eyes. "Get on your knees and don't move." She got on her knees. She looked at him with begging eyes. He moved his finger in a circle across her plump lips. He moaned. "You're gonna use that mouth, okay?" She nearly vomited at the thought. "I've never done a cop, so I'm going to enjoy this most of all." He unbuttoned his black jeans. Brianna eyed the protrusion from his white jockey shorts. "Ask me what I want you to…to do." He rubbed his crotch.

"No." Brianna tried to look away. He forced her eyes on him again.

"Do it, Brianna." He rubbed her neck. "I don't want to hurt you, but I will, if I have to. Ask me what I want you to do."

"No." She shut her eyes. He pulled her hair, snapping her neck back. She howled in pain. "What…what do you want…me to do?" Her voice shook.

He smiled through the cap. "Good girl. I want you to suck my dick, okay? I want you to suck it until I come. You understand me?" He let her hair go. "And if you don't, I'll kill you." She tried to shake the fright. It seemed impossible. He frightened her beyond belief. She could only imagine how the other women felt. He pushed his underwear into his jeans. "See the head? Do you see it?"

"Please just…"

He moved closer to her. "I won't fuck you if you don't want me to," he whispered. "I'm making you a special offer. I just want you to suck my dick. If you don't, I'm gonna stick it in your pussy. So, which do you want?" He chuckled. "You were gonna spray that pepper spray at me, huh? Well, I'm gonna spray something in your lovely black mouth." He pulled out a knife.

"I won't be your victim." She shook. "And I won't let you hurt anyone else. You can fuck me if you want to, but believe me you won't leave here alive. I promise you that, limp dick." She gasped at her own words.

"What did you say to me?" He stepped back. "Who do you think you're talking to, huh?" He held her neck. "Who the fuck do you think you're talking to, bitch?"

She grinned. "Call me what you want, but you aren't gonna live for long, if I have anything to say about it."

He knelt beside her. He rubbed his crotch. "You know, I like you." He ran his hands down her face. "You got guts. I knew you would. Tell me something. You ever fucked a white guy before?" He circled his thumb around her nipple. It hardened beyond her control. "Answer the question, Brianna."

"You've obviously been watching me. So you probably know things about me. Probably been asking around." He nodded. "You should know who I've fucked, shouldn't you? White guys or not."

"But I want to hear it from *these* lips." He cradled her plump mouth in between his fingers. "You have no idea how hard this makes me. It's your partner, Steven, right? You used to have some heated love affair." He grinned.

"May I ask how you got that information?" She stared at him.

He pulled her from the floor. He played with her hair. He held her in his arms. "It's going to be a real treat having *you*. Why don't you try some of those self-defense moves on me, huh? Or am I still one step ahead?"

She struggled in his arms. "Tell me about the women

you raped. I want to know why you did it. How you got into their homes, everything."

He kissed her neck. "Why you want to know that? What difference does it make now? I think tonight I'll do things different." He ran his tongue down her neck. She struggled. "I'm not leaving you as my next victim." He tore off her T-shirt. Her luscious breasts stood in midair. He gazed at the black nipples. "I can see why Detective Kemp's so taken with you." Brianna gaped. "Know why I love that sweet black pussy of yours? All that soft curly hair…the smell."

"Let…go." She struggled.

He sucked her left breast. She tried her best to hold it together. She needed another plan of action. She couldn't come up with anything. If only she could get to her gun upstairs. He continued to suck her nipples. His knit mask moved softly against her shivering skin.

"Tell me you want me to fuck you." He gripped her buttocks.

"No." She shut her eyes. "You're gonna have to take it! I'm not giving into your sickness!"

"Fine." He dragged her to the small table in the hall-way. He tied her hands behind her back with a black scarf, binding her to the table.

"I won't let you. You're gonna have to kill me first." She glared. "Why just black women, huh?" She stared at him. He fondled her breasts again.

"I guess chocolate's always been my favorite flavor.

You're going to be surprised, Brianna. As you can see, I'm kind of big. So I might tear you a bit. But it'll be worth it."

He pulled his pants down to the ankles.

Brianna maneuvered her body against the table. He positioned his long legs around her. He pulled her on top of him. The table scooted against her from the force.

She stared into his eyes. For some reason she couldn't stop looking at them. She wondered if he had hungered for the others like he had her. Brianna figured she'd been the biggest challenge for him. The possibility of raping a cop obviously turned him on beyond belief. She knew he enjoyed playing this game with her. Mind fucking his victims probably got him off faster than the physical act.

"A or B?" he whispered. She grimaced. "A, means we do things nicely. B, means not so nicely." He grunted, scooting her toward his crotch. She jiggled to block his entrance. "It's not going to work." He sweated through the cap. "I know what you're trying to do. I'm fucking you tonight, so you might as well relax. You might as well."

Brianna waited until he got into the perfect position. She thrust her knee into his crotch.

"Ahhh shit!" He threw her off. She bounced against the table. She used the bounded table for leverage. She reached up and kicked him in the face. He flipped backward. She hurriedly rubbed her wrists together to free her hands from the scarf. The predator scrambled around on the floor. He cradled his bleeding face. He headed for the front door.

"No!" Brianna grabbed his leg. "You're not leaving, you son of a bitch!"

"Let go!" He smacked her. She fell backward. Blood slithered from her forehead. She batted furiously to keep the blood out of her eyes. She refused to let him leave, no matter how hard it would be to keep him there. He limped out the front door.

"No! You son of a bitch…" She held her sides. Weakness prevented her from going any farther. She heard a car alarm from down the street. A few dogs barked. The stuffy night air invaded her home. She struggled to catch her breath. She scooted onto her porch on her hands and knees. "No," she gasped. "No!" She didn't see *anyone*.

"Meow." Davis scampered up behind her. He rested at her feet.

"Damn…it." Brianna rested on the porch in agony.

❊❊❊

Officers scrambled throughout Brianna's home an hour later. She didn't like being the "victim," but tonight she had been. She held her favorite blue blanket across her shoulders to shield her torn clothing. She didn't anticipate having to hand her clothes over to her peers. She knew the drill. Hell, she lived the drill. Being a cop ran through her blood. She couldn't escape it.

She moved onto the front porch and she slipped through a line of passing officers.

Steven ran up the driveway. Captain Jersey's car pulled in behind the four cop cars parked on the street. Brianna took a deep breath. Yep, she hated being the victim.

Steven asked a uniformed cop some questions about the situation. He joined Brianna on the porch. He stared at her. She turned away. So, the "treatment" had started already? She could never stand the thought of a man protecting her. Steven's usual handsome face seemed torn with worry that had been all her fault. She knew it. Situations like these made it difficult to be his lover.

They butted heads about this damn job continuously. Brianna had always been stubborn. She knew that. She never wanted a man to protect her and Steven knew that. Brianna sighed. Knowing what had caused past mistakes hadn't made them easier to deal with for either of them.

Steven held his waist. He looked at the pavement as if he wasn't sure of what to say. Brianna moved her curly hair from her face. The night wind ruined the neat look she tried to preserve. She rocked on her heels. She'd rushed to put on socks before the police got there.

"So..." She chuckled. "Hell of a night, huh?" She held the blanket tightly. "Hell of a night."

"My God, Bree." Steven looked at her. "Are you okay?"

"Why wouldn't I be okay?" She watched Captain Jersey converse with a group of cops on the lawn. "I was just almost raped. It's no big deal."

"Bree." He turned her toward him. "Let's not do this."

"Do what?"

"Play this game. It's cute at other times, but it isn't now. You don't know how I felt when they told me what had happened." She looked away. "I nearly crashed my damn car. All I could think about was that monster in your house with his...his hands all over you and..."

"Don't, Steven." She shoved her mouth into the blanket. "This is just part of the job, right? We're cops. We're supposed to handle anything that comes our way." She looked at the bright moon. Funny how a night so beautiful could end up being one of the worst she'd ever experienced.

"We're supposed to handle even attempted rape?" he whispered. She didn't answer. "Did you give your statement, yet?"

"About eighteen times. They've been crowding around me like I'm a newborn baby. Look. *Five* cop cars for this, Steven? You see the fuss they're making?"

"They're worried about you, Brianna. How do you expect them to act? You better be glad every fuckin' cop in the city isn't here." Steven looked at Captain Jersey.

"Only because I'm one of them, right? Have we gone through this much trouble for the other victims? Is it supposed to be comforting to realize all this is being done because I'm a cop, and we all know that cops look after their own."

"Yeah, maybe we do, but nothing's wrong with caring for one another. And we *have* done this and more for the victims. You know that, Bree." He sighed. "It's just different when you're close to someone. Being a cop... it's like a family, Brianna. You automatically have that acceptance and protection, you know?"

"I just feel so damn...helpless. I hate this feeling!" she shouted. The officers briefly witnessed her outburst, then went back to business. "I guess I better go inside and take these clothes off for evidence."

"Wait, Bree." Steven rubbed his chin. "Tell me what happened."

"To make a long story short, the Albany Predator was waiting in my home." She moved for a female officer to pass. "He may have been here the entire time. I'm not sure. I heard a noise when I went to feed Davis." She gestured inside. A muscular black officer played with the tired feline. "He ran off somewhere and I heard someone in my home."

"Did you know it was the Predator?"

"Not at that time. I didn't know what the hell it was, really. I just got the feeling that something was wrong. I tried to go back upstairs for my gun, but I ran short of time so I got the pepper spray. But that was like getting nothing because I didn't get the chance to use it." Steven shut his eyes. "So uh..." Her voice shook. "He grabbed me, he said a lot of things I don't care to repeat, tied me to that table." She pointed. "Tried to rape me, I fought back. He ran out...end of story."

Steven scoffed. "It's only the beginning, Bree. I knew this would happen! It's all my fault."

"What? How the hell can it be your fault, Steven?"

"It's my fault because I kept letting you push me away. I knew you needed me. But I let you go on with this fantasy that you can take care of everything yourself. It's the same bullshit that killed what we had!"

"I don't have time to listen to this." She waltzed into the living room. He followed.

"I want you to admit it; you can't handle everything on your own. I want you to once admit that you're not some super cop and that you get scared, too! I need to hear this from you, Bree!"

"Steven, I can't believe how selfish you're being. I was almost raped tonight! The last thing I need is to be interrogated by you!" She sighed. "What do you want from me?"

Captain Jersey walked inside. She looked back and forth at Steven and Brianna.

"Morris, are you okay?" Captain Jersey's voice held its usual stiffness, yet Brianna could tell she cared. She wouldn't have rushed over if she didn't.

"I'm fine." Brianna looked at Steven. "I was just about to tell Steven that I can take care of myself, and that I know what I am doing." He scoffed.

Jersey sighed. "I'm not so sure. I mean, I know you're a damn good cop, Morris, but this is just a little too close for comfort. I'm thinking that maybe I need to take you off this case, and let Kemp go at it alone."

Chapter Six

"Excuse me?" Brianna nearly dropped the blanket. She rushed to catch it after remembering her torn clothes. "Captain Jersey, you cannot be serious. I have put months and months of time and effort into catching this man. I know this case better than Steven does! How the hell can you even think of taking me off it?"

"I can think of it because you were almost raped tonight. Not only that, you're damaged goods."

"Damaged goods?" Brianna gaped. "What the hell are you talking about?"

"She's talking about how you're gonna be when you start to face this, Bree." Steven squinted. "I mean, really, face it. You haven't faced it yet."

"I'm facing it fine! I know what happened to me! It has nothing to do with me being able to do my job! I can handle myself, Steven!"

"You were almost raped tonight!" he yelled.

"But I wasn't! And this is the fuckin' job, right? We are cops! We know the dangers like the back of our hands!" She looked at Jersey. "Captain Jersey, you can't pull me out now. You can use me as bait even."

"What?" Steven shrieked.

"I mean, he knew I was a cop. He knew everything about me, Captain. He even knew Steven and I used to be together. I am no different than any other woman he's wanted to control. The only difference is that I got away. Don't you see? Rapists don't just walk away. They don't just quit. Captain Jersey, I can draw him out."

"How?" Steven scoffed.

"He wants me, Steven." Brianna's voice shook. "And he'll be back."

"So what'cha saying?" He rubbed his chin. "Huh? You want to put yourself out there for this sick mother-fucker? Why can't you just walk away, Bree? Why do you always have to prove that you're better than every-one else?"

"I'm not doing that, Steven!"

"You can't just wish tonight away, Bree. I don't care what you do; this has happened! You were almost raped tonight!"

"I know that!" She cried into her hands. Steven reached for her. Jersey gestured for him to let her be. Brianna calmed down. She took a deep breath. "I am not in denial. No matter what you both think, I can do my job, regardless of what I went through tonight. I'm a cop." She looked at them. "Okay?"

"You're a woman first, Bree." Steven shook his head. "Why can't you realize that? There's nothing wrong with being scared or confused. No one expects you to be perfect, except yourself! No one else expects you to be anything more than what you are."

"I can take care of myself, Steven." He paced. "Captain Jersey, let me finish the case."

Jersey rubbed her forehead. "I…"

An officer ran into the room. "Detective Kemp, you got a phone call from the station." The officer threw the cell phone to Steven, then ran back outside. Brianna and Jersey watched in silence.

"What?" Steven looked at the ladies. Brianna and Jersey exchanged glances.

"Wait, when…this evening?" He rubbed his face. "Yeah, I'll be there. Did you dispatch some officers already? Okay, yeah. I'll be at the scene in five minutes. Yeah, Detective Morris is fine. Okay, bye." He stared at the phone.

"Kemp, what is it?" Jersey glared.

He exhaled. "Monica Cartwright…is dead."

"What?" Brianna covered her mouth.

"Who is Monica Cartwright?" Jersey fixed her glasses.

"The woman we brought in for questioning about the rapist. The one that got away." Brianna looked at him. "Steven, what happened?"

"Apparently it happened this evening. A neighbor found the body. Monica's body's all bruised up. She was raped, too. The blows to her head may have caused her death. They say it looks like the work of the Albany Predator."

"Shit!" Jersey stared at the carpet. "Homicide. You

know what that means, don't you? Oh, if you think Commissioner Reynolds has been riding our asses about this guy so far, then you just wait until he hears this! A fuckin' homicide!"

"Captain Jersey, you can't take me off the case." Brianna exhaled.

She shrugged. "Morris, weren't you listening? The man may have *killed* that young lady. So the homicide guys get the case, you know this. It's changed directions, Morris. We're no longer dealing with just a rapist. Sorry, but you and Kemp's days are numbered on the case." She rushed out the living room.

Steven shook his head. "And if we find out he's killed others it may even go to the FBI. He'd be a serial killer. Fuck! How did things get this far?"

Brianna sighed. "He was here. He was so damn close, Steven. How could I let him get away like that?"

"You did the best you could."

"But he could be a killer, Steven. I had him. I was so close and I just let him get away."

"I got to get to the scene. I'll call you with the information soon as I can." He rubbed her arm. "Are you really okay?"

"Yeah," she sighed.

"You sure?" She nodded. He kissed her forehead. "See you, Bree." He quickly headed toward the front door.

"Steven, wait!" Brianna struggled with the blanket. "I got to get changed and…"

"You kidding me? You're not going, Brianna! This man nearly raped you, and he may have murdered Monica Cartwright! You're not going anywhere near that place!" He ran into the yard.

"Oh yeah? Try and stop me." Brianna ran upstairs to change.

❊❊❊

Melody arrived for her first day at Caper a few days later. She felt more at ease since Lucas's visit last night. He claimed he'd come over to wish her well for her first day. She grinned. She tugged on the lapel of her crisp tan pantsuit. Courtesy of Sarah's newest credit card. If Lucas's intentions had only been about the job, then how come he hadn't mentioned the job once?

Melody scampered to the floor she'd be working on. She'd do her best not to appear cocky, though she'd figured out how to navigate the building already. With such a complex building that hadn't been an easy accomplishment. She stopped in a hallway encased by beautiful, top-notch offices. She wondered if she'd become acquainted with everyone here.

She doubted it. Even though Caper Enterprises took up less than half of this skyscraper, Melody had a feeling that it boasted the most employees in the building. And that seemed to be *a lot*. Well-dressed men breezed past her like gnats. Two women flew around a corner chattering. Melody would have made their acquaintance, but couldn't keep up long enough to say hello.

The ladies darted around another corner talking about coffee and a new brand of perfume. She passed Dave's empty office. His secretary stacked papers on his desk. Melody continued down the hall. She looked for her office and the trainer Dave had assigned her. He'd been nice enough to take care of things personally for her. Once again, she couldn't help wondering if it had been more for Lucas's sake than for hers.

At this point she couldn't afford to care. All she'd think about would be this job from now on. She anticipated working here more than she thought. She liked the busyness. She liked the organization. She liked keeping to a schedule. Hell, she just liked feeling important and needed. She would be leveling things out for all of Caper's employees. She vowed to do her best. She'd become a top necessity, if she had anything to say about it.

Her trainer turned out to be a forty-year-old clerk named Mario Lamos. Melody glowed at seeing another Hispanic on the premises. She assumed if she would see one, they'd be pushing a bucket. Maybe her ideas were prehistoric, but Caper didn't seem like it hired many of her kind. Mario presented her a girlish smile the moment she entered the office.

He told her about the business within minutes. She could see why Dave spoke so highly of the chipper clerk. Mario knew everything about files, answering phones

and setting up meetings. She wouldn't have been surprised if he knew how many staplers were in the building.
She grinned at the thought. Her mind drifted to the
news reports she'd caught over the last few nights.

She'd become so sick of this rapist she didn't know
what to do. It didn't matter to Melody who he targeted
specifically. Black or not she felt like a potential victim.
She didn't know how much longer she could deal with
being so on edge. Maybe this job would get her mind
off things. At least it would keep her busy.

Mario shared personal tidbits about himself after
explaining the job to Melody. He got a pretty hefty sum
for his duties. He first started at Caper at twenty-three,
too. Melody didn't find that part too comforting. She
did *not* want to be an assistant for the next seventeen
years, high pay or not. Mario openly admitted his
homosexuality though Melody had picked up on it
immediately. He boasted that he knew everything about
everyone in the company. Melody took this as another
chance to do her own digging. If Mario knew the goods,
it would be in her best interest to become a friend.

She waited until he went on about some boat he and
his boyfriend Luis were buying. They'd been saving up
for a trip to Costa Rica. The two had been together for
four years. Mario claimed they'd finally make it official.
Melody pretended to care long enough to get to the
good stuff...what *she* wanted to talk about. Mario un-
packed newly delivered office supplies for her desk.

Melody liked the office, though it lacked the prestige of Dave's. She walked around the back of her desk. She also had a window where she could see around the city.

She ran her fingers down the cool glass. She belonged here. She could feel it. Maybe this had been what she needed all along.

"So, you're a quiet chica, huh?" Mario winked. "We can talk all the Spanish we want in here, but in the halls, let's keep it English."

"I speak primarily English, anyway, unless I'm pissed."

Mario chuckled. "Then what'cha do?" His accent became apparent after every three words.

"I curse in Spanish." She grinned. "There's not a lot of Latinos where I live or where I go and all, so it's easy for me to curse folks in Spanish and walk away."

He laughed. "I'm gonna like you, girl. I really think we'll become fast friends. I like your style, mama. That suit's to die for. I think I saw it in a catalog from one of them fancy stores. Girl, if you got that kind of money, why are you an assistant *here*?"

She shrugged. "First off, my sister paid for this suit. She's the one with the dough in the house. Hell, she's the one with the house, period." Mario grinned. "Soon I'll be making my own money, and I won't need her to support me. I just want to do all I can. I think working here is going to be a great opportunity for me." She sat in the leather chair behind her desk. "Mr. Lawson is very nice. He seems very fair and professional."

"Oh yes, he's the best," Mario gushed. Melody wondered if he held more than admiration for his employer. "Mr. Lawson believes in helping the underdog, you know? He gave me a chance when no one else would. I hadn't even finished college and he offered me a place here. After he saw my qualifications, of course. He's one in a million. I wouldn't want to work for anyone else." He smiled.

"Well, if it's all it's cracked up to be, then maybe I made the right decision to work here." She smiled.

"Yep." He yanked a box of folders from the floor. "Pardon me for staring but...you are Sarah Johnson's sister, right?" Melody nodded. "You guys don't look anything alike."

She grinned. "Believe me, we know. We get this all the time. I mean, we say we're sisters, yet people are always dead set against believing us." She chuckled.

"I mean, I didn't even know Sarah was Latino until probably recently. And I still can't believe it." He slapped the box on the desk. He held his thick waist. "Your father was white, right?" She nodded. "What exactly was your mother?"

"A woman." Melody grinned.

He chuckled. "Her *race*."

"Mexican." She smiled.

He tilted his head. "Ah, I'm Chicano myself. I got a lot running through my blood." She smiled. "Got any kids?"

"Who me?" She chuckled. "I can't even keep my own room clean. You think I can tell someone else how to run *their* life?"

Mario laughed. "I can see you'll be fun to have around already, Mel. Looks like we're hitting it off well. So, how did your parents meet? Was your mother born here or Mexico?"

"She was born here." She looked at the ceiling. "Actually, I kind of forgot how my parents met." She grinned. "I think they met in college. My dad was a dentist and my mother a pharmacist."

"Wow, very good jobs, huh? You come from good stock. I know Sarah makes that good dough where she works."

Melody shrugged. "Now it's time for me to make some decent money for myself, hopefully."

"Lucas told me that your parents died in a car crash when you were young, right?" She nodded. "I'm sorry. It must have been hard growing up without parents. My parents are the center of my world. I'm so close to my mother, I could be a pimple on her ass." He laughed.

"Wow, well…I guess that's a good thing." Melody chuckled. "So you really know a lot about the people here?"

"Nothing gets past me. I guess every workplace needs a good gossip, huh?" He rested his large frame against the file cabinet. Melody couldn't help thinking why the most alluring men seemed to be gay. Mario had looks, charm and a sense of humor. Too bad she'd been the wrong damn gender to even experiment with him. "Something on your mind?" he asked.

She shook from her daydream. "What do you know about Keith Taylor?"

He sighed. "Besides the fact that he's fine as hell?" She grinned. "Well, he's probably the only one here I don't know much about." He opened the box of folders. "I don't think the CIA could get into his business. He's very private. He doesn't give people the opportunity to know what he doesn't want them to."

"What do you mean?" Melody nibbled her lip.

"Well, with other people you can just read them, you know? You can listen to their conversations. You can see how they react, and you can watch them and find things out. Not Keith. It's like he's always...always guarded somehow. Like he goes out of his way to make sure he doesn't lend extra information. It's not normal, if you ask me."

She leaned up. "What do you mean?"

"Well, I hate to say things about people, but I never really liked Keith Taylor. He just doesn't come off as being on the up and up." Melody raised an eyebrow. "It's like he always has some kind of angle, and I can't figure it out for the life of me."

"Angle with this job, or in general?"

Mario wiped sweat from his forehead. "He always manages to make things work out in his best interest, you know? I mean, he gets perks around here that people who have been working here for years don't even get. It's like everyone is snowed. The employees flock to his every move. The women around here, oh, they can't get enough of him. And Mr. Lawson acts like he's Jesus." He shook his head. "I'm probably the only one around here who doesn't think twice about him."

Melody stood. "Until now." Mario looked at her. "I think you're on the right track, Mario. I don't like Keith Taylor, and I'd die before believing a word that came out of his mouth. I think he's a manipulative liar." She looked into the hallway. "He scares the hell out of me, and for that, I want to make sure he stays away from my sister."

Mario sighed. "I think you should definitely stay away from him, too, Melody."

"If only I could get Sarah to see a reason, but he has her snowed like everyone else."

"Hi." Keith leaned at the door with his arms crossed. His fancy white shirt, blue tie and black slacks were straightened to perfection. Melody wondered if he'd heard. Somehow she felt it hadn't made a difference either way. She wanted him to know how she felt. Maybe then he'd leave Sarah the hell alone.

"Uh, hello, Keith." Mario waved nervously. "I was helping Melody get settled in. How are you this morning?"

Keith squinted as he glanced at Melody. "I'm fine, Mario. Just heading to my office. Please don't stop talking about me on my account." He smiled at Melody.

"Melody, I'll be right back. I need to get you the manual so you can read up on your duties." Mario slid past Keith.

"Oh, boy." Keith chuckled. He scooted on top of the desk. "Nothing more flattering than a woman checking up on me."

"Believe me, I wasn't doing it for the reasons you think, Keith." She glared at him. His eyes skimmed her large breasts through her suit jacket.

"Any reason you'd take time to know more about me is music to my ears, Melody." He smirked.

"I have to go to the bathroom and…" He blocked the door.

"You're not going anywhere!" He shoved her in the chair.

"Get out of my way, Keith!"

"Shut up!" He opened her suit jacket. He tore open her blouse.

She screamed. "Oh! What are you doing? My blouse!" She tried to shield herself with her arms.

Keith held her to the chair. "Yeah, I did it," he whispered.

"Get away from me!" she begged.

"I said, shut up." He glanced at her plump breasts encased in the lacey white bra. Melody could barely breathe. She sure as heck couldn't confront him. Her heart pounded. She started to see double and became woozy.

"Oh, what's the matter…huh?" Keith panted. "What,

having a panic attack, Mel? Sarah's told me all about those." He struggled from staring at her breasts.

"Keith...I...I can't breathe."

"What, huh?" He got on his knees in front of her. He continued to hold her arms to the chair. "Besides being gorgeous with great legs, you've also got a very bad habit. You're nosey as hell. At first, I assumed that was part of your charm. So I tolerated it. But I won't tolerate it much longer." He stood erect. His eyes narrowed until she saw no evidence of the green pupils.

"Are...you...threatening me?" She gazed at him between pants.

"At first, I found it cute how you've been acting, but I quickly grew tired of it. You don't have to like me, Melody. But you are gonna stay out of my business. You stay the fuck out of my business. Do you understand me?"

"Oh...I...Keith...I can't breathe." She bent over.

"I don't want you asking questions about me. I don't want you snooping in my things. I don't want you bugging Sarah about me...nothing."

"Keith!" she panted. "I can't breathe!"

"It's hard, isn't it, Melody?" He stood. "It's hard when you're cornered, isn't it? When you realize you aren't in control of what's around you. I hate that feeling myself. So I make sure I'm always in control." He leaned over her.

"Keith..." The panting slowed. Her heart settled. She focused on the gray carpet. She exhaled. Finally her body naturally relaxed. She forced her hands from Keith's. She immediately closed her blouse. She held her suit jacket closed over it.

"I must admit, this is kind of fun." He touched her hair and she jerked away. "I'm incredibly attracted to you. Do you know that?"

She shoved him away. "If you come near me again, I'll call the police. I'll tell Mr. Lawson and you'll be fired, Keith. You'll have nothing!" Her arms shook over her breasts.

"If you stay out of my business, and be a good girl, Melody, then things will be fine." He slumped to the door. She held her mouth. She fought the urge to vomit right then and there. Keith turned from the door. "I love that perfume, by the way. The more you wear it, the more I look forward to it." She shut her eyes. "Sorry if I scared you, Melody." He left.

"Oh…oh…" She leaned back in the chair. She didn't know what in the hell to do. She just knew she had to do *something*.

"Melody?" Lucas stood at the door. She hurried to make herself presentable. He rushed inside after noticing her strange behavior. "Jesus, why is your blouse open?" He turned away.

"Uh…" She could have easily settled things by being honest. For some reason she didn't see it the time or the place. Besides, she wanted to keep her problems with Keith away from Lucas. She'd waited a long time to meet someone special. She had no idea that she'd known him all the while Sarah had been right. Maybe Lucas had been the man of Melody's dreams.

She wouldn't let her feelings about Keith fuck that up. She deserved happiness like everyone else. She just needed time to think about what to do. Somehow, she could make Sarah see reason about her new "perfect" boyfriend.

"Melody!" He snapped his fingers. She looked at him. "I asked you why your blouse is opened. What in the hell is going on in here? You look a mess." He touched her hair. "Still a beautiful mess."

"Uh…" She knew damn well she couldn't think of a convincing lie. She'd do her best to try. "I was, uh, in here with Mario, unpacking things. Uh…" She grinned. "And I opened my jacket because it was kind of warm. I bent over to pick something up and my blouse snagged on the desk. It just popped open. I'm so embarrassed." She chuckled. "And thanks for saying I look a mess."

"Well, I came to welcome you on board. I couldn't wait until you got here." He looked around. "I picked out this office for you. I hope you don't mind." She shook her head. "I hope you enjoy your time here, Melody." He gestured to the door. "I saw Keith leaving a few seconds ago. Was your blouse open then?"

She scoffed. "Uh, are you getting at something?"

He shrugged. "Am I?"

"Lucas, what are you saying?"

"It just looks suspicious, that's all. Keith was in here

and I come in here and your blouse is open. You give me some flimsy excuse and…"

"It's not an excuse." She straightened her jacket. "God, I had an accident, Lucas. It's nothing to even mention. Am I being accused of something?"

"It's just that you're so tense around Keith. When we were at Jayson's, I got the feeling something was going on between you two. Like, I don't know, some kind of secret. Am I right?"

"No." She crossed her arms. "Not in the way you mean. I'm not attracted to Keith, if that's what you mean, Lucas."

"Is he attracted to *you*?"

She scoffed. "He's with Sarah."

"I didn't ask you who he was with. I asked you if Keith was attracted to you."

"He's my sister's boyfriend. Do you really think I'd go there, Lucas?" He sighed. "Damn, I thought you of all people knew me better than that. I already told you I don't like Keith. There definitely isn't anything romantic between us. I could never do that to Sarah. What kind of person do you think I am?"

"I didn't mean to offend you. I was curious, that's all. Mel, you gotta admit that this looks pretty strange, don't you think?"

"Maybe it does, but it's not like I have to explain myself to you. You're not my boyfriend or anything, Lucas. Look, I like you, okay? But I don't need yet another person second-guessing me or treating me like a child.

Now, I said nothing is going on between me and Keith. At least not in the way you may think. I don't like him. I can't *stand* him. Are you happy now?"

"I just had to check."

"Why?" She glared at him. "What difference would it make to you?"

"It makes a big difference because I think I'm falling in love with you." He kissed her. She moved away. The kiss produced the same fire as the one at Jayson's. He rubbed the back of her smooth neck. Melody leaned against him, praying that he'd get the hint to take her mouth again.

"Lucas, this feels so strange. Everything feels so strange these days. It's like things are moving so fast and I can't keep up."

"I said, we can take it slow, and I meant it, Melody. But I want to explore this."

"There's only one way we can."

"How?"

He wrapped his arms tighter around her thin waist. "For starters, let's go out on a *real* date, just the two of us." He nibbled her neck. She moaned at the action.

"Lucas, I gotta ask you something." She moved away. His lips dangled in mid-air. "Did you want me to take this job just to get close to me?"

He rubbed his nose against hers. "Would you be offended if I said I did?"

She smiled.

❖❖❖

Melody enjoyed the dinner at the fancy restaurant that night. Lucas claimed it would be nothing compared to his next surprise. She couldn't get over how gorgeous he'd become over the years. While so many things changed, they still stayed the same. No one made her laugh like Lucas. No one made her comfortable like Lucas. No one made her feel beautiful like he did.

Melody always felt that she wasn't worthy of being in the company of some people. She didn't feel like that with Lucas. He acted as though *she* had been the prize. He clung to her every word. He asked her about her every thought. Some women bitched about men paying them too much attention. Melody felt nothing could sour such treatment. Lucas could ask her anything if he held her how he did tonight.

She loved the blue silk shirt and black slacks he'd worn. She wore her white skirt and jacket set. Sarah begged her to wear it. She thought nothing suited Melody like the color white. Melody found that bullshit, but since Sarah had the fashion sense in the family she didn't question the opinion. She touched the sides of her head. She pinned her hair up in a sophisticated ball.

Melody couldn't wait to see the surprise. Lucas walked alongside of her with his hand over her eyes, and the other held her waist. He ordered her to keep her eyes shut until they reached the destination. Melody took such light steps that she felt like she was walking on air. She couldn't tell where they were. They were somewhere very quiet. She could hear every breath Lucas took.

She became flattered at his anxiety. If he was nervous due to the surprise, that meant he truly cared what she thought. It obviously meant as much to him as it did to her.

Lucas picked up the pace. She struggled to keep up while stumbling on the pavement. She realized they were on some kind of sidewalk. She grinned. At least they were still close to civilization. She heard laughter far off. She imagined a crowd of people standing around, gawking at the strange-looking couple. They made it to a crooked walkway that felt like gravel.

"Lucas!" She laughed. He held her waist to keep her from stumbling. "I'm sick of this! Show me what in the hell you want to show me already."

He laughed. "We're almost there, Melody. Believe me, it's worth the wait."

She struggled to keep her eyes closed. The suspense had long been killing her. Melody thought she recognized the place, but couldn't be sure. The crooked gravel path suddenly converted into a smoother walkway. Lucas whispered for her to watch her step.

"Whoa." Melody stumbled. She felt him lifting her into his arms. He steadied his feet and carried her on. "*Now*, Lucas!" She laughed. "If you don't show me what this is, I swear I am never going out with you again." He stopped. "Can I open my eyes now?"

He chuckled. "You can open them now." She clung onto him for leverage. She heard loud, rhythmic breathing. She stood on some sort of wobbly platform. She opened her eyes. She tumbled back. She grabbed onto Lucas. "Whoa, you okay?" He laughed.

"Ahhh!" She laughed. "I can't believe this!" They stood in a fancy white horse carriage. A beautiful mare turned around to check out the excited couple. "Oh my God, Lucas." Melody held her chest. "Oh…this is beautiful." They settled into the seat. The carriage driver tilted his hat to her. "Jesus. I can't believe…you did all of this for me?"

He shrugged. "Well, I wanted our first date to be something you'd remember. I couldn't think of anything more romantic than a carriage ride in the park, could you?"

"Oh no." She kissed him. "No." She leaned against his chest. Lucas gestured for the driver to go down the path. "I can't believe you'd do all of this for me." The beautiful horse neighed.

"I wish you could see how important you really are, Melody. You've always been a big part of my life. You were like my best friend." He looked ahead. "I know Aileen and Craig were always there with us back then…" He took her hand. "But sometimes it felt like you were the only one I saw." She smiled. "Maybe I've been in love with you all this time, Melody. I never stopped thinking about you. I can't believe I stayed away."

"Lucas, this…this is just incredible. Tonight has been

amazing. I can't even take all of this in!" She turned all around. "I, this is just too much. Lucas, I…oh, I don't know what to say."

He pulled her close. "I figure if you've got the money, you might as well use it in the best ways. And you don't have to thank me, Melody. This wasn't a favor, okay? I wanted to do this. You deserve all of this and more. Don't let anyone make you feel that you don't. I wish I could make you see how wonderful you are."

He wrapped his arms around her to shield her from the night's chill. People gawked at the attractive young couple in the carriage. Melody felt like royalty. She usually didn't like to show off, but tonight she thought she deserved to. She imagined how jealous Aileen and Sarah would be to hear of this night. She grinned. Why couldn't she have something special for once? If Lucas felt she deserved it, didn't that mean something?

Melody turned from Lucas's intense gaze. "You're staring." She grinned.

"I always stare at you."

"Not like that. Something on your mind?"

"You never told me how you felt about me. Better yet, how did you feel when I said that I've been in love with you all this time?"

She wiggled in the seat. "Strange, I gotta admit. I mean, we haven't seen each other in a while. It's going to take some time for me to know exactly what I feel for you, Lucas. I hope you understand."

"But, you do want to explore this, too, right? I know you said you aren't good in relationships, but can we just do this? I mean, can we give it a try on your terms?"

"It shouldn't just be on one person's terms, Lucas. A relationship is a partnership. It takes two to commit. I do want to take it slow, but I don't want you to hide your feelings because of me. I'm very comfortable about how you feel."

He smirked. "Really? Because you got this strange habit of running away from things that could ultimately make you happy."

"Really?" She tilted her head in the air. "Very presumptuous of you since you haven't seen me since high school."

"Did I offend you again?" He sighed.

"You damn right, you did!" The driver looked around. Lucas grinned. "And it's not funny. Don't just assume how I'm gonna act, Lucas. I may surprise you." She smirked.

"Oh really?" He held her closer. "What kind of surprise do you have in mind?"

She gently pushed him away. "Uh, the night is romantic but not *that* romantic."

He laughed. "Don't think just 'cause you swept me off my feet you're gonna get laid."

"I wasn't thinking that." He grinned. "Anyway, I wouldn't want to have sex with you unless it was official, you know?" He touched his lap. "I mean, we'd have to do the girlfriend and boyfriend thing first."

"So what are you saying? You want us to become an official couple?" The horse neighed.

"I guess, if you want us to." He shrugged. "Do you?"

"I guess, if you want it." She pouted.

"Fine." He grinned. "Then we're going together officially. We won't date other people."

"Uh-oh, commitment, huh?" She bit her lip.

"Yeah. Can you handle that, Melody?"

She pulled him close. "I'd at least like to try." They kissed.

"Well, that's what I'm talking about." Lucas wiped lipstick from her mouth.

"You're not as smooth as you think." She tugged his shirt. "I know you did all of this to seduce me." She lay against him.

"Well…" He felt his hair. "I didn't do it to get you into bed, Mel. I did it because doing good things for you makes me feel good. I've never wanted to be like this with anyone else before. I wanted to impress you like no one ever has."

"Thought you said that you didn't want me to think of you in terms of your money, Lucas. But then it's okay for you to use it to seduce me?"

His head rocked with the movement of the carriage. "Anyone ever tell you you're a pain in the ass?" She laughed. "No, I mean a man can't even try to be romantic around you, huh? You're suspicious about even that." He chuckled.

"It's just that men don't usually do things like this for nothing."

He sighed. "Okay, maybe I was hoping to get some loving out of this." She laughed. "But I'd rather wait. Being with you is not anything to rush or take lightly. I want it to be special when it's time."

"And who says we're gonna get to that point?" She grinned. "A little cocky, aren't we, Luke?"

"If I didn't know you wanted me, too, I'd be offended, Mel." He laughed.

"You aren't getting these panties tonight, no matter how many horses and carriages you buy." He laughed. "Nice try with the seduction thing, though."

"Is it working?" He raised an eyebrow.

She looked at the glorious bright moon. "When it works, you won't have to ask."

Chapter Seven

"Oh, I cannot believe this!" Melody stomped through the upstairs hallway. She'd had a perfect time with Lucas only to come home to Sarah's unreasonable temper. Apparently, Keith had told Sarah his own version of his and Melody's last meeting. Melody ripped her bedroom door open. Sarah stayed heavy on her heels. Melody grabbed her long T-shirt from the drawer.

Sarah slammed the door behind her. "Why are you closing the door when we're the only ones here, anyway?" Melody snapped.

Sarah opened it again. "Don't change the subject. I want to know why you've been asking questions about Keith! And before you deny it...don't!"

"I told you when you jumped down my throat, when I first walked in here that I need to know more things about him."

Sarah scoffed. "You act like Keith's *your* boyfriend, Mel."

"Oh, please." She walled her eyes.

"No, really." Sarah leaned against the dresser. "You're not working at Caper to keep tabs on my boyfriend!"

"Well, seems to me that someone needs to. He's not this 'knight in shining armor' guy you think he is, Sarah. You honestly think someone could be that perfect? I see the signs every time I look at him. I don't understand why you're letting him treat you like a fool! He's playing you, Sarah. He's hiding something. Something, something's not right with him."

"You're way out of line, Melody. I'm not gonna take this anymore."

Melody threw her bra on the dresser. "And why are you treating me like *I'm* in the wrong? Didn't he tell you what happened in my office today? Yet you stand here yelling at *me*?"

"Why wouldn't I be when you damn near scared the shit out of him?"

Melody gaped. "Excuse me?"

"Don't act like you don't know what I mean. You not only decided to spy on Keith, but had the nerve to threaten him when he confronted you about it!"

"I didn't threaten him!"

"Oh, Mel, save it, please." Sarah waved her hand. "He told me all about it. You don't have to lie. I know you did it. I know you hate Keith enough to pull some trick, but it won't work this time, baby girl. I'm not letting you run Keith away like you ran all my other men away."

"Sarah, he's lying! I didn't threaten him." Melody sighed. "You don't understand what he's doing, Sarah. He's manipulating both of us. The only problem is that he has no trouble getting you to believe what he wants you to believe." Sarah turned away. "Sarah, Keith threatens me every time we're alone."

Sarah looked at her. "What are you talking about?"

"He does things every time your back is turned. I didn't want to mention it because I knew you wouldn't believe me. I don't see why not, since I'm your sister, and he's some guy you just met! Anyway, I won't go into all the details, but Keith assaulted me in my office this morning."

"What?" Sarah sneered.

"I'm dead serious, Sarah. He closed the door, shoved me in my seat and he...he ripped open my clothes."

"What?" Sarah gaped.

"I couldn't believe it, either. He was trying to intimidate me. Sarah he practically told me he'd do something to me if I didn't stay out of his business. Does that seem normal to you?"

"Wait, you mean to say all of this shit happened, yet you didn't tell me?"

"Sarah, I couldn't." Melody sighed. "Sarah, look, I knew you'd say I was just starting trouble. I was hoping that you'd see what Keith was doing fast enough that I wouldn't have to keep going on like this! Sarah, he's sick, okay? I know something is wrong with him."

Sarah looked at her fancy fake nails. "So, he, uh, ripped your clothes and threatened you? That's quite different from what he said."

"I don't care what he said. Anyway, I'm your sister. Who are you gonna believe?"

"Well, you know, Melody, it would be easier for me to believe you if you didn't pull this stunt every time I have a new boyfriend, you know?"

"This isn't like the other times! Besides, I was telling the truth then, too! All of your guys have been jerks, Sarah! You couldn't pick a decent guy to save your life! You take the first well-dressed, charming dog that slumps up to you! You don't think twice!"

"Well, at least they slump up to me," Sarah scoffed. "Which is a lot more than I can say for you, Mel."

She rolled her eyes. "We're past this childish shit, Sarah."

"No, obviously we aren't! I've had it up to here with this shit, Melody! You do this every goddamn time, and I'm sick of it!"

"I just told you that Keith Taylor assaulted me, and you're yelling at me?"

"He didn't assault you! I don't believe a word you said!"

"He's done that and more, Sarah." Melody stood against the dresser. "See, I didn't want to tell you any of this because I love you. I didn't want to hurt you, but I guess I'll have to come clean." Sarah crossed her arms. "Today wasn't the only time your boyfriend has put his hands on me."

"Get to the point."

"Okay, if you want it this way." Melody sighed. "You

won't want anything to do with Keith Taylor after this. Sarah, the other day, you remember how flustered I was when you came home? Remember, when Keith was waiting for you?"

"Of course I remember." She exhaled.

"You kept asking me to say what was wrong, but I just couldn't get it out. You said I was more frightened than you ever saw me. Well, that was because of Keith." Sarah's arms dropped. "When I got home, he followed me to my bedroom. When I got undressed, I realized he'd been watching the entire time. I told him to leave and he wouldn't."

"What?" Sarah whispered.

"That's why I was so shaken up that entire night. That's why I didn't want to be two feet near Keith Taylor. And it didn't stop there. He also grabbed me in the kitchen and wouldn't let me go. And that's not all. He's also kissed me, Sarah." Melody looked at the carpet. "I'm sorry." Sarah chuckled. "What in the hell are you laughing at, Sarah?"

"You're pathetic, Melody. So this is the next stage, huh? You can't get me to believe your version of Keith, so you end up lying? How could you do this?"

"Oh no, wait, wait, wait, wait." Melody shook. "I'm not lying, Sarah. You know me. I don't lie! Well, I mean, at least not about anything serious. Sarah, I wouldn't make any of this up! I can't believe you'd even think that way."

"Melody, am I supposed to believe that Keith's been doing all this shit and you didn't tell me? Look at the sense that would make!"

"Sarah, I didn't tell you because I know you care about him! I wanted him gone, but I didn't want to hurt you in the process!"

"You never gave a shit about telling me about my other boyfriends' so-called problems. Why wouldn't you tell me about Keith? Especially when you hate him? Wouldn't it have been easier for you to tell me this stuff first off...if it had actually happened?" Sarah squinted.

"It did happen! Sarah, look at me. I'm your sister! You, you said that I've been acting weird lately, right? All of that is because of Keith! Sarah, he can't keep his hands off me." Sarah laughed. "So what, is it hard to believe a man would want me that much?"

"No, it's not. But what you say about Keith is impossible to believe, and I don't!" Melody gaped. "Why would you even take a job with Keith if he'd done all these things to you? Melody, I cannot believe you're standing in here lying!"

Melody grabbed her. "Look at me! Would I have been so frightened if I made all of this shit up?"

Sarah broke free. "All I know is that Keith's scenario seems to be the logical one. Melody, how can I believe you now? Why would you put up with this stuff from Keith if it truly happened? Unless..."

Melody squinted. "Unless what?"

"Unless, all of this happened and you enjoyed it."

"Get out of my room."

"I'd believe that before I believed that you didn't."

"You know what, fuck you, Sarah, okay? If you don't want to believe me, then it's okay. You'll see what he is soon enough. I'm telling you the truth and your stubborn ass will have to live with that one day."

"Melody, the bottom line is that I'm not taking this shit from you anymore. You're not running Keith away like you ran away all the others. He's special, I love him."

Melody got in bed. "More than you love me?"

Sarah shook her head. "I don't know why you have this attitude like everyone's against you, Mel. That's just not the case. Look, everything in my life doesn't revolve around you. Keith is not gonna take your place, okay?"

"It's not even about that, Sarah! Something is wrong with him. He's dangerous."

"Oh." Sarah laughed. "So he's dangerous now. He's gone from being an asshole to now being dangerous?"

"Do I look like I'm laughing? He scares me more than anyone I've ever met. I'm not misreading a damn thing, Sarah. What I feel about Keith is real. It's all there, and you're gonna see it one day." Melody sighed. "Maybe we both will. I just hope it's before it's too late."

"Here's the deal, okay? Stay out of my relationship with Keith. I love you, Melody, but I'm not going through this shit again with you. My love life is my business. You want me to respect your privacy and you living your own life, then do the same for me." She went to the door. "And just to clear all confusion, why don't you stay away from Keith from now on?"

"I was trying to do that, but it's not gonna be easy seeing how you gave the prick a key!" Melody slapped her pillow. "And without even telling me."

"Melody, honestly, I can't believe a word you said about Keith. It makes no sense. I love him. He is a part of my life now and you won't change that."

"Good night, Sarah." Melody walled her eyes.

"Melody, get yourself together, okay? There's nothing wrong with Keith. It's all in your head."

"I'm trying to help *you*, Sarah. I've always been on your side."

"Really? How come right now it doesn't feel like you are?" She left the room.

"After all the time we've worked together, you hand me this flimsy excuse, Kemp?" Captain Jersey reached for the coffeemaker behind her desk the next morning. She poured a steaming cup of coffee. Steven ran his hands over his rugged face. He'd never been late one day since being on the force. Too bad he'd chosen the wrong day to oversleep.

"Captain, I don't know what to say." He shrugged. "My alarm didn't go off. You know me, I'm never late!"

"Too bad for you, it's the wrong damn day." She

shuffled through papers. "There was another rape last night. Morris is questioning the victim now. That's why I was calling your ass all morning."

"I didn't hear the phone!" He waved his hands. "Come on, Captain." He sat down. "This case is taking a toll on me. I couldn't *steal* sleep these days."

"You should be used to it. Besides, sleeping should be the least of your worries. Look at me. Do I look like I sleep? Shit, Kemp, I never sleep. I spend my time riding cops' asses while trying to stop the commissioner from riding *mine*." She pointed to the wrinkles under her eyes. Steven couldn't tell if they were from lack of sleep or age, but he'd humor his superior.

"So there was another rape, huh?" He sighed. "Well, since this is my case, too, you mind filling me in on the details?"

She clasped her hands on the desk. "The victim is Cheyenne Wilson. She's twenty-three, black and she dances at the Flamingo bar on Southmore."

"A stripper?" Steven scratched his head.

Jersey shrugged. "We won't know more until Morris comes back from talking to her. She should be back soon. She's been at the hospital about an hour. Cheyenne is supposed to be released to go home later this afternoon."

"Is it really our guy?"

"Looks like it." Jersey sipped coffee. "She was raped at home and beaten in the face with a flashlight."

Steven sighed. "Oh man."

"The cop who took the report said she was so battered he couldn't make out the left side of her face. Said he was surprised the blows didn't kill her. I suppose the blow didn't cause any major trauma, or else they wouldn't be releasing her today. As for the rape, I'm sure that's not anything pretty to hear about either but..." The door opened. Brianna walked in. Jersey sat erect. "Morris. What's the deal with Miss Wilson?"

Brianna looked at Steven. "Well, uh, it was definitely the Albany Predator. Uh, she described his face, then when I showed her the sketch she hadn't any doubt. She said it was definitely the man who raped her."

"She's a stripper?" Jersey asked.

Brianna shrugged. "She says she's just a regular dancer, and doing it to pay the bills."

Steven scoffed. "I don't know nobody who 'just dances' at a titty bar without taking something off."

"Stripper or not, she doesn't deserve to be raped." Jersey tapped her pencil.

"Of course not, Captain. I didn't mean nothing by that. I'm just saying that my experience with titty bars, these women usually take it all off for quick cash. Some even do more than that. Anyway what happened, Bree?" Steven crossed his arms.

"Well, apparently he offered her a ride last night after she finished dancing. She said he was sitting on a bench. She said now that she remembers it, she thinks she saw him in the bar, too."

Jersey bit her lip. "Was the bar crowded? Did she say if there were people outside that may be able to identify him, too?"

"Come on, Captain." Steven grinned. "The Flamingo is the most popular titty bar around. Believe me, it was crowded and there's never been a night it wasn't."

Brianna raised an eyebrow. "I didn't know you were into titty bars, Steven."

He cleared his throat. "I'm not. Uh, I mean, I may have stopped in occasionally." He ignored their judgmental expressions. "This isn't about me, anyway. What else did Miss Wilson say?"

"She said that he took her home, they had cake, talked and he raped her."

"What?" Steven chuckled. "I don't mean to laugh, but is she in the habit of having picnics at her home with guys she doesn't know?"

Brianna shrugged. "She said she started to feel uncomfortable with him. She asked him to leave but he wouldn't. She said he forced her to her bedroom. She tried to fight him and he beat her with a flashlight... then raped her."

Steven shook his head. "Why in the hell would she go off with him in the first damn place? Jesus! Aren't these women even thinking these days? I mean, doesn't she know about the Predator? Hasn't she been listening to the news? Why in the hell would she get in a car with someone she didn't know?"

"I was thinking the same thing myself until she told me…" Brianna sighed.

"Told you what?" Jersey leaned back in her chair.

"Until she told me he was a cop."

"A cop?" Steven scooted to the edge of his chair. "A *cop*? What the fuck…"

Jersey gaped. "A *cop*? Is she, uh…is she sure?"

Brianna nodded. "He showed her his badge. I tried to see if she could give me the badge number so I could run it, but she didn't pay attention to any of that. Besides, she was so shaken she could barely talk to me."

"This can't be right." Steven stood. "This man can't be a cop. I mean, why would he be a cop now? Wouldn't this shit have come up before…months ago? We've been investigating him for months! None of the other victims said shit about a badge!"

"Maybe he hadn't shown them his badge then." Brianna shrugged. "He had to show Cheyenne something for her to get in the car with him."

Steven looked at Jersey. "What do you think, Captain?"

"Well, uh…this is definitely surprising. But I'm willing to bet he isn't a cop. Anyone can get a badge underground these days." The officers nodded. "Anyway, we need to work on her some more because she may be the one to tie things together. Morris, does she seem like she'll cooperate?"

"Well, she did give me her home number and told me she might want to talk to me when she gets home. She was scared as expected, but she seems to be avid in wanting to get this guy off the streets."

"We need to go to the Flamingo, too." Steven held his waist. "I mean, if he was there last night, this could be a regular hangout for this guy. I'm willing to bet on it. Something made him pick out that side of town. Maybe it's the clue we need. He may even live over there. We'll go tonight, Bree. That way we can see what really goes on there."

"Sounds good to me." Jersey nodded. "Go to the *Flamingo* and see what you can find out. Who knows, he may have already approached another woman who works down there. Either way, the ladies on that side of town should be terribly aware."

Steven nodded. "You mean 'black' ladies."

"Yes," Jersey sighed. "I mean 'black' ladies."

Melody accompanied Lucas to his place that evening. She'd already gotten used to being an employee at Caper. She felt she'd had a decent day until she got home to find Keith and Sarah snuggling on the couch. She couldn't remember a time when Keith wasn't around these days. Her hopes of breaking them up seemed impossible with the attitude Sarah showed the night before.

Lucas quickly showed her around his fabulous, two-story bachelor pad. She loved how he appreciated the simple things in life. Lucas could have lived anywhere in New York with his money. Yet he chose to live in a quiet, ordinary and extremely peaceful neighborhood. He showed Melody the upstairs. He then showed her the large living room and immaculate kitchen.

He admitted he had a maid that came in twice a week to keep things tidy. Melody chuckled at the thought. She wondered if the lady would like to do *her* chores for her. Lord knows, Melody could use someone to pick up after her. Lucas's home wasn't fascinating like his charm, good looks and wardrobe. But Melody hadn't ever felt so comfortable before.

They hadn't talked much on the way over. She knew he sensed her tenseness about Keith. She refused to get into the subject today. Lucas had become a great distraction. She'd use the time with him to her advantage.

They walked into the den hand in hand. Lucas gestured for Melody to sit on the couch. She did. She noticed the fireplace when he lit the incense. The aroma of cinnamon and pine soothed her as if she'd had a glass of warm tea. She stared at the brown walls and at the marvelous maroon carpeting. He'd obviously hired a private decorator. So much for his quest to be "common."

Lucas turned on the television. Melody groaned at another report about the rapist. She figured the other criminals in the city were having a field day. They got zero airtime, while the Albany Predator could soon have his own talk show. Melody didn't see what sense it made to continually broadcast the rapes if the police weren't doing much about it.

"So, how do you like working at Caper so far?" Lucas asked with his eyes glued to the latest news report.

She grinned. "You've asked me that a million times." She stared at the blond news reporter. The reporter walked around some shabby bar. The scene cut to a bald reporter who stood in front of the hospital. He went on about the recovery of Cheyenne Wilson. Melody had been so busy avoiding the news that she hadn't heard about the latest rape.

"What did they say?" She sat up to hear. "She was raped in her home, too?" Lucas nodded. "Wonder why she's still in the hospital."

"She was banged in the face with a flashlight."

"Wait…" Melody turned the volume up. The bald reporter rattled on about Cheyenne's recollection of events. "Did he say she got in the car with him?" Lucas nodded. "Well, is she stupid or just crazy?"

"Mel." Lucas chuckled.

"Well, I can't feel sorry for someone who is that careless. Why would she get in the car with someone she didn't know?"

The bald reporter pointed to the hospital. "Apparently, Miss Wilson says the perpetrator showed her a badge and admitted that he was a cop. Police are further investigating…"

"This is making me sick." Lucas turned the volume down and he pulled Melody close.

"A cop?" Melody gaped. "She said he's a cop?" She looked at Lucas. "Wait, can that be possible? Can a cop be doing this and the police *still* not know it?"

"Yeah, but it's hard to believe isn't it? But maybe it explains why it's taken them so damn long to find the guy. I always had my suspicions that something was going on with the police. Like they might have not been doing their best to catch this guy."

"You mean, like they may have known it was a cop and are protecting him?" Lucas shrugged. "Oh no, I don't believe that, Lucas. I mean, I don't think they would go that far. Granted, some forces are quite corrupt, but I've never heard much about Albany's department being that way."

"Just because you don't know the cat ate the fish doesn't mean he didn't eat it, right?" She sighed. "How long can all of this go on? I barely recognize my own hometown now. Seems like everything's at a standstill because of this guy. I hope they find this bastard. How can someone be so hateful? How are these women going to deal with this for the rest of their lives? Some of them were married and have kids. I just can't see how people can be so...so heartless. These women didn't do a damn thing to him but he's ruining everything for them, Mel."

"You really think the police are hiding something?"

He scratched his head. "Who knows? I wouldn't be

surprised at anything that people do these days. Shit, the main ones you think you can trust are the ones you can't.

"I know they are hiding something big, though." He nodded. "See, my father has a friend on the force at the precinct that's handling this case. He says that the lady detective investigating the case was attacked by the rapist herself."

"What?" Melody covered her mouth.

"Uh-huh, and the police hid it from the public. Now what kind of shit is that? Why hide that when it can make people more aware of what's going on? If a police-woman is not even safe from this guy, then who is?"

"Oh my God." Melody looked at the television. "So he raped her and…"

"No, he didn't rape her. He broke into her home and she fought him or something, and he got away." Lucas sighed. "I heard he tried to make her give him a blow-job. He's one sick motherfucker. My father's friend says it's other things they're not sharing with the media, too."

"Well, Lucas I know a little about police investiga-tions." She thought of her favorite pastime of watching cop shows. "They can't just go blabbing everything because it could hurt the investigation. The key is to stay one step ahead of this guy. How could they do that if they tell the public every damn thing? You know how the media takes things and runs with it. The situation would get even more out of control. Also, they have to worry about copycats and…" She rubbed her face. "Especially since that other lady was murdered."

"Monica Cartwright wasn't murdered." Lucas straightened up. "Turns out she had a heart attack when the rapist came back. He raped her *after* she died." Melody held her stomach for fear of vomiting all over the floor. "They just thought he'd killed her at first. I can see you haven't been watching the news, huh?"

"I can't believe someone could be so sick."

"Can you imagine how frightening it is for them to be face to face with this guy? I mean, have you ever met someone who scared you beyond comprehension?"

Melody thought of Keith. She decided to keep her opinion to herself. "Is the lady detective black, too?" she asked.

"Yeah, from what I hear, this man is dangling the cops from a string. I mean, he's pulling all the shots. Makes me wonder if this *will* go on forever. Will he be caught, or will he just move to another place and continue? It's some scary shit for me and I'm not even a woman. I can imagine how they feel."

"I'm so scared about what I've been feeling, Lucas. I hate women's intuition, sometimes. And you know I can predict things more than most. I hope to God that it's wrong this time. I can't bear to think what I'm feeling will come true."

"What are you feeling?" He rubbed her shoulders. She looked at him.

"That Aileen might be next."

"I'm worried, too, but just because you think something will happen doesn't mean it will." He smiled. "You trust me?" She nodded. "Then believe it when I say that Aileen will be okay." He held her. In his arms everything seemed okay.

His hands suggested that he wanted more than to hold her. She sure as hell wanted the same. But every time she thought of taking him without thinking twice, something inside screamed it wasn't the right time. She didn't know how long she could hold out. She longed to have her body smashed against his in a heated frenzy. How long would cold showers do the trick?

Lucas's patience had been what she appreciated the most. But sometimes, a small part of her wished he could be more like Keith. She ached at the thought. Keith was an asshole hands down, but he knew passion. Melody could tell by the way Sarah whimpered every time Keith walked into the room. She couldn't imagine Sarah having *any* complaints.

Even though Keith went out of bounds, Melody liked how he took charge when it came to romance. If he wanted Sarah, nothing stood in his way. The time or place didn't matter. He didn't even care if others were in the room. Many times he grabbed Sarah and kissed her into undying passion right in front of Melody. He did anything he damned near pleased to put out that fire Sarah ignited in him. Melody hated to admit that she admired that about him.

She looked at Lucas. He kissed her forehead. Patience

also had its rewards. The lovemaking would have no choice but to be perfect if they waited. He took her hand.

Deep down she knew she had the better man. She imagined him picking her up and throwing her over his shoulder like the sex-crazed bucks in old western movies. She laughed as if it were true.

Melody wasn't surprised that Keith hadn't left when she returned home. He was massaging Sarah's feet on the couch. He flashed that sickening grin when he looked up and saw Melody. She fought the urge to puke. Every time she looked at Sarah, she remembered their argument. She advised Melody to stay away from Keith. How could she when the man practically lived at their place?

Sarah waved a bowl of chips. "Chip, Mel?" She smiled.

"No thanks. Good night." She made sure not to look Keith's way.

"*Good night*? Mel, this is your favorite movie." Sarah grinned. Melody caught a scene with Mimi Rogers flicking a cigarette. "You love Mimi Rogers, right?"

She scoffed. "Yeah, maybe in the early nineties." She headed toward the stairs. Sarah rushed after her.

"Mel, wait, please."

Keith waved. "Sarah, let her go. She needs her rest."

Melody couldn't take his sly attitude any longer. She wouldn't even pretend to be polite from now on. If Sarah intended on bringing Keith to the house, Melody would make it damn tough on the both of them. She turned around.

"Yeah, I do need my rest, which is something I can't get since you're always here." She walked toward him. "You think you're so smart, don't you, Keith? Running and lying to Sarah when you know damn well what happened in my office yesterday!"

"Let me guess." He crossed his arms. "In a bad mood again, Mel? What, the time with Lucas didn't go well? Did something spoil it, like your attitude?"

"Keith," Sarah sighed.

"No, my attitude isn't the problem here, Keith. You may have Sarah believing you shit gold, but I know different."

"Oh yeah?"

"Yeah! I'm not going to let you manipulate me like you manipulate her."

"He doesn't manipulate me, Melody!" Sarah huffed. "Look, I want us to forget about the argument we had last night, okay? I'm sorry for how I talked to you but you had no business asking questions about Keith."

"And why is that?" Melody squinted. "Why is it so horrible for me to know more about this guy? Keith, it's bad enough that you act a jerk when Sarah's back is turned, but it's completely unreasonable to expect me not to want to know things about you."

"Well, I tried to be nice and *let* you get to know me,

didn't I?" he scoffed. "You didn't want to be nice, Melody. Why didn't you just ask me what you wanted to know, instead of harassing the people at my job?"

"Because I don't believe a thing you say."

"You know, Mel, I don't give a shit what you think of me."

"Keith, please." Sarah moved in front of him.

"No, that's the problem, Sarah! Why do you feel you gotta do everything to suit her? It's not your fault how things turned out for Melody! If she's not happy, I can see why. How could she be?" He chuckled. "She's so wrapped up in *your* life she can't have one of her own! You're pathetic, Melody."

"Keith!" Sarah shoved him.

"She is, and we all know it!" He looked at Melody. "Say I'm wrong. You wish you could be half the person Sarah is, don't you? Well, you can forget it because you're nothing like her, Melody. You're not even fit to be in the same family with her."

"Keith, stop!" Sarah shook her head. "I don't understand what it is about you two but I don't want to be caught in the middle anymore. Can't we just let things pass and start over?"

"If you can still be with him after the nasty things he just said about me, then there's no way in hell we can come to common ground, Sarah."

"Melody, please." Sarah took her hand. "You're not being fair. I really think you and Keith could settle things if you got to know each other. Please, just give it a chance. I love him, Melody."

Melody moved away. "Then you should be ashamed of yourself, Sarah. Keith is going to ruin your life. How many times do I have to say it?" She went to the front door.

"Where are you going, Mel?" Sarah exhaled.

"I can't stay here another minute with him around. I hope you two have a nice night." She opened the door.

"Melody, where are you going?" Sarah ran to the door.

"Let her go." Keith sat on the couch. He turned around. "I really do want to be your friend, Mel. I hope you realize that before it's too late."

"You're something else, Keith. I wish I knew how to lie as well as you do."

He scoffed. "See, Sarah? What good is it to be nice to her when she's gonna hate me no matter what?" He stood. "Melody, what in the hell do I have to do for you to accept me?"

"Leave." She glared. "And never come back. That's the only way I can accept you, Keith."

"Well, I guess we just have to learn to be civil because I'm not going anywhere." He held his waist.

Sarah took Melody's hand. "Melody, he's trying to make an effort. Please do the same."

"I honestly don't know if I can, Sarah." She kissed Sarah's cheek. "I'm going to Craig's if you need me." She left.

Chapter Eight

"Let me handle this." Steven held the door of the Flamingo open for Brianna later that night.

"Why should you handle this when we're on a case together?" She walked inside. She felt she could at least get to the bar without bumping into someone. She'd made a terrible assumption. The Flamingo seemed to live up to its reputation of being wild and popular. Groups of people crowded the floors. Beautiful, busty ladies of all nationalities stood on a stage twisting to Prince's "1999." Brianna could barely hear it for the men howling.

Steven clapped to the music. For someone who claimed he didn't frequent the place he sure seemed comfortable.

"I know you're uncomfortable, right?" Steven yelled over the music. Brianna watched a big-busted blonde swing her thong-covered behind in twelve different directions. "That's why I said you should let me handle this, you know?" Steven winked at a topless waitress. She offered him and Brianna drinks. They quickly announced that they were on duty.

"Well…" Brianna shouted over the music. "This is some kind of place!" A group of rowdy men bumped into her. One winked on his way to a dinky table in the corner. "Doesn't look like much! I mean, the bar itself, you know?"

"Nah, it's a dump!" Steven snapped his fingers to the music. "But the people don't come here for the bar itself, know what I mean, Bree?" He winked. "Like I said…" He twirled to the music. "You should let me handle this if it bothers you, you know?" A big-busted redhead ripped off a leather bra. She threw it toward the bar. The men howled. A man wrapped the sweaty garment around his face.

"Steven, I don't know why you think I can't handle this!" Brianna moved for people to pass. "I've been in strip bars before."

"Oh really?" He grinned. "Care to elaborate?"

She grinned. "Maybe later if we have the time. We need to get to work and get the hell out of here. My ears are beginning to pop." Brianna scoped the place. "I can't imagine any of these people being too cooperative with the cops. Can you, Steven?" A man slapped another man on the head with a beer bottle. They rolled around on the floor laughing.

"Hell no!" Steven laughed. "But that's what I love about being a cop the most, Bree. Making folks cooperate!"

They went to the bar. Steven quickly made himself at home on a center stool.

"You sure you don't come to this place often?" Brianna sneered.

"No, I mean, I've been here before but a long time ago."

Brianna grinned. "Uh-huh."

A man scooted beside her. "Can I buy a beautiful lady a drink tonight?" He winked at her.

She rolled her eyes. "Sure, if you can find one that will *let* you buy her a drink tonight." The man moved to another lady at the end of the bar.

"Ouch." Steven grinned. "Glad *I* didn't ask to buy you a drink."

She laughed. "That's why I hate bars. A woman can't be in one for two seconds without some creep hitting on her."

"He only asked to buy you a drink, Bree."

"Yeah, but we both know he wants more." She turned to see the man laughing it up with the woman at the bar. "I guess she'll be the one to give it to him." Brianna grinned.

The flabby bartender turned around. Sweat dribbled from his bald head. All the men sweated. Brianna wondered if the cause had been the lights, or the naked girls. "Hey, Detective Kemp!" the bartender guffawed. "How you doing, Steve?"

"Uh…" Steven looked at Brianna. She crossed her arms. "How you doing, Tim?"

"Fine, man!" The bartender slapped Steven's arm. "The usual?"

"Usual?" Brianna gaped.

"Uh." Steven straightened his collar. "No, I'm on duty tonight, Tim."

"Ah, what a shame. Some of the girls will be disappointed. Especially Sunshine." Tim pointed to the busty blonde dancing at the end of the stage. She waved at Steven.

"You know she's got a big case for you, Steve." Tim cackled.

"Really? Seems interesting." Brianna sat down.

"Uh…" Steven grinned. "He's just playing, you know?"

Brianna smiled at Tim. "He was just telling me he never hardly comes in here, but that doesn't seem to be the case."

"He used to come in here all the time! Right, Steve?" Tim laughed. "He started a couple of years back. See, he had this bitchy girlfriend he used to complain about. Said he'd come here to get some peace." Tim chuckled. "I think the lady's name was 'Brenda' or…no 'Brianna'! That's right, huh, Steve? According to him, she was a real bitch."

Steven groaned.

"Oh?" Brianna ogled Steven. "Well, if he thought she was a bitch back then, I'm sure it doesn't compare to what she'll be from now on."

"I'll bet." Steven sighed.

"Well, it's nice to meet you, Tim." Brianna held out her hand.

Tim kissed it. "Always nice to meet such a lovely woman, too, ma'am. I didn't catch your name."

"Detective Brianna Morris." She looked at Steven. He turned away.

"Bri…" Tim looked at Steven. "Oh, ha, ha, ha! Know what I just said? I think I got that wrong, you know? He actually said you were the best girlfriend he ever had. Yep, I think so." Tim wiped sweat from his forehead.

"Yeah, I'm sure." Brianna grinned.

"Tim, can I get some help here or what? The place is packed." A female bartender passed truckloads of drinks to groups of men.

"In a minute. Got a special customer."

"Hey Steve, good to see you!" The female bartender winked. Brianna looked at him. Steven once again avoided her gaze.

Steven cleared his throat. "Uh, Tim, we're investigating the rape of Cheyenne Wilson. We wanted to ask some quick questions."

"It's a damn shame." He sighed. "Cheyenne's probably the sweetest thing to walk in here. She never said a bad word about anyone. The customers go crazy over her routine even though she doesn't strip. She keeps her act clean and is just here to pay off some college loans or something. Says she's heading for New York City as soon as she gets the cash."

Brianna looked at Steven. "Well, uh, were you working yesterday?" she asked.

Tim nodded. "But I worked only about an hour yesterday evening because I had a doctor's appointment. I was probably gone around seven. Cheyenne hadn't even come in then. She usually comes in at eight and dances for about an hour, so she's usually done by nine."

"Shit. So you weren't here to see if she may have caught the eye of the Albany Predator, huh?" Steven sighed.

"So it *is* the same guy? Why the hell can't you catch him?"

"Well, it takes time, Tim." Brianna smiled.

"All I know is that Cheyenne didn't deserve to be beaten and raped like that. She's a good girl, even if she is working in a place like this. But who can judge her, you know? Shit, she's probably the only person I know who's already got a roundtrip ticket to Heaven." Brianna and Steven exchanged glances. "I wish I'd been here to see if this guy had been in the bar."

"Well, was anyone here that may have been here last night?"

"Uh…" Tim pointed to an extremely thin waitress scrubbing a back table. She did her best to ignore the catcalls coming from the customers.

"Juney." Steven nodded.

"So you know her?" Brianna scoffed. They walked toward her. "Steven, for someone who doesn't come here often, you sure have a fan club."

He walled his eyes. "Okay, so I come here sometimes. Are you happy now?"

"No, I'm not happy to know my ex-boyfriend spent a bulk of his time at titty bars. Especially when he was with me. But since this is business I'll let you off the hook, for now." She smiled. "Excuse me?" She tapped Juney's shoulder. The skinny brunette nearly toppled over.

"Yes?" She looked at the handsome man beside Brianna. "Detective Kemp! It's always good to see you."

Brianna shook her head. "I'm Detective Brianna Morris, Juney. We need to ask you some questions. It has to do with the Cheyenne Wilson case."

"Uh…" Juney laid the rag on the table. She gestured for them to follow her. She led them to the restroom area. "How is Cheyenne? I tried to call the hospital but no one would say anything."

"Well, that's standard procedure during a police investigation." Steven nodded. "The hospital has been notified by us not to give information, unless it's family. She's recovering, though we don't know how long it will take. She was supposed to be released this evening. I'm sure you can visit her at home, but I'd give her some time. She's been to hell and back."

"Jesus. Cheyenne is probably the sweetest person you'd ever wanna meet. I was always telling her she's too good for this shithole. I truly admire her."

"Why?" Brianna glared.

"Because she has dreams and she goes after them. If I could do that, you think I'd be wiping up beer in this joint every night?"

"So you're close friends?" Steven took out a notepad and pencil.

"Well, we don't hang out too much after work, but we're pretty cool. She stays to herself. She talks to me, and she used to be friends with Sheila who was another dancer here. She doesn't work here anymore."

"Oh, got a better gig, huh?" Steven smiled.

"I wouldn't say that. She died last year. She had kidney failure. Cheyenne was pretty torn up about it. They were very close."

Brianna sighed. "Well, uh, we don't want to take up much of your time. We believe the man who attacked her was the Albany Predator. We hear a lot of regulars come in here. Did you get someone in here last night that may not have been here before?"

Steven interrupted. "Or even a regular who seems kind of strange?"

Juney grinned. "All the men who come in here seem strange. But I didn't notice anyone."

"Juney, did you pay any attention to Cheyenne last night?" Brianna asked.

"Well, she finished her set and she talked to some guy at the bar. Other than that, nothing seemed different."

"Well, what did he look like?"

"The guy at the bar?" She grinned. "You tell me, Steven. You saw him, too."

"Excuse me?" Steven chuckled. "Where did you get that from? How would I have seen who she talked to?"

"Oh wait…" She batted. "Guess that could have been around the time you left. You left around ten, I believe."

Brianna gaped.

"Juney, what in the hell are you talking about? I wasn't here last night."

"Steven, yes, you were." She laughed. "I didn't work your table, but I saw you." She pointed to the table in front. "You sat right there. The next thing I knew you were gone."

"Steven, what is she talking about?"

He sighed. "I haven't a damn idea, Bree. Juney, I was not here last night. You got me mixed up with someone else."

"With those baby blues?" She pointed to his eyes. "No chance. Why, were you on duty or something and you didn't want someone to know you were here?"

"I wasn't here last night." He sighed. "What the fuck is going on here?"

"Juney, are you sure, or do you just think you saw Steven?"

"Detective Morris, I'm looking at him now and I looked at him last night. I've seen Detective Kemp many times before." She looked at him. "You were here and you sat right there. But you were gone probably by ten. Didn't you see who Cheyenne spoke to at the bar?"

Steven lowered his head.

"Uh, thanks for everything, Juney. If you can help us out, give us a call." Brianna passed her a card. Juney went on her way. "Steven, what in the hell is going on here?"

"Bree, I have no fuckin' idea! I wasn't here last night!"

"Well, she must have you mixed up with someone else."

"Damn straight." He shook his head. "I don't know what that's about but I don't have time to wonder. I'd like to question Cheyenne Wilson since I didn't get a chance to with you this morning."

"Okay, but I don't think we should tonight. She's been through enough. Let's let this all ride and we can head over there in the morning."

"Good, because I got some questions of my own I'd like to ask." Steven led the way out the bar.

"Say what? Melody, this is insane." Mario stood outside Keith's office the next morning. Melody would get rid of Keith if her life depended on it. For five minutes Mario had been protesting her plans to search Keith's office. She knew he'd go along with it after minor convincing. Mario had become a friend already.

The fact that he couldn't stand Keith, either, made knowing him even more worthwhile. Melody felt she'd been lucky to find at least one other mortal immune to Keith's charm.

"Mel, are you trying to get fired the same month you were hired?" Mario held his waist. "I can't stand Keith any more than you can, but this is not a good idea."

"Why not?" She rocked back and forth.

"Because you could get fired and this is against regulations, Melody. You can't go into another employee's office like this. You might as well be breaking in!"

"Shh!" Melody smiled at a janitor passing through the halls. "I'm doing this, Mario. I won't get caught, believe me. I have no choice. Please, just wait outside the door and let me know if Keith comes, okay?"

"Melody, I need my job, okay? This isn't just some hobby for me."

"Mario, I wouldn't do anything to jeopardize your job. But you just gotta trust me. Anyway, you know in your heart that Keith's a rat. Don't you want to help me find out what he's hiding, at least?"

"I said, I thought he was sneaky, but that doesn't necessarily mean he's hiding things, Melody."

"Just wait outside the door. If I take longer than two minutes you have my permission to report me." She smiled. He walled his eyes. "Don't forget to let me know if Keith's coming." She unlocked the office.

"Where did you get those keys?"

She shrugged. "I took them from the main office downstairs."

"Jesus! Melody, do you know what kind of shit you could get us into?"

"This is for my sister's well-being, Mario. I have to do this." She peeked inside the immaculate office. Keith had always been neat, yet the shape of his office surpassed volumes.

"Well, what the hell do I do if Keith comes?"

She grinned. "Distract him. I'm sure you'll think of something."

She slunk inside the office. She got a chill. She felt like Keith was standing in the room with her. Talk about being frightened. The walls seemed to watch her. The floor seemed to make note of her every movement. As terrified as she felt, she didn't care. Nothing would stop her from finding out more about him.

She thought of that briefcase he carried around like law. She hoped to find it in the office. She had no such luck. She twisted back and forth as she looked at the black file cabinets. She tried to ignore the smell of his expensive cologne that hovered around his desk. She quickly searched his desk drawers. Nothing seemed out of the ordinary.

She found some files. She got on her knees to search his last drawer. She found four pictures of Sarah and a stick of gum.

"Wait a minute." She struggled from the floor. "There's gotta be something." If she couldn't find anything here, she'd search his house next. She'd stop at nothing. She glanced in the tiny mirror on Keith's desk. She barely recognized herself or what she'd been doing. Maybe Craig's theory had been correct. *Was* she obsessed? Honestly, she didn't give a damn at this point.

She thought of those cop shows. Maybe this wasn't the right idea. Keith wasn't your average twenty-something-year-old. He'd been graced with superior intelligence. He had the talent to manipulate the smartest people. He'd done it to Dave Lawson. He'd even done it with other bigwigs of the company, from what Melody had heard. She would have to fight fire with fire.

She hadn't the slightest idea how to put out a rising flame like Keith Taylor. It wouldn't be easy. She thought of giving up. Maybe she should let Sarah handle this. She leaned against the desk. No matter how angry Sarah made her, Melody couldn't let her fall in love with such danger. Keith was dangerous. She didn't know how she knew it. She just did.

She searched the first few drawers of his file cabinet. She found a middle-sized black box stuffed behind a folder. She grabbed it. She'd overlooked the suede box. She grinned. This had to be a sign. If Keith went through so much trouble to hide this, it must have been important.

"Mel!" a woman yelled from behind. Melody nearly fell over. She threw the box on top of the file cabinet. She turned around to see Sarah glaring at her.

"Sarah!" Melody leaned over. "Jesus, you gave me a heart attack!"

"What in the hell are you doing in here?" Sarah looked at the box. "Answer me, Melody. What's going on here?"

"Well, I work here, for one!" Melody struggled to catch her breath. "You scared the shit out of me, Sarah. What in the hell are you doing here yourself?"

"Don't ask me questions with your hand caught in the cookie jar. What are you doing in Keith's office?" Sarah crossed her arms.

"I, uh…" Melody looked at the box. "Looking for Keith. Why else would I be in here?"

"And you thought he'd be in the file cabinet?" Sarah sat on his desk. Her piercing green eyes had the power to make anyone crumble. Melody hated getting caught but she didn't necessarily feel guilty. Keith had the problem here. Soon everyone would know it. "You told me to trust you. Isn't that what you said, Melody? But I come here and find you going through Keith's things?"

"I was not doing that, Sarah. I was…"

"Don't you dare lie to me. I saw you with my own eyes! Now I wanna know what in the hell you're up to, and I want to know now!"

"Jesus, what the hell happened to Mario?" Melody mumbled. "Okay, I was looking through his things, Sarah. But can you blame me? Even if you can I don't care. I'm doing this because I love you." Melody grabbed the box.

"Put that down," Sarah ordered. "Melody, do you even think before you do things?"

"I don't know. Do you even think before you start sleeping with a man and realize that you don't even know him?"

"Well, the way things are going these days, I feel like you're the one I don't know, Melody. I don't recognize you anymore. You're beginning to scare me."

She laughed. "*I* scare you? What the hell does Keith do then?"

"Melody, I'm beginning to think you're obsessed."

"What are you doing here, anyway, Sarah?"

"Keith spent the night at our place." Melody walled her eyes. "After you stormed out, I was so upset. I didn't wanna be alone, so he stayed the night. He left his cell phone this morning and I was bringing it to him." Sarah sighed. "Mel, what did you expect to find by doing this?"

"Something," she whispered. "Something to make you believe that what I say is true."

"Melody, I'm asking you to please stop this."

"Are you going to stop seeing Keith?"

"No!" Sarah looked away.

"Then let me do what I got to do. You've protected me before so it's my turn."

"Melody, I don't need you to protect me! You're way off base here!"

"Sarah, why are you so against me finding out things about Keith if you're so sure about him?" Melody stared at her. "Unless…unless you have doubts about Keith yourself."

She turned away. "That's ridiculous."

Melody shook her head. "Doesn't seem that way to me. Maybe you want me to stay out of his life because you're afraid of what I might find."

"That's not true! I want you to stop this because it's my life and I love him!"

"You don't even know who he really is! How could you love him?" Melody yelled.

"I know what he is," Sarah whispered.

"If that's true, then what are you so afraid of?" Melody stood in front of her.

Keith whistled into the room. "Wow." He looked at the sisters. "Both of my beauties are here. You don't know how thrilling this is." He looked at Melody. "Melody, you look beautiful." He set his briefcase on the desk. "May I ask why you're in my office?"

Sarah slid from the desk. "Well, *I* came to return your cell phone, and I caught Melody in here snooping."

Melody shook her head. "I can't believe you'd call me out like this, Sarah."

"Well, it's the truth. If you can do something so sneaky you should own up to it." She took Keith's hand. "I apologize for this, Keith."

"Sarah, I don't need you to apologize for me. Yes, I was sneaking, Keith." He smirked. "I don't care what happens to me beyond this point. You can tell Mr. Lawson or whoever else, but I had just cause to do this."

He played with his car keys. "I'm not gonna tell anyone, Mel. I guess I understand why you did it."

"What?" She grimaced.

"I want to apologize for what I said to you last night, Melody. I was way out of line. I love Sarah too much to come between you two. I care about you, too, you know? I wouldn't want you to lose your job."

"See how he cares for you, Melody? How can you keep treating him like this?"

Keith held Sarah. "She doesn't trust me and maybe that's my fault. I should have been more open from the beginning. Melody, I really hold no hard feelings for you. I hope we can put this behind us."

She rocked. "Oh, you're good, Keith."

"Excuse me?" He blinked.

"You are good. I can see why people don't dispute what you say. You almost had me going up until that last part. You should quit while you're ahead, buddy."

"Melody, I wish I could make you see that I do want us to all get along."

Sarah glared at her sister. "Melody, why can't you at least make an effort?"

"Keith, I may not have found enough, but I did find this." Melody handed him the box. He looked at Sarah. "Seems to me such a fancy-looking box wouldn't be in the back of a file cabinet unless, say…you wanted it hidden?"

"Mel." Sarah grunted.

"Wow." Keith looked at the box. "Seems to me you're pretty good yourself, Melody." She nodded. "I *was* hiding this. I hate that you found it but I can't do anything about it, now, can I?"

"You can come *clean*. What's in the box, Keith?" She smirked.

"Well, uh…I was hiding this from Sarah."

"I know that!" Melody grinned. "Why, though? What's in it? A picture of your wife or something about your prison record?"

"Melody, shut up." Sarah stared at the box.

"Neither." He grinned. He handed the box to Sarah. "Go on and open it." She pulled out a diamond necklace. Melody nearly hit the floor. She didn't know exactly why. Could it have been because it was such a lovely gift? It also could have been because she looked like the biggest turd on the planet at that moment.

"Oh, Keith." Sarah examined the astonishing necklace.

"What the…" Melody sighed.

Keith nodded. "Sarah, I remembered how much you liked it when we passed that jewelry store that time. You kept going on and on about it, but said you could never afford it. When I saw it, I knew it could never look as beautiful on anyone else as it would on you."

"Oh, Keith." She hugged him. They exchanged sloppy kisses. Melody turned from the disgusting display of affection. She felt absolutely beaten.

"You like it?" Keith smiled.

"Keith, this is the most beautiful gift I've ever seen!"

"Good." He pulled Sarah close. "Because you're the most beautiful gift I've ever had." They kissed.

"Oh." Sarah pulled away. "I'd better get to work myself." She looked at Melody.

Melody rolled her eyes. "I suppose you're at a loss for words, huh, Sarah?"

She twirled the necklace around. She put it back in the box. "Seems to me I should ask *you* that, Mel. I was pissed at you, but you'd better be glad Keith's gift took my mind off that."

He smiled. "And there's more where that comes from." He kissed her. Sarah glanced at Melody, then left. Keith shut the door behind her. "What a woman. Well..." He walked toward Melody. "Bravo, Mel. I gotta give you an A for effort."

"Get out of my way."

He blocked her. "You not only have Sarah's beauty but her spunk, too. I like your tactics but they need a little work. What were you expecting to find, anyway?"

"Anything to prove that something is wrong with you!" She reached for the door. He picked her up. He forced her against the wall. "Let me go, Keith!"

He exhaled. "You have any idea how much this turns me on?" He shoved his lips against her face. She struggled. "Any idea how much I like playing this game with you?"

"Let go!" she shrieked. He kissed her. She tore her lips away. "Don't! Get off me!" He held her tighter.

"It's time for the next phase in our game, Melody. Maybe then we can see how much you might like it. I really think you'll enjoy the things I have planned."

"Get off me, Keith!"

He held her against the wall. "I gave you a chance to be nice. But then I got to thinking, maybe I liked it better that you weren't playing so fairly. Wanna know why?"

She grunted.

"Because even though it got on my nerves at first, this thing we've got going is the most exciting thing I've ever experienced. You don't know how much it gets me going, Mel."

"Get...off!" She struggled.

"See, you didn't know that, did you?" he panted. She felt his hardened crotch against her thighs. "Didn't know that I'd end up liking all you're doing to get rid of me? The harder you try, the better it all feels." He kissed her again. She jerked away.

"No! I swear to God, Keith! I swear I'll call the police!"

"Oh yeah? And what would you say, huh?" He shoved his hands underneath her skirt.

"I'll tell them everything! I'll tell Mr. Lawson, too, and you'll be fired! Is that what you want?"

"I don't think anyone would believe you, Mel. You've got no proof." He grinned. "Besides, any outsider would probably feel you enjoy this. I think you may in the long run. Who knows? You probably already do."

"Stop!" She pushed him off. She ran to the door. She looked back at him just to see if this could have been real. These days she wasn't sure. He sat behind his desk. He shuffled through papers as if nothing had happened.

"Have a good day today, Melody." He smirked.

She ran out the office.

Chapter Nine

Cheyenne Wilson turned from her bedroom window. The bruises on her face had already begun to heal. Brianna knew that would be the least of Cheyenne's worries. After all, she may never be able to heal the wounds she held inside.

Brianna rushed to help Cheyenne as she stumbled from the window. Brianna hated seeing a young woman so distraught. The minute Brianna walked into the house Cheyenne studied her as if Brianna had the power to make her pain go away. It hurt Brianna like hell that she couldn't give any comforting news to the broken woman. The police were stuck.

The rapist still ran around free, while his victims crumbled beyond control. Brianna sighed. Cheyenne wasn't the only one who needed positive reassurance.

"So." Cheyenne moved her fluffy hair from her face. She had a vibrant smile that even her traumatic state couldn't hide. She sat on the bed. "Detective Morris, I just want to thank you for all you're doing. On behalf of me and all the ladies."

"I'm just doing my job." She smiled. She wanted so much to let Cheyenne know that she too had been attacked. Brianna didn't have the heart. She couldn't kill Cheyenne's hope by having her develop doubt toward the police when she needed them the most.

"I still want to thank you. I was surprised when you said you were coming by this morning. I was hoping it meant you had some good news." Cheyenne looked at the carpet. "Can't say I'm not disappointed, you know? I feel so stupid."

"You don't have anything to feel stupid for, Cheyenne. You didn't do anything wrong."

"I was…so…so trusting." She wiped her eyes. "I'm not a fool, Detective Morris. Yet I acted like one the other night. Why? Why in the hell did I get in the car with him? I knew better! I knew better!" She cried. Brianna held her. "I'm just so mad and…confused. I've never felt like this before." She shook. "I've been scared, but nothing like this."

Brianna rocked her. "I think you're doing very well, Cheyenne. You're a strong woman and you'll get through this. Remember that number I gave you?"

Cheyenne sniffed against Brianna's chest. "For that rape center?"

"It's the best in the city. I want you to contact them whenever you need to."

She moved away. "I'm not ready for that, Detective Morris. I can't even understand what happened yet. How can I talk to others about it?"

"They can help you understand, Cheyenne. That's what they're there for."

"Detective Morris, have you..." Cheyenne swallowed. "Have you ever been raped?"

Brianna exhaled. "No." Yet she'd almost been. That had been hard enough. Sometimes she wondered if she thrust herself into Cheyenne's case to forget what happened to *her*. She'd been determined not to be a victim. It hadn't been easy. She was already one whether she liked it or not. She hadn't been raped, but judging by the newfound fear she felt, she might as well had been.

Brianna had been so scared of being alone in her home. Even having a gun hadn't given her comfort. Brianna could easily say she hadn't been in Cheyenne's shoes. But did that mean she could escape fate? If the predator came after her again...could she escape? She could easily be in Cheyenne's shoes. Could she deal with such fear when she stood on the opposite side of it? She prayed she wouldn't ever find out.

"Detective, are you okay? I hope I didn't upset you."

"Uh no." Brianna stood. "Uh, I almost forgot. The reason I came is because my partner wants to speak to you. He's downstairs."

"Oh." Cheyenne glanced at her bedroom door. "Uh..." She held her shirt. "I don't know if I am..."

"I know you're afraid of being with a man right now, but he's here to help you. Cheyenne, you have to cooperate with us as best you can. We need to get this guy off the streets before he has a chance to hurt anyone else."

She sighed. "I don't know if you can catch him. He seems invincible."

"No one is invincible, and we won't stop until we get him." Brianna nodded.

"You can believe that."

"I'll talk to your partner, but only if you're in the room, too."

Brianna smiled. "Then let's go." Steven paced around Cheyenne's little white living room. Brianna walked in first. Cheyenne huddled in back. She kept her head to the floor. She hadn't taken a glimpse of Steven yet. Brianna walked toward him.

"Is she doing okay?" he whispered.

"As good as to be expected. I think she's holding up well considering what she's been through. She's talking, which is more than I can say for the other victims."

He nodded. "We just need to go over some things."

"Cheyenne?" Brianna gently grabbed her arm. "This is my partner, Detective Steven Kemp." Steven held out his hand with a smile. "He just wants to ask you some questions."

Cheyenne's mouth dropped as if it weighed a thousand pounds.

"Hello, Miss Wilson. I hope you're doing okay." Steven put his hand in his pocket when she didn't take it. "I know this is a hard time for you so we won't be long. I just wanted to go over some things…"

"What the…" Cheyenne looked at Brianna. She shook unlike anything they'd ever seen before. She screamed uncontrollably. She ran across the room. "Monster!

Monster, this monster right in front of me!" She gripped her head. "Oh, no, no, no, no!" she cried hysterically. "No!"

"Cheyenne!" Brianna ran to her. "Cheyenne, what's the matter?"

"What's the matter?" Her eyes filled with tears. "You're asking me what the matter is?" She charged Steven. "Get out! Get out of my house!" She hit him repeatedly. He used his arms to shield his face. "Get out! Get out! Get the hell out of my house!"

"Hey!" Steven tried to move away. She continued to hit him any place she could.

"Cheyenne!" Brianna grabbed her by the waist. She had so much strength she nearly threw Brianna off. "Cheyenne, wait! Cheyenne, please! What's wrong?"

"Get out! Get out of my house!" She ran to the kitchen. She came back with a butcher knife and charged Steven. "Get out right now, you bastard! You son of a bitch!" she wailed. "How dare you come into my home? Get out! Get out!"

Brianna ran to the front door. She gestured for the uniformed cop they'd brought along. He ran inside and charged Cheyenne until she waved the knife his way.

"Put the knife down, Cheyenne!" Brianna begged.

"Miss Wilson, are you okay?" Steven exhaled.

"How dare you?" Her eyes danced with fury. "How dare you come into my home after what you did?"

"What...what are you talking about?" Steven hollered.

"You know what!" She waved the knife toward him. "Goddamn, I'll kill you, you motherfucker! You sick, disgusting perverted motherfucker!" She ran toward him. Steven found himself blocked against the wall.

"Stop, please!" He held his arms up. Brianna and the uniformed cop held Cheyenne back. Yet the knife had easy access to Steven. "Miss Wilson, I'm a cop who just wants to help you! I know you've been through a lot but I am here to help!"

"Put the knife down, Cheyenne!" Brianna shouted.

"No chance." She wiped tears as she glared at Steven. "You come into my home? And the cops brought you here! Get out of my house, you motherfucker, or I'll kill you!" She leapt on top of him. The uniformed cop pulled her off before she could cut Steven. "Get out! Get out of my house! Get out!"

"Go, Steven!" Brianna pointed to the door. He followed the order, though he didn't know the hell why. Brianna followed him outside.

"Bree?" He waved his arms. "I…I don't know what that was! My God, she wanted to kill me. What the fuck is going on?"

"Just let me see. I'll be right back. Rape victims can get very distraught, Steven."

He looked at the door. "She wasn't distraught; she wanted to *kill* me, Bree! Jesus Christ." He held his head. Brianna went back inside. Cheyenne huffed and puffed. The cop stood over her.

"Cheyenne, what happened?"

"I want you out of my house, Detective Morris! I don't want to see you ever again!" Cheyenne ran to the stairs.

"Cheyenne, what's the deal?" Brianna begged. "I think you need some help. I know you're hurting right now, but that doesn't excuse you attacking my partner. Please talk to me so I can help you!"

Cheyenne turned around on the stairs. "I don't need your help, Detective Morris. Not as long as you're with trash like that!"

"You have a problem with my partner?"

"Oh, I have a *big* problem with your partner!" Cheyenne shrieked. "I could have killed him dead right in front of you! I didn't give a damn! He deserves to die! I'll kill him if he comes near me again!"

"*Why?*" Brianna yelled desperately. "Just tell me what's going on!"

"Okay, I will." Cheyenne came down the stairs.

Steven jerked when Brianna came outside. He noticed a red car speeding down the street. Other than that the neighborhood appeared unusually empty. The uniformed cop walked out. He looked at Steven, then headed for the car. Brianna shut Cheyenne's door. She avoided his gaze.

"What was that about?" Steven pointed to the uniformed cop. "What's going on, Bree?"

"Steven…"

"So did she say why she charged me in there?" He

wiped his forehead. "Look, I understand she's distraught but she was out of line, Brianna. If I didn't feel sorry for her, I would have arrested her."

"She's very upset, Steven."

He scoffed. "Yeah, I kind of figured that out, Bree. I want to know why." She looked away. "Brianna, what in the hell is going on? Talk to me." He took her hand. She looked at him. "Talk to me, baby."

"I don't know how to say this, Steven." She ran her hands through her hair. "I'm too shocked to absorb it myself."

"Just tell me." He moved back.

"Steven, Cheyenne Wilson said that you...that you were..." She groaned.

"I *what*, Bree?" He crossed his arms.

"She said that *you* were the man that raped her."

He lightly chuckled. "What?" He blinked wildly.

"Cheyenne Wilson said you raped her. That's why she went so crazy." Brianna shrugged. He leaned against the house. "Steven, why would she say that? It makes no sense and it's absurd. Why would she say that about you?" She stared at him.

He rubbed his mouth. "I wish I knew, Bree." He stared in complete shock.

"Kemp, I'm telling you, don't let this bother you so much." Captain Jersey shuffled through the morning reports. "Don't take it personal."

"Captain, how can I not?" He leaned over her desk. Brianna watched silently in the corner of the office. "I mean, what in the hell makes Cheyenne Wilson think I raped her? I'm gonna go back over there and talk to her."

"No, you're not." Jersey took off her glasses. "Let me explain something to you, okay? She's in a very confused state right now. She's vulnerable mentally, Steven. She came down those stairs and saw you, a man who looks like the man who raped her." Jersey waved her hands. "She started swinging a knife at you and I don't blame her. I mean, I can only imagine what I'd do if I saw a man who I thought had raped me in my home and beat me with a flashlight. I would have been swinging a knife too and probably some furniture."

Brianna grinned.

"I understand that, Captain. But it doesn't make me feel any better about it. I went there trying to help this girl and she treats me like I'm some kind of monster. I know what rape victims go through, but this didn't seem excusable. I was scared, Captain."

"She was, too, Steven," Brianna whispered.

He sighed. "Why do I feel like the bad guy here when I was the one who was attacked?"

Jersey leaned back in her chair. "Kemp, put yourself in Cheyenne's shoes. She's the victim, not you. And you gotta admit…" Jersey studied a sketch of the rapist. "You do look a lot like the rapist. I mean, we can't deny that."

"Captain, I didn't rape her."

She laughed. "Kemp, please! Of course you didn't, and

I don't need you to explain any of this to me! I wouldn't believe that in a second! Cheyenne will come to her senses and realize she overreacted. Don't give it another thought."

He gestured toward the door. "I think I should go and explain things to her."

Jersey waved a finger. "Stay away from her and that's an order. In fact, I want you both to give Cheyenne some room. If she's waving knives at people, it's definitely not the time to be questioning her. Follow up on the other victims and try to come up with more leads."

Steven sighed. "It's not that easy, Captain." He left the office.

Jersey looked at Brianna. "Since when is being a cop supposed to be *easy*?"

"He did *what*?" Aileen turned from Sarah's stove that night. Melody dipped up two giant bowls of buttered popcorn. She gestured for Aileen to follow her to the den. She invited Aileen over to talk about Keith. Since Sarah worked late tonight, there couldn't have been a better time. Melody took the remote as he cradled the bowl of popcorn in her lap. She almost laughed at Aileen's shocked expression. Aileen ate two kernels before repeating the question. "Keith did *what*?"

Melody nodded. "He molested me right there in his office." She shrugged. "Believe me, I was as shocked as you are. So I called you over because you always give the best advice." Melody switched the channel.

"Why are you being so nonchalant about this guy, Mel? My God, the shit he does gets worse and worse. You gotta go to the police now."

She scoffed. "Right. And say what? I mean, how in the hell could I prove anything? Plus, would the police really care about some woman who's having problems with her sister's new boyfriend? Hell no, Aileen. I can see it right now. They'll label me jealous the minute I walk into the room, then wonder why I had the nerve to bother them with something so juvenile. The police are not an option, believe me. Keith hasn't really done anything against the law."

"He put his hands on you, didn't he?" Aileen crossed her legs Indian-style. She swallowed a fistful of popcorn. "Girl, if it was me, his ass would be outta here."

"Easier said than done with Sarah thinking he's heaven sent." Melody waved her hand through the popcorn. "You know, we aren't even close like we were since Keith came into the picture. Sarah and I used to share so much. Now it seems like she shares everything with Keith. We can't have one conversation without her bringing him up. And the way she thinks of him is pathetic. Oh man, she runs when he calls. When he doesn't call, she acts like a big nut. I don't know what to do."

"I told you before that if Sarah won't listen, you need to take the initiative." Aileen chewed.

"Before it gets out of hand?" Melody whispered.

"Melody, it has gotten out of hand and passed out of hand! When a man starts grabbing you like you're his property, something is seriously wrong. He has no business putting his hands on you any damn way, but at work…" She shook her head. "Melody, this fucker seems to think he can do whatever the hell he wants, but you gotta make him see he can't. Some men are like that. They push and push until you give in to them."

"Give in?" Melody stopped flipping the channels. "What, you think this is some kind of seduction thing Keith's doing?"

"Would you be surprised? Melody, he had his hands under your skirt today. Don't you see that he's attracted to you?" Aileen walled her eyes.

"He actually told me that he was. I just wanted him gone. I never thought about *why* he was acting the way he acts. You think he is trying to be with me on the side or some shit?" Aileen shrugged. "So that's it?" Melody sighed. "He thinks I'll play this game, huh? I've told him repeatedly to leave me alone, and I'm sick of talking!"

"You should be. It's time to take action. There's something you can do about this, Melody. You hit him where it hurts. Hit him so that he gets the point that he can't keep doing this to you." Aileen raised an eyebrow. "Get my drift?"

"No."

"Dang, girl, do you need a crate to fall on your head to get a clue?" Aileen chuckled. "What's something that

Keith needs and can't afford to lose? And I'm not talking about your bouncy blonde sister, either."

Melody smirked. "His job?"

"That's right. Hit his ass where it hurts. Tell Mr. Lawson exactly what he's been doing. I bet you that'll put Keith in his place."

"It definitely will and piss him off in the process." Melody grinned. "He's so damn cocky. I'd love to stick it to his ass and let him know he can't push me around."

Aileen shrugged. "And there's only one way to do that. I don't care how great he may think he is, but Keith probably needs that job either for money or clout or both. This will not only make him leave you alone, but he'll see that you're no one to mess with. You go to Mr. Lawson and this shit will end real quick, believe me. Anyway, what choice do you have?"

"You're right, this is the only choice. I warned Keith that I'd report him. I think Mr. Lawson would at least listen to my claims. After all, why would I have reason to lie? Mr. Lawson has to be objective, anyway, because if something like sexual harassment is even suspected, he could end up in trouble himself for not paying attention to me. Shit, I may even get Keith fired." Melody grinned.

Aileen winked. "The bastard would deserve it any damn way. Mel, reporting his ass is the only way to prove to him that you mean business. He isn't listening to words so you gotta use action."

Melody nodded. "You're right, girlfriend. I have a feeling this is the only thing that will finally put Keith Taylor in his place."

Aileen winked. "Just do your thing, girl. Do it."

Melody held the fat stack of papers to her chest the next day at work. Out of all the rooms Melody regularly visited at Caper, she disliked the file room the most. Still, filing papers was a big part of her job. She couldn't escape it. She wondered if anyone else found the room creepy. She hated that dim light that only lit up half the room. The room seemed to be the size of two conference rooms. It would have to be. It housed every piece of written information Caper needed or would ever need.

Mario had done a miracle by training her on the system. A computer, with every gadget known to man attached to it, sat on the desk in the middle of the room. She preferred searching for files manually while others relied on the computer. She didn't trust computers. Since humans programmed the damn things in the first place, what made people think computers were any more reliable?

The room smelled of old dust. She sneezed on her way to the back file cabinets. She squeezed through rows and rows of tall, fat, overstuffed cabinets. She came to the giant black ones in the back. They had to reach at least six feet. Anyone shorter than her would proba-bly have to use steps. She hurried to find the files. She didn't want to be here any longer than necessary.

She heard something by the door, yet she didn't know why she jumped. She *was* in a crowded building. Anyone had access to this room. Why in the hell did she feel it could be more than that? Maybe she should switch to decaf after all. She heard footsteps. She thought of calling out, but that seemed silly. She didn't know why this room frightened her so much. She rushed to find the files.

She got on her knees to check the low drawers. She pulled the Thompson files from the front. She smiled at finding them quickly. She stacked the fat files under her arms and turned to leave. She gasped. Keith stood in front of her. He swatted the files from her hands, and papers flew in all directions.

"Keith!" She went to pick them up. He grabbed her. She ripped her arm from his grasp.

"You think you're clever, don't you, Melody?" He sweated. She'd never seen him so angry. Usually his cockiness kept him grounded. She took a deep breath. Going to Mr. Lawson *had* knocked Keith into place. Too bad that she got the feeling she would regret it. She loved Aileen, but sometimes her advice got people into trouble.

"Keith." She looked at the scattered papers. "Did Mr. Lawson talk to you today?"

"Oh, you damn right he did." Fury ran through his

gorgeous face. His eyes were so piercing Melody had to turn away.

"Look, I didn't want to do that, Keith, but you left me no choice. I told you not to mess with me. I deserve to be able to come to work without you bothering me. You took it too far. You've invaded my personal life, and now you're in my face at the job."

He smirked. She trembled. She wondered if he made anyone else feel this way.

"So this is how you want to do things, Melody? The hard way?"

"Look, you made that choice and not me. I want you to stay away from me, Keith. I don't care about what you do with Sarah, just stay the hell away from me!"

"And...if I don't?" He squinted.

"Then next time I won't be going to Mr. Lawson. If you lay a finger on me or think of doing something because I went to Mr. Lawson, then I'll go to the police." He scoffed. "Think I'm playing, just try me, Keith. I'm not taking any more of your shit."

He straightened his Omega on his wrist. "I don't appreciate being threatened, Melody. You went too far. You do what you have to do, okay? But if you think you're getting away with this, you are wrong. You've fucked with me and now you've fucked with my job. I'm not just walking away from this. You can believe that, okay?"

"I'm not afraid of you, Keith. But if you're as smart as

you want people to think, you will leave me alone! I will go to the cops next time, I swear I will." She shook.

He leaned closer to her. "Maybe that's a good idea, Melody. Because from now on, you're probably gonna *need* to." He walked away.

Melody leaned against the cabinets, breathless.

Chapter Ten

Melody read the message Sarah left on the refrigerator when she got home from work that Friday. The note instructed her to heat up dinner. Once again she'd be eating alone. She didn't mind. She loved the solitude that accompanied an empty house. It gave her time to think, which was something she longed for. Melody stared at the note.

Sarah hadn't mentioned if she'd be working tonight or hanging out with Keith. She heated up the frozen dinner of fish sticks and cheesy macaroni. Sarah rarely worked late on Fridays. Even Mr. Pepskin wasn't that cold. Just imagining Sarah cuddling next to a naked Keith made her sick to her stomach. She refused to think about them anymore tonight.

She thought of the other day in the file room at Caper. Surprisingly, Keith managed to keep his distance over the last few days. Every now and then he shot her a threatening glance, yet he hadn't dared to touch her or even speak to her. He hadn't even been to the house. Had she really put that slick, slimy, egotistical SOB in his place? Melody loved to believe that she had. But still she wasn't sure.

She looked out the kitchen window. Driveways were vacant. Fences were locked for the night. The streets were bare. Even the old folks across the street were out. Lucas had plans with his parents. Tonight would be the perfect time to invite him over to embark on both of their fantasies. She couldn't believe Lucas had plans tonight of all nights. She couldn't call Craig, either. He taught paint techniques at the community center on Friday nights. Aileen spent her Friday nights at her book club meetings. Melody had no choice but to pamper herself.

Sarah claimed milk baths helped women relieve stress. Melody decided to try one. She got the dried-milk packages from the kitchen cabinet. Sarah made trips to the spa with girlfriends from work now and then. She brought back plenty of beauty products. Sarah had a special drawer for her spa products. Melody searched through facemasks, brushes, hair removal gels, vegetable face creams, body oil removals and everything else that Sarah claimed brought out a woman's natural beauty.

Melody headed toward her bathroom with some delicious-smelling lotions and facial creams. She loved taking scalding hot baths. She had been blessed with smooth yet tough skin. She could take the heat. She sucked in the fog from the steaming tub.

Her clothes practically melted from perspiration. She leaned against the sink. She enjoyed the dirty thoughts about Lucas. No telling what she'd have done if he'd been here. She may have taken him up on his offer of going all the way. God knows she got hornier by the second. She found it typical to want him when he wasn't there. She grinned.

She turned off the water. She searched for a gown in her bedroom. She didn't want to wear the boyish T-shirt tonight. She'd been in a sexy mood for days. She wanted something silky, lacy and seductive. She found a lacy pink nightgown she'd bought when she dated Enrique. She ran her hands through the soft silk. He'd gone crazy with her in it. She wondered if Lucas would ever do the same.

Being alone felt deviously exciting. She grew incredibly aroused. She had a feeling she'd end up doing more in that tub than washing. Melody didn't see a thing wrong with masturbation. Others shied upon it. To her, not touching yourself seemed unnatural. She never believed a person who said they hadn't masturbated. She knew how aroused she got from slipping into a comfortable pair of panties.

She knew how hot she got if she accidentally tickled her nipple while sliding on her bra. Masturbation brought a girl such undeniable pleasure. She couldn't see anything being wrong with that. Many times she'd enjoyed masturbating more than actual sex. For some reason, when she made herself cum, she appreciated it more than some guy that couldn't last more than three minutes.

Thirty minutes later she emerged from the bathroom

feeling refreshed. She thought about taking in a movie. She couldn't remember the house being so quiet. She went to her bedroom. She left the curtains open so that she could see when Sarah got back. She ran her hands down the nightgown. She had masturbated during her bath. It had been absolutely heavenly. Yet she remained aroused.

She knew the gown had something to do with it. The sensuous fabric hugged her cleavage. She slid her hands across her breasts. She tickled the edge of her nipples until they peaked. She moaned. She couldn't believe being alone could feel so good. She started to wish Sarah would never come home. She shut her eyes. She slipped her hands toward her buttocks, cupping them. She slipped her hand toward her vagina.

She wanted to fully make love to herself. All the while she'd think of Lucas. She moaned. A loud truck passed, interrupting the moment. She opened her eyes. Her arousal vanished. She concentrated on how exhausted she'd been the last few days. She couldn't remember such a beautiful night. The full moon provided the perfect amount of light.

She stood at the end of her bed. She noticed something moving underneath the sheets. At first she thought her eyes played tricks on her. The movements grew faster.

She heard a light hissing sound. Whatever swerved underneath the sheet moved rapidly. The mattress wobbled in the center. "What the fuck?" Melody whispered.

Something told her to call the police before moving that sheet.

She didn't know what the hell to think. She would turn back the sheet now or never. She wouldn't call the cops unless she knew what to tell them. She took a deep breath as she lifted the end of the sheet.

Sssss! A snake hissed.

"Ahhh!" Melody jumped back. She tried to catch her breath. She felt a panic attack coming on. Sweat ran down her face. *Snakes!* A pile of small brown and black snakes slithered around the center of the bed. They made their way to the floor. They coiled themselves around the bedposts. Melody hopped on the chair beside her endtable.

She snatched the phone. Snakes slithered from under the bed. Melody huffed and puffed. She couldn't call anyone if she couldn't breathe. "Oh, oh, oh God." Her hands shook. She tried to dial despite her shaking fingers. "Oh my God, I don't believe this." She trembled. "Oh… oh God. Ahh!" She noticed a snake slithering up the leg of her chair. "Oh shit!" She nearly dropped the phone.

She noticed a few snakes slithering against the walls. She didn't know how many there were. Right now she didn't give a damn. She couldn't gather enough courage to even scream. Everything happened so fast. She jumped off the chair. She ran downstairs. She bent over to control the panic attack. She finally made the call.

❖❖❖

Sarah tore through the front door. She darted past the group of officers in the living room. She busted into the kitchen. Police searched the hallways, entrances and bedrooms for any key to where the snakes came from. Melody shivered in the chair beside the kitchen table. She waited for someone to offer any reasonable explanation.

She calmed down when she saw Sarah.

Sarah knelt beside Melody's chair. They embraced. They tried to block out the overlapping voices from the officers in the living room. A group of bewildered animal control officials scattered past the kitchen. Sarah kept her eyes on the officers by the kitchen doorway.

"Mel, what in the world is going on? Are you all right? Shit, I saw all the cop cars and I didn't know what had happened!"

"I tried to call you but..."

She sighed. "Damn it, I turned my cell phone off this evening and forgot to turn it back on."

"Well, at least you're here now. Sarah, I've never been so scared. It was like some kind of nightmare! Sarah, snakes were all in my room! I don't know what in the hell is going on!" Melody huffed.

Sarah gaped. "*Snakes*?" She glanced at the officers at the kitchen door. "Okay calm down, sweetie." Sarah rubbed Melody's hand. "We don't need you to go into a panic attack right now."

"Believe me, I've already had about ten." Melody held her chest. "And you know I'm petrified to death of snakes.

Sarah, how in the world could something like this happen?"

"Well, what did the animal control people say?" Sarah pointed.

"They've been looking upstairs for about thirty minutes. They haven't said anything to me yet, but a policeman said they could have come through a small hole in the wall or floor. Hell, I don't know. He claims that this happens a lot. Especially in this area."

Sarah nodded. "We got that big swamp about two blocks down. Some neighbors have complained about snakes in their homes a couple of times. That may explain it. Snakes can come in all kinds of ways, Mel. Sometimes they can come in with something brought into the house, you know? And they can easily get somewhere and hatch. Especially in the walls."

"No, Sarah, we would have seen something. Look, I know you're just trying to comfort me, but do you really think this is just a coincidence?"

She grimaced. "Melody, what am I supposed to think? I mean, that's Mother Nature. You can't control it. Bees, snakes, rats, raccoons, you name it…they get in people's homes all the time. I don't believe this is any different." Melody shook her head. Sarah stared at her. "But *you* seem to. Is there something you want to say, Melody? You think this is more than a coincidence?"

The tall cop Melody spoke to earlier walked in. A short, sweaty bald guy followed.

The cop looked at Sarah. "Are you Miss Johnson, Miss Cruz's sister?"

"Yes, I am. This is my house. Can you tell us anything about the snakes?"

"This is Mr. Loggia." The cop pointed to the sweaty guy. "He works for the animal control department."

He dabbed his bald head. "Hello, ladies." He laid his hands on his wobbly belly. He wore a yellow-and-blue suit that made him look like a human burrito. "I took a look at the room and our men are taking the snakes out. Wasn't that many, really." He looked at Melody. "Though, I can understand even five snakes will seem like a million to someone who may have a fear of them. Uh, they are completely harmless." He shrugged.

"Not poisonous?" Sarah asked.

He grinned. "Not at all. But I am sorry for the trouble, Miss Cruz."

"Thanks." Melody slipped her hands between her thighs. "Uh, but how could they have gotten in like this and me not know it?"

Sarah interrupted. "I told Mel that snakes are common in this area because of that bayou a few blocks down. We've had complaints of snakes before. Uh, this is common, right? Sometimes snakes can just get into homes, right?"

"Certainly, Miss Johnson. But that isn't the case here."

"What do you mean?" Melody glared.

"Well, the snakes found in Miss Cruz's bed aren't

snakes that are found in this part of the USA. No, these were more like Midwestern snakes. Or snakes you would find in the desert or country." Melody and Sarah exchanged glances.

"So what are you saying exactly?" Sarah crossed her arms.

"Uh, well, these would have to have been purchased from a pet store. These types of snakes are just not found here. Also, I've studied snakes for years and these were bred to be pets. Children far and wide love this specific type of snake. Uh, but you couldn't find them around here."

"Not even in the bayou, huh?" Melody contemplated Loggia's theory.

"No, not even in the bayou." He shrugged. "So, uh… we'll be gone in probably about twenty more minutes. Any questions?"

"Uh, you searched all around the room, right?" Melody asked.

Loggia nodded.

"I know you said the snakes don't come from around here, but did you see any holes?"

"I saw no holes that any snakes would have been interested in. Anyway, snakes don't just crawl into someone's bed and stay there." He grinned. "They're adventurous, curious creatures. They get bored easily, and Miss Cruz's bed wouldn't have been that entertaining to them, unless a rat was in it."

"Oh God." Sarah held her chest. "I'm scared to death of rats." She looked around.

Loggia laughed. "I was just kidding, Miss Johnson. I'd better stop talking or neither one of you will be able to sleep. What you can do is track down the pet store that may have sold these. Then you can find out exactly what happened."

Melody leaned up. "Are you saying that you think someone *put* these snakes in my room?"

Loggia looked at the officer. "Uh, maybe you should speak to the policeman about that." He left the kitchen.

Sarah looked at the officer. "This is just a simple situation, right?"

He took off his hat. "Miss Cruz, you may want to make a report of this."

"Report…" She looked at Sarah. "So you really believe this wasn't accidental?"

He cleared his throat. "All the facts are telling me that it's probably not. So since I'm here you might as well do a report. Judging from what Loggia said, and he's the expert, these snakes being here was no accident." He tapped his pencil on the table. "You said you're very frightened of snakes, Miss Cruz?"

"Very. I only have to see a picture of one and I go crazy."

"Uh-huh. Do a lot of people know you're afraid of snakes?"

Melody shrugged. "Of course my friends do. And Sarah. Wait." She grinned. "My friends wouldn't do this."

"Not as a practical joke?"

"No. Believe me, my friends wouldn't do something that would scare me half to death."

He crossed his legs. "Would anyone else? Do you, uh…have any enemies, Miss Cruz?"

Sarah stared silently.

"No, I…" Melody exhaled. She certainly did have an enemy. And she'd definitely pissed him off. A feeling came over Melody that told her she had to be right. Keith Taylor put those snakes in her bed. She looked at Sarah. Melody no longer entertained any other explanations. The bastard did it. Even though it seemed incredibly farfetched, it had Keith written all over it.

"Miss Cruz, were you going to say something?" The officer stared at her.

"I know who did this." She looked at Sarah. "His name is Keith Taylor."

"*What*?" Sarah shouted.

"Yes, I know he did it, Sarah!"

"You are unbelievable!" She paced in front of the stove. "You can't stop blaming Keith for anything, can you? This is completely ridiculous!"

"Who is Keith Taylor?" The officer gawked.

"It's not ridiculous, Sarah. Keith hates me, okay! He has every reason to get back at me!"

"For what?"

Melody sighed. She hadn't mentioned that she'd reported Keith for sexual harassment. With Sarah's current state, she chose to work around that.

"Sarah, you know Keith hates me. We both know he wants me out of the picture!"

"Who's Keith?" The officer yawned.

"Keith doesn't hate you, Mel! Anyway, what do you think this is, a fuckin' movie? Who would be insane enough to put snakes in someone's bed?"

"You heard what Mr. Loggia said! He said they couldn't have gotten here by accident. Why won't you listen to reason, Sarah? You refuse to see Keith for what he really is! I don't understand you!"

"Stop it! You just stop it right now, Melody! Keith did not do this!"

"For the last time, who is *Keith*?" the cop shouted.

"My sister's boyfriend and possibly the devil," Melody muttered.

Sarah scoffed. "Melody, you're scaring me. You can't give up this animosity you have toward Keith. And why? He never did a damn thing to you!"

"No, he does things, but you just won't pay any attention to them! He did this, Sarah! I don't care what you think!"

"Well, this is very interesting." The cop jotted down Keith's name. "What's his address and phone number?"

Sarah sighed. "Officer, this is not necessary! It's hearsay at best. I know Keith did not come in here and put those snakes in Melody's bed!"

"How do *you* know?" Melody shouted.

"Because I was with Keith all evening, okay?" Melody gawked. "When would he have had time to do this,

Melody? Can't you see how sick this seems? You cannot spend your life blaming things on Keith."

"Then explain how the snakes got here, Sarah. Explain it!" Sarah looked away.

"You can't can you? Keith has this in him, Sarah. He's dangerous and you're gonna learn that soon enough. I just hope it's before it's too late." Melody looked at the officer. "I won't press charges." The officer gazed. "Does that make you happy...*sis*?" Melody ran upstairs.

Sarah sighed.

"Yes?" Aileen peeked out the keyhole Saturday night. A handsome man smiled at her. He waved his hands through silky blond hair. The darkness of night couldn't hide those magnetic blue eyes. Aileen never opened the door these days without peeking. A girl could never be safe with the Albany Predator at large. He hadn't hit anyone in Aileen's neighborhood yet, but she didn't take chances. Melody would have been proud to see how careful she'd been lately.

"Uh, hello." The man smiled. "This may sound strange, but maybe you could help me. I'm looking for a Mrs. Aileen Andrews. Can you tell me which house is hers?"

"Oh, that's me." She smiled. "I'm Aileen Andrews."

"Oh. Well then, this must be my lucky day. I'm doing a routine check tonight, ma'am. Uh, actually I'm investigating a crime that's been committed not far from here. I'm a detective and…" He held up his badge. She nodded. "I just wanted to come in and ask you some questions."

"What's your name?" She squinted.

"Detective Kemp. May I please come in for a second? I've been investigating the Albany Predator. If you aren't sure, you can call my precinct. They'll vouch for me."

She grinned. "That won't be necessary." She hurriedly opened the door. She looked over his badge. "I'm just being careful these days. Especially since they said the rapist may be a cop."

"Yeah, you should be very careful." He walked inside without waiting for an invitation. He looked over the tidy living room. He leaned to get a glimpse of the hall toward the kitchen. "Beautiful home you have here, Mrs. Andrews. You seem so young to have such a beautiful home."

"Yeah, well…" She pushed her fluffy hair behind her ears. She stroked the sides of her thin housedress. "Will this take long? I planned to take a nap."

"Oh, not at all." He took out a pad and pencil. "I just needed to ask you some questions. There was a woman assaulted a few blocks down." They sat on the couch.

"Got your name from someone in the neighborhood. They said you stay home during the day, and the lady was attacked Friday morning."

"Yes, I'm a stay-at-home mom, if you want to call it that." She smiled. "All this talk about this rapist scares the hell out of me."

"And it should because he's very dangerous." His eyes twinkled. "He's a lot more dangerous than the cops are letting on. We have to do that, you see, in order to catch him. We also don't want to scare the victims."

"Well, I'll definitely do my best to help. I don't know if I saw anything."

"No one strange going around the neighborhood?"

"Uh, no. I mean, if someone walked down the street, I'm sure I didn't notice them. Not with a two-year-old taking up most of my time." She smiled.

"Ahh, you got kids?" He blushed.

"Yes, a little girl, Danielle." She pointed to the picture by the lamp.

"Oh, she's beautiful. Enjoy being married?"

She showed off her ring. "Yes. My husband is a truck driver. He's in Texas right now."

"I see." He looked around. "Uh, are you all alone?"

"It's just me and my daughter. She's sleeping." She gestured upstairs.

"Don't you hate being alone on Saturday nights?"

"Well, I'm getting used to being alone all of the time. I mean, my husband is always away working. I guess I shouldn't complain when some wives' husbands are too lazy to even take out the trash." She chuckled.

"But it still doesn't compensate for him being gone, huh? I bet you're very lonely, aren't you, Aileen?" He paced around the living room.

"Yes. I am. But you didn't come here to talk about my boring life." She stood.

"Are you guys any closer to catching him?"

"Who?" He glared at her.

"Well, the rapist." She waved her hands. "You getting any closer?"

He smirked. "Hard to tell. But if the victims keep cooperating, things will turn out better in the long run. So, I can imagine how hard it is with your husband always being away, huh?" He leaned against the door with his hands in his pockets. "Makes no sense to me. Thinking of leaving him?"

She laughed. "Funny. But uh, we'll make it through. Hopefully, he won't have to work this hard much longer."

"So you have to juggle time with him, huh? Are you two still able to have fun together?"

She rubbed the back of her neck. "Uh…we do what we can. Is there anything else I can help you with, Detective?"

"Huh?" He gazed.

Aileen remained beside the couch. She now knew what Melody meant about that "frightening" feeling. She experienced it with a vengeance at this moment. Something about the way this man looked at her terrified her. She hardly listened to her gut feeling these days. Tonight, she would. "Uh, you know what? I'm expecting some friends over."

"Are you?" He raised an eyebrow. "Well, I just have one more question, if that's all right with you."

"Then you'll leave," she politely ordered.

"Of course." He nearly bumped into her when he stood

from the door. "Now this question is very important, Aileen."

"Okay." She crossed her arms.

"You said you and your husband have to compensate for a lot of things, right?" He rubbed his hands.

"Wait, I thought this was about the rapist."

He smirked. "Oh, it is. Is sex something you and your husband have to compensate for, Aileen?"

She trembled. This definitely wasn't right. "You know, I uh, forgot I have somewhere to be."

"Oh really? A few seconds ago you said you had friends coming. Which one is it?"

"Both. See, uh, I have to get some food for the get-together, you know."

"All women?" He smiled.

"Yes."

"Then maybe I should stick around." He grinned.

She pretended to take the suggestion as a joke. "Uh, maybe you should come back another time. I'll call your headquarters if I know something…"

He grabbed her. "No need."

"Let go!" He held her by the waist. "Help!"

"Things were going so well with us, Aileen. Just like a woman to start acting all crazy." He walled his eyes.

"You're the rapist! You are!" She struggled in his arms. "Someone, help!"

He carried her to the couch. "Damn, aren't you a sweet little brown thing, huh? I'm gonna enjoy this, you can believe me!"

"Help! Someone help!"

"Oh, come on, baby. Just relax, huh?" He grinned. "It'll be over before you know it. No, better yet, I want to take my time with *you*." He ran his tongue down her face. She whimpered. "I'd like to take my time and get it right." He threw her on the couch.

"Help!" She jumped up. He shoved her down. "Help! Someone help!"

"Aw, why you screaming? I mean, you're in good hands now, baby." He sat beside her. "Might as well enjoy it." She screamed. He slapped his hand over her mouth. "I don't want to hurt you, Aileen. I like you a lot already. There are ways we can do this, sweetheart. You understand?" He pulled her up.

"You're...you're a *cop*?" She shook. "My God, you're supposed to protect people! How can you do this?" He lifted her and slung her over his shoulder. "Put me down!"

She fought viciously.

He panted. "You'll understand me once you get to know me better, Aileen. And believe me, darling, that's most of the fun."

He took her upstairs to her bedroom.

Chapter Eleven

Melody had anticipated this Saturday night for days. She found dinner with the Lawsons interesting. It didn't compare to what happened afterward. She knew Lucas would try to get her to go back to his place. She did. She didn't know where things would lead. She still wasn't ready for sex. She couldn't understand why she held out. She'd known Lucas for ages.

He would always be special to her. She found it terribly difficult to balance the bond of friendship and love. Tonight appeared perfect. Hell, it should have *felt* perfect. But Melody still wasn't any step closer to making that move with Lucas. His living room signified the perfect romantic setting. Candles, light music, wine, fresh fruit, two blankets by the fireplace. Yep, idle perfection.

Lucas admitted that his maid helped him set things up. It didn't matter to Melody. They could have been in the bathroom. The moment would have still been magical to her. She slipped her shoes off. Lucas led her to the blankets. She sat down. She didn't think he could get more beautiful until she saw him in candlelight.

"What do you think?" He wore a silky black shirt

that nearly gave Melody hives. Maybe Lucas's perfection had been what stalled her toward sex. Maybe she unconsciously felt she couldn't live up to his expectations. She sipped her wine.

"Did you have a good time at dinner?"

"I don't call eating at your parents' townhouse a 'good time,' Lucas. It was perfect. Everything is so damn perfect." She sighed.

"Uh." He leaned toward her. "You're upset?"

"Yes." She looked away.

He grinned. "Because the night was perfect?" She nodded. "And this is a bad thing?"

"Sometimes," she exhaled. "You're mad?"

"No." He walled his eyes.

She grinned. "Yes you are. Why can't you just admit that you're mad?"

"Okay, I am!" He stood. "I'm furious! I can't get a handle on you, Mel! I can't figure you out to save my life!" She sat on her knees. "I try to show you a good time, to be the best boyfriend I can, and all you do is whine!"

She grinned. "Okay, go on."

"I'm sick of it! I want you to put out something, Melody. Shit, I'm not talking about sex; I'm talking about your damn emotions! Sometimes I feel like I could get more affection from a rock." She covered her grin. "I mean, I try and try to do things to make you happy, and I end up feeling guilty! Sometimes, I feel like I should just give up! You should be damn glad you got a man who goes through so much trouble for you, Mel! You know how many women would want that?"

"Ha, ha, ha!" She rolled over.

"What...what's so damn funny? I'm pissed as hell, Melody! I'm sick of this shit and you're laughing at me? I just gave you the business! What the hell's so funny?"

"Ha, ha, ha! You!" She pointed. "Oh God!" She strutted around, mocking his rant. "Oh, you...oh, Lucas." She smiled.

"Wait a minute." He grinned. "You mean, I act a gentleman all the damn time and you act like you're on PMS." She laughed. "Then I get upset and you're *happy*?"

"Yes! Yes, I am!" she guffawed.

"Why?" he yelled.

"Because you're not fuckin' perfect after all!" She kissed him. They fell over on the blankets. Melody laughed until her stomach ached. Lucas laughed until he turned red.

"Mel, I..." He chuckled. "I don't understand you."

"I don't want you to be perfect, Lucas." She looked into his eyes. "I just want you to be my boyfriend. I enjoy the romantic settings and the carriage rides. But you don't have to be that way all the time." He looked away. "Sometimes trying too hard is worse than not trying at all."

"I understand. I thought women wanted this kind of shit. I mean, 'stuff.'"

She grinned. "No, 'shit' was the right word." She kissed him. "Lucas, each day I fall more in love with you."

"You do?" He smirked.

"Yes. And now that I know you're not perfect your-self, I can relax. I mean, I don't have to feel like I'm under a microscope."

"Jesus, I made you feel like that?" He grimaced.

"No. It's just that my idea of you being perfect started to wreck *my* self-image. That's probably why I wouldn't give more to the relationship. And I'm not talking about just sex."

He held her. "You give enough." He kissed her cheek. "Anyway, this is a relief to me, too. I got sick of trying to be so damn perfect all the time. Now I can relax." He belched.

"Eeuuw, Lucas!" She frowned.

"What? You told me not to be perfect." He laughed.

"I didn't mean be a damn pig in the process." She fanned her hands. "God, smells like a dead dog."

"It does not!" He laughed.

"Don't do that again, I swear." She grinned.

"Can I have a kiss?"

"Not after belching in my face." She pushed him away. "I'm glad we got this cleared up, Lucas."

"Me, too. I wanted to talk to you about something else. It has nothing to do with us."

"Okay. Sounds serious."

"Well…" He unhooked his leg from underneath the other. He sat down flat. "I want you to settle this thing with Keith."

"Excuse me? Why are we all of a sudden talking about Keith?"

"Because he's told me some things and I am concerned about how you two are together. Melody, uh, Caper is my father's company. Everything that happens there reflects him. I wanted to make sure you know that."

"Wait, Lucas, how come I feel like this is a damn lecture?"

"Don't get upset. I'm just saying that I see what's going on. Keith says he's worried you're going to do something to jeopardize his job, and frankly, I'm worried about that, too."

"Lucas, I'd never hurt someone out of spite or anything. Is that what you're implying? Did Keith tell you to talk to me? What the hell did he say, anyway?"

"He asked me to keep it in confidence, Mel. He's my friend, so of course we talk sometimes. Since you're my girlfriend I guess he wanted to come to me. There's no harm done." He rubbed her hair. She pushed him away.

"The hell it's not. I'm leaving." She gathered her shoes.

"What?" He stood. "Melody, it isn't that serious!"

"Oh, believe me, it is. I get this shit from Sarah and now I gotta get it from you, too? I don't need yet another snowed person trying to tell me how great a guy Keith Taylor is, Lucas. I know what he really is!"

"Is that why you went behind my back and reported Keith to my father, Melody?" He squinted. "And you're always harping about trust!"

"That son of a bitch told you?" She sighed. "Did he tell you why I reported him?"

"He thinks to make trouble."

"But what do *you* think?"

"I…I don't know what to think, Melody. I've seen how you are with Keith at work, and I know how much you can't stand him."

"Lucas, I have just cause! I don't believe this! So you think Keith is this great guy and I'm just causing trouble?"

"Melody, Keith is my friend. I've known him for four years."

"But you've known me forever!" She waved her shoes. "So much for trying to make this night perfect, Lucas. I think you're on a roll with being able to fuck up moments like these." He grabbed her. "Let me go!" He backed away. "Lucas, I need you on my side about this. I need you to believe me about Keith."

"Believe what? You haven't said a damn thing except that you don't like him! What has he done to you, Mel? Why can't you just tell me that? I find it suspicious that you can't."

"I don't want to involve you. You won't understand."

He shook her. "Try me, and let me make that decision! Melody, you don't ever come to me with anything! What am I supposed to think when Keith tells me that you're out to get him?"

"You're not supposed to think I'd really do it! I'm your girlfriend, Lucas! I thought you're supposed to be on my side!"

"And look how pissed you always get when Keith's name's mentioned! It's not normal, Melody. You're not being rational about this. Melody, it doesn't look right to me. I think you have a problem and it has nothing to do with Keith."

She shook her head. "Fuck you, Lucas." She went to the door.

"Melody, I brought you! Wait!" He grabbed her. She knocked him to the floor.

"I don't need anyone else pointing out my mistakes, Lucas! And most of all, not my so-called perfect boy-friend." She sighed. "Or ex-boyfriend. Whatever the hell you wanna call it!" She slammed the front door. He opened it.

"Melody, wait! Mel, I wasn't accusing you of anything! Melody!"

She didn't look back.

Steven awoke to someone banging on his front door. He didn't bother putting on a shirt. He rushed down-stairs in his boxers. He opened the door to a solemn-looking Detective Cunningham.

"Hey, man." Steven rubbed his eyes. He ran his hands through his straggly hair. Cunningham didn't seem his usual jolly self.

"Hey, Steve," he muttered.

Steven grinned. "Cunningham, I know this has to be

important. I mean, it's almost midnight. I know something's gotta be up. I mean, you haven't been over here in about two years." Steven chuckled.

"Yeah." Cunningham gestured inside. "Steven, this is serious. I never thought I'd have to do this, but…" Two cars sped into Steven's driveway. He leaned to get a better look. Captain Jersey and a uniformed cop got out of the police vehicle. Steven cringed when he saw who got out of the second, shiny black car.

"Cunningham, what in the hell's going on?" Steven stared at a tall, hard-faced black man with a thick mustache. He walked with the poise of power. He straightened the lapel of his light jacket. He followed a white man who appeared in his early forties. The white man stomped out a cigarette before they reached the porch. "Cunningham, I asked you a question." Steven exhaled. "What the hell is Commissioner Reynolds doing here?" Steven pointed to the regal black man.

"Steven, something terrible has happened. I came because I thought it would comfort you seeing me and…"

"Is it Bree?" Steven grabbed him. "Did something happen to Bree?"

"No, Morris is fine." Cunningham lowered his voice when the others walked up behind him. "Steven, there was another rape. You…uh…"

Captain Jersey looked at the three men behind her. She made her place beside Cunningham. "Detective Kemp, you already know Commissioner Reynolds."

Reynolds kept his eyes ahead as if looking at Steven sickened him.

"Commissioner Reynolds, sir. What's going on here, Captain?"

"I'm Agent Parsons." The white guy held up his badge before Jersey could introduce him. "Internal Affairs."

Jersey shook her head.

"Internal Affairs?" Steven gasped. "What the hell's going on here?"

"Didn't Detective Cunningham fill you in?" Reynolds gestured. "Then let us do the honors. Steven Kemp, you are under arrest."

"Under arrest?" He chuckled. "Is this some kind of joke?" He looked at Jersey. "Captain, what the hell is going on here?"

"Steven, I'm afraid this is no joke. You're being arrested." She sighed.

"Uh..." He gaped. "Mind telling me what in the hell for?" He laughed. "Okay, I've been the butt of many practical jokes, but this takes the cake!"

Reynolds squinted. "Do you see anyone else laughing here, Kemp?"

Parsons popped in a stick of gum. "You're being arrested for the rape of Aileen Andrews."

Steven's shoulders fell. "What did you say?"

"You heard him, Detective." Reynolds squinted. "You're being arrested for the rape of Aileen Andrews." Reynolds looked at Jersey. "Parsons and I will be at the station, Captain Jersey. We expect Kemp to be there in five minutes."

Parsons grinned. "And not a minute *later*." They walked off.

"Captain." Steven turned all the way around. "What in the hell is going on here?"

"Steven, we just need to get you to the station. I'm sure everything will be sorted out there. It's probably a misunderstanding."

"Did this woman say I raped her?" Jersey and Cunningham looked off. "It's not true! I didn't rape anyone!" He grabbed Jersey. "Captain, you gotta believe me!"

"I…I believe you, Steven. We just have to deal with this now. I have no choice but to put you under arrest. I'm sure this will be straightened out tonight. Cunningham can bring you down. Just get some clothes on and be there as fast as possible." She walked off with the uniformed cop.

"Jesus. Cunningham, I don't know what's going on. Please help me understand this, man. I didn't rape anyone."

"It'll be all right, Steve." Cunningham patted his shoulder. "I'll wait for you in the car."

Steven looked at the party in the interrogation room. He couldn't believe this. He thought of all the suspects he'd questioned in here. He hadn't dreamed he'd ever be on this side of the table. Reynolds looked like he wanted to string him alive. Parsons held a grin that Steven couldn't figure the reason for yet. Captain Jersey looked like someone killed her puppy.

Steven couldn't see himself to notice how he must have looked. He could only guess that he looked shocked. Maybe later he'd be scared, too. Right now, he couldn't even think past the time in this room. He'd do the best he could. He was innocent. He knew that. He'd only have to make them believe it. At least Captain Jersey seemed on his side. For now.

Parsons lit his third cigarette. Steven couldn't believe he'd already been in the room an hour. Reynolds and Parsons spent most of the hour conversing in the hall. Steven couldn't have guessed what they talked about. He just knew it wasn't good for him. Parsons did most of the questioning. Steven disliked the man already. He held a chip on his shoulder for cops. Most of these Internal Affairs folks did. Steven wouldn't let the man get to him. He didn't care what questions he had to answer. He wouldn't give in.

"Okay, uh, let's go over this again, Detective Kemp." Parsons flicked his cigarette in midair. "You said that you were at home between the time of five-thirty and eight tonight?"

He sighed. "Yes, I was."

"Can anyone vouch for that? I mean, anyone who can be a witness to your alibi?"

"It's not an alibi, Agent Parsons. It's the truth, okay?

I was at home all day. I didn't have to work. I was glad to finally get a day off. Especially a Saturday. Believe me, I enjoyed it."

"Mmm." Parsons smirked. "So you don't know if anyone saw you at home? Like your neighbors or anything?"

He shrugged. "I'm sure they saw my car. Other than that, I don't know. I mean, you don't know if someone's watching you or not. I don't know where you live, but in my neighborhood we don't have a ritual of watching each other. People can come and go as they please."

Parsons didn't seem to appreciate the sarcasm. Steven heavily enjoyed knocking the agent on his ass. Parsons scribbled on a piece of yellow notebook paper.

"Well, this doesn't look too good. Saying you were at home all day seems flimsy at best. Let's just get to the point, shall we?" Parsons straightened his tie. "Did you rape Aileen Andrews?"

Steven tapped the table. "No," he exhaled.

"Well, she says you did."

"I don't care what she says. I didn't rape Aileen Andrews. I didn't even know she'd been raped until you came to my house and rounded me up like the Calvary." Parsons grinned. "I didn't rape anyone." Steven looked at Reynolds. "Commissioner, you got to believe me, sir."

"This is a very personal case for me, Kemp." Reynolds glared at him. "You see, I have two beautiful teenage daughters at home. Lately, my wife and I have been scared to even send them to school because of this man.

They can't live a normal life because I'm afraid some nut is gonna grab them off the street and rape them. You probably can't understand this, but to me it's a hate crime, plain and simple."

Reynolds rubbed his face. "He's targeting women of my community and it burns the hell out of me. Everywhere I go I'm blamed because I'm black, and people think I should be doing all I can to get him. Well, I am. Yet, I got organizations on my back. I got black leaders on my back, and what do I have to give them…nothing. Not even peace of mind."

Steven shook his head. "Commissioner Reynolds, I'm sure no one blames you personally, sir."

"They're my people so they definitely blame me for not protecting these women. I blame myself! So when I got the call about Aileen Andrews today, I went nuts that she'd accused an officer of doing these things. Do you realize how furious and sickened I am to see that one of my officers has been accused of this crime? I'm sorry if I don't seem to be giving you the benefit of the doubt right now, Kemp. But I have a frightened young woman who was brutally raped by a man claiming to be you."

"Commissioner, I…"

"He raped her with her daughter standing in the hallway! This is the same man who has committed sodomy, beaten and raped over twenty-five women, total! These women will live with this for the rest of their lives! In their eyes, they can't even begin to accept this! I've been praying that some sign would fly from the sky so we could get this motherfucker!" Reynolds sighed. "So imagine how disgusted I felt to find out that one of my officers is the prime suspect."

"I did not rape Aileen Andrews!"

"Well, she says you did!" Reynolds pounded the table. "She says you did, and that's all we need to know! She described your ass down to the wire, Kemp! She even said your name! Why in the hell would she say these things if you didn't rape her?"

"I don't know!" Steven held his head. "I can't understand any of this! All I know is that I didn't rape Aileen Andrews, Cheyenne Wilson or any of the other women! I swear! I've devoted my life to helping people! I've put more rapists behind bars than most of the officers in this damn precinct. Why would I turn into something that I hate?"

Parsons flicked his cigarette. "What would you do if you were in our shoes, Kemp? Would you find it odd that Aileen named a cop the rapist, and then it all seemed to turn out that he may be?"

"Put myself in your shoes? How about you guys putting yourselves in *my* fuckin' shoes, huh? Shit, I thought cops were supposed to be on each other's side!" Steven looked at Captain Jersey. "You guys have already convicted my ass! I might as well have been electrocuted the minute I walked in here. It isn't fair. How can you not believe me? I have never hurt anyone. I'd never do such a terrible thing. Do you really think I could?"

"I believe you, Kemp," Jersey said. The others looked at her. "I know you'd never hurt anyone." She looked at Parsons. "None of my officers would."

"Detective Kemp, can you give us one reason why Aileen Andrews would name you as the rapist then?" Parsons shrugged. "Because we're stumped."

"I don't know, but I want to speak to Mrs. Andrews."

"You're not going anywhere near her," Reynolds warned. "She's been through enough. The last thing she needs is to look at your face. She's at the hospital and she needs to focus on getting herself together the best she can."

"Commissioner Reynolds, I didn't rape her! You gotta believe me."

"Kemp, all I have to do is put the rapist behind bars. And right now that looks like it's going to be you."

"I didn't rape her! You can't arrest me!"

"You've been named by Aileen Andrews as the man who raped her tonight. We can do more than that if we want!" Reynolds bellowed. "You obviously don't realize the shit you're in, Kemp. It doesn't matter what we think. What matters is what Aileen Andrews has said. She says you're the man who raped her. Can you explain why?"

"No." Steven lowered his head.

"Captain Jersey, I want Kemp held tonight," Reynolds ordered.

"Commissioner!" Steven shouted.

"And that's an order!" Reynolds shouted. "I want his

ass in a cell tonight! Do you understand me, Captain Jersey?"

"Yes, sir." She looked at Steven. "We'll deal with the rest of this tomorrow." Reynolds opened the door.

"Commissioner Reynolds, this is a mistake." Jersey sighed. "Steven wouldn't rape anyone."

"We'll see." He left.

"I don't believe this." Steven wiped his forehead. "What in the hell am I gonna do, Captain?"

Parsons winked. "I'd start by getting myself a lawyer, Kemp. And I'd make sure he was damn good." He left.

"I can't believe this is happening to me. Captain, this man, this rapist is playing with my life. He's trying to make it look like I did these things!"

"Why, Steven?" she whispered.

"I don't know! You think if I knew I'd be getting arrested? Captain, we gotta find this man. If not my whole future could be at stake. I didn't rape those women. You gotta believe me."

"I believe you, Steven. It's just that right now I can't do a damn thing about it."

Chapter Twelve

Sarah and Melody rushed through the halls of the hospital the next morning. Aileen had become the Albany Predator's latest victim. Melody was completely devastated. Just when she thought Aileen would be safe her worst nightmare came true. She loved Aileen like a sister. She couldn't imagine the pain she felt. If Melody could take on Aileen's worries she would in a heartbeat.

Sarah tried her best to console her sister. Melody couldn't put her thoughts into words. She couldn't get Aileen out of her head. How scared she must be. How badly had she been attacked? Had he beaten her like the others? Had he hurt Danielle? Would Aileen ever recover? She couldn't get the overwhelming thoughts out of her head. Sarah kept saying when Melody could see Aileen she'd feel better.

Melody wasn't so sure. What if Aileen's state confirmed Melody's frightening assumptions? Could she handle it? She'd have to be strong for Aileen. But who would be strong for Melody? Tons of reporters from the local news stations surrounded the side entrances of the hospital. The Albany Predator had become one of the most talked about criminals.

It had been easier to deal with when the locals had only known his terror. Now everyone knew. Melody realized how big it was when she caught a story on CNN the week before. The biggest networks started clamoring to bring attention to what people called one of the most vicious rapists to ever hit the streets. He hadn't just scared an entire city, but scarred it for life.

It no longer mattered when he'd be caught. His reign of terror would forever change the citizens of Albany, New York. Melody would never look at her hometown with the same amount of pride and admiration again. She saw it as a place of contempt, pain and violence. She could have accepted things before Aileen's attack. The rapist had hit too close to home this time.

They made it to Aileen's floor. A police officer stopped them at Aileen's door. He informed them that the police were questioning her. Melody did her best to calm her anger. It wasn't easy. She kept seeing a frightened, shaking Aileen being grilled by some overbearing, male police officer who didn't know the first thing about being raped.

The door opened. Melody and Sarah overlooked the striking black woman who walked out. She slipped a tiny notepad into her tweed jacket. Melody didn't have to guess. She knew this had been the detective the Albany Predator had attacked.

"Hello." Brianna smiled at the two young ladies. "I'm Detective Brianna Morris. I'm the investigating officer on the Albany Predator case."

"Uh, hello." Sarah gestured to Melody. "I'm Sarah Johnson, and this is my sister, Melody Cruz. We're friends of Aileen Andrews."

"Sisters?" Brianna stared. Melody and Sarah were so used to that reaction they no longer paid it much attention. "You must be very worried. I was just questioning her. She's been through a lot."

"How is she?" Melody asked.

Brianna sighed. "She's very upset and sad. I don't know if she wants to see anyone right now. She wouldn't even look at *me*."

"Yet you felt it important to grill her when she hasn't even had time to understand what's happened to her?" Melody squinted.

"Mel, please." Sarah sighed. "I'm sorry, Detective."

"You don't have to apologize, Ms. Johnson. You both have every right to be angry and sad. I am, too. It never gets easier, no matter how many rape victims I talk to. I, uh, have to get back to the station."

Melody blocked her. "Any leads?"

Brianna sighed. Melody felt she knew something. She figured Brianna wouldn't share it. Melody had watched enough police shows that she knew their methods by heart.

"We are, uh…following up on some leads."

"Are you just saying that to make us feel better?" Melody crossed her arms. "If you know something about Aileen, then we deserve to know."

"Ms. Cruz, I admire how much you care about your friend. But this is police business. We're doing all we can. I hope you ladies have a nice day."

"So is it true that this guy could be a cop?" Melody squinted. "Are you still doing the best you can knowing that?"

Brianna sighed. "Whether he's a cop or not makes no difference to me."

"I bet, since you were attacked by the predator yourself, huh?"

Brianna stood in front of her. "Who told you this, Ms. Cruz?"

"It doesn't matter. What matters is helping Aileen and the women he's raped. Since you've been in their shoes, I hope you'll do everything you can."

"Melody, you're offending her." Sarah sighed. "Detective, I apologize. We know you're doing all you can."

"I am." Brianna kept her gaze on Melody. "I promise you, I'll do what I can to help your friend and the other women."

"Even if it means arresting a cop?" Melody raised an eyebrow.

"Ms. Cruz, you seem to have a dirty perception of police officers. We're not all corrupt, you know? Some of us really care. I'm one of those people."

"I hope so." Melody walled her eyes.

"Just be warned if you don't recognize your friend right now. She's been through something you can't imagine."

"Thanks, Detective Morris." Sarah smiled. Brianna left. "Melody, what was that about?"

"What?" She turned from Aileen's door.

"She was attacked by this guy, too?" Sarah pointed in the direction Brianna walked off in. "How did you know?"

"Lucas's father has a friend on the force, and he told him." Sarah gasped. "And from what Lucas says, it may not be the only thing the police are hiding."

Sarah squinted. "You think this guy really is a cop or just using that to get his victims?"

Melody bit her lips. "I don't know. But I definitely feel like the cops are hiding something huge from the public about this case."

"Even her?" Sarah pointed down the hall.

Melody nodded. "*Especially* her." She went into Aileen's room.

"I don't understand how it happened, Arlen." Steven glared at his attorney. Arlen Sumpter rubbed his bald head while contemplating Steven's words. "All I know is that everything is pointing to me." He glanced around the interrogation room. "I've been up all night trying to figure out why, but I can't. The rapist has to be targeting me specifically. He must know we look alike and that's giving him all he needs to do his thing. Hell, whatever that is." He sighed.

Arlen tapped the shiny table. "Steven, I'm trying to understand but I can't. It makes no sense. Why would he pretend to be you?"

"Arlen, if I knew that, I wouldn't be here! Look, Commissioner Reynolds won't give me the benefit of the doubt for a second. And Agent Parsons is the biggest asshole on the planet. He has it in for cops or something. He already has me tried and convicted."

"Yeah, Agent Parsons didn't exactly strike my fancy, either." Arlen reflected on meeting the agent earlier that morning.

"Arlen, you're my lawyer aren't you?"

He sighed. "Steven, I want to be."

"What do you mean, 'want to be'? Arlen, you're one of the best attorneys around. If anyone can get me off, it would be you."

"So you assume you'll have to stand trial?"

Steven rubbed his face. "I'm just thinking realistically. The bottom line is, I didn't rape anyone. I just can't prove it."

"Well, they don't have any physical evidence but Aileen's claim is damaging. It is still your word against hers. You're a pillar of the community. You have excellent standing in the department. You've arrested hundreds of sexual predators and been up for some prestigious awards. You got some good points, Steven."

"I feel a 'but' coming on."

"Well, Aileen Andrews seems to be a decent person herself. She's a housewife with a young daughter and hard-working husband. They're an educated, young couple trying to make it. The only problem is that she's the victim in all this. That automatically means trouble for you. People are gonna see this frightened woman and picture how her two year-old stood in the hallway, listening to her mother being raped for about two hours." Steven shook his head. "If we go to trial, that's what the jury will see in their minds. It's my job to put that picture out of their heads."

"I don't want to even think of going to trial right now." Steven sighed.

"Well, you ought to. Steven, I've known you for years. I believe in you. No one in the department has ever uttered anything bad about you. You're a hard-working detective who's making waves. I don't think people can easily just call you a rapist and call it a day."

"Commissioner Reynolds and Agent Parsons seem to be doing that easily enough. It's not easy defending myself when Reynolds keeps looking at me like I'm a member of the Ku Klux Klan." Steven sighed. "And Parsons acts like I fucked his wife in another life or something."

"Yeah well, Agent Parsons doesn't know you. Don't take him personally. Commissioner Reynolds is a good person, but you gotta see where he's coming from. He's getting the bulk of blame for this guy terrorizing the city. The mayor wants answers and he expects Reynolds to give them to him. That's not good for you because Reynolds is desperate for a suspect, so he won't let up for a minute."

Arlen shrugged. "The facts have to speak for themselves, Steven. They have no physical evidence against you. They have twenty-five victims, half who refuse to talk. Out of the ones who will talk, the rapist was masked throughout the attack. Cheyenne Wilson and Aileen Andrews are the only ones who saw a face."

"Mine." Steven scoffed.

"So far it looks good to me, Steven. I don't think Aileen has a case against you. And the part where she says he said his name was 'Kemp.' That's flimsy at best. You can easily get around that, Steven."

He sighed. "Arlen, I want to prove I'm innocent but I don't want the rapist to go free. I don't want these women dragged through the mud. They've been through enough. Besides, I'm still supposed to be the cop on the case."

"I understand."

"I can find this motherfucker but I need to be outta here to do it. Can you get me out?"

Agent Parsons and Captain Jersey walked in before Arlen could answer.

"I want my client released. You have no reason to hold him." Arlen stood.

"Only the claim that he raped Aileen Andrews last

night." Parsons glared at Steven. "Since when is the victim's word not enough to hold a rapist?"

"I am not a rapist," Steven growled.

"Aileen says you are. She's gonna come into the station later to go over her statement. We want Steven to do a lineup. If the man is just a mere lookalike, then she should be able to tell."

"A lineup is not a good idea at this point, Agent Parsons," Arlen insisted. "Mrs. Andrews is distraught. Anyone who looks like the rapist is a target for being accused. I want Steven released. Aileen hasn't brought official charges against him yet."

Parsons shrugged. "Commissioner Reynolds has granted me precedence over this case. He told me to act as I see fit."

"You cannot hold him like this." Arlen glared. "Aileen hasn't pressed formal charges. You had no business holding him last night, either!"

"We'll get Aileen Andrews down here immediately then. Detective Kemp, if you're so innocent, then you won't object to waiting to do a lineup. If Aileen doesn't press formal charges against you, then you'll be free."

"She won't because I'm not the rapist. I am confident she'll be able to tell the difference when she sees me."

Brianna walked in. "Steven?" The others gaped at her. He smiled. "Pull up a chair, Bree. This is one show you won't wanna miss."

"I'm glad you find it so entertaining, Detective." Parsons

grinned. "Let's see if you can continue to amuse yourself in the process."

"Morris, did you speak to Aileen Andrews?" Jersey glared.

"Yes. I wanted to tell Steven what she said."

"Why don't you tell us all?" Parsons grinned.

"Hold your horses, Parsons." Arlen grinned. "You can't step into their investigation. It's official police business. They don't have to discuss what she said in front of you. You want to get something on Steven, find it yourself."

He chuckled. "Now I remember why I hate lawyers." Arlen grinned. Parsons smiled at Brianna. "I don't think we've been introduced."

"Detective Brianna Morris. I'm Steven's partner." She shook Parsons's hand.

"I see. Well, have your little meeting. I'll be back later." He left with a cloud of smoke behind him.

"Who was that?" Brianna pointed.

"The biggest asshole on the planet," Jersey muttered. They grinned.

"Agent Parsons with Internal Affairs. He's handling the investigation. And he can't stand me, but since I hate him too it's understandable." Steven chuckled.

Brianna sat at the table. "How are you doing, Steven? I can't believe this. You didn't rape anyone. How can they even think this?"

"I've been wondering the same thing. Anyway, I feel a lot better now that you're here."

"What did Mrs. Andrews say?" Arlen asked.

"Bree, this is Arlen Sumpter, my attorney." Steven gestured.

"Hello." Brianna took his hand.

"Nice to meet you, Detective." Arlen smiled. "Did Aileen Andrews say anything that could help Steven?"

"Well, she said the same thing but she seems to be a little shaky. She still says he said his name was 'Kemp.'" Brianna shrugged. "Other than that she told me about the rape and that was it."

"Once I do the lineup today, then this should be over with. Even if the guy looks a little like me, Aileen should know the difference. He can't look that much like me, right?" Steven chuckled.

"No." Brianna smiled. "Anyway, we all know how silly this is." She grinned. "There's no way anyone would believe you're a rapist."

"I hope so." Steven took her hand.

Aileen hung up the phone in her den. Sarah and Melody had accompanied her home that evening to help with anything she needed. Melody knew it would take time for Aileen to come to terms with the rape. Yet she hated seeing her friend like this even for a day. She tried to put herself in Aileen's shoes. When that became impossible, she vowed to just be there for her.

"You all right?" Melody rubbed Aileen's shoulders. They stared at the phone.

"They want me to come to the station and to do a lineup later. Uh, they want to see if I can identify Steven Kemp as the rapist. Melody, I don't know if I can." She shook.

"Leen, it's hard I know, but you gotta do it. If this man is the rapist, you have to do your part."

"Oh, easy for you to say. What in the hell do you know about it?" Aileen shook her head. Melody ran her fingers through her hair. "I'm so sorry, Melody. I didn't mean that." She cried. Melody rocked her. "I can't even think about what happened to me for dealing with all this other shit right now. I mean, the cops and not to mention that exam. It was humiliating, Melody. I felt like I was being raped all over again."

"Shh, it's okay. Just take it one step at a time. I'll be here for you as long as you need me to be."

Sarah walked in with a tray of sandwiches and chips. Melody appreciated Sarah's concern.

"Is everything okay?" Sarah overlooked the touching scene.

"They want Aileen to do a lineup at the station later on."

"Oh well," Sarah sighed. "Uh, are you okay with that, Aileen?"

She sniffed. "No, but I guess I have no choice. All I can think about is how scared I was. How scared I still am. I can't let another woman go through this. And if this officer is the rapist, he needs to be put away. Look at all the pain he's caused all of us. If he goes free, he may never stop." She wiped her eyes. "I just gotta be strong, right?"

"And we'll be there to help you." Melody hugged her.

"We will?" Sarah gaped. Melody looked at her. "Oh sure, we will. We'll come with you, Aileen."

"Yeah." Melody smiled.

"I don't know how to thank you guys. Your support is… well, it's all I could hope for right now. I love you both."

Sarah smiled. "We love you, too."

"They'll get him, Leen." Melody pushed Aileen's curly hair behind her ears. "This is just something that has to be done."

Steven followed the officer from his cell. He met up with Brianna and Captain Jersey on the way to the lineup area. In less than twenty minutes, Aileen would forever clear his name. He wasn't upset. He wasn't anxious. He was very, very confident.

"Ladies." He smugly followed them down the hall. Jersey and Brianna grinned at each other.

"Well, you're the first person I've seen who looked forward to a lineup, Kemp."

"Oh, I got no worries, Captain." He cracked his knuckles. "I'm not the rapist and soon Mrs. Andrews will prove it. I just can't wait to see the look on Agent Parsons's ugly-ass face."

Brianna grinned. "Let's not get too cocky, okay? We want you to be cleared, Steven. But we should all remember Aileen is the true victim in this. We want to help her." They walked down a long hallway.

"Bree, there's nothing I want more than to find this man. That's why I got to hurry up and prove I didn't do it. How can I help them if I'm stuck in here? The entire thing was just ridiculous, anyway. I can't believe it even got to this point."

"But why did the rapist say he was you?" Jersey glanced at him. "That's what I want to know."

"I told you he's using me to benefit him. Like he knew that shit about me and Bree being together. Obviously, he's keeping tabs on the whole damn precinct." Brianna nodded. "Who knows what else he's doing. Shit, he could be a cop and we don't know it. He just looks like me."

Brianna sighed. "Hopefully, he doesn't look so much like you that Aileen can't tell the difference."

They reached the lineup area. Six cops who resembled Steven sat on a little bench by the door.

"Don't worry, Bree." Steven winked. "I got this."

She hoped so.

Sarah, Aileen and Melody made their way through the police station. Melody admired Aileen for doing this. Just *being* in a police station scared the hell out of

Melody. They came to the room where the lineup would be held. A uniformed cop escorted them into the room. They noticed a small group of people. The group turned around when Aileen approached. A somewhat handsome man extended his hand.

"Mrs. Andrews? I'm Agent Parsons with Internal Affairs. I'm handling the investigation." She nodded. "I just want to say that I'm very sorry for what has happened to you. I'm gonna do my part in making sure the man who raped you is brought to justice." She quietly nodded.

"Aileen, I'm District Attorney Zachary." A tall, attractive brunette held out her hand. "It's wonderful to meet you, Aileen." Melody recognized the elegant lady from many newspaper articles. "I look forward to doing my part to help you. I hope I can make this easier for you to deal with. That depends on what happens here tonight."

"You mean, this could lead to the actual trial?" Aileen held Melody's hand.

Zachary nodded. "If you identify Detective Kemp as the rapist, then we'll definitely start the proceedings. Does that make you uncomfortable, Mrs. Andrews? We want to make this as easy for you as we can."

"I appreciate that." She shook. "These are my friends, Melody and her sister, Sarah." Parsons and Zachary tilted their heads in respect. "I just want this over with." Aileen looked at the glass. "Will I have to be in the same room with him, at all?"

"Oh no, no, no." Parsons smiled. "Absolutely not. He'll stay behind that glass, and he can't even see you. No need in worrying. We'll be right here with you the entire time."

"We want you to take your time and try to be as accurate as possible, okay?" Zachary smiled.

"I'll do my best. It's just not easy, you know?" Aileen tugged at her clothes. "Just, well, none of this is easy." She looked at Melody.

"We think you're very brave, Aileen. And we'll be with you every step of the way. We're not going to let anyone get away with what he's done to you ladies. Whether he's a cop or not." Parsons assured.

"Hello." An older plain-Jane looking lady with red glasses walked up. Brianna Morris followed with a tall, bald gentleman. "I'm Captain Jersey, Mrs. Andrews. How are you?" Jersey took Aileen's hand.

"Honestly, I've been better."

"I quite understand, and my precinct will do all we can to help."

Melody squinted. "Really?"

"Yes." Jersey smiled. Melody didn't bother introducing herself. She held a special contempt for anyone in this precinct already. "You remember Detective Morris. This is Arlen Sumpter, Detective Kemp's attorney."

"Hello, Mrs. Andrews. Are you feeling okay?" He smiled.

"Yeah." She walled her eyes.

"Well, uh, I think we're ready." Parsons waved to a cop. The cop went to gather the men for the lineup. Aileen, Melody and Sarah sat at the table. The others stood behind them.

"So what happens if Aileen identifies Kemp?" Melody asked.

"Well, then Steven Kemp will be held in jail. But he'll have a bond hearing probably tomorrow."

"So he can get bail even if you arrest him." Aileen rubbed her forehead. "So he can be the rapist and just walk free until God knows how long?"

"Aileen, I'm going to ask that Kemp be denied bail at the hearing if you identify him," Zachary promised.

Brianna and Jersey exchanged glances. Neither liked that idea but at this point felt it important to keep quiet.

"Aileen, are you ready?" Parsons asked.

"As ready as I'll ever be. I just want to get this over with so I can go home. I haven't been able to rest at all today."

"We understand, and we won't take up much of your time. We just want to do what's comfortable for you." Parsons smiled. "Please take your time." He spoke into a small microphone in front of the glass. "Bring the men out, please."

"Mel, I'm so nervous." Aileen nearly ripped the skin off Melody's hand.

"You're doing the right thing, Leen."

"Yeah." Sarah smiled. "You really have no choice. If

this cop is the rapist, no one can afford to have him walking around free. You wouldn't want that on your conscience, would you?"

"No." Aileen shut her eyes.

"Then just know you're doing the right thing." Melody held her.

The men walked out behind the glass. Aileen kept her eyes shut. She waited until Parsons instructed the men to look straight ahead. She turned to see Brianna, Jersey, Arlen, Parsons and Zachary gazing as if she held their life in her hands.

"Aileen?" Parsons gestured to the men. "Do any of these men look like the man that raped you last night?"

"I…" She couldn't bear to open her eyes.

"Take your time." Zachary smiled. The D.A. looked at Steven Kemp, who was number four in the line. Brianna and Jersey exhaled. They wished Steven didn't look so cocky at the moment.

Parsons pointed to the first two men. Aileen looked at them carefully. They were dismissed. Parsons pointed to the third man. She leaned forward. He had a similar rugged look and build, yet his eyes weren't nearly as intoxicating as the rapist's had been. She couldn't forget that shade of blue, no matter how much she wanted to. She shook her head at the third man.

"Aileen, what about number four?" Parsons stared at her. "Does he look like the man that raped you?" She looked up. She felt as if an imaginary hand pulled her from the chair.

She stood. She stared at the cunning face of Steven Kemp. Those blue eyes that already haunted every fiber of her being. That soft, blond hair that immediately took her back to being in bed with him. Those hands that had stripped her against her will. Those strong, hard legs that held her down while she screamed for help. Those lips that had drained her dry with one kiss.

Those eyes that she'd never forget in a million years. They made her afraid to go home and they made her afraid to *leave* home. Those eyes that would forever be engraved in her mind.

"Aileen?" Melody found it impossible to hold the shaking woman. Steven Kemp stared ahead. They claimed he couldn't see her. Aileen wasn't so sure.

"Oh God." She wept into her palms. She viciously shook her head. "It's him." Brianna and Jersey moved closer. "It's him. Oh God, it's him. I'm sure of it."

"Are you sure?" Brianna gaped.

"Shut up, Morris." Parsons rolled his eyes. "Don't you dare try to influence this."

"I wasn't doing that. I wanted to make sure she was definite."

"I think her jumping out of the chair and shaking like a leaf seems pretty definite to me." Zachary rubbed Aileen's shoulders. "The man you identified is Steven Kemp. Are you saying in front of all of us that he is the man who raped you?"

"Yes!" Aileen backed away. "When I looked up, something came over me. It was a fear I couldn't explain! Just like last night! There's no mistake. He raped me! I want him in jail! I want him in jail!" She cried into Melody's arms. "It's the eyes." Aileen shivered. "The most evil eyes in the world. I don't want to see him! Get him away from me, please!"

Parsons ordered the men to be escorted from the room.

"So she did it." Melody looked at them. "She identified the man who raped her. What happens next?"

"He'll be held on the charges," Parsons stated. "And we're gonna make sure he pays for what he's done."

"Aileen?" Brianna stood in front of her. "There must be some mistake. I have known Steven for years. He has dedicated his life to helping rape victims. He couldn't hurt anyone. I'd trust him with my life. You have to be wrong."

"I'm not." Aileen shook. "He raped me, and if you weren't so blind by how you obviously feel about him, then you'd see it too, Detective Morris. I was the one he attacked and not you! How could you tell me it's not him? I know it!"

"There has to be some kind of mistake." Jersey shook her head. "Mrs. Andrews, Steven Kemp is not a rapist."

Melody shook her head. "If she says he raped her then he raped her! The question now is how much time will the bastard get. I can't believe this. The main person who was put on this case to help the victims is the same man that's assaulting them? What kind of police force is this?"

"You're wrong." Brianna sighed. "Steven Kemp is not a rapist! Aileen, we want to help you, but you're not thinking clearly."

"How *dare* you? How in the hell do you know how I'm thinking? Steven Kemp is the man who came into my house and raped me with my daughter in the hallway! I'm gonna make sure he goes to prison and stays there! You're supposed to be protecting us, Detective Morris! Not him!"

"So it's true?" Cheyenne Wilson whispered from the doorway. Everyone stared at her. She walked up where they could see her in the aura of the lights. "It's true, isn't it? Detective Kemp is the rapist after all?"

"Cheyenne, what are you doing here?" Brianna whispered.

"Funny I came to talk to you, Detective Morris. I was waiting outside until I heard someone yelling." She looked at Aileen. "I assume you were raped by the Albany Predator, too?"

"Yes." Aileen nodded. "Or in other words, by Steven Kemp. May I go now? I've had enough of this for one night."

"Yes, and please try to get some rest, Mrs. Andrews. I'll show you and your friends out." Parsons led Melody, Sarah and Aileen out of the room. Arlen rushed out behind them.

Cheyenne glared at Brianna and Jersey. "I thought you were on our sides, but I see you're not, Detective."

"Cheyenne, I don't know what you think you heard, but I am on your side. I'm just trying to find out the truth, that's all."

"Right. Why do you go to such extremes to defend this man? I heard what she said out there. She identified Steven as the rapist. And you stood here and defended him. How could you do that? You're supposed to protect the victims and not the criminals!"

"Cheyenne, we have to be sure! A cop's life is at stake here."

She chuckled. "A cop's life? What about our lives, huh? How do you know he didn't rape us? How do you know? Tell me how you can be so sure? Were you there? You don't give a damn about us."

"Cheyenne, that's not true. I'm doing all I can for everyone! Please see that I am. I want to help you!"

She scoffed. "I can't see that at all. As a woman you should be ashamed of yourself."

Brianna sighed. "Please, you've got the wrong picture of me, Cheyenne."

"All I see is someone determined to defend that man no matter what we all say. Maybe you'd think different if you were standing on this side of the fence, Detective. I hope you never have to go through something like this. I wouldn't wish this on my worst enemy. Not even on you."

"Cheyenne, please understand where I'm coming from," Brianna pleaded. "I *am* on your side, but I know Steven and he's not a rapist! Please believe that."

Cheyenne shook her head. "All I believe is that you will do anything to protect that man, Detective Morris." Cheyenne turned to Jersey. "I'm gonna do my part to make sure Steven Kemp gets what he deserves. You can count on that." She stomped away.

Jersey touched Brianna's shoulder. "Morris, are you all right? She didn't mean what she said. It's a difficult time for her right now." Brianna sobbed. "Morris?"

Brianna left the room.

"I didn't do it!" Steven slapped the wall of his cell.

"She's identified you, Steven!" Arlen paced. "What in the hell is going on? Do you realize the shit you're in?"

"Oh Jesus." Steven rubbed his forehead. He sat on the little bed. "Arlen, how could this be happening to me? I was just going along and now I'm accused of rape? I could lose my badge and be kicked off the force." He held his head low.

Arlen held his waist. "Steven, losing your badge is the last damn thing you need to be worried about now. You could to go prison!" Arlen leaned against the wall. "Steven, I want to believe you, but..."

"*Want*? So you think I'm capable of rape?"

"All I know is that Aileen Andrews identified you as easy as the white on snow! And she didn't just point you out, Steven. She nearly had a heart attack because she was so frightened. You can mistake someone's judgment but you can't question fear. Steven, you gotta be honest with me here. That's the only way I can put together a decent case."

"It's really going to trial?" Steven exhaled. "Arlen, we gotta stop it from going to trial!"

"What do you think this is, some fairy tale? You were just accused of being a serial rapist! Of course you're going to trial, unless you can prove that you're innocent! And you wait until they bring the other victims in here. Steven, you gotta give me something to work with!"

"I didn't rape anyone, Arlen! That's all I can say!" Arlen sighed. "I'm innocent. You have to believe that."

"Steven, it's not what I believe; it's what everyone else believes. This isn't looking good at all. I thought for sure that the lineup would go our way but it was a disaster! There has to be something you're not telling me!"

"I…did…not…rape…anyone! If you can't believe that, then don't defend me!" Steven leaned against the wall.

"I do believe you, Steven. That's why this is so scary. I can't bear the thought of an innocent man going to prison. I mean, I represent plenty of guilty clients, but I work my ass off extra hard when I believe the person is innocent."

"Arlen, I just need to get outta here, man. I need you to get me a bail hearing for tomorrow. Can you?"

He shrugged. "I'll try my best. But the DA's going for no bail, Steven. That means, if I don't convince the judge that you're safe enough to put on the streets, then you'll have to figure out what the hell you're gonna do from inside this cell."

Captain Jersey walked up.

"Captain." Steven sighed. "I'm glad you came. What's going on?"

"I uh, just got off the phone with Commissioner Reynolds. Steven, I have to put you on suspension."

"No! I have to be on this case in order to clear my name!"

"Steven, you were just charged with rape. There is no way around this." Jersey clasped her hands.

"Do you believe that I'm innocent, Captain Jersey?" He stared at her.

She smiled. "Of course I do. There isn't a doubt in my mind, Steven. You would never hurt anyone. I'm going to do everything in my power to help you prove it."

Chapter Thirteen

That night Melody dropped Sarah off at a friend's, then headed home. She couldn't ignore how beautiful the night had been. Even Aileen's ordeal hadn't dirtied the fantastic moonlight. Melody rarely had time to appreciate nature's beauty. She'd always loved looking out her bedroom at the moon and stars. Nighttime had always been her favorite.

While others slept through it, she always received pleasure from lying in her bed and listening to the still of night flowing through the house. She noticed Lucas's car before she moved from her jeep. She had forgotten their argument while dealing with Aileen. He would always be the most handsome man she knew. She could imagine thirty years passing, yet Lucas would still probably be the only man she really loved. They shared more than most couples did during a lifetime.

They'd been kids together. They'd shared more than people of the opposite sex ever could. Lucas had been one of her dearest friends. No matter what happened in their romantic lives, nothing would ever change that. He would forever have a special place in her heart. She walked to the porch. He sat on the little bench with his head low. He seemed as tired as she felt.

He immediately looked up when she approached. It seemed so automatic how she got his attention sometimes. He claimed he lived just to be near her. Just to please her. Melody didn't have to question the sentiment tonight. Him being there proved how much he cared.

"Hey." He waved. She couldn't ignore how fascinating he looked under the glare of the porch light. She twirled her keys.

"Uh, what are you doing here?" She didn't know why she asked. She didn't give a damn *why* he'd come. She silently thanked God that he had.

He nodded. "I know I'm the last person you want to see." Melody opened the front door. Lucas kept his eyes on the flow of her denim skirt. Lucas had a way of looking at her that couldn't compare to flattery from words. "I've been waiting for a while. I think it was still light when I came." He chuckled. "I called your cell phone."

"Yeah, I didn't have it on. I've been busy, you know?" She rested against the door as she swatted a gnat from her face. "You didn't say why you were here."

He stood. "I'm just here to apologize. I also rushed over when I heard about Aileen. Craig called me. He said you told him." Melody nodded. "He wanted to go see her, but didn't know how she'd react."

"Yeah, it's best that he waits. She just needs some time."

"I can't believe it, you know?" He stuffed his hands in

his pockets. "Aileen's like family to me. You all are. We grew up together. I mean, you know someone for years, and you never dream that something so terrible could happen like this. I wanted so much to go see her. But how could I? What would I say after not being around all this time?" He sighed. "Anyway, it's ridiculous that I lost touch with you all. You guys were a part of me, Melody. You all mean so much to me. It's like something's been missing since school."

"No one blames you, Lucas. Like you said, people drift apart."

He stepped up to her. "But not from family. It's no excuse, Melody. I should have always been there. I'll never forgive myself for that."

"Yeah, but why are you bringing this up now? I mean, tonight?" She gestured for him to come inside. He did. She offered him some refreshments. He refused. They sat on the couch. "Luke, talk to me."

"I guess Aileen's rape made me realize that I was taking things for granted. I took *you* for granted. You've always managed to be there for me, even in spirit. And I can't be a more supportive boyfriend?" He shook his head. "After you left my place last night, I was so confused. It didn't make sense for us to fight, and about Keith." She turned away. He took her hand. "Melody, I don't ever want you to feel you can't come to me. You can come to me with anything, baby. Anything."

"I need you to be my boyfriend, Lucas. I don't need

you tearing into me and lecturing me. I get that shit enough. I need to know you're on my side, because right now, I feel like no one is."

"That's not true, Mel. We're all on your side. That's why we want to make sure everything is okay."

"Sometimes you look at me like you expect me to fall apart, and I hate that feeling, Lucas. I'm not gonna explode or get to where I can't handle things. I wish you could accept that I can handle things for myself. I don't need a guardian, Lucas. I need a lover."

He nodded. "You're a complicated woman to love."

She chuckled. "Well, I never said loving me would be easy. You wanted to hitch on for the ride. I didn't invite you."

"Wow, that's honest." He bucked his eyes. She kissed him.

"Doesn't mean that I don't want you to come along." She lay her head on his shoulder. "See, this feels good. Just holding each other like this. I spend too much time worrying, Lucas. I can't live like that anymore. When I'm with you, I want no worries. Can we just be happy and enjoy being together?"

"Melody, I will support you in anything. I want you to come to me. I will also respect what you say about Keith." She stared at him. "I don't have a beef with him personally, but if you do…then I'll respect that. After all, I don't remember you ever lying. So if you believe something about Keith, then I'll support you."

"You mean that?" He nodded. He spoke with such honesty. Melody hadn't ever met a man like that before. Anyone could say they cared. But her *feeling* Lucas's adoration spoke volumes. "I love you, Lucas."

He took her into his arms. He guided her thin body onto his lap. He held her for the longest time. Neither thought it could be long enough. They resumed conversation after moments of cuddling.

"Where's Sarah?"

"I dropped her off at a friend's house. A lady from her job."

"Oh." He sucked his lip. "So, will she be gone for the night?"

She smiled. "Lucas, I want to..."

He laid the tip of his finger to her lips. "Melody, I *really* want to."

"But I'm exhausted, you know?" She stood. "It's been a long day. I'm sure you understand."

"Mel," he sighed.

"You do understand, don't you?" She got her purse from the couch.

"Yeah." He stood. "I guess this is good night then." He looked as if he wanted to cry. She couldn't help chuckling at his puppy-dog expression.

"I need a little help with something. Could you come to my room for a second?"

He stared. "Uh, sure. What do you need help with?" They made it to her room. She gestured for him to come inside. He looked around like a kid at the North Pole. "Nice room." He nodded with approval. "Comfortable and quaint. Oh, big bed, huh?" She grinned. "So what did you need my help with?"

"I know this is gonna sound silly, but my wrists have been bothering me a lot today. Sometimes they get so tired. I think I got a tinge of carpal tunnel from all that typing at work."

"Oh, you might want to get that looked at."

She rubbed them. "Yeah, I just don't know if I can get these snaps." She pointed to the snap in the back of her skirt. She lifted her top. "See?"

"Uh…yeah." His voice cracked.

"Think you could help me with it? I hate to bother you."

"Oh no, it's no bother." He sweated. "Uh, let me see." He bent down. He tugged at the tight snap. He unhooked it. He took the liberty of pulling the zipper down along the way. She turned around. "Anything else?"

"Well, since you mentioned it." She sighed. "I don't want to embarrass you."

He wiped his forehead. "I won't be embarrassed. What is it?"

She slipped off her blouse. Lucas glared at the luscious, plump breasts inside of her black lace bra. "My bra. I can't get it in the back."

"Mel, uh…" He exhaled.

"Oh, uh…" She looked him in the eyes. "If you mind, I'll understand."

He groaned. "No, I don't mind." She grinned. He un-hooked the three snaps. He stared at her flowing breasts. She didn't do her best to keep the bra from slipping. Men were so easy. "Anything else?" His voice cracked again.

She grinned. "No."

"See you tomorrow then."

"Oh, Luke?" She snapped her fingers. He sighed at the doorway. "There's one more thing."

"Yeah?" He slowly turned around.

"Could you help me with my panties?"

"*What*?" He scoffed.

She slipped her fingers down the sides of her white panties. "It's hard to move my fingers because my wrists are so tired." She pretended to have a hard time slipping the garment down. "I mean, if you don't mind a little nudity." Her bra dangled from the sides. She knew damn well that it would.

"No." He cleared his throat. "Uh, Mel, maybe you should wait until Sarah comes back."

"But I don't know how long she'll be gone. She stays late at her friend's sometimes. She may even stay over."

He walled his eyes. "Well, do you *have* to take your panties off? Can't you just sleep in them for tonight?"

She shrugged. "I wanted to take a shower." He sighed. "Lucas, I'd scratch your back, you know?"

"Yeah, but I'm not looking at your *back*." He stared at her half-naked body.

She pouted. "Well, that's okay then."

He rubbed his face. "Jesus, I'll do it. But you're killing me here." She smirked. He walked over, gazing at her underwear.

"Just slide them down for me. Then you can go."

"Heaven help me," he muttered. She chuckled under her breath. He knelt down. He turned away while he slid down her underwear. "Okay, uh…are they off now?" He refused to look. Melody looked at the panties on her feet.

"Yeah, they are. Thanks so much."

"Damn, you're welcome." He stood. She grinned. "Now can I leave before I end up having a seizure?"

"Yes." She held her bra across her breasts. She didn't bother hiding her naked bottom. Lucas rushed to the door. "Uh, Lucas?"

"Damn it, *what*?" he shouted.

"I need your help with one more thing."

He huffed. "Melody, I think I've unsnapped everything in this room."

"Not *everything*."

He turned around. She threw her bra to the floor. He ran his hands across his mouth. Melody knew that if you could categorize an expression as lust, Lucas's current one would fit the title perfectly. "Close the door," she instructed.

He followed the order without another word.

Melody enjoyed running her fingers through Lucas's hair. He'd been asleep for almost an hour. She had no idea of the time. It didn't matter. Nothing mattered on such a perfect night. Lucas slightly moved. She enjoyed teasing him with her fingertips. She rubbed his nose. He pried his eyes open. It felt like heaven for Melody to look in the eyes of the man she loved.

She couldn't categorize the lovemaking if she tried. She'd taken the initiative, which had made the act even more enjoyable. She'd have waited forever to experience such passion again. She didn't know he'd take her body so masterfully. That he'd respond to her feverish demands from mere instinct. She'd shocked herself, too.

She hadn't imagined that she would let loose like she did. She thought she'd feel uncomfortable embarking on a new lover. She hadn't in the slightest. In fact, she had taken control of the situation in bed like she had outside of it. He moved the covers from his firm chest. She ran her hands across his medium-sized pecs. She curved her fingers against his nipple. He cupped her breast in his hand.

Melody ran her hand down his arm. For the first time, she felt like the most beautiful woman in the world. Usually Sarah fit that description. Tonight Melody played second to none. Lucas put his hands around her waist. He guided her to his jutting crotch. He perched her on top of him. Melody squealed with avid delight. Before they realized it, the lovemaking took on a world of its own.

Lucas left around midnight. Melody decided to take

in a late-night movie in the den. Who could sleep after such mind-numbing lovemaking? Anyway, she knew she'd only dream of Lucas. She'd probably get so hot she wouldn't be able to sleep anymore before work. She opened a can of sliced peaches. She sat Indian-style on the sofa. Suddenly she felt guilty. She'd had one of the best nights of her life, but how was Aileen holding up? She hadn't thought about her since she got back home. She wanted to call, but with Aileen's current state she wasn't sure if waking her in the middle of the night would be smart. Then again, she probably wasn't asleep, anyway. Melody knew if she had just been raped in her home, she wouldn't be able to sit down in the damn place long enough, let alone sleep.

She remembered how Aileen shook when they took her home that evening. She'd acted like she didn't even recognize her place. Melody kidded herself if she assumed Aileen would be all right now. Rape victims could easily stay calm in public. But how did they act when they were alone? Aileen swore she felt all right when Melody and Sarah dropped her off. That didn't mean shit.

Melody dropped her legs over the couch. Aileen had been alone all night. She'd been alone in that house with her daughter. Who knew the scary thoughts going through her head? Who knew how close this attack already pushed her to the limit? Rape victims weren't very stable after being attacked. Aileen seemed to be worse than most. She not only insisted that Steven Kemp raped her, she'd almost died when she saw his face.

Melody *knew* Aileen's fear. She easily identified it because that's the same way she felt about Keith. Aileen needed someone to hold her. She needed her best friend there to let her know everything would be all right. How could Melody succumb to sex tonight when Aileen needed her more than anyone, right now? Jesus, what kind of friend was she?

She grabbed the phone by the couch. She hooked the receiver between her ear and shoulder. She began to dial when the front door opened. Keith stood in the doorway with two suitcases. Melody jumped from the couch. She hadn't realized that her pink nightgown had hooked between her thighs. A breeze swept between them.

"Well." Keith gazed at her figure. "So you do wear gowns to bed after all? I knew that T-shirt was covering up something fantastic."

"What in the hell are you doing here?" Melody threw the phone down. "Where's Sarah?"

Sarah walked in. She shut the door behind her. "Melody, uh, Keith's staying with us for a while. He has a gas leak in his neighborhood. The police and everything were there. It was a big mess, and they're suggesting the residents leave until they get a handle on the problem."

Melody shook her head. "Didn't I drop you off at Pam's? How the hell did you get to Keith's in the first place?" Sarah and Keith looked at each other. Keith grinned.

"Oh, I see. You had no intentions of visiting Pam, did

you, Sarah? You only said that so I wouldn't know you were with Keith!"

"Look, I didn't want to lie but we'd had a hard day and I didn't feel like arguing with you about it, Melody. Also, with what happened, I didn't want to upset you."

"Sarah, you don't give a damn about me!"

"Melody, I love you more than anyone!"

"Bullshit! Since Keith has wormed his way into your life, I don't know you! I can't take this anymore." She crossed her arms. "Sarah, it's gotta be him or me. I mean that. Right now you gotta make a choice because I can't take being around here anymore."

"Is this about the snake thing? Melody, you gotta know that was an accident. Keith would never do anything like that."

He chuckled. "Yeah, putting snakes in your bed. Why would I do that, Melody?"

"You know, you both are completely fucked up. All this time I thought you were too good for this asshole, Sarah. It's finally dawned on me that you belong with him! If you want to be with him, then go on! He can stay here for as long as you like because I won't be here!"

"Melody!"

"No, that's it, Sarah! Make a decision right now! You stop seeing Keith or I will move out...now."

"Mel, you can't mean that." Sarah exhaled. "Baby girl, I love you. You can't think that a man would change that." Keith looked at Sarah. "Melody, think about what you're saying."

"No, I usually think and have everything I say planned out. Maybe that's why it doesn't seem to hit any chords with you. Me moving out just came to me. Maybe that means it's the right thing to do."

Sarah sighed. "You know you can't make it on your own."

Melody scoffed. "Just like you to think I can't even take a piss without you holding the toilet, huh? I *can* make it without you, Sarah. I can do many things without you, contrary to popular belief. And I am sick to death of you throwing it in my face that this is your house and that you took me in! I never asked you to, did I?"

"I wasn't throwing anything up in your face! Melody, with what happened to Aileen, you can turn around and get angry over something so minor?" Sarah held Keith's waist.

"Well, it's not minor to me, Sarah. Over and over I've told you how I felt about Keith and you don't care. If you don't care what I think, then I don't need to be around you. I'd believe you in a heartbeat, Sarah."

"Mel, I…"

She held up her hands. "No, if you came to me repeatedly with things about Lucas, I'd listen. I'd put your opinion over my own selfishness."

"Mel, don't do this. You know I love you. No man could ever take your place."

"You just can't make the choice, can you, Sarah?" Melody sighed. "Then I'll make it for you. I'm leaving. I'll go to Craig's tonight and I'll figure out where I'll go from there." She went to the stairs.

"Melody, don't do this!" Sarah rushed after her. "You're the one who's wrong, Melody."

She turned around on the stairs. "Sarah, it's all on you now." Melody glanced at Keith. "I hope you can live with the decisions you've made." Melody ran upstairs.

"Mel?" Sarah whispered.

Keith held her. "Everything will be okay, Sarah. You just gotta let her finally grow up."

"This is tearing me apart, Keith." She went into the kitchen.

Keith stood at Melody's door a second later. She shoved enough clothes into a suitcase to get her through a few days. She hated herself for not locking the door when she noticed Keith in the room.

"For some reason you like coming into my room un-announced." She'd changed into jeans and a sweatshirt.

"So you and Craig must be closer than I thought if you're going to his place. Why not Lucas's?"

"Why are you all in my business?" She struggled to close the stuffed suitcase. Keith grabbed a small wrapper from the floor. Melody would have been embarrassed if she didn't hate him so much. Anyway, this was her room. Sarah may have owned the house, but she couldn't control what went on behind *this* door.

Keith overlooked the torn red condom wrapper. "Well, how come I get the feeling that Lucas has already been here tonight?" He smirked. "Glad to see you use pro-tection, Mel. So Lucas won't mind you spending the night at Craig's? I can't see him not having a problem with that."

"Craig and Lucas are old friends. We all grew up together."

"Yeah, but back then you all weren't so…" He stared at her breasts. "Grown up, if you get my meaning. Is Craig a faggot or what?"

"What in the hell are you talking about?"

"You mean he can have you over there and not be tempted to make a move?"

"Contrary to popular belief, Keith, every man isn't out to get pussy, okay?"

He grinned. "We're all out to get pussy, Melody. It's just that some men dress up their methods better than others. You seem to think Lucas is better than the average man. Don't be so sure, Mel. I get the feeling he'd be jealous as hell to know you're staying with another man. Especially after the hot, passionate, sensuous night you two obviously had." He laughed.

She leaned over on her suitcase. "Is there something you wanted?"

"There's always something I want, Mel." He threw the wrapper in the tiny wastebasket. "I hate it when Sarah's upset, you know? I mean, you can do what you want with me, but I don't like it when she's hurt. Do you understand me?"

"I'm going to the police, Keith. I'm going to tell them that you put the snakes in my bed."

He grinned. "Kind of farfetched, right? Mel, you tell a story like that and you'll end up locked up. No one is gonna buy that I'd do anything like that."

"They will once they see what kind of person you are."

"Sarah didn't believe you about the snakes, did she?" He sat on her bed, watching her closely. "Anyway, I told you that I wouldn't take you snooping into my business and going to Mr. Lawson. Oh, that was a huge mistake, Melody."

"Oh, and one more thing, Keith." She grinned. "Your little plan of trying to cause friction between Lucas and me didn't work."

"What are you talking about?" he groaned.

"He told me you told him that I went to his father about you. I can't imagine you telling him the honest reason, so I'm sure you lied through your teeth. It didn't work. You're trying to control me, but you can't, so you went to Lucas?"

"That's right, and that's nothing compared to what I can do if you don't back off!"

"My God, Keith, what's wrong with you? You have a big problem. I am dead serious. I think you need mental help. You can't take not being in control. But you're not in control with me, are you? That's why you continue your sick little games behind Sarah's back."

"I can control you in more ways than one, Melody," he whispered. "Anyway, this became war when you went to Mr. Lawson."

"After you assaulted me, Keith! You may do this with other women, but you won't do it with me! Since Sarah refuses to listen, I no longer feel obligated to her. That means that if you fuck with me this time, I'll pull out all the stops! And I *will* go to the police if I have to."

"Then let me oblige." He smirked.

"What?"

"No need in going to the police without a reason, huh? Why don't I give you one next time? It would make everything easier for you, Mel."

"My God, you are sick. Stay away from me, Keith." She tried to leave. He blocked her.

"Can't wait to see you at work, Melody." He walked away, grinning.

Sarah walked in. Melody couldn't believe that a total stranger could break a bond between sisters. That bond should have been stronger than steel. She stared at her sister's torn face. Maybe Sarah regretted Melody's sudden decision. Yet that wasn't enough.

"Good-bye, Sarah." Melody picked up her suitcase.

"Melody, think of how unfair this is! How would you feel if I asked you to choose between Lucas and me, knowing you love us both?" She sniffed.

Melody fit the suitcase underneath her arm. "Sarah, the point is that you'd never even have to ask." She left.

❖❖❖

"So this is supposed to be the Albany Predator, huh?" Craig gobbled down cereal at his kitchen table Monday morning. He stared at the black-and-white picture of Steven Kemp on the front of the newspaper. His arrest had made headlines. "He doesn't look guilty." A cornflake fell from his lips.

Melody sipped a glass of orange juice. "And how does someone *look* guilty?"

"You know what I mean." He chewed. "I know guilty people, and this cop doesn't look guilty to me."

"Well, Aileen and Cheyenne Wilson identified him as the rapist. They saw him as clear as day. I believe Aileen with all my heart."

"I believe her, too, Mel. Aileen is one of my dearest friends." She chewed toast. "Then why are you defending her rapist?"

"That's not fair, Melody. We can't just lock up an innocent man, thinking this will make everything go away."

"And what makes you think he's so damn innocent? That's the part I don't get, Craig."

He sighed. "Why would this cop just start raping women? It makes no sense. Look here." He read Steven's statement. "He claims the rapist could be some looka-like."

"Isn't that a bit farfetched? He raped them, Craig. Case closed."

He shook his head. "Nah, I don't buy it, Mel. I don't think Steven Kemp is guilty of those rapes. It just wouldn't make sense. I know I don't know him, but I don't think he'd risk his career and everything he built, do you?"

"Look, you weren't there to see how torn up Aileen was. The minute she saw his face she freaked, Craig. Believe me, there's no mistake that Kemp raped her." She stood. "Anyway, the DA and judge at the bail hearing obviously believed it. He was denied bail." Craig stared at the newspaper. "I gotta get ready for work."

She left the kitchen.

Held without bail. Steven couldn't get the words out of his head. How could he prove his innocence while stuck in a jail cell for who knew how long? He tapped his fingers against the dirty wall as he looked up at the crusty little window. Streaks of dirt prevented him from seeing the beauty of the sunlight. He sat on the hard bed. If he didn't find a way out of this, he may never see the sunlight again. At least not in the same capacity.

Now he knew how some of the people he had arrested felt. He hadn't always made the best choice. He'd arrested some innocent people in his day. But he'd always realized that before prison came into the picture. He blew into his hands. He'd never felt so alone. He used to think being a cop meant everything. He knew staying behind these bars would wreck his high opinion of law enforcement.

His faith in the system grew dimmer as the hours

passed. He questioned how he could dedicate himself to something that had crucified him without hesitation. It hadn't mattered that he built his life on catching sexual predators. It hadn't mattered that he'd always been one cop the force could trust. What had they done in return? Arrested him? Dragged his good name through the mud for all to see? Refused to hear his side? He looked at the dingy toilet beside him. A drunken man howled from the cell down the hall. Everything he worked for would be wasted.

Steven had to get out of jail if he had any hope of surviving this nightmare.

"Steve?" Brianna stood against the bars. Funny how she could erase even the worst times for him. He wondered if she truly knew how much he still loved her. He'd do anything to go back to that time when they were more than partners and friends. If he could only hold her for one more night, it would somehow be enough.

"Bree." He slumped to the bars. "So I guess you heard about me getting no bail, huh?"

"I can't believe this, Steven. This makes no sense! What about that organization that fights for cops, whose rights have been threatened? They could make a stink, and they may even be able to get you out, Steven."

"Bree, the judge has ruled. It doesn't matter what anyone else does. It only matters what I do from this point."

"Sounds like you have a plan. Mind sharing?"

"I don't have anything solid, except that I need to get

this man. He's a clever son-of-a-bitch. While keeping tabs on you, he kept tabs on me. I bet he was ecstatic when he learned we looked so much alike. Shit, it became all he needed to have an edge on the cops."

"It's so scary, Steven. I couldn't get yesterday out of my head. I kept seeing you behind that glass. I kept hearing Aileen and Cheyenne calling you a rapist in my dreams. And to think that this monster could look so much like you, I…" She leaned against the bars. "I'm so sorry, Steven."

He rubbed her fingers through the bars. "You believe me, Bree?"

"Of course! Steven, there was never a doubt in my mind. Jesus, we know each other more than anyone else on this earth. We were lovers. I know you, and I trust you. I believe in you and I know you're not a rapist. I'll never forget how I felt being caught up in the danger of almost being raped. He's nothing like you, even if he looks like you. He's pure evil, Steven. There's no other way to describe him. I know that you'd never hurt anyone the way he tried to hurt me. Soon, everyone will know it, too."

"I could do a better job of getting Commissioner Reynolds to see reason if Parsons didn't have his dick in my ass. He acts like I killed his mother or something. Can't they see he's doing this because he can't stand me? Shit, I gotta get out, Bree." He pleaded. "I gotta go and take care of this myself. Parsons is just waiting to hang me! I can't just sit in here and wait."

"I never thought I'd say this, but I kind of hope there's another rape."

"Jesus why, Bree?"

"Because that would be the only thing that can prove you're really innocent. If the man claims another victim, then you'll be free. I know, it's a terrible thing to think of but I can't help it, Steven. You don't deserve to be in here for what that bastard has done. He's ruining your life and all you can do is sit here and take it."

"Maybe Arlen can tell me something I can do." He leaned against the bar. "Meanwhile, I want you to work the hell out of the case. Don't let up on anything, Bree. You could be my only chance out of here right now. If I can't get the rapist, you gotta try your best to. Bree, you have to. Talk to the victims. Make them cooperate. Arrest them if you have to." She nodded. "Find anything and anyone who could lead us to this guy, Bree. My life and future depend on it."

She sighed. "I'll do all I can, Steven. Meanwhile, I want you to just stay grounded. I know it's hard." She looked around the dirty cell. "But it's all you can do at this point. No need in driving yourself crazy." She felt his hair. The action shocked him. "You got to keep your sanity, Steven. No one's gonna believe a nut."

He nodded. "As long as you're on my side I know I can do anything."

She smiled. Jersey walked up with Arlen.

"What's going on?" Steven stared at his attorney.

"Well, there may be a light in the tunnel after all."

Arlen smiled. "Steve, I need to speak with you for a moment, then they want you back in the interrogation room." The guard opened the cell. Steven and Arlen sat on the little bed.

"Morris, I want you to come up, too. I need to speak to you." Jersey took Brianna by the arm. They made it to the room a minute later.

"What's up, Captain? I get the feeling this is good news."

"It is. Arlen wants Steven to do a DNA test." Jersey's eyes danced. "That way there will be no mistake!"

"Jesus, I wasn't even thinking about that!" Brianna guffawed. "Oh, this is great! Once he takes the test, then there will be no question!"

"Well, Parsons was dragging his feet, the little weasel. I think he thought Arlen was too stupid to go the DNA route. But what choice would he have in getting Steven off? It's the only way. We're going on the DNA for Cheyenne and Aileen specifically, but it won't make a difference which victim we compare Steven to. He's innocent."

"That's right." Brianna grinned. "I can't wait to see that rat Parsons's face."

The door opened. Parsons walked in looking like the cat that ate the canary.

"Did I hear my name?" He smiled at Brianna. "Detective Morris, how are you? Uh, is it just me, or do you have something you need to be doing? Like your job?"

She walled her eyes. "I'm doing it. In case you've forgotten, this is my case. Any developments that go on here, I need to know. I'll find the right rapist and when I do, I hope Steven shits down your throat."

He lit a cigarette. "Well, I hope none of this offends you. Why are you so interested in what happens to Kemp, anyway?" He smirked.

"He happens to be my partner and my friend."

"Sure that's it?"

"What are you getting at, Parsons?" Brianna sighed.

"I think you know." He stared at her chest. "You and Kemp seem to have a connection other than professional. Am I wrong?"

Brianna looked at Jersey. "We used to date. It's no big secret. But that was a long time ago. I don't see what it has to do with anything, now."

"Just wondering, you know?" Parsons flicked his cigarette in midair. Jersey had become sick of the habit. "If I had such a beautiful and sexy partner like you, crime fighting would be the last thing on my mind. I wonder how he even concentrates."

"There's nothing between Steven and me, okay?" She held her waist.

He winked. "If you say so."

"You won't be so cocky once you leave here. You'll be too busy apologizing to Steven. But with all you've put him through, I'm sure apologizing isn't enough." Brianna smiled.

"On this DNA test thing?" Parsons rolled his eyes.

"Let's wait until he takes it before we start celebrating hey, Morris?"

"You're gonna eat your words, Parsons. I promise you that." Brianna squinted.

"I find this tension between us mighty sexy." He laughed.

"Asshole," she muttered. Jersey grinned.

Arlen, Steven and a uniformed officer walked in. The officer sat Steven behind the table. Arlen set his suitcase on the table.

"You told him yet, Arlen?" Jersey asked.

"No, Captain." Arlen smiled at his client. Steven waited wide-eyed. "Steven, there is one definite thing you can do to prove, once and for all, that you're not the rapist."

He looked at the company in the room. "I'm not the rapist, Arlen." Parsons walled his eyes. "Has the commissioner finally realized that? Have I been released?"

"Not so fast." Parsons flicked his cigarette.

"Steven, we want you to do a DNA test." Arlen grinned. "That's the sure-fire answer."

"Isn't that great, Steven?" Brianna grinned. Parsons looked at her.

"A DNA test would be the answer." Arlen looked at Parsons. "Once the tests come back negative there is no case."

"Still got Aileen's and Cheyenne's statements." Parsons winked.

"Agent Parsons, why are you so determined to lock Steven up for this?" Brianna crossed her arms. "You know once the DNA test is done you have nothing. Is that what you're worried about? Instead of arresting Steven, you should have been helping us find this asshole. We've wasted valuable time putting needless energy on Steve." Brianna pointed.

"You're out of luck, Parsons." Arlen gestured to Steven. "The DNA test will vanish all possibility that Steve's the rapist. It won't matter what the ladies say. It's all up to hard evidence. His DNA won't match the rapist's and we all know it. Which means there will be no case."

"That's right." Brianna nodded.

DA Zachary sashayed in with her assistant. She hurriedly passed the shaken young man her briefcase. "Well, looks like I got here just in time."

"As you did." Arlen nodded. "Once Steven takes a DNA test, you will have no case. I guess that's a lost cause for you, huh, Debra?"

Zachary grinned. "I wouldn't be so cocky if I were you, Arlen." She looked at Steven. "From the way Kemp is sweating, I don't know if a DNA test would work in his favor."

"He didn't do it and the DNA test will prove that." Brianna smiled.

"We'll get it done now." Jersey ordered. "Steven, you can meet with the…"

"No." He stood. Everyone looked at him. "No, Captain

Jersey, this isn't going to happen this way. I'm not going to take a DNA test."

"*Excuse* me?" Arlen gaped.

Steven gulped. "You heard me, Arlen. I won't take a DNA test."

"Steven, have you lost your damn mind?"

"May seem like it, Bree, but I haven't. I'm innocent and I don't need to take a damn test to prove that."

"Hold on." Parsons waved his hand. "Let me get this straight, Detective. You're innocent and that's why you won't take the test?" Steven nodded. "That has to be the dumbest thing I've ever heard in my life."

"Steve, what in the hell is this?" Jersey walked to the table. "Do you understand what you're doing? You're refusing to do the one thing that could free you!"

"Take the goddamn test, Steven!" Arlen yelled.

"No. I'm not taking a damn test because I did nothing wrong! I got my pride! I've put years into this department and this is the way they pay me? I cannot believe that my word isn't good enough! I've been sworn to uphold the law, yet that same law hasn't listened to my pleas, demands or reason! I know it looks funny to not take the test. I want to prove my innocence more than anything but I will not take a DNA test! Not now and not ever!"

"Steve." Brianna scoffed.

Zachary shook her head. "Do you realize you're playing with the rest of your life, Detective?"

"Steven, I've always admired you for standing up for your beliefs, but this is not one of those times! You cannot be serious about what you're doing."

"I am, Bree. I gotta do what's right for *me*, no matter how it looks to all of you."

"I don't believe this." Arlen shook his head. "Steven, this is your life. Forget your damn pride! If you keep going on like this, you won't have a life, career or future! Do you realize the pile of horse shit you've stepped into?"

"Steven, this is not the time to pull this hotshot-cop shit!" Brianna sighed. "Take the damn test and worry about getting your point across later."

"No, Bree. I've done things their way since I've been in here."

Parsons scoffed. "Man, this is too easy."

Zachary raised an eyebrow. "So, you're actually refusing to take the test, even if it could free you? Detective, do you realize how guilty that makes you look?"

"Yeah, maybe. I don't care." Steven looked at his weary attorney. "I appreciate everyone who believes in me. But I'm not taking a DNA test. I know I'm innocent and I shouldn't have to do some test to prove it. It's not fair to me at all. I have rights and one of them is to refuse this test. I'm sorry, Arlen." Arlen stayed silent.

"Then you stay in jail." Parsons grinned. "You realize you're headed for a trial, Detective Kemp?"

"So be it." He shrugged.

"Steven?" Brianna waved her hands. "Why are you doing this?"

"I don't care if this whole city thinks I'm a rapist, Bree. I can risk what others think of me, but I can't risk what I think of myself."

Arlen felt his forehead. "So you're giving up your future for self-respect?" he shrieked. "Take the test and take it today, Steven!"

"No."

"Then get yourself another attorney!"

"Okay, if that's the way you want it." Steven sighed. Arlen left.

"I don't understand you at all right now, Steven."

"Well, you got company then, Bree. There's a lot of things I don't understand right now, either."

Chapter Fourteen

A Week Later

"**M**elody, it's for you." Craig brought the portable phone to the couch. Melody hated being interrupted during the end of a classic film. She sat Indian-style on the couch with a plate of steaming spaghetti on her lap. The clock struck six p.m. This Wednesday had been the first day off she'd had since working at Caper. She intended to enjoy it until at least midnight.

"Who is it?" she asked with a mouthful of spaghetti.

"Keith." Craig threw the phone on the couch. He headed to the bedroom area.

"Craig!" He turned around. "Why didn't you tell him I wasn't home? I don't want to talk to Keith. It's bad enough I gotta work with him."

"He says it's important. Something about Sarah." Craig left the room.

She grabbed up the phone. She hadn't seen her sister in a week. Being away from Sarah nearly killed her. She enjoyed staying at Craig's, but it didn't compare to living at home. She'd talked with Sarah on the phone every other day. It wasn't enough for either of them. Melody couldn't help feeling depressed each time she thought of how close they used to be.

She hated herself for giving Keith the power to break them up. She and Sarah were sisters. Melody had an obligation to that bond. She blamed Sarah for not choosing her over Keith. But had that been fair? Hadn't she been the one that allowed Keith to destroy her life with Sarah? Had it been right to let Keith run her away from her own home? So far, Keith had kept his distance at work. It wasn't enough.

Melody wanted him *gone*. Nothing would ever be the same unless Keith disappeared from both their lives.

"Keith?" she sighed.

"Hey, Mel, uh…" he exhaled. "I, uh…am I interrupting you?"

She sighed. "No," she lied. If it involved Sarah, it had to be important.

"How did you get Craig's number, anyway?"

"I saw it in the address book at your house one day." She sighed. Like she suspected, he *had* been spending even more time there since she left. "Melody, I…you gotta come over here quick."

"What's going on, Keith?" She set her spaghetti on the table. "You're breathing hard, panting and it's scaring me."

"It's Sarah. She's…Mel, she's not moving."

"What? What do you mean she's not moving?" She jumped from the couch.

"She's not moving! Shit, I mean…we were talking and she started breathing funny." Melody covered her mouth. "Before I could call someone, she passed out! I tried to revive her but she isn't moving."

"Is she breathing, Keith?" Melody panted.

"Uh, yes…I think she is."

"What do you mean you *think*? Go check!"

"She's breathing!" He huffed. "Oh God, Melody, you gotta come over here. I already called the ambulance."

"I'll be to our house in a few minutes." She started to hang up.

"No," Keith exhaled. "Uh, we're at my place. You gotta come to my place." He rambled off the address. He lived in a very upscale neighborhood. "You know where that is?"

"Yes."

"Good." He let out a relaxing sigh. "I have a feeling everything will fall into place once you get here." She wondered what in the hell he meant by that. She didn't have time to think. She grabbed her purse and ran to the door. Craig stomped from the back room.

"Mel, what's wrong?"

"It's Sarah!" She threw on a jacket. "She's at Keith's. She's passed out or something."

"What? Is she all right?"

"I don't know, uh…he already called the ambulance.

Hopefully they'll make it before I get there." She opened the front door.

"You need me to come with you?"

"No, I'll call you if I need to." She slammed the door.

Keith lived in prestigious Madison Hills. Melody had no idea. She'd never bothered to find out where he lived before. Living in Madison Hills meant he had more money than she'd thought. You had to be above upper-middle class just to rent in the area. She turned on the street to Keith's house. Lights shined from security posts at every corner.

She couldn't get Sarah out of her head. Just when she thought things were looking up, she'd been thrown a loop. It never failed. What in the hell had happened to Sarah? The woman hadn't had a cold in her life! Now she'd passed out without explanation. Every frightening thought in the world passed through Melody's mind.

Had Sarah contracted some disease?

She didn't regularly go to the doctor. Who knew? Had she developed some respiratory problem? Had her lungs collapsed? How serious could this be? Would doctors be able to help her? Melody slapped the stirring wheel. She had a knack for worrying herself into frenzy. Yet how could she help it? If she lost Sarah… "Oh God." She shut her eyes. Why did the worst thoughts always come at the hardest times?

Melody constantly got on Sarah about working so hard. Sometimes Sarah seemed so tired she could barely breathe. Melody wouldn't be surprised if she'd suffered from over-exhaustion. She prayed that it hadn't been anything more. Apparently, Sarah hadn't ever worried about her health. She never worried about anything, which made Melody worry about them *both*.

Keith lived in a huge two-story home on the far corner of his block. Melody knew Keith appreciated this location. No through streets meant he didn't endure noisy traffic. Melody caught a sign that forbid big vehicles to drive through after a certain hour. It seemed like the residents of Madison Hills had been gladly locked away into their own self-absorbed planet.

Melody didn't resent people with money. They just didn't make it easier for her to like them. She parked in Keith's wide driveway. She didn't see Sarah's car. She figured Keith brought her. Sarah complained about gas constantly. Melody figured she'd walk all the way over here if it meant saving a few dollars. Melody wondered how Sarah managed to live above her means being so cheap.

She stepped from her jeep. She stared at Keith's colossal, beige brick home. A garage that could probably house eight families sat over to the side. A pristine lawn suggested he had a gardener at least twice a week. Melody squinted down the street. The next house sat about a block down. The lawn looked the same as Keith's. It wasn't hard to figure out the perks of living in Madison Hills.

She stepped to the front door. Keith's sophisticated style extended from how he dressed to how he lived. Melody hadn't expected his place to be so remarkable even for an upscale neighborhood. She took a deep breath. Concentrating on Keith's beautiful home kept her mind off Sarah. Why hadn't the emergency vehicles made it yet? Melody lifted a fist to knock. She stopped.

Something felt strange about all of this. Why *wasn't* the ambulance here, yet? Melody's drive had been at least fifteen minutes. She'd never known an ambulance taking their time before. She thought about Sarah's car again. For some reason, the explanation of her coming with Keith seemed unreal. Melody felt a nagging chill. That damn intuition. Yet, that intuition had saved her many times. But why now?

Something told her *not* to go into the house. But she had no choice! Sarah needed her. Should she listen to reason for Sarah's sake, or intuition for her own? Even nature seemed to contribute to her growing anxiety. She hadn't remembered it being so dark at six p.m. before. She couldn't remember the air being so still.

Her heart pounded. She didn't have time to think. Sarah needed her. Battling with her soul on the porch had been silly at best. She knocked on the door. No one answered. She called for Keith. No one answered. She peeked in the windows. The living room lights were off. What was going on here?

She leaned against the door. It easily swung open. She

stepped inside. She'd never been in a room so still. She could taste the air. She called for Keith and Sarah. No one answered. Maybe they had taken Sarah to the hospital. That would be the logical thing to do. She chuckled for nearly scaring herself to death. But why had Keith's door been unlocked? Had he been in such a rush that he'd forgotten to lock it?

Melody turned to leave. The lights popped on. She stood in a fantastic living room that would put Martha Stewart's decorator to shame. Keith stood against the large bookshelf. He moved his hand from the light switch. Melody overlooked his serene behavior. If Sarah had been hurt, how could he be so calm?

"Keith, you scared me." She held her chest. "Where's Sarah?" He walked past her. He shut and locked the front door.

He leaned against the door with his arms crossed. "Jesus, Melody. I can't believe how fuckin' easy it was to get you here."

"What's going on?" She trembled. He cracked his knuckles. "Where's Sarah?"

"She's fine. I imagine she's at home resting after a hard day's work."

"What?" She sucked in her anger. Something told her this wasn't the right time to confront him. "I don't believe this. You set me up? You made me believe that Sarah was hurt so I'd come over here?" He nodded. "*Why?*"

"Well…" He stepped toward her. She moved back. "I enjoy playing with you, Mel. Didn't you know that?"

"Goddamn you!"

He chuckled. "It amazes me how easy it is to fool you. You claim I won't manipulate things but I keep doing it, don't I? I got Sarah to believe me over you many times. I even got it where you moved out. I got it where you can't break us up, and I got you here tonight. Do you finally see how this is going, Melody? You can't win. I hope now you realize you'd better give it up."

"You sick bastard. What is the point of all this now? I've been gone for a week! If you loved Sarah so much, then why would you want to come between us?"

"I never did, Melody. But when you kept making things harder for me, I needed to eliminate the problem. And we all know that's you." He lowered his eyes to her skirt.

"What do you want from me, Keith?" She held her purse for protection.

"I only want to be your friend." He looked at her breasts underneath her white blouse. "That's all I've ever wanted. But you had to act like some little child and keep Sarah all for yourself!" He hit the wall. She shrieked. "I wanted to love you both, Melody. It could have been so beautiful. I know that you really want that, too."

"You stay away from me, Keith." She shook.

"I know you want that." He moved toward the couch. "You've always wanted that, haven't you? You wanted a taste of what Sarah had, didn't you?"

"No!" She ran to the door. He blocked her.

"You're tired of being in her footsteps, aren't you? You wanted to know why she always got everything! You resent her, just admit it!"

"No!" She held her head. "I love Sarah with all my heart!"

"Is that why you try to manipulate all of her relationships, Melody? You couldn't get the point that I'm not going anywhere." He grabbed her.

"Let me go!" she screamed.

"I told you not to fuck with me, Melody. I meant it."

"Please, Keith!" she sobbed. "You're scaring me!"

He licked his lips. "I guess I never told you how beautiful you are when you're scared." He firmly held the back of her neck. He shoved her body against him. He moved his mouth to hers.

"No! No…" She shook her head to thwart his kisses. He shoved his hand under her skirt. He tugged at her panties. "Stop! Keith, please!"

"You know you want this. You've wanted it all along."

"No!" She tried to move. She didn't know anyone could be so damn strong.

"You smell so good." He sniffed her neck. "I love that perfume. Do you wear it just for me?"

"No," she whimpered, sobbing. "Keith, let me go, please!"

"No." He stared in her eyes. "No, Melody, tonight you're gonna learn why Sarah loves me so much. That's the only way I can get you to understand." He tried to kiss her again. She moved her head to stop him.

"Please, don't do this, Keith," she cried. "Please!"

"It's okay. Shh." He slid his arm underneath her bottom. He tried to hoist her into his arms. Melody desperately fought him. She couldn't believe no one heard her scream. She should have listened to intuition. Why tonight of all nights had she not? Keith pulled her to the couch.

"No! No, what are you doing?" she gasped.

"You know exactly what I'm doing." He pulled her to his mouth. He brutally kissed her. She tore her lips away. "Someone, help! Help!"

"Shut up!" He covered her mouth. He pushed her on the couch. He got on top of her.

"No!" She kicked and swatted her arms. He grabbed them. He held her down on the couch. "Stop!" She wiggled her legs underneath his body. He seemed to weigh a ton. "Keith, please!" He locked her hands underneath her head. "I'm sorry! I'm sorry! I won't interfere anymore, I swear! Please, just get off me!" she bellowed. "Please!"

"Enjoy it, Mel." He nibbled her earlobe. "I want to show you what makes Sarah want me. I want to convince you. I know you just don't understand how she feels about me. I'm gonna make you understand."

He pulled up her skirt. He slid his hand to her panties. Melody jiggled underneath him. She couldn't believe this. She, Melody Cruz, was being raped! The evil look in Keith's eyes told her he wouldn't stop. He'd planned this for who knew how long. Melody just couldn't accept this as reality. Keith Taylor was raping her? Was that how sick he actually was? Was that how dangerous?

All this time she thought she could handle him. She had no idea he'd hurt her like this. He threw his sweaty hand over her mouth. He sucked her neck. She cried, kicked and begged. He paid no attention. He maneuvered her legs underneath his.

"You're so beautiful," he panted. Melody nearly choked from tears. He licked the sides of her face. His hardened crotch jabbed her thighs. Before she knew it, Keith tore off her underwear.

"No, Keith! No!" She shook uncontrollably. "You can't do this! Think about Sarah!" He looked at her. "Think about how much this will hurt her!" Melody sobbed.

"I am thinking of Sarah." He fondled her breasts through her blouse.

"Keith, please. You don't want to do this. This is *rape*."

"No, it's not," he panted. "Because you want this. You've wanted it all along. That's why you did the things you did."

"No!" She bounced underneath him. She did all she could to throw him off. She might as well have been under a pile of bricks.

"Mmm." He unbuttoned his shirt. His muscular legs held her firmly to the couch. Melody's body burned from being pressed against the fabric. She screamed many times. It didn't do any good. Keith would rape her tonight. She knew it by the look in his eyes; by the words he said; by the ravenous way his hands invaded her body. "Did Lucas make you feel like this?"

"Keith, please." Tears ran down her face.

He ripped her blouse open from the bottom up. He unzipped his pants. Melody gyrated to interrupt his movements. He pulled his pants and underwear down to the ankles. Melody kept her eyes on the fine assets in the room: the entertainment system, expensive vases, fancy overhead light, computer, phone, Asian-style lamps...

Why stop the unstoppable? How much screaming could she do? Keith had gotten what he wanted up until this point. He wouldn't stop now. She thought of Craig warning her to mind her business. She thought of Aileen's rape. Did Aileen feel this afraid? The fact that Melody knew Keith didn't make her like it. She nearly threw up over them both.

Keith slipped her breasts from her bra. He sucked her nipples. Melody quivered violently beneath him. He ran his hand down the side of her thin body. He brought his hands to her middle. He stuck his fingers against her clitoris, forcing her to accept them. She trembled. Her legs, hands and head shook violently.

"Melody?" Keith gripped her head. He forced her eyes on his. The panic attack subsided. "It's okay. It's all right."

"Don't do this, Keith! I'll tell Sarah!"

He held her neck. She shrieked. "You won't tell Sarah shit. Besides, she'll only think you seduced me if she ever found out."

"I'll go to the police, I swear! Keith, you'll be in jail by morning! Please, think about this!"

"Shut up!" He shoved her down flat. He covered her mouth. He moved his legs underneath her thighs. He plunged inside of her. Melody shrieked from the pain of his entrance. She shut her eyes. Keith pumped her slowly at first. He hooked her leg over his arm. He shoved himself deeper inside.

"Mmm!" Melody screamed from pain.

Keith rolled his eyes in the back of his head. "Oh, you sweet thing. God, you feel so good. You're so tight."

"Mmm! Mmm!" She tried to bite his hand. He held her mouth tighter.

"Oh God, you feel so good." He shut his eyes. He pumped her harder now. Melody felt she'd rip in two. She didn't imagine anything being so humiliating and uncomfortable at the same time. She tried to throw him off of her. She failed to interrupt him for even a moment. Keith leaned against her. He readied his mouth to take hers. When he moved his hand Melody screamed louder than she ever had.

"Stop!" Keith held her leg higher. Melody violently bounced underneath him.

"You son-of-a-bitch!" she wailed. "Get off!" She grabbed at his shirt. "Keith, please! Keith, you're hurting me!" She realized he probably wanted to. He had planned this after all. The degree of pain only meant more power to him.

Keith continued as if the rape were mutual. "Oh God, you feel so good, Melody." She screamed. "Oh…God." Sweat dribbled from his forehead. "I'm gonna cum." He slipped his hands underneath her. He pushed her against his crotch.

"Get off me! Get off!" She beat his chest with her fists. Once again, her efforts were lost.

"You're so beautiful, Melody. You're just so goddamn beautiful. I wanted you like this for so long. I always did. Now I know you want me, too." He tried to kiss her. She turned away. "Come on, don't save it for, Lucas." He kissed her. She shoved him away.

"No! No!" She continued to hit him.

"Don't fight me," he grunted in between movements. Melody felt herself stretching to fully take him. She couldn't remember such pain. The longer he lasted, the worst it felt. "Look at me," he exhaled. "I said, look at me."

"No!" she cried. "Someone help me! Help me!"

"Look at me. Look at me while I cum," he moaned.

"Help!" Melody slapped him. He held her hand down.

"Say something, Melody. I can't cum unless you say something. Oh, look at me."

She finally gave up the fight. She fooled herself to think she could win, anyway.

"Say…say my name, Melody."

She sucked in tears. "It hurts, Keith! Please stop!" She tugged at his shirt.

"Tell me you like it," he begged. "Tell me you like it Melody, please. Oh!" He tightened inside of her. Liquid shot out of him with such force that Melody quaked underneath him. He collapsed on top of her. He lightly chuckled. His chuckle turned into heated laughter.

"Guess I won the game, huh?" He touched her messed-up blouse. Melody could barely see him for the blinding tears. "Mel…" He leaned toward her.

"Get off me!" She punched him. Keith flipped off the couch in pain. She grabbed her purse from the floor. She slapped tears from her face. "I'll kill you if you come near me again! I swear to God, I will!"

"Kill me." He struggled from the floor, grinning.

"You sick motherfucker! You're gonna lose everything! You're gonna lose Sarah, your job, your freedom!" She ran to the door.

"We both know I won't!" Keith stood. He fixed his pants. "No one would believe you, Melody."

"Sarah will!"

"I don't know about that." He straightened the pillows on the couch. "I know you won't tell. Not unless you want our next meeting to take on the same turn as this one." He lifted an eyebrow. "You'll keep your mouth shut if you know what's good for you, Melody."

"You stay away from me," she whispered. "Stay away!" She ran out the door.

Keith looked at his feet. He picked up the gold, dangling

leaf-shaped earring from the carpet. "*Melody*," he whispered. He took the earring upstairs.

Melody flew through red lights. She skidded in other people's lanes. She didn't give a damn. For all she knew Keith had decided to follow her. Everything she looked at reminded her of the rape. The lights in parking lots, broken beer bottles on the streets, cars...every damn thing reminded her. She nearly choked to keep from vomiting. She could not care less about the dangerous driving.

She ignored the people who honked at every move she made. She didn't pay attention to anything! She couldn't think of anything but what had happened. When she closed her eyes, she saw Keith's face. She rubbed her raggedy skirt. She could actually feel him inside of her, even *now*. She couldn't make out red lights from white ones due to her unruly crying.

She lost contact with everything in the world. She couldn't feel herself driving. She couldn't feel herself moving. She couldn't think of anything but this nagging newfound terror. A terror she hadn't ever experienced. A terror she didn't dream existed. A terror that would change her life forever, because now, it would be the only thing she'd ever remember.

"God." She sniffed. She jumped back into reality. She

tried to shift into another lane. Her wrists locked. The wheel twisted and turned underneath her control. She couldn't see. She couldn't hit the brake fast enough. The car drifted to the side. Someone honked from the right. Melody froze. She shut her eyes. She completely lost control of the jeep.

"Melody?" She awoke in a hospital room with Craig standing over her. She wasn't sure which hospital. She didn't care. He took her hand. She flinched. He immediately moved away. He sniffed. "Mel, are you all right?"

"Do you know what happened to me?" she whispered through a hoarse voice.

"The police drove you to the hospital after the accident, Mel."

"I'm not talking about the accident." She stayed turned away from him. She couldn't bear to look at his face. "I was raped." She nearly threw up just saying it.

"Yes, I know that, too." His voice shook. "I spoke with the doctor just now. She said you've already had your exams and everything. Do you remember?"

"Vaguely. What, did I pass out from shock?"

"No, they gave you something to relax you. You were irate when they brought you in. Oh, Mel." He reached for her. She moved before he could. "Can you look at me so I can see if you're all right?"

"I love you, Craig," she whimpered.

"Mel, I love you, too. I feel like this is my fault. I should have gone with you." She finally turned to face him. "With it being so dark and with all the strange things that's been happening. Damn it." He hit his thighs. "You, uh…" He wiped tears. Melody couldn't remember him ever crying. At times, she'd forgotten how close they really were. "You know you can come to me, right? With anything?"

"Craig, uh…" She wiped tears. "You gotta understand that this is very uncomfortable, okay? I can't just talk to…you just…can you understand?" He smiled.

"I appreciate you for being here, but I can't talk to you about it. I just can't."

"Not about any of it so that I can help?" She recognized the pain in his voice. "You shouldn't be alone right now. You can come to me with anything." She nodded.

"Is, uh…is this gonna change you?" he whispered. Honestly, she didn't know. Everything resembled pain to her. She knew she'd done more damage than help by rejecting Craig's offer. She'd never felt so helpless and unattractive in her life. Already, he looked at her like a victim. She found that worse than what she'd been through. She'd been violated. With that came a humiliation she couldn't put into words.

She shut her eyes.

She remembered being carried from her jeep by two officers. She remembered the blank looks when the doctors first saw her. She clenched her hospital gown. She'd remember every piece of this night. She wouldn't ever have the power to forget it.

"What are you thinking?" Craig leaned against the bed.

"My jeep. Silly, huh?"

"They drove it here. There wasn't much damage."

"Did I hurt anyone?"

"No, you just skidded to the side, but stopped before hitting anyone or anything. At least that's a good thing. But it's you I'm worried about."

"The accident won't break me, Craig."

"But will the rape?" he whispered. She looked at him. "How did it happen?"

Sarah walked in. Craig did a double-take. Melody had forgotten that Craig believed Sarah had been sick. Melody rubbed her forehead. She thought dealing with Craig had been difficult. It wouldn't compare to explaining things to Sarah. She loved Sarah with all her heart. How could Melody hurt her by telling her Keith raped her?

"Sarah." Craig stepped from the bed. "Are you okay?" he asked.

She stared at Melody. "Why wouldn't I be okay?" She rushed to the bed. Melody turned from her gaze.

"Craig, can you give Sarah and I some time to be alone?"

"Sure, Mel," he sighed. "I really am sorry. I wish there was something I could do."

"I know." She smiled. He left. She looked at Sarah's torn face. "Who told you?"

"The police called me. They saw the address and phone

number when they took your purse." Sarah shivered. "Mel, I don't know what to say. I can't believe this."

"Sarah, please don't cry."

"I have to! You're my little sister! How could this happen to you? All these years I thought I did my best to protect you, then this happens."

"Sarah, this isn't anyone's fault except for who did this to me." Melody shook her head. "I don't ever want to blame you for it."

"But if you had still been at home this wouldn't have happened."

"It easily could have, Sarah."

"No." She took Melody's hand. "It's *my* fault because I abandoned you. I turned my back on you and look what happened! I cannot believe this. Why would someone hurt you like this?" She rubbed Melody's hair. "Melody, I'm so sorry. I'm going to do everything I can to help you through this."

It wasn't easy looking into Sarah's eyes and not telling her what Keith had done. Melody swore she'd tell everyone about tonight. But something prevented her from it when she realized the consequences. She just couldn't bear to tell Sarah the truth. She still couldn't hurt her, even if it meant making Keith pay for this terrible crime. She only looked at Sarah's sad green eyes to know that telling her right now wouldn't be the answer.

"Melody?" Sarah kissed her hand. "How did it happen? Do you know the man who did this to you?"

She cleared her throat. "I was driving down Valley Road."

"Valley Road? Keith lives close to there. Where were you going?"

"I needed some fresh air so I left Craig's. You know how driving helps me think. I've had so much on my mind considering what had happened between you and me. Sarah, I've missed you so much."

"I missed you, too, Mel. But that's over now. Nothing's gonna break us apart." *Not even Keith?* Melody wondered. "Mel, I promise you we are gonna get the bastard who did this to you. I don't care what we have to do! He won't get away with this."

Melody continued with the story. Lying seemed to come so easily at this point. "My jeep started hesitating. I got out to see what was the matter with it."

"You got out on the street alone at night?"

"I know, it's the dumbest thing I could have done. I had to check under the hood."

Sarah cuddled Melody's hand. "You always did know a lot about cars."

"Yeah, well everything seemed okay. When I was going to get back in, uh…a man grabbed me. He ordered me back inside." Sarah panted. "He told me not to scream or anything. I think he had a knife but I can't be sure. He had something I believe. Then he…" She stared at the wall. "He raped me."

"Oh God," Sarah sobbed. "Oh, Mel."

"It happened so fast, really. I couldn't comprehend what was going on until it was almost over. I just kept screaming and begging for him to get off me."

"And no one saw you being attacked right there on the road?"

Melody hadn't thought of that. She shrugged. "Well, it was on a desolate part of Valley Road, away from the traffic." Sarah nodded. "Plus, it was so dark tonight I don't think anyone could have seen us in the jeep."

"Cops pass through that area religiously." Sarah bit her lip. "And not one passed through tonight?"

"Obviously not." Melody shrugged.

"How did he look?" Sarah gazed into her eyes.

This would be the hardest part. She couldn't reveal the real rapist. Would Sarah even believe her if she had? She loved Keith. Worse of all, Sarah felt she knew Keith more than anything. She wouldn't accept Melody accusing him of rape. It just wouldn't add up with her. Keith had set Melody up with sheer brilliance. He'd planned to rape her knowing damn well that she wouldn't tell Sarah the truth.

He knew she could never hurt Sarah. Telling Sarah the truth would hurt her unlike anything. She couldn't shoot a hole in her sister's heart. She couldn't tear through Sarah's soul and watch her bleed to death. This had been the one person who loved her unconditionally. Sarah had always been there when Melody needed her. She'd been a friend, mother, and confidante.

She'd taken her in. She made sure she had everything she needed. She even put up with Melody's strange disposition and smart mouth. So how could she destroy Sarah's love, though it sickened Melody, for Keith by telling the truth? People always said Melody looked out for others more than herself. She supposed they were right. She'd do it again, right now.

She couldn't hurt Sarah just to make Keith pay. And he'd known that. The bastard played her like he invented the game.

"Honey, take your time," Sarah whispered. "Can you tell me anything? We need to know what to tell the police."

"Sarah, I don't want to go to the police."

"Mel, you have to! This man could hurt someone else. Besides that, he raped you! I'm not gonna let him get away with this. Now please tell me what you remember about him."

"I'm trying to forget it, Sarah."

"Melody, you have to do this. Can you tell me anything about the man who raped you?"

"Sarah, please, I don't want to talk about it right now." She still wasn't sure if she should say it had been Keith or not. She just knew she couldn't deal with this now. She needed at least tonight to rest.

"Okay, I won't pressure you. But we gotta go to the police as soon as you're comfortable, Mel." Sarah rubbed her hair. "The doctor says you can leave when you get ready. Are you going to Craig's or coming home with me?"

Melody sobbed. "You don't even have to ask." They hugged.

A middle-aged blonde lady walked in. "Melody Cruz?" The lady smiled. "Hello. I'm from the Rape Center."

Melody sighed.

Sarah snuggled beside Keith on his couch later that night. She hadn't wanted to leave Melody alone. Melody insisted she'd be fine. Sarah figured a need for solitude came natural with a rape victim. She sniffed into her teacup. She loved the aroma of mint and cinnamon tea. Keith had been the only guy she knew who could whip up homemade tea recipes.

She glanced around the gorgeous living room. He'd created the perfect setting with candles and light snacks. She hadn't been sure of things before she came here tonight. Keith's arms always rescued her from the worst moments. She looked into his intense, mysterious eyes. He smirked. She loved that sly smile of his. He had the power to unleash all of her emotions with just a glance.

He took her hand. She laid her head on his shoulder. She'd never been so in love. She actually felt guilty for being happy while Melody went through such pain.

"You okay?" Keith whispered. She nodded. "I hope

you don't blame yourself. Sarah, you couldn't have pre-vented it."

"I made so many mistakes with her, Keith."

He stared into his tea. "Because of me, right? If that's the case, then this is just as much my fault as anyone's."

"No, honey." She kissed him. "This is the rapist's fault." He looked away. "You probably don't understand the bond between sisters. With sisters, you feel like that's the only person in the world you have…each other. You're not that close to your brother so you may not understand."

"So I did come between you two?"

She sighed. "If you did it was my doing, Keith. I was the one who made the choice."

He touched her chin. "Do you regret the choice you've made? Because all I want to do is be with you, Sarah." He kissed her. She relaxed in his arms as if nothing else mattered. He gently pulled her away. "How much do you love me, Sarah?"

"Oh, Keith, I've never loved anyone like you. Melody could never understand the hold you have on me." He smiled. "I can't understand it, either. All I know is that when I look into your eyes, I know everything will be okay. I know we were meant to be together. By this time I usually get bored." She grinned. "But I could never get bored with you. I love you so much, Keith."

"Sarah, I hope I never disappoint you."

She grinned. "How could you? You seem to live to make

my dreams come true. Keith, the only way I could be disappointed is if this ended." She wrapped her arm around his shoulder. She rested her head against his chest. She even loved how he smelled. A manly, hungry scent that left her breathless.

"I have a feeling you want to say something else." He rubbed her thick crinkles.

"Keith, from now on, I want to do what's best for Melody. I hope you understand that."

"Oh, of course, Sarah. I know how hard this must be for her. It's terrible what happened. I hope she really is doing okay."

"It's too soon to tell. She's being strong, but that's how Melody is. She doesn't break easily."

"I've noticed. You must be proud of the kind of woman she turned out to be."

She nodded. "Keith, would you mind not coming to the house for a while? I want Melody to be able to heal and I don't want her dealing with any conflicts so..."

He pressed a finger to her lips. "You don't even have to ask. I completely understand. This is gonna take some time. I'll do whatever makes you happy." She smiled. "But what about work? It will be impossible for me to stay away from her all the time. We have to butt heads at one point or another."

She bit her lip. "I didn't think of work. She can't not go. It's too soon for a vacation. Shit, and she's been doing so well."

Keith looked at his watch. "It's no problem, Sarah. I think I need some days off."

"Oh, Keith, thank you." She hugged him.

"You sure you're okay?" He rubbed her back. She nodded. "Did Melody tell you anything about the attack?" She moved away from him. "Did she say anything about the rapist?"

"She says she'll share that with the police and I didn't want to pressure her." He gaped. "You okay? You look like a train ran over your foot." She grinned.

"Oh yeah, I'm fine." He rubbed his head. "Just got a lot on my mind these days."

Chapter Fifteen

"This is an outrage!" Commissioner Reynolds paced around Captain Jersey's office. Agent Parsons lit a cheap cigarette. "Jersey, you damn well better have an answer for this or you'll be answering to the mayor yourself!"

"Commissioner, I don't know how this happened! I had no idea!"

"You had no idea?" Parsons winked. "Come on now, Captain. He's one of your officers and you strike me as the kind to protect her officers, no matter the case."

She stood from her desk. She held her straight hips. "Are you implying that I had something to do with this? I don't know who in the hell you think you are, but I have spent most of my life working for law enforcement. I sure as hell wouldn't go along with something like this! I was probably a cop before you were born!"

"How could you not know Steven Kemp has escaped?" Parsons glared. "We're waiting."

"I don't go traipsing through the holding cells every damn minute." She walled her eyes. "And I am not about to stand here and take this in my own office!"

Parsons grinned. "Getting mighty huffy for someone who claims she doesn't know the deal." He walled his eyes. "The fact is that Kemp escaped sometime this evening. I just can't believe you didn't know."

"You think I went down there and let him out, Parsons?" Jersey huffed. "I really don't give a damn what you think! Commissioner, I refuse to take this from this little weasel!"

"Hey!" Parsons grinned.

"Enough!" Reynolds rubbed his forehead. "Jersey, you'd better not have anything to do with this." She sighed. "I've known you a long time. I'd hate to think you'd aid Steven Kemp in escaping jail."

"Sir, I wouldn't! I honestly didn't know he was gone until now!"

Parsons chewed his cigarette. "But I bet there's someone who does know. Someone who may have even helped Kemp escape."

Jersey squinted. "Now wait a minute. I see what you're getting at and you're barking up the wrong tree, Parsons. Besides, Detective Morris had the day off. And Brianna wouldn't go along with this kind of thing, anyway. As much as she cares for Steven, she'd want him to do the right thing."

"Sounds noble, Captain Jersey. Too bad I don't buy it. Do you buy it, Commissioner?"

He exhaled. "I think we should at least pay Detective Morris a visit." He headed for the door.

"But, sir…" Jersey waved her hand. He turned to look at her.

"And Jersey, if you did have anything to do with this, then believe me, you won't have to *wait* to retire." He walked out.

Parsons smirked. "Have a nice night, Captain." He shut the door.

"Little weasel." Captain Jersey relaxed in her chair.

"What the hell?" Brianna grabbed her dinner from the kitchen counter. Davis sat beside the microwave licking his paws. Brianna wasn't exactly shocked to see her piece of meatloaf missing from the plate. She stared at Davis. Apparently he'd grown quite an appetite today. First it started with that missing waffle left over from breakfast, then the three homemade peanut butter cookies she made for snacks.

She swore some grapes were missing from the fruit bowl, too. She sighed. Now her meatloaf? She didn't know what had gotten into Davis. She vowed to put an end to this very quickly.

"All right you little thief." She tapped her fingers on the counter. "Now I could excuse everything else, but when you put your paws on my meatloaf, it's on." Davis turned around. "Don't you turn away from me." She grabbed him up. "What's the deal, huh?" He purred. "I know you can't be pregnant unless you know something I don't. Why are you stealing all my food?"

She noticed a glass of milk on the table. She looked at Davis. She could see him getting the cookies, grapes and meatloaf. But she couldn't remember the last time a cat could go into the refrigerator and pour a glass of milk. Especially when someone drank out of it. Davis galloped on the table. Had she lost her mind? Had she become so stressed that she couldn't remember doing things? "Meow." Davis cuddled against her arms as if he wondered the same thing. Someone knocked on the door.

"Okay, cool it." She carried Davis to the door. "You're not exactly off the hook yet." She thought the missing food struck her off course. It didn't compare to her surprise at the door.

"Commissioner Reynolds!" Brianna dropped Davis. He scurried into the den. Parsons stared oddly at the feline.

Brianna pushed down the ends of her flimsy shorts. She straightened the curls that had fallen from her fluffy ponytail. She looked a mess. She had more important things to deal with at the moment.

Reynolds looked past her into her home. "Detective Morris, we're here on official business. This is very important." She knew it had to be. *Since when did the police commissioner make house calls?*

She fiddled with her hair. "Sir, uh, is something wrong?" Two uniformed cops walked up behind Parsons.

"We're here to search your home." Parsons held up

his hand. "Before you dispute this, we've got a warrant." He passed it to her. "Step aside, please."

"Search my home?" She stared at the warrant. *Only the commissioner himself could have gotten this done so fast.* She looked at them. "Commissioner Reynolds, sir, I don't know what this is about! Am I being accused of something?"

"It's funny how all these people suddenly don't know things."

"Agent Parsons, are you getting at something?" Brianna held her hip.

Reynolds glared at her. He walked in without an invitation. The others did the same. "Steven Kemp has escaped from jail." Brianna gaped. "Just disappeared into thin air, it seems. We figured you'd know something about that."

"Commissioner Reynolds, I swear I didn't know about this! How could Steven be so stupid? You have to believe me, sir! I was off today! I've been around the house. I had no idea!"

"Well, even if we bought that, which we don't, we're gonna search your place. We figure you may know more than you're letting on." Parsons ordered the officers to begin their search.

"Now wait a minute! Commissioner?" Brianna exhaled.

Reynolds went into the living room without a word.

Parsons headed upstairs. "I think I'll check the bedroom. Seems the best place to look." He grinned.

"Hey, you can't just come in here and search my place

like this! I'm an officer of the law! You're treating me like a damn criminal! I know my rights!" She followed Parsons upstairs. "Who in the hell do you think you are?" They went into the bedroom.

"Get out of my house!"

Parsons looked at the pictures on her dresser. "You realize how much trouble you could be in if you did help Steven Kemp escape, Detective?"

"I did not help him escape! I told you I didn't know a damn thing about this until you showed up!" Parsons opened the top dresser drawer. "Get out of there!"

"Just checking." He smirked.

"In my panty drawer?" She slammed it shut. He went to the closet. "Oh, this is insane! Steven is not here!" She crossed her arms. "And you know what? I wouldn't tell you if I *did* know where he is!"

He stood in front of her. "For some reason I don't trust you, Bree."

She scoffed. "First thing, get out of my face with your breath smelling like ass!" Parsons covered his mouth. "Second, don't call me, 'Bree.' It's 'Detective Morris' to you, jerk!"

He blew his breath into his hands. He blushed from embarrassment. "Where's Kemp?"

"For the last damn time, I don't know!"

"There's no one here, sir." A uniformed cop stood in the bedroom doorway. They all went downstairs.

"See? I didn't have anything to do with it!" Brianna

insisted. Reynolds came from the kitchen. "Sir, I swear I don't know where Steven Kemp is. But can't you see this proves he's innocent?"

"And how do you figure that?"

She ignored Parsons. "Commissioner, Steven would never break the law unless he had good reason. He knows that if you all won't believe he's not the rapist, then he has to find the rapist."

"Then in that case, all he has to do is look in the mirror." Parsons lit a cigarette. Brianna snatched it. "What are you doing?" he growled.

"No smoking in my damn house!" She flicked the cigarette back at Parsons.

"Commissioner, I swear I don't know what's going on."

"I tell you what, Detective Morris. We'll be talking to you tomorrow. And by then you'd better know damn well where Kemp is." Reynolds rubbed his mustache.

"And if I don't?" She shifted back and forth.

"Then you'll take his place in that cell for aiding and abetting a fugitive. Let's go, Parsons." They went to the front door.

"Sir!" Brianna scampered behind them on bare feet. "I had nothing to do with this! You can't hold me accountable!"

"Yes, I can! I don't believe a word you're saying, Morris. But you'd better have something tomorrow, or you can forget ever working on any police force again!"

"But, Commissioner!" she shrieked.

"If we find out you did help Kemp somehow, then I swear Morris, your black ass won't be able to get a job as a security guard at Wal-Mart! Let's go, Parsons!"

"Yes, sir." Parsons grinned at Brianna. Davis ran from the living room. He doused Parsons' foot. "Hey! Shit!" He shook his leg. The uniformed cops laughed.

"Your damn cat just pissed on my foot!"

Brianna walled her eyes. "Well, you'll have to excuse him, Parsons. I guess since your breath smells like kitty litter, he got confused."

"Ha, ha!" The cops laughed out the front door.

"Yeah?" Parsons pointed at her. "Let's see how funny you are tomorrow." He slammed the door.

She paced, muttering to herself. "Damn it, Steve! How could you do something so stupid?"

"Well…" Steven came downstairs. "I didn't have a choice really." He wore shabby oversized sweats.

"Steve!" She did a double-take.

"Now don't get mad, Bree. I had to come here."

"Steven, I could wring your neck! You know how much trouble I almost got into? What in the hell are you doing here, anyway?"

"Well, I couldn't go to my place! I had to come here to regroup. I've been here all day. Haven't you noticed? Getting slow in your old age, huh, Bree?" He grinned.

"Damn you. So this explains the missing cookies,

grapes, meatloaf and glass of milk?" She held her waist.

"Yeah." He held his stomach. "Those cookies were out of this world. How come you never baked when we dated? The meatloaf was a little salty, though."

She grumbled. "I sure as hell wouldn't know since you ate mine!"

Steven looked at Davis. "Did you rat me out, buddy?" He picked the cat up. "He missed me. Been a while since we hung out together."

"Steve, what the hell do you think you're doing?" she screamed.

"Saving my life, Bree. Besides, I'd been in that place more than a week and I couldn't take it anymore. I'm innocent and I'm gonna get the rapist."

"You could have been out a week ago if you had taken the DNA test. Steven, this is only going to get you in more trouble! It's going to get *me* into trouble! Did you hear what Commissioner Reynolds said? I could lose my job because of you!"

"I won't let that happen, Bree. I could never jeopardize your career."

"Well, that's exactly what you're doing just by being here!" She felt her forehead. "Wait, how come they didn't find you when they searched?"

He grinned. "I was in the linen closet. Guess they didn't think to look there." He nuzzled Davis with his chin. The cat meowed happily. "I'm sorry, Bree. Just let me lay low here. I promise it won't be for long."

"Steven, it's already been long enough." She sighed.

❖❖❖

Melody lay in bed the next morning staring at the ceiling. She hadn't slept all night. Every now and then she leaned to get a glimpse of the clock. The time didn't matter. It would be impossible to even pretend she could go on with her normal routine. She'd been raped? It had happened to her. She'd been there. She'd lived it but she still couldn't believe it.

It wasn't that she felt it couldn't happen to her, but it had been the shock that prevented her from facing reality. She thought of Aileen. The situation had been totally different. Which had been worse? Being raped by a serial rapist, or your sister's boyfriend? She had no idea things would go this far. She wondered how long Keith had planned the attack.

Had it been when she reported him to Mr. Lawson? He threatened her with a vengeance that same day. Told her flat out she'd need to call the cops. How insane could he really be? She felt a menacing chill. The situation with Keith had gone from annoying to treacherous in a few short months. Melody sat up in bed. She finally saw the big picture. It scared her half to death.

Of course! The game he played with Melody had nothing to do with her. Keith wanted to keep control over Sarah. Melody slipped the covers from her legs. She stared at the floppy T-shirt she'd worn to bed. He'd always said he loved Sarah like no other. Melody didn't know how many women he'd actually loved. She didn't know a damn thing about his past.

She didn't know anything about his family. She didn't know anything about where he'd come from. Nothing. All she knew was that he raped her. That he'd do all he could to keep Sarah. Sarah jumped like a puppet on strings when Keith paid her attention. He manipulated people like no other. He had manipulated Sarah to the point where she'd sided with him.

Melody rubbed her mouth. It took being raped by the bastard to catch on to his game. It wasn't normal the way he paid so much attention to Sarah. It wasn't normal the way he'd popped into her life and made all of her dreams come true. It certainly hadn't been normal how he acted with Melody. Melody always knew she could see something in Keith no one else did. Even after all he'd done to her, this revelation frightened her the most.

Keith hadn't raped Melody simply for sex. Sure, the asshole had obviously enjoyed violating her, knowing he'd hurt her in a way that would scar her forever. But that hadn't been his main reason. All this time, all the shit he did had been for Sarah. Melody knew it went way beyond admiration on Keith's behalf. He always said he'd let no one take Sarah away from him.

Didn't that borderline on obsession? Keith went through life controlling everyone around him. When he couldn't control them, he became violent. He'd done it with Melody last night. So, why wouldn't he do the same thing to Sarah, too?

Melody paced. Sarah would be in more danger than Melody ever could. Sarah didn't know how sick Keith could be. She didn't know how far he'd go. Melody sighed. She'd spent all this time trying to convince Sarah to leave Keith without realizing how dangerous that would be. Her antics only pushed Sarah further into the devil's arms.

Something told her the rape had only been a sample of what he could do. Who knew where it ended if he didn't get what he wanted? He wanted *Sarah*. Keith being dangerous was hard enough. But worse than that, he believed he could do anything he wanted and get away with it. Melody saw firsthand how he acted when people refused him. She'd lived through a terror she'd never face because of it.

Yet something told her Sarah would pay a bigger price. Melody rubbed her quivering thighs. Every time she shut her eyes, she ended up back on that couch being raped. She couldn't stop thinking about Keith tearing inside of her. Ignoring her screams. Inflicting more physical and emotional pain than anyone could deal with. She got back into bed. She wasn't going to work. She nearly died *thinking* of Keith. She damn well couldn't be in the same building with him!

She didn't know what to do at this point. She only knew that Sarah would end up in terrible danger if Keith stayed around.

❖❖❖

Okay, this was it. Brianna stood from her desk. The other detectives stopped in mid-sentence to eye the spectacle. Brianna had been raised to be a lady. It wasn't too easy with men like Agent Parsons. He stood beside her desk with a cigarette cocked from the side of his mouth. Ooh, that smug smile. She didn't know how Steven controlled himself from punching Parsons.

She nearly had to be held back from killing him. He could say what he damned well pleased in private, but Brianna wasn't going to take him disrespecting her or Steven in front of their peers.

"You know, I've had just about enough of you, Parsons." She threw her pencil on her desk. Cunningham gaped. "You don't give a damn about helping those women. You just want to lock up Steven so you can add another notch to your file. Steven Kemp is not a rapist! How many times do I have to say it? I'd go to prison for him if I had to prove he's innocent myself!"

"That's right!" a detective yelled. "Steve's not a rapist!"

"Yeah, asshole!" Another detective waved. "Steve's one of the best damn cops in this place!"

"So I see, cops really do stick together." Parsons grinned.

"Yeah." Cunningham stood. "Maybe *you* should try it."

Parsons grinned. "Before tearing into me, Detective, you should have asked why I came."

Brianna scoffed. "I know why. You came to cause trouble for Steven. We've all had enough of you, Parsons! You don't give a shit about finding out the truth."

He sighed. "Well, that's not the most important issue this moment, is it?"

Brianna glared. "What are you talking about?"

"Let's see how much you stand up for Steven Kemp once you hear this. There was another rape around three a.m. this morning. A young black schoolteacher named Candace Bridges was raped in her home." Brianna's anger slithered into shock. "Oh, that's right, Detective. I wouldn't sprout off so easily next time before I heard the facts."

"Well…" She cleared her throat. "It doesn't mean anything. What does that have to do with Steven?"

"You know exactly what. You think it's just a coincidence that this happened? Steven is the Albany Predator!" He looked around the room. "When are you all gonna stop protecting him and realize the truth? Just because you've known him doesn't mean a damn thing! He's out there raping women! If you all called yourselves true cops, you'd help bring him into justice!"

"That's not true!" Brianna looked at her fellow officers. The detectives sat dumbfounded. She could see the doubt filling the heads of the men and women Steven had known for years. This wasn't a good thing. What worried her most had been the doubt she felt in hers. Steven left her home in the middle of the night. Why would he have done that? She thought she had an answer before Parsons dropped this bomb.

"Still sticking up for Kemp, Morris?"

"It doesn't mean a thing, Parsons."

"Well, look at the damn picture, would you? Stop playing me, Morris! You see the connection here! While Steven was in jail, there were no rapes!"

"You don't know that!"

He shook his head. "Well, we haven't had any that seemed to be connected to the Predator, have we?" Brianna turned away. "So explain to me how there's another rape the minute Kemp escapes from jail!"

"I..."

"You can't, can you? And here's another thing that you might want to know, Morris. Candace Bridges lives about two blocks from Steven Kemp." She stared at him.

"Oh yes, it's true."

"I don't care what you say, Parsons. Steven didn't rape anyone." She sighed.

"Oh." He grinned. "You don't seem so sure now, Morris. Okay, how do you know he didn't rape Ms. Bridges? Do you know where he was at three in the morning? You know where he ran off to when he escaped?"

"I told you I had nothing to do with that." She sat down. He leaned over her. The detectives watched in silence.

"Why don't you just realize that Steven Kemp is not the man you thought he was, Brianna. This man is a sadistic rapist. He doesn't give a damn who he hurts. If he was so innocent, why didn't he want to take that DNA test?" She rubbed her forehead. "How come Cheyenne and Aileen can identify him to a T? How come he escaped from jail? What kind of 'innocent' guy would do something like that?"

"You don't know what you're saying, Parsons. I...I know Steven."

"Yeah? What about when the Predator attacked *you*? How in the hell did he know that you and Steven used to be lovers? Was it ever in the newspapers? I don't think so." Parsons squinted. "You know damn well how he knows. He knows because he's Steven! And what about how Steven fits all the sketches? Lookalike, my ass! He's the rapist! When are you gonna see that, Brianna?"

Her hands shook.

"You okay, Morris?" Cunningham stared at her. She didn't answer.

Parsons stood erect. "She's fine. She's just finally absorbing the truth. I'm sorry, Morris. I know you really care about him. But you have a duty to protect these women. You gonna help us find Kemp or not?"

"I don't know where he is," she whispered. She stared ahead as if she were in a trance.

"Okay, fine." Parsons straightened his jacket. "But I have a feeling this will end up affecting your life more than anyone else's. I'm just doing my job, Detective. Maybe it's time you do yours." He left.

❖❖❖

"Stop," Melody whispered to herself. She stood by her bed. She abandoned unpacking when the rape forced its way into her head for the millionth time today. Craig had been very attentive. He happily brought her things over for her. He, of course, asked if he could do anything to help. Melody could only ask him to leave. Even being close to Craig seemed unnatural right now.

She took her red blouse from the suitcase. She did her best to block out the horrible recollections of the rape. Once again, she couldn't stop it.

Keith's hungry dark eyes stared into hers. He plunged his middle against her thighs. She slapped her fists on his chest to keep him at bay. He became stronger the more she fought him. "Stop!" Melody screamed. Keith entered her despite protest. Melody cringed and moaned from merciless pain. "Stop!" He jabbed his crotch inside of her. Melody twisted and turned on a couch that felt as rough as a bed of nails.

"You're mine, Melody. All mine tonight…" Keith smirked.

Someone grabbed her from behind! She felt herself being lifted off the floor.

"Oooh, I got you! I won't let you go! You're all mine now!" Someone kissed her cheeks. She struggled in his arms.

"Stop!" she bellowed. She grabbed the open suitcase. She whirled around before she had a chance to think. She smacked him. He twirled on the carpet. "Don't you ever touch me again! Don't you dare touch me again!" She held the suitcase high. She stopped when she saw the trembling hands. His eyes begged for mercy.

"Melody!" Lucas shielded his face from another attack.

"Oh God." She lowered the suitcase. She rested on the bed. "Oh, Lucas!" she wailed.

"Melody." He rushed to hold her. She thought she'd feel uncomfortable in his arms. She didn't. She felt safe. She needed that right now. "Mel, what's wrong?" He moved her hair from her face. "Huh? What's going on?"

"Oh, I'm sorry!" She cried into her hands. "I'm sorry!" She wrapped her hands around his neck. She forced him closer. "I'm so sorry, Lucas!"

He rubbed her back. "It's okay, Melody. I don't have a clue what you're talking about, but it's okay. I'm not hurt. I shouldn't have sneaked up on you like that, anyway, baby. I'm the one who's sorry. What was I thinking? Did you know your front door was unlocked? You gotta be more careful."

"Oh, Lucas." She lay against his chest.

"I missed you at work today. I wanted to see what was going on. I started to call first but I thought surprising you would be better." He chuckled. "Guess that idea stunk, huh? Well, this is certainly one time when you can't accuse me of being perfect." He smiled.

She touched his soft skin. She looked into his charming eyes. "Lucas, I love you so much. I don't want to lose you."

"You're not gonna lose me, but I do want to know what's going on. I know I scared you but you damn near killed me just now." He chuckled. "And you're shaking, Mel." He touched her hands. "You're breathing hard. I know something's wrong. You can tell me anything."

She wanted so much to tell him. Lucas made everything all right when no one else could. She just didn't know how he'd react. He'd always understood things, yet this would change their entire relationship. Once he found out she'd been raped, he'd never look at her the same way again. He'd never smile at her the same way. He'd always be too cautious. Always treat her like a helpless victim. He'd want to protect her first thing.

Melody didn't want his *protection*. She just wanted someone, anyone to make what happened go away. If Lucas could do that, then he'd have her heart for life.

"Mel, talk to me. We're all alone now. When I said you could come to me with anything, I meant it." He touched her face. "I mean it, baby."

"Not with this." She sniffed.

"Anything." He nodded. "I love you, Melody. That's not gonna change."

"Lucas, it's not easy at all." She stood from the bed. "We were doing so well. We were getting so close. Now all of that's gonna change. You won't look at me the same. You'll be guarded around me all the time. I don't want that!"

"Melody, I don't know what's happened to you, but I promise it won't change us."

She looked at her fingers. "It's gonna definitely change some things, Lucas. You will start to resent me, even if you don't want to. It's only natural!"

He grabbed her. "No, I won't." He stared into her eyes. "Melody, I love you like I never loved any woman. I always have. You're always pushing me away and I want that to end tonight. I'll be there for you. No matter what you say, baby, I'll be there for you no matter what. I love you and I'll do all I can to be with you."

"You can't mean that."

"I do." He touched her chin. He wiped her tears with his fingertip. "You can tell me anything, Melody. We'll just get through it together. Nothing could be that bad, okay?" He guided her to sit beside him again. "Now tell me what's going on with you."

She exhaled. She looked at the dresser. She looked at the carpet. She looked at her Jennifer Lopez poster on the wall. Anything to ignore looking into his eyes. She finally gave in. "Lucas." He nodded. "I was *raped*."

Melody passed Lucas a bowl of ice cream twenty minutes later. They sat at the kitchen table. She couldn't believe how easy it had been to explain things to him. She found it hard to even talk to Sarah about it. She wanted to go one step further and tell Lucas who had raped her. She wasn't ready for that yet. She stared into his eyes. He didn't smile. She didn't expect him to. Anyone would be shocked right now. What guy expects his girlfriend to tell him something like this?

He stirred the large spoon through the clumps of vanilla ice cream. Melody understood when he pushed the bowl away. She hadn't eaten much today herself. It seemed like everything died when Keith raped her. She had no real emotions, appetite, drive or interests. She just kept thinking of the rape hour on the hour. She wondered if that would ever end.

"Do you, uh, want to say something?" she whispered.

He rubbed his chin. "Did you go to the police?"

"No. I, uh, I don't know if I wanna even go that route."

"Melody, you can't let this guy get away with what he's done. I tell you, if I ever meet up with him, I'll kill him." He pounded his fist to the table. "I will absolutely kill him!" That alone made her want to reveal Keith. "I just can't believe this. Aileen was raped, now you?"

"I'm sorry I didn't tell you earlier."

"You don't have a damn thing to apologize for, Melody. God, this is…it's just a shock. I can't even grasp it yet."

"Me, either." She played with her fingers. "Lucas, I don't know if I will be able to come back to work." He stared at her. "I don't think it's right for me."

"Melody, you belong at Caper. You're doing so well. Don't let this stop you from living your life."

She scoffed. "It already has."

"Not as long as I'm still here." He took her hand. "We'll get through it. It's not just your problem, but it's mine, too. I really want you to reconsider going to the police. You may be able to help other women from being raped."

"Rape, rape, rape." She sighed. "Is that all that ever happens in this city anymore? When will it all end?"

"When victims like you make a stand." He sighed.

"Damn it, Mel. I wish so much that I could change what happened."

"Shh, you can't, believe me."

"I tell you, if I ever get lucky enough to see this motherfucker, I'll kill him." He stared at the wall. "As sure as the sun shines, I'll kill him without looking back."

"I think I need to be alone now, Lucas." She stood.

"I wish you would reconsider coming back to work. You don't have to make up your mind now. I'll talk to my father, okay?"

"Don't tell him I was raped."

"No, I won't." He took her hand. "I'll just tell him you'll need some time to deal with some personal issues."

"And if he asks for details?"

He sighed. "I'll just have to make something up." He kissed her.

Chapter Sixteen

Brianna opened her front door to Steven around one a.m. She never could sleep during rain. The storm had faded into drizzling. She noticed the tiny droplets of water that clung to her porch light. Steven looked different somehow. He seemed relax. Lately he'd been so tense. She had hoped he'd come back to explain things. She had so many questions.

She hated thinking negatively about him. She was only human. You can only take so many unanswered questions.

No one could hold a candle to Steven's good looks in her eyes. He reminded her of the tanned, blond guys on the cover of romance novels. She hadn't really been attracted to a white man until Steven. He soon became someone she'd always love. No one, black or white, would ever take his place. She couldn't help hating herself for what she thought.

She kept telling herself she had an excuse. That he wasn't being completely honest, so it wasn't her fault if she doubted him. Somehow that didn't wash with her. She felt the sides of her flimsy blue nightgown. Steven's eyes drifted from her face to her breasts. He swatted raindrops from his forehead. He wasn't wearing those baggy sweats. He wore a fitted black shirt that hugged his muscular chest. Those black slacks reminded Brianna of his fantastic body. She looked down at the soaking black, leather combat boots he wore. She'd never seen him in all black before. He'd obviously had time to go shopping on the run. She wouldn't waste any time. She wanted answers. She intended to get them.

"Hello." His voice sounded hoarse, yet still held its usual charm.

"Hello, Steve. Uh, I'm glad you came back."

"Oh, you are?"

"Yes, we have some things to talk about. Come on in."

He smirked. He eagerly followed the command. He accidentally brushed up against her when she shut the door. She never remembered Steven looking at her this way before. She figured him seeing her in a nightgown might have been too much to handle. She felt her nipples tighten against her gown. Her thighs quaked. Her mound ached with the thought of giving in and ravishing him. She'd always been attracted to Steven. She just couldn't be with him. Or so she thought.

"Steve, come on into the living room." He followed. She turned on the lamps. They sat on the couch. Steven hadn't broken his stare once. "Steve, uh…" She caught the stare again. "What is it?" She chuckled.

He cocked his head to the side. "God, you're so beautiful." He brushed his warm hand against her left cheek. She shut her eyes. She couldn't afford to get lost in what they used to have. Not with so much at stake. She moved his hand. "Brianna?" He laid his hand on her naked knee.

"Steven, we have to talk, okay?"

He grinned. "We *are* talking." He caressed her knee.

She moved his hand. "I'm serious, Steven." He nodded. "Why did you leave my place last night?"

"Uh…" He scratched his head. "I just needed time to think. I…I didn't want to further involve you in this. I saw that my escape was in the papers this morning." He grinned. "Guess I'm getting a lot of attention."

"Steven, I'm serious. Why did you leave?"

He turned toward her. "Brianna, I've never cared for anyone the way I care for you. I didn't want to put you through this. I came back because I was fooling myself. I miss so much what we had."

"Steven, I want to believe in you. But there was another rape. A woman named Candace Bridges and she lives close to your neighborhood."

"Brianna, I swear I had no idea." He sneezed.

"Are you all right?"

He sneezed again. "Yeah, uh, just allergies, I suppose." He sneezed again. "God, excuse me."

"Oh, let me get you something." She passed him a tiny box of tissue from the drawer in the table. He sneezed again. After three more he finally relaxed. "You all right?"

"Yes, uh, I must be allergic to something in this room." His eyes turned red.

"I haven't done anything different. You didn't sneeze last night. Maybe it's the weather." He nodded. "Steven, you can't just run forever. Do you have some kind of theory other than the lookalike story?"

"What's wrong with that theory? You already know the rapist looks exactly like me." He gawked. "Oh, I get it. You're having doubts?"

"Steve, I care about you very much. But it's not easy to stay objective with what's been going on."

"I didn't rape anyone, Brianna." She grimaced. "Please believe that." He kissed her hand. He rubbed his other hand down her caramel thigh. He brought his mouth to her neck. He sucked gently, yet hungrily. "Now tell me…you don't want this."

"I…" She did want it. She still wanted him. She couldn't deny that forever. His touch awakened the past. She thought of how good it felt to lie naked in his arms. How handsome he looked when he came after making love. How he could bring her to slopes of ecstasy untouched by any man. She had forgotten that soothing tongue. Those commanding fingers. Those satisfying lips.

"God, I want you so bad, Brianna," he whispered in her ear. "You gotta know that. How could I get over a woman like you?" He slipped his hand inside her gown. She moaned while he took her nipple between two fingers. "You like that?" he whispered. She moaned desperately. "Want me to suck it? Huh?" He flipped her nipple with his thumb.

He slipped the gown from one shoulder. She put her hand on his chest to stop him. "Steven, wait. Uh, this doesn't feel right."

He grinned. "What the hell you talking about, Brianna? It feels right to me." He brought his mouth toward her hard black nipple. She gently held him back. "Brianna, we've already done it before. What's the big deal now?"

"*No*, Steven," she sighed. "I'll be right back. I gotta go to the bathroom."

She ran to her bathroom. She dabbed her face with warm water. She couldn't let him get to her now. She needed answers. She couldn't afford to be reminded of how great it had been to love him. The bathroom door opened behind her. She felt his breath on the back of her neck. He grabbed her hips. He roughly shoved himself against her.

"Come on now." He sucked the back of her neck. "Brianna, I love you so much."

"Steven, don't." She tried to move his hand from her sides. "Steven." He turned her around. He kissed her hungrily, to the point where she almost couldn't breathe. He lifted her gown to the level of her panties. She kept her hands on his to stop the action. All the while Steven continued kissing her. "Steven…we can't do this," she mumbled with her lips to his.

"Yes, we can. We both want it. It's natural. I know how you feel about me. You don't have to be afraid, Brianna." He pressed her against the sink. "Just tonight, Brianna. You can go back to your regular life. Just let me remember how it was for tonight." He kissed her. She pushed him away.

"I can't, Steven." She wiped her mouth. "Please just go."

"I want to make love to you, now." He went for a kiss. She moved away. "Brianna, you honestly can say you don't want me?" He chuckled.

His blue eyes didn't hold their usual compassionate flicker. Had being accused of rape changed him? Could Steven really be the rapist? She held her mouth. "Please go, Steven. You can come back another time."

"Yeah." He stood up straight. He wiped his mouth. "Yeah, I can come back, Brianna."

She stared at him. "Steven, are you all right? You seem different."

He winked. "I'm always all right." He kissed her. "I can't wait to make love to you again. The next time we meet, I will. I won't leave here until I do." He went downstairs. She slowly followed, gripping her gown along the way. He definitely knew how to twist a girl's emotions.

"Steven, where will you go? And you gotta be more careful coming around here."

"You'll be hearing from me again."

"Steven, you can't run forever."

"From them or from you?" He wrapped his arms around her waist. He pushed his lips to hers. His tongue forced her mouth open. He nearly sucked the breath from her. Suddenly he began gagging. Brianna moved away.

"Steven, are you all right?"

"I…I can't breathe!" He coughed and sneezed. "Oh God, you must have something in here I'm allergic to!"

"No, I don't."

"You must!" He coughed. Davis scampered from the living room. "The cat," he sighed. "Can't go two feet near one." He ran out the door.

Brianna glared. A brick on the head couldn't have shocked her more than this moment. She laid a finger to her trembling lips. She thought of the man she'd just made out with in the bathroom. The air tightened around her. Perspiration popped from her forehead. She ripped the door open. "Shit!" She slammed it shut. She ran to the phone. She dialed Jersey's number.

"Captain, this is Brianna!" She leaned against the living room wall.

"Morris?" Jersey exhaled. "Are you all right? You sound like you're struggling to breathe."

"I am. Oh Captain, Steven's not the rapist. I know that for sure now."

"Well, I do, too. I always did."

"No, you don't understand! I *know*!" she exhaled. "Steven hardly ever calls me 'Brianna'! He always calls me,

'Bree'! Shit! I should have realized it from the beginning!"

"Morris, what the hell are you talking about?" Jersey groaned.

"Captain, the rapist! The rapist was just here!"

"*What*? Are you all right? Did you get him?"

"No! He left before I realized it. I thought he was Steve the whole time! Captain, they look exactly alike! It's impossible to tell them apart. They could be twins!"

"Okay, take a deep breath, Morris. Tell me how you know for certain that that man is not Steven."

"Because Steven isn't allergic to cats! The man who was just here… is." Jersey nearly dropped the phone. "I can't believe I let him get away, Captain. I was so close again!"

"Believe me, you've done good enough, Morris." Jersey crossed her fingers.

"I believe we've finally got the asshole where we want him. And we'll use the perfect bait to bring him out."

"What's that?" Brianna panted.

"*You*," Jersey whispered.

Brianna and Jersey watched each other from across Jersey's desk the following morning. Commissioner Reynolds and Agent Parsons exchanged quick glances. Brianna knew her disclosure about the rapist had thrown them off balance. She couldn't have been happier for Steven's sake. The revelation still hadn't eased her recurring anxiety about the situation. Only catching the *real* rapist would do that.

Brianna looked at Reynolds. He stroked his mustache in thought. "It's the truth, sir. I know for a fact that that man in my home last night was the rapist." Reynolds sighed.

"And we're really supposed to believe this?" Parsons shook his head. "Morris, you're pathetic! You'll obviously do anything to help Kemp!"

"Why are you so against believing that Steven is innocent?" Jersey shouted. "Is that so hard to believe? Why would you want to hang a man for something he hasn't done?"

"A damn lookalike?" Parsons shouted. "We're supposed to believe this? Morris, explain why the so-called look-alike showed up at your place last night of all nights! How the hell did he know Kemp wouldn't be there, huh? And how are we supposed to believe you when you lied about Kemp being in your home in the first damn place? None of this makes any sense!"

"So you don't believe me?"

"Hell no, I don't believe you!" Parsons walled his eyes.

"I do." Reynolds cut his eyes to a shocked Parsons. "You have a problem with that?"

"Uh, no, sir." Parsons shifted awkwardly. Brianna and Jersey grinned. "But, sir, this is…it's not likely to me."

"They say everyone has a twin." Jersey shrugged.

"And they really look that much alike?" Reynolds crossed his arms.

Brianna nodded. "Exactly, sir. I wouldn't have known it wasn't Steven if he hadn't been allergic to my cat.

They talk alike, walk alike…but you know something?"

"What?" Jersey rested her elbows on the desk. She propped her hands underneath her chin.

"I kept getting the feeling that something was strange the entire time. It just didn't feel like it always did to be with Steven. Of course, with them looking so much alike, how could I know? It's amazing that he could even fool me." She shrugged. "I know Steven more than anyone. Yet, I couldn't tell even from a kiss."

"Well, look…" Parsons gaped. "A *kiss*?"

"He kissed you?" Jersey grimaced.

"Yeah, and he wanted more." Brianna crossed her legs.

"Goodness, Morris, what the heck happened in that house last night?" Parsons sighed.

"So we got a lookalike, huh?" Reynolds paced. "And Jersey, you want to use Morris as bait?" She nodded. "Morris, do you think you could get him?"

"Yes, I believe so, sir. He thinks I think he's Steven. He already said he'll be back. I got a feeling he meant very soon."

"Then what?" Parsons grimaced. "You gonna pull out the old charm, huh? Get him to admit he's the rapist? It'll never work! Jesus, you did some shabby work last night, Detective!"

"Excuse me?" Brianna stood.

Parsons shook his head. "You have one of the most wanted criminals in the nation in your house and you just let the man walk on out into the *street*? What kind of shit is that?"

"I didn't know he wasn't Steven until it was too late! He'd already left when I figured it out!"

"Just like before, huh?" he scoffed.

"I don't need this shit from you, Parsons. The bottom line is this man is still out there and we need to get him before he hurts someone else! And that could even be me."

Reynolds glared. "And how do you know he really thinks you think he's Kemp? How do you know he wasn't just playing you?"

Brianna thought of how he held her. How he'd kissed her. How he'd wanted so much more. Men rarely just left such a passionate scene without an afterthought. He may have even cared for her in some sick, sadistic way. She could only go on his claim that he'd be back. She knew in her heart that he would.

"I just know, sir." Brianna shrugged.

Jersey stood. "He'll be back and now we're a step ahead. He doesn't have a clue that we know he's not Steven." She smiled. "Morris is a brilliant officer. Nothing better than using a fine cop as bait. Especially when she's what the rapist wants. It's like dangling cheese in front of a rat."

Brianna smiled at her superior's vote of confidence.

"Okay, fine." Parsons held up his arms. "I can't step in on how you handle your case, Detective. But I'm not saying that I believe any of this, okay? So don't think that everything's outta the clear with me." Brianna grinned. "I just have one more question. If this man last night really *was* a lookalike and supposed rapist, then where the hell is *Kemp*?"

Brianna sighed. "That's the one thing I haven't figured out."

A Month Later

Lucas brushed past Keith's office door. Keith stacked files on top of his desk. He wondered. What would cause Lucas not to say hello? He hadn't seen Melody in a month. People speculated she wouldn't return to work. What would he do if she told the truth? He rubbed his face. No, she *wouldn't*. He smiled. She didn't have the guts.

Anyway, what would she say? If she did tell, he could easily dispute it. Even if that didn't work, he could make it look like they'd been having an affair. She had lied about the entire night from what Sarah told him. *Raped on the side of the street by a man she didn't know.* He'd obviously given her more credit than she deserved in the brain department. Did she realize how she'd sunk her own ship already?

Just too many lies. Not to mention an entire month has passed. She'd been known for crying wolf. No one would believe her. Keith had nothing to worry about. He caught up with Lucas in the hall. Lucas spoke with another co-worker. He headed to his office. Lucas hadn't been the same since the rape. He'd been distraught for weeks. Keith had only wanted to teach Melody a lesson. He hadn't intended on hurting Lucas.

"Hey, Luke!" Keith smacked Lucas's back. Lucas jumped.

"Hey," he muttered. He blew into his Styrofoam cup of coffee.

"Man, I've known dead people who look happier than you," Keith cackled. "Something on your mind?" They entered Lucas's office. He slunk behind his desk. He straightened his navy-blue tie. "Luke?" Keith sat down. "What's going on, man? You look like you haven't slept all night."

"I haven't." He pushed a button on his fancy office phone.

"Well, you know you can tell your boy if you're having a hard time." Keith grinned. "Nothing you can't tell me, man. I'll try to help if I can."

"It's personal, Keith." Lucas searched his desk drawer for his stapler.

"Personal." He sucked his lip. "Well, if you need me, you know where I'll be." He headed out.

"Keith," Lucas sighed. "Wait, uh, close the door." Keith did. "I appreciate you being there for me, man. You know I do. But since this involves Melody, I'm uncomfortable talking about her after what's gone on."

Keith put his hands in his pockets. "Anything you say to me won't leave me. You know that. You can trust me, Luke."

"Everything's just falling apart." Lucas rubbed his hands. "I knew she would change, but I had no idea this much in such a short while. Keith, I want to be there for her, but she's pushing me away. I know she doesn't mean to, but I can't help wondering if we should be together, after all."

"Well, I'm sorry to hear that. I haven't seen Melody since before she was raped. I've been thinking a lot about her. Sarah asked me not to come around the house a while ago. I've respected her wishes. Uh, is Melody even coming back to work?"

"Who knows?" Lucas looked at his computer. "She doesn't stick around me long enough for me to ask. Every time I call or go to see her, she makes up some flimsy excuse. No one could be as busy as she claims she is. Man, I feel like she somehow blames me for what that asshole did to her. All I want to do is be there for her. How can I, when she treats me like this?"

"Lucas, she just needs some time."

Lucas twirled a pencil. "Yeah, but I am beginning to think I don't have that amount of time to give her. Keith, I feel like I'm at a standstill. The rape has changed everything! I can't even get ahold of my own life. I feel like I'm wasting away, waiting on Melody to recover. Funny thing is that I don't know if she ever will."

Keith sat down. "This is tearing you up, huh?"

"Of course it is. She's my girlfriend. What burns me is that this motherfucker is just walking around free. I love her so much, man. I could kill anyone that hurt her."

Lucas looked at his computer. Keith hadn't ever seen his friend this distressed. All of this had been Melody's fault from the beginning! If she hadn't made things so difficult, then this wouldn't have happened. Keith wouldn't have had to teach her any lessons. She always left him no choice. She just pushed, pushed and kept pushing!

It had always been her fault. Besides…

Keith crossed his leg. She'd wanted him from the minute they met. It wasn't rape. Okay, maybe he *had* forced her at that particular moment. But she deserved everything she got. He looked at Lucas. She'd probably fuck up his friendship with Lucas. When would the little bitch stop messing up his life?

"I know how you feel." Keith spoke after moments. Lucas looked as if he'd forgotten about him. "If anything happened to Sarah, I don't know what I'd do. I love her so much."

"Melody's so different from other people, Keith. Most women like being protected and cared for. Melody doesn't. She's a loner. She likes to handle things on her own. It's not easy being with someone like that." He sat back. "God, I keep wondering why this had to happen! Why would someone hurt such a sweet person as Melody? She never did anything to anyone."

Except ruin their lives, Keith thought.

"She'll heal in time, Luke. Did she, uh…did she say if she was going to the police or anything?" Lucas shook his head. "Maybe that's best. It's probably nothing they could do, anyway."

"What?" Lucas looked at him.

"It's probably better if she just lets it go. I mean, so much time has passed, anyway."

"Lets it go?" Lucas threw the pencil on the desk. "Keith, what kind of shit is that to say? Melody was raped! This is gonna change the rest of her life. It doesn't matter how long ago it happened. Do you realize this gets harder for her every day? Every decision she makes from now on will be because of what that asshole did to her. Why should she let it go when even *I* can't? I could kill this bastard with my bare hands, Keith! He took the Melody I fell in love with away forever! She'll never be the same! Why the fuck should she let it go? How can any of us let it go?"

"Lucas, calm down, man." Keith waved his hands. "I was just saying…"

"No, obviously you don't know a damn thing about rape if you can say some shit like that. It's not just the physical, Keith. It ruins a woman inside and out. Melody will never be the same again!" Lucas trembled. "No matter how much I want her to be."

Keith exhaled. "Contrary to popular belief, I'm on your side, Luke. Now I know Melody is hurting. But she will get through it in time. I didn't mean to sound insensitive. You don't have to remind me how she was after it happened." He shut his eyes. "I'll never forget how she looked. But we can't change things for her, Lucas. She just has to accept this in order to move on." Keith shrugged. He couldn't categorize Lucas's expression. Why had it changed? Shit. Keith realized he'd made a big slip.

Lucas tapped the desk. "What did you just say?"

"Uh, I said, that in time Melody will heal and…"

"No, you said, 'I'll never forget how she looked.' You mean, after the rape?"

"No." Keith cursed himself for making such a mistake.

"Then what did you mean then? Did you see her the night she was raped?"

Keith fiddled with the fancy buttons on his long-sleeved white shirt. "No, I just meant that Sarah and I talk about it all the time. We talked about it when it first happened. I remember how Sarah said she was. That's all I meant."

"You're lying." Lucas shook his head.

"Lying?" Keith grinned. "How can I be lying? What about?"

"If you saw Melody that night, then why can't you just admit it?"

"Okay, I might have seen her that day. I mean, at work." He walled his eyes.

Lucas shook his head. "I don't think so. Melody was off that day. I remember and it was a Wednesday. I'll never forget that day as long as I live. You saw her that night?"

Keith stood. "Look, we can talk about this later, okay? Uh, I have to get some work done." He went to the door.

"It can wait."

Keith twitched. "Lucas, I have a meeting to get to in about an hour, man."

Lucas stood. "It can *wait*."

"Luke, man…"

Lucas walked from around the desk. "Don't give me any bullshit now, Keith. I want the truth. I've been trying to figure out this thing going on between you and Melody. I couldn't figure it out for the life of me. Something happened that made her act the way she does around you. Did you see her the night she was raped?" Keith sighed. "And don't lie to me, man."

"Yes. But it was before it happened."

Lucas looked off. "Sarah said that you hadn't seen Melody since before the day she was raped. I remember because I asked her if you'd been to the house. She told me she requested that you didn't come and you hadn't been."

"Yeah, and…I respected her wishes. I haven't seen Melody because I didn't want to upset her."

Lucas raised an eyebrow. "Why didn't you just tell Sarah you saw Melody that night?"

"Because it wasn't a big deal! Melody came over my place."

"Why would she do that?"

"I don't know! She thought I did something to her as always. She's always had it in for me, you know that!"

Lucas nodded. "Yes, she has. And I think it's time to find out exactly why. What went on between you and

Melody back then, Keith? Why does she dislike you so much?"

"Lucas, I really can't tell you that, man." Keith chuckled. "Because I don't know. She never liked me from the beginning. You meet up with people like that from time to time. You don't always know why they don't like you. You just accept it."

"I'm gonna ask you straight out, man." Lucas shifted. "Did you and Melody ever have something going on?"

Keith guffawed. "Lucas!"

"I'm dead serious, Keith."

"No, man! You know how much I love Sarah! She's all I've ever wanted. And you're my friend! I wouldn't mess around with Melody like that! You've known me for years. How could you accuse me of something like that?"

"How come I don't believe you?"

"Hell, I don't know! I guess I got one of those faces that makes me look guilty."

"Do I look like I'm in the mood for jokes, Keith? I want to know what's going on! Why was Melody at your place the night she was raped? Answer me!"

"I told you she came over there to talk!"

"To *you*? Keith, Melody hates you, or so she claims! But I'm beginning to wonder why. Were you stringing Melody along while being with Sarah?"

"Luke!"

"*Were* you?"

"Man, fuck this! See what she's doing? She tried to

break me up from Sarah; now she's messing up our friendship!"

"Keith, something is going on here. I want to know what it is!"

"You want to know so badly, then go ask your little girlfriend!" He stomped to the door. "Just remember that it all started with her. Everything has always been her fault! You keep that in mind! I don't need to be second-guessed by you, Lucas. If you and Melody are having problems, then take it up with her!"

"Did you ever sleep with Melody?" Lucas bellowed.

Keith slammed the door.

"Hello, Sarah. Glad you could make it." Lucas stood by his door later that night. Sarah sashayed in. She overlooked the comfortable décor. She smiled. Lucas politely took her purse. She couldn't help noticing the lines running through his bothered face.

"Please, sit down. Would you like a snack or something to drink? My maid just picked up a refrigerator of groceries."

They sat on the couch.

"No, thank you." Sarah looked around the room a second time. "Uh, is everything all right? I found your invite strange since you asked me not to mention it to Keith or Melody." She crossed her legs. "Is something wrong?"

"Look, Sarah, I'm not gonna beat around the bush, okay? I want to talk about Keith and Melody." She nodded. "I think there is a lot we both don't know. Something is going on, and I intend on finding out what as soon as possible."

"You're angry?"

"I'm sad and confused and hurt because of what happened to Melody. I'm also sick and tired of being led by the nose. Sarah, this just isn't right. Keith claims Melody has no cause to distrust him or not like him, but you don't hate someone the way she hates Keith unless they've done something to you. Melody hates Keith with a passion and would do anything to get him out of both of your lives. I can't believe it's just on Melody's doing."

"What are you saying exactly?" She didn't want to hear this. She decided to entertain Lucas since he loved Melody so much. She didn't know why they were having this conversation. So, Melody didn't like Keith. Is it really that big of a deal? Lucas curved his fingers into a reddish fist. Suddenly, Sarah understood that it had been.

"I'm saying that we have to get to the bottom of things, Sarah. Well, probably, mainly, *you* do. Keith, hasn't been exactly honest with you."

She scoffed. "And how do you know this?"

"Did he tell you that Melody was at his house the night she was raped?"

"What?" She stared at him.

Lucas shrugged. "He didn't tell you that, did he?" Sarah felt like someone had kicked her in the head with steel-toed shoes. "He hid it from you, which makes that lying in my book."

"You must have been mistaken. Keith would have told me if Melody had been to his place that night. *Especially* on that night. He tells me everything."

"You can't say that now, Sarah. He tried to hide it because he made a slip. He said Melody was upset and that in time, he knew she'd heal. I caught the slip and he admitted that she was at his place. I accused him of having an affair with Melody."

"That's insane, Lucas! Melody wouldn't do a thing like that to me!"

"I know she wouldn't. But at that moment I was so hurt by Keith lying that I thought I needed to ask him about it. He of course grinned and pretended it was the most insane thing he'd ever heard."

"That's because I'm sure it is! Lucas, what are you getting at? Why am I really here? And if you have doubts, why didn't you talk to Melody about all this?"

"Because we both know Melody wouldn't have opened up about it. She's gone for months not disclosing why she feels the way she does about Keith. Why would she tell me something now? Sarah, this secrecy can't go on. Something happened between them and we need to find out what it is!"

"It's nothing, Lucas!" She flipped her hair off her shoulder. "Look, it's been a weird time and I know you're stressed because of Melody being raped. But this is insane. You have doubts about Keith, someone you've known for four years?"

"That's just it, Sarah. Do I really know Keith? In all this time, I still don't know even the most common things about him. Don't you think that's strange?"

She walked around with her arms crossed. "You know a lot about him, Lucas. You know he has a brother. You know…"

"No, for us to be friends for this long, Sarah, I don't know enough!" She turned away from him. "I don't know about his family. And what *about* his brother? I've never even seen the guy! I've been to Keith's house many times! What's that about?"

"So what, huh? You think Keith made up a brother, now? Lucas, you know him! He's your friend. Why are you turning on him like this?"

He sighed. "I don't mean to, but Sarah…" He stood. "Sometimes it takes another person to point out that you don't know someone as well as you may think. For me, that's been Melody. She knows something about Keith that we don't. Sarah, you mean to say you don't have any doubts? You don't wonder why he doesn't share all he can with you?"

"He shares enough." She rolled her eyes.

"I think you just don't want to see what's going on here. I think you're scared."

She pounded her chest. "Look, I love Keith, okay? I love him and I trust him, Lucas!"

"Do you trust your sister?" Sarah shut her eyes. "Sarah, please think about what I'm saying. Something isn't right. I think everything going on with Melody is connected to Keith. He couldn't even lie straight when I confronted him this morning."

"Maybe he wasn't trying to lie! Maybe he was shocked that one of his dearest friends has decided to give him a hard time!"

"Listen to me!" He shook her. "I know you got doubts, too. If you love Melody you'll find out all you can about why she hates Keith so much!" She broke from his grasp. "Sarah, we both know he tried to hide that Melody was at his house when she was raped. Why?"

"When she said Valley Road, I…I knew it was near Keith's." She rubbed her head. "But this doesn't make any sense. Why are you coming to me with this now? I'm trying to help Melody through this. Lucas, I got enough to deal with! I don't need this on my shoulders, too."

"I never wanted to make things hard for you, Sarah. But I love your sister. I'll do all I can to make things easier for *her*. You aren't stupid, Sarah." She turned away from him. "You know in your heart that something is going on." He turned her toward him. "Don't you think it's time you faced it?"

"Lucas, I…"

He nodded. "Sarah, you're probably the only one Keith would be completely honest with. Sarah, he is in love with you. He'd probably tell you just about anything."

She sighed. "So you want me to investigate my own boyfriend, now?"

"If he loves you as much as he says he does, he should have no problem with that. Don't you want to know why he didn't tell you Melody was at his place that night? Why did he hide it from you, unless he felt it needed to be hidden? And what was she doing there in the first place? Sarah, we have all of these questions and no answers! At least not any that fit. It doesn't make sense to me. Sarah, it may be hard but you gotta talk to him. You know you do."

"Uh, I gotta go, Lucas." She grabbed her purse from the coat rack by the door.

"Sarah."

"Good night." She left.

Lucas leaned against the door. "Do the right thing before it's too late, Sarah. Because you're probably the only one who can," he whispered.

Chapter Seventeen

"Oh, hello, Sarah." Jeff Williamson greeted Sarah at Keith's office door at Caper the next morning. She straightened her tan suit and skirt that hugged her voluptuous hips. Passing men gawked at her magnificent shape. Jeff smiled brightly. She got the feeling that Jeff had a crush on her. She remembered when Keith first introduced her to Jeff. He'd been so nervous he dropped his soda.

She figured he'd jump to help her if he could. For some reason, Keith took to Jeff. She knew he probably told Jeff things he hadn't told Lucas. Keith probably found Jeff to be a "safe" friend—one you could confide in, but they weren't so close that they'd go blabbing all your business. Sometimes she'd surprise Keith at work to find he and Jeff in mysterious conversations.

Sarah figured Jeff had the information she needed. In that case, it didn't hurt if he wanted her. She could use that to her advantage.

"Hi, Jeff."

"You look beautiful," he panted. She looked away from his gaze. "Uh, how are you?"

"Fine."

"It's Keith's off day, you know?"

"Yes, I know." She smiled. "I, uh, came to talk to you."

"Me?" He rubbed his curly brunette hair. He blushed. "Why would you want to talk to me, Sarah?"

"Can we go to your office?"

"Sure. It's right this way." They walked six doors down to his office. He shut the door for privacy. Sarah wondered how they could get so much work done with people constantly hanging around in the halls. Jeff sat at his desk. "What can I do for you, Sarah?"

"I wanted to talk to you about Keith. But, could you keep this between us?"

He stared at the tiny spot of cleavage peeking from her blouse.

"Jeff?"

"Huh?" He ran his eyes down her breasts. "Oh yeah, you want to ask me something about Keith? Sure, that's fine." He smiled. "Boy, he's lucky to have a woman like you." She smiled. "Especially after all the trouble he went through to get you."

"What are you talking about?"

He chuckled. "Well, he just knew you were made for him the first time he saw you. He came to work with glowing eyes, skipping over clouds." He laughed. "Man, I don't think anything flips Keith's world like you do."

"We met in a coffee shop." She shrugged. "It was nice for me too but nothing that would cause that much of a scene."

"Oh, the shop by your job, right? Oh yeah." He grinned. "He used to go there every day during lunchtime, and believe me, it wasn't for the coffee. He always said that was the only time he could watch you and not feel guilty. He said that watching and wanting you without you knowing was incredibly exciting."

"Uh." She chuckled. "Are you saying that Keith knew me *before* we met at the coffee shop?"

"Oh, absolutely! I'd say probably a year before he got the guts to talk to you." Sarah's mouth dropped. "He never told you this?" She shook her head. "Sarah, knew where you lived even before he knew where you worked."

"What?" she gasped.

"Well, he was determined to find out your address." Jeff grinned. "We dared him that he couldn't do it. Said he followed you home one night and soon he was driving over there quite often. We told him it would look strange and he'd scare you off, but Keith always goes by his own methods."

Sarah gripped her chest. She felt like her heart would drop from her body.

"He never told me any of this. I don't believe this. He was stalking me."

"No, Sarah, look…"

"No, you can't call it anything else, Jeff! He followed me home! He knew where I worked? He approached me like it was an accident but it wasn't like that at all! He planned this entire thing?"

"Sarah, most women would be flattered that a guy like Keith would go through so much trouble to meet them."

"Flattered? It's insane, Jeff! Keith is not some high school kid who followed the cheerleader to the game! He's a man who knew me, knew things about me, watched me before I even knew his name. I can't believe this." She shook her head. "This entire thing has been a lie."

"Fuck." Jeff walled his eyes. "Boy, is Keith gonna fry my ass. Sarah, look, it's not that big of a deal. He just didn't know enough about you and that was his way of finding things out."

"Jeff, you ask people things if you want to get to know them. You don't follow them home or to the coffee shop! And all this time I had no indication that he'd done this." She shook her head. "It's not normal, Jeff. I thought I knew him. I don't know him at all."

"Sarah, uh, do you remember getting any flowers or gifts at any time that you didn't know where they came from?" He bit his lip.

"As a matter of fact, I do. Please don't tell me Keith…" He nodded. "Oh." She guffawed from shock. "Oh God, this can't be happening!" She laughed.

"Sarah, are you okay?"

"Melody was right." She shook her head. "She was right and Lucas was right." Jeff stared. "All this time, Melody told me he was hiding something. It may not have even been this but now I know it's something." She stood.

"Sarah, I didn't mean to cause trouble between you and Keith. He loves you so much. You're a beautiful woman. Honestly, I can't blame him. What man wouldn't go after you? Granted he should have picked a better way but he wanted to make you fall in love with him, and you did. If you love him now, then it shouldn't matter."

She sniffed. "Lying, stalking, manipulating…that's not love, Jeff. Not the kind I want." She left.

He wasn't Steven. Brianna knew it the minute she opened the door that night. She took a deep breath. She had a plan, though she wasn't sure if it would work. She wouldn't be as crisp on it as she would have a month ago. Still, she had no choice but to give it a try. He stepped inside. Every night she'd hidden Davis in case the rapist came back. She did the same tonight.

She didn't want the rapist to realize she knew he wasn't Steven. This would be her last chance to get him. She could feel it. He'd escaped her twice already. She wasn't letting him get away again—no matter how frightened she may have been.

She wished to hell that it had been Steven. She couldn't figure him out! Why would he just leave like that? He hadn't tried to contact her in a month. She could understand him hiding from the cops, but not from *her*. Maybe she didn't know him as well as she thought. Had he wondered about her once in all this time? Didn't he care that she'd be worried?

Why couldn't he even call? He knew he could trust her. They'd grown distant in more ways than one. She didn't even know if he was okay.

Steven walked in. He shut the door. He took her by the waist, and he kissed her even rougher than he had before. "I missed you so much, Brianna." She smiled, realizing he wasn't Steven for certain. "I can't tell you how hard it's been not being able to hold you." He wrapped his other arm around her waist. He seemed to want to pull her straight inside of him. "Every time I see you, you get more beautiful. How did I ever let you get away from me?"

"Steven." She played with his collar. "I had no idea where you'd been. I wasn't sure if you were safe or not." Thunder roared. He looked toward the door. She grinned to keep his mind on her. "The last time you were here, it was raining, wasn't it?"

"Yeah." He nibbled her neck. "I want you so bad, Brianna. Remember what I said the last time?" He smirked. "That I wasn't gonna leave until we made love?"

"I remember." She smiled.

"I meant it." He scooped her into his arms. He stopped at the stairs. She steadily watched him. He cut his eyes to her. She could tell the bluffing had become difficult for him. He didn't even know where her bedroom was. And he *should* have.

She waved her arm nonchalantly to the first room at the top of the stairs.

"You remember where it is, don't you, Steven?" She kissed him. He smiled. He headed for the bedroom. He smirked at the sight of her bed. Brianna couldn't stop trembling inside. She couldn't botch this up. Yet the man scared her half to death. She couldn't believe she stood in her bedroom with the same man who had attacked her and beaten other women. He may have even killed a few. She glanced at her end table by the bed. Her gun sat in it as always. She wanted to take the fucker in so he could get what he deserved in prison. He needed to suffer. But if he made one wrong move on her, she would shoot him in a heartbeat.

"Come here." He pulled her close. He slipped her nightgown from one shoulder. "No need in waiting, Brianna."

"Mmm, no need." He cupped her buttocks. "Oh, Steven, this feels so good."

"It can feel even better, Brianna." He ran his hand down her thigh. "You're so hot, aren't you? I feel your heart beating so fast. I don't think I've ever wanted someone so much."

"Steven, Steve?" She pushed him away. "It's been a long time for me, you know? Especially with you. You're so special to me. Let's take our time." He grimaced. "We could have some wine first."

He nodded. "Wine, huh? Where do you keep it?"

"You don't remember? In that little cabinet in the kitchen, above the microwave." She pointed to the door. "You know wine really gets me going. It did for you, too."

He rubbed his hair. "Believe me, I never need anything to get me going." She frowned at the crude remark. He didn't seem to pick up on it. "I'll be right back." He turned toward the door. He opened it, then slammed it shut again. Brianna jumped back. He grabbed her by the hair. He ripped a knife from his back pocket.

"Steven, what are you *doing*?" she shrieked.

"Just cut the shit, Brianna! You think I'm stupid, huh? Do you?" He yanked her head back. She felt like her neck would cave in. "Well, I must be kind of smart since you cops haven't been able to catch on to me, right?"

"Steven, I only want to help you! I care about you!"

"Come off it! You know damn well I'm not Steven! You really think I'm stupid, don't you, Detective? Like I didn't know you probably figured me out! Why do you think I stayed away so long? I knew you guys were planning something!" He shoved her on the bed. He leapt on top of her. He placed the knife under her chin. "Well, let's see who gets the last laugh *tonight*."

Brianna cut her eyes to the end table. She vowed to get that gun.

"Oh, Sarah." Keith pulled her into his arms before she got in the front door. He didn't seem to notice her stiff reaction. He brushed rain from her jacket. He took her umbrella. "Oooh, this weather!" He chuckled. "How come when it rains in Albany it seems to pour every time?" Sarah stared, stiff-faced. "You look so beautiful. I got the dinner set up in the kitchen."

"Keith."

"We can eat it there, or if you want to watch television, I understand." He grinned.

"Keith."

"Or we can eat in the bedroom." He pulled her close. "Since we're gonna end up there later, anyway." She moved away. He studied her eyes. "Sarah, is everything okay?"

"No, Keith, I don't think it is. We need to talk."

He stepped back. "Okay, fine. We can talk, but can we do it during dinner?"

"This is not the romantic-dinner-by-candlelight kind of discussion, Keith."

"Sarah, what's the matter? Did I do something wrong?" He took her arm.

She snatched away. "Let go of me, Keith."

He stared. "You never told me to let go of you before."

"Well, I'm saying it now! I look at you tonight and I realize I don't even know you, Keith. Maybe I never did."

"Sarah, you know me more than anyone! I know you, too. Baby, what's going on? What's happened?"

She exhaled. "Apparently, a lot of things have been happening where you're concerned, Keith."

"Sarah, I have baked salmon and champagne, those

little strawberry tarts you love so much. Can we please just discuss this after dinner?"

"No."

"Oh." He grimaced. "Well, what the hell's the problem, Sarah? I hope I can straighten it for you, because so far it's ruined a perfect evening."

She rubbed her chin. "Hmm, let's see. For starters I spoke to Jeff Williamson today. He told me some very interesting things about you."

"You went to the job?" She nodded. "Checking up on me now?"

"Jeff told me that you knew me a year before we met. Is that true?"

"No."

She nodded. "Uh-huh. So Jeff just made it up?"

"Probably when you spoke about *how* we met, he might have just gotten confused. How would I have known you before then?" He shrugged.

"You know, I'd buy that, Keith, except for one thing. Jeff volunteered the information before I had a chance to ask. In fact, I wasn't even going to speak to him about that. But I sure as hell am glad he told me."

"What did he say exactly?"

"Oh, that you'd been following me home and that you'd purposely go to the coffee shop we met at, just to see me. In other words, he told me you planned meeting me, and started a plan for me to fall in love with you, too. Is that true?"

"No, it's not."

"Keith, stop it!"

"Stop what?"

"Goddamn it, I know it's the truth! Jeff wouldn't have a reason to lie to me!"

"Oh really? News flash, Sarah! Jeff wants you for himself! He always did! What the hell are you doing speaking to him behind my back, anyway? What the hell is going on around here? You're acting suspicious and sneaky just like Melody." He sighed. "What the hell difference does it make how we met? You love me now!"

"It makes a big difference because you weren't honest! None of this was honest, this relationship, nothing!"

"Sarah, how can you say that? I love you! Everything I did I meant it! You couldn't tell that? You're going on something that doesn't even matter!"

"It matters to me!"

"All right, fine! I was so in love with you that I wanted to make sure when we met it was perfect! I didn't want to mess things up." She turned away. "Is that so wrong? I did it for you, Sarah."

"Moving on."

"What is this, a courtroom?" He grimaced.

"I don't know but you're about to be put on trial, Keith." She crossed her arms. "You've lied about another thing, haven't you?"

"No. I've never lied about anything." She grinned. "It's the truth, Sarah!"

"How come you didn't tell me that my sister was here the night she was raped?"

"What did you say?" he whispered.

"I'm sorry. Did I *stutter*, Keith?" she shouted. "Why didn't you ever tell me that Mel was here the night she was raped?"

He tilted his head in the air. "I guess Lucas told you this." She nodded. "First, my friend accuses me of things, and now my girlfriend? I wish I knew what was going on."

"You're not the only one. You still haven't told me why she was here."

"She came over because she was angry at me. Big surprise!"

"Why was she angry with you?"

"Does Melody need a reason? She hates me, Sarah!"

"Okay, well, why didn't you tell me about it?"

"I forgot! It's not even important, is it? Damn, I mean, she was over here the night she was raped! Big deal! What's the problem about that?"

"The problem is that you never told me, Keith. And I thought I could trust you more than I can trust myself."

He reached for her. "Sarah, you know you can. I love you so much."

"Then why have you been lying to me?"

"It's Melody! Sarah, is it always gonna be like this? Is Melody gonna constantly interfere in our lives? Sometimes I wish she was..." He paused. Sarah squinted.

"Go on, Keith." Her voice trembled. "You wish she was *what*?"

He shrugged. "I wish she was dead."

She gaped. "How can you say something so cruel? And about my sister?"

"Sarah, she hasn't pulled the punches with *me*. I'm sick of making an effort and all she does is ruin things. She has tried to ruin my life and now she's trying to ruin our relationship! Well, I won't let her." He grabbed her. "I know you love me, Sarah. With that, nothing matters."

"I can't stay here any longer. This is sickening."

"Don't go." He held her. "Please just...look, I bought something for you. It's upstairs. Please just come and get it. Then if you still want to go, you can."

She exhaled. "Keith."

"Please, Sarah." He kissed her.

"Okay," she muttered.

"You're gonna love it, I promise." He led her upstairs.

The rapist climbed from the bed. Brianna lay still.

"What do you think you're gonna do?" she asked. "Like you said, I obviously have a plan, right? The cops are waiting to make their move on you. They're hiding outside."

He grinned. "Bullshit." He waved the knife. "But I'll tell you how much about you I know." He walked to the end table. He got her gun. Brianna buried her head into the bed. "Didn't know I knew where you kept it, did you?

I told you I know everything about you, Brianna. I knew everything about all the women I pleasured."

"Is that what you call it?" She grimaced.

"They might not have wanted it but they enjoyed it after they got it."

"You're disgusting. You are a rapist! The lowest piece of shit to walk the planet! I cannot wait to see your ass in prison, shaking and scared like the women you raped! You're not as smart as you think. You shouldn't have come here, because this time, I won't let you leave!" She charged him. She punched him. He toppled over. The gun flipped from his hands. "Freeze!" He threw the knife at her face. "Ahh!" He grabbed her by the waist. Brianna dropped the gun.

"Stupid bitch!" He grabbed her. "Who do you think you are, huh? Get on the bed! Get on the fuckin' bed, you stupid cunt!" He shoved her on the bed. He grabbed the gun and knife from the floor. "It's gonna happen this time, Brianna. But with only one change! I'm not leaving you alive." She shook. He climbed on top of her. "Tonight you're gonna die! How do you like that, huh?"

"Freeze, motherfucker!" a voice bellowed from the hall. Steven stepped inside with his gun held high. The rapist gaped at Brianna. He held her gun in one hand, his knife in the other. "Put it down now!" Steven ordered.

"Steve." Brianna gasped. The rapist glared at her.

"I said…" Steven stepped closer. "Put the gun down now."

"Steven, be careful," Brianna whispered.

He winked. "No thing, Bree." He grinned. "Hate to bust up your little party, though." The rapist groaned.

"No apologies necessary." Brianna exhaled.

"And?" The rapist grinned. He held his hands up. Steven went for the knife. The rapist swung his other arm toward him. He cocked the gun.

"Steve!" Brianna screamed. Steven ducked. She kicked the rapist off the bed.

He shot the ceiling. He rolled on the floor. Steven held him up by his collar. He punched the rapist in the face. The rapist kneed Steven in the gut. Steven fell over in pain. Brianna couldn't tell them apart!

"Think you're so smart, huh?" The rapist kicked Steven in the chest. Steven's gun fell from his hands. The rapist grabbed it. "Fuck! A little pussy like you should have been flattered they thought you were me!" He kicked Steven again.

"Ahh!" Steven held his stomach.

"Damn, we really could be twins, huh?" The rapist cackled. "Maybe we are brothers, you know?"

"Fuck you." Steven spat. "I'm nothing like you!"

"No, you're *not*." The rapist pointed Steven's gun at him. "There's a major difference. I'll be alive and you won't! " He cocked the gun. It jammed. Brianna crept behind him. She held her gun firmly. She pointed it straight into his back.

"You were saying?" she whispered.

He turned around. "No one will believe any of this! I'll disappear like before!" He ran to the hall.

"Shit, get him, Bree!" Steven held his stomach. Brianna heard footsteps charging upstairs. A group of uniformed officers stood smack dab in front of the Albany Predator. He twitched and turned as if he couldn't believe he'd been cornered. Brianna rested against the bedroom door. Two cops grabbed the rapist by his arms. They turned him around where he faced Brianna.

It seemed all over. For some reason she couldn't celebrate. The rapist smiled.

His eyes searched her body like they had many times before. He flinched while the cops snapped the handcuffs on him. She walked toward him. Steven limped from the bedroom. The group of officers gasped. Some did a double-take at the lookalike cop and rapist.

Brianna stared into the Predator's eyes. "Guess you didn't get me like you hoped. Sorry things were messed up for you." She snickered.

"I still won, Brianna. Because I'll be in your life forever from now on." He looked at Steven. "In both of your lives. You'll never forget me. You probably won't be able to look at each other the same way again." Brianna looked at Steven. "I put a doubt in your mind that will always be there, Brianna. Even *you* can't change that. I may not have left my mark on your body, but I have left it on your life. I left it on all of their lives! They'll never forget me! So whose work is more important, hmm?"

"I just can't understand why after all you've done, I still feel sorry for you," Brianna whispered.

He licked his lips. "You would've *loved* it, sweetheart. Every time you close your eyes you'll think of me kissing you. You'll think of how you almost made love to me." Steven gaped. "I can handle being in prison, being behind bars. I can handle anything!" The cops stared at him. "But tell me, Brianna. Can you live with your memories of me?" He grinned. "'Cause I don't think you can."

"Get him out of here!" Steven ordered. Brianna turned to Steven when the others left. Brianna lifted her arms to hug Steven. He moved away. She watched him in awe.

"So uh, it's over." She smiled. "That's great, huh? At least now we can resume to our normal lives." She crossed her arms. "Until our next case." She chuckled. He stared at her. "Steven, what's wrong?"

"'Kissing you,' 'making love to you.'" He scoffed.

"Steve." She touched his face. "Are you jealous?" she whispered. "Steven, I had to do those things to get him."

"I'm not talking about that, Bree." He removed her hands from his face. "I'm talking about the fact that he could do those things and you not be able to tell the difference."

"Steve."

"Yeah." He sucked in tears. "You couldn't tell his kisses from mine? As close as we were?" She looked away. "Bree, how is that supposed to make me feel?"

"Steven, I never meant to hurt you," she whispered. He limped downstairs.

"But I guess I *did*." She sighed.

"It looks so beautiful on you, Sarah." Keith looked over his shoulder at the diamond bracelet on Sarah's arm. They slow-danced around his bedroom. Sarah couldn't believe how emotions could change in just a day. A day earlier she had yearned for Keith's touch. She depended on his kisses. She lived for his veneration. Tonight she simply felt dead. His touch meant nothing more than being with a stranger on the street. She moved away from him. He seemed to sense the distress in her eyes.

"You don't like it, do you?" He turned off the little stereo on his dresser.

"The bracelet is beautiful, Keith. But I'm still not satisfied with what you've told me. I'm also not satisfied by how you cooked all of this up."

"I haven't cooked anything up, Sarah." He sat on the edge of the bed. "I love you. Why can't that just be all that matters?"

She sighed. "It used to be, Keith. But tonight it's not. I can't be with someone who's not honest with me. How can I build a relationship with someone like that?" She took off the bracelet. He raised an eyebrow. "I think this belongs to you."

"What are you doing?" he grumbled.

She held the bracelet in front of him. "I'm giving you back your…"

He grabbed her hand. "No you're not."

"Let go." She sighed.

"No. I don't want the damn bracelet back, Sarah! I bought it for you as a symbol of how much I care for you!"

"I don't want it, Keith!"

He waved his arms. "Why the hell not? Sarah, I don't get this! Things have been great! It's been the best! Why in the hell are you stopping now?"

"Didn't you hear a word I've said, Keith? I don't want the damn bracelet!" She threw it at him. She walked to the dresser. "It's over."

He smirked. "The fuck it is. You can't just walk in here and break this off without giving me a reason. Even then, I won't let you."

"There's so many reasons I can't count them, Keith! The main one is that you haven't been honest! The other is that being with you has destroyed my sister's life! I can't keep hurting her like this. It's time I finally do what's best for her."

"Shit, you've done that your whole damn life, Sarah! That's the point! You do everything to suit Melody but she doesn't give a shit about you. If so then she wouldn't want us to break up! Don't let Melody ruin this. You said I loved you unlike any other man and that you loved me the same."

"I do."

He grabbed her. "Then that's the only thing we need, Sarah! We belong together. What about all the plans we made?" She looked away. "We even talked about getting married! What about...what about Europe?"

She rubbed her face. "Keith, stop, please."

"No, we made all these plans to be together, Sarah! Think about the trip, baby."

He held her. "We can go on it even sooner than we planned. We can go this month if you want." She scoffed. "Sarah, we can go there and you'll see that this is right. That it's always been right. It'll just be you and me. No one to interfere. That's the way it's supposed to be."

She turned toward the dresser. She'd been afraid that his charm would sway her. God, she'd never met anyone like Keith before. He could make the worst times seem like blessings. Every word he said ran like a song in her ears. She shut her eyes. Going to Europe with him had been all she could think about for weeks. She thought it would be good to give Melody some time on her own. It would be so perfect. Sarah knew that.

Until she saw the earring.

She batted her eyes. Her mind had to be playing tricks on her. She picked up the little golden leaf. She examined it closely. She'd know this earring anywhere. It belonged to Melody. She faced Keith. His face twisted into what Sarah could describe as only confusion. He didn't have to bother to explain this. Finding the earring somehow put all the pieces together.

"Sarah..." He held up his hand. "What, what do you have there?"

"Why is this here?" She shut her eyes from disgust. "*Why*, Keith?"

"Uh, I found it. It was so beautiful that I kept it. I just..."

"Do you ever stop lying? Can you for once just be honest with me? Who in the hell do you think you're fooling, Keith? You did not just find this earring! This is my mother's earring, Keith!" He gaped. "I know damn well it is! My father had these earrings custom made for my mother on their last anniversary before they died! I received these earrings in the will! I gave them to Melody on her sixteenth birthday!"

"Sarah, I..."

"Why is this here, Keith?" Tears filled her eyes. "Oh God, is it true? Were you sleeping with my sister?"

"No!"

"Then tell me what the hell this is doing here, Keith!" Sarah paused. She glanced around. Her mind went to Melody's description of the rape.

She remembered how upset Melody had been that she'd lost her earring that night. That had been strange. Melody couldn't give a decent description, though she claimed she saw her attacker's face. That had been strange. She nearly fell out whenever Sarah mentioned Keith. Sarah held her mouth.

Melody couldn't describe her attacker or wouldn't?

"Sarah, what are you thinking?"

"I'm thinking..." The earring shook in her hand. "The worst thing I could ever think in my life. Keith, I'm begging you to give me an answer I believe. Now, what is Melody's earring doing here?"

"Okay, she left it that night she came over here. Must have been then because she was only here once."

"Why did she take her earrings off in the first place and in your bedroom?"

"She left it by the couch, Sarah. Of course she wasn't in my bedroom." He sighed. "Sarah, I meant to give it to her but I guess I forgot I had it."

"You forgot with it sitting right on your dresser? Tell me the truth! What is Melody's earring doing here, Keith?"

"It fell off, okay! I mean, damn! I didn't know she'd left it. By that time you'd banned me from the house."

She rubbed the back of her neck. "Then why didn't she come back to get it?"

"What?" He stood.

"You heard me, Keith." Her tone stayed level. "If she simply left it, why didn't she ever come back? Or better yet, why didn't she tell me she left it here?"

"She probably didn't know."

She squinted. "And why would she not know?"

"Sarah, she was raped that same night! You think she cared about an earring? She probably thought she lost it when she was attacked!"

"She did, Keith." He glared. "You see, she told me she lost it when she was raped. She figured she must have." He turned away. "So I guess that explains it, huh?"

"Sarah, I know you're not accusing me of…"

"I am, you motherfucker!" She trembled. "I'm accusing you, you bastard! You raped her, didn't you, Keith? You raped her! It was you! All this time!" Tears filled her eyes. "Oh God! You sick, pathetic bastard!"

"Sarah!"

"I know it was you!"

"I can't believe you're accusing me of raping Melody! That's insane! Sarah, how could you do that?"

"Because it's the truth!" she shrieked. "I know it! Melody didn't leave her earring! She lost it when you raped her, didn't she? You sick bastard! Oh!" She gripped her head. "How could you do this? What kind of monster are you? Oh my God!" She walked around the room. "And I kissed you! I made love to you after what you did…," she wailed.

"Sarah." He tried to hold her.

"Don't touch me! Don't you ever touch me, Keith! You are gonna pay for this!"

"I didn't rape her!" He shook her. "Do you realize how that sounds? Sarah, I love you!" She tried to break free. "How could you say something like this about me?"

"It's the truth!" She pushed him with a force both couldn't believe. "These earrings mean the world to Melody, Keith! For her not to come back here, she had to be scared to death! And she said she lost it when she was raped! Stop lying to me! Admit it!" She hit him. "Admit it!"

"All right!" he bellowed. Sarah shivered. He looked at her. "All right. I did it."

"You..." She struggled to breathe.

"Oh, Sarah, baby." He rubbed his hair. "I know it seems horrible but I did it for *you*. Everything I did was for you."

"You did it for me?" She sighed. He nodded. "You did it for *me*?" she screamed. She charged him. "She's my sister, Keith! She's my little sister! The person I love more than anything and you did it for *me*? You son-of-a-bitch!" She pounded his face and chest. Keith ducked for protection. "You sick asshole! You son-of-a-bitch! I hate you!" Sarah slapped Keith with her purse, causing him to lose his balance. He fell to the floor and held his arms up for cover.

"I hate you! I hate you, you bastard! You raped my sister!"

"Sarah!" He tried to grab her swinging arms. She could feel herself going insane every time she hit him. Nothing could ever be enough. She wanted him dead. She wanted him dead for all the pain he'd caused. For all the lies he'd told. For the tentative, painful future that his actions would place upon her sister's life forever. She wanted him dead for making her trust him. For making her believe in him over Melody. For making her fall so heavily in love, that she couldn't see what lay smack dab in front of her face. She now hated him with every fiber of her being.

The more he begged, the more she hit. She wanted to inflict the most pain she could, hoping that he'd get a glimpse of what he had caused Melody.

"Sarah!" Keith jumped up. He wrapped his arms around her. "Sarah, please calm down!" She wailed in his arms. "I never meant to hurt you."

"Get away!" She shoved him. "I hate you! I hate you! How could you do something like this, Keith?" Her eyes widened with terror. She held her shaking hand to her mouth. "Oh...I can't believe this." She cried. "I can't believe it." She bent over to stop from throwing up. "I swear, this is one of the worst days of my life. And my Melody. My sweet Melody. She has dealt with all this pain because of you. The man I loved."

"Sarah," he sighed. "Just let me hold you."

"You stay away from me!" She held up a fist. "You stay away from me and from both of us." She glanced in the mirror. "I can't even look at myself," she whispered. "I kissed you. I made love to you. I let you touch me after..." She covered her mouth. "I'm gonna be sick."

"I love you, Sarah!" He shook her. "I didn't mean to hurt Melody but she left me no choice!" He held her close. "Stay with me, huh? Just stay with me tonight and..." She grunted in his arms. "Stay with me, please," he whispered.

"No!" She turned from his kisses. "Stop, Keith!" He pulled her toward the bed. "You gonna rape me, too, huh?" He moved away.

"How can you say something like that? This is all Melody's fault! You couldn't handle the situation so I did!"

"Yeah? Well, we'll see how the police handle the situation, won't we?" She slapped him. She ran downstairs. He ran after her. He pulled her back. "Let go of me!"

"No, Sarah, no!" He shook her. "You can't just leave like this. It's only us in this world, okay. That's all that matters, remember? We don't need anyone else! We never did."

"How could you do that to my sister? How could you do it to anyone?"

"I'd do anything to keep you, Sarah. *Anything*."

"Let me go, Keith." He did. She ran out of the house.

"You can't be serious! You're going to the police?"

"Oh, you're damn right I am." She ran to her car.

"And say what? You have no proof."

"They have medical evidence on file, Keith."

"Melody lied." He shrugged. "And she'll lie again. She won't tell."

"You bastard. You threatened her, didn't you? My God, she's too scared to leave the house because of you, isn't she, Keith?"

He rubbed his face. "Just be with me, Sarah. I can make all of this go away. You always said I could make anything go away!"

"Not this time, Keith."

"Sarah, you go to the police and you have nothing! They won't believe Melody because she's wasted too much time!" She shook her head. "Besides, money talks, Sarah. And I got enough of it to say anything I want. You know I'll get the best attorney. And with my connections I'll get off, Sarah." She figured he probably would. But that wasn't reason enough for her not to try. "Sarah, think about this. The police will believe me over what you or Melody say. I can get people to believe anything I want." He squinted.

She wiped tears. "And to think that I once admired that about you the most." She got in her car.

He stepped off the porch. "You belong with me, Sarah. Nothing I've done will ever change that. You'll come back to me. You know no man will love you the same way I do."

She started the car. "I hope not." She sped off.

"Sarah!" Keith ran into the driveway.

Chapter Eighteen

"Ahh!" Melody moved her head from the pillow just in time. The huge knife swung past her face. The blade instantly shattered her pillow. She turned around to see Keith standing by her bed. She couldn't describe his twisted expression. She would have said angry or mad. But that didn't even seem to fit. His hair and clothes were neatly in place.

A man like Keith never seemed to unravel in any circumstance. His cool-no-matter-what attitude had always alarmed Melody. She hadn't seen him since the rape. Right now she wasn't thinking about that. She thought about the knife in his hand. She wondered why she hadn't heard from Sarah all night. She had no idea where she'd gone. Keith yanked the knife from the pillow.

He rubbed it against his leg. He dug the point into his skin until tiny drops of blood covered the blade. Melody stared at those icy green eyes. Could he not feel the blade? Could you not feel pain once *insanity* kicked in?

"So are you happy now, Mel?" He sighed. "You happy now?" She slowly moved against her bedroom wall. She held the sides of her floppy T-shirt. The clock barely struck nine. Where the hell had Sarah gone? "I asked you if you were happy now, Melody." Keith's voice trembled.

"Keith." She sobbed without warning. "What...what are you doing?" She kept her eyes on the blade, while quickly cutting her eyes to the door. Keith shut it closed before she could make it out of the room. He stood in front of it.

"Sarah knows." He sweated. Melody gasped. "I tried to explain to her that this was all your fault. She didn't believe me. It's the first time in my life that I had to prove myself. I didn't enjoy the feeling."

"Keith..."

"Shut up!" He held the knife toward her. Melody shook against the wall. "This is all your fault, Melody. Your pain, my pain, Sarah's pain! It's your fault! I wouldn't have raped you if you hadn't insisted on taking Sarah away from me!" he sobbed. "Did you even care about how I felt about her? Did you care I loved her? No, because you're so damn selfish!" He swung the knife at her.

"Oh!" she shrieked.

"Selfish bitch! You're not even worth being alive!" He swung the knife at her face.

"Oh God!" she wailed. "Keith! Ahh!" He swung again. She clung to the end table by her bed. "Keith! Please!"

He looked at the knife. "I've never loved anyone like I love your sister. There have been others, Melody. But none of them made me feel like Sarah does." He rubbed the blade. "I don't like hurting people! But I've always been taught that you do what you have to do to stay in control! You…" He wailed. "You gotta stay in control or nothing matters."

"Keith." She held out a shaking hand. "Keith, I… look, this has all gone too far. Even after all that's happened, I'd like to help you." She stared at the knife. "I'm so sorry. I had no idea you were in so much pain."

He acted as if the knife put him in some sort of trance. "You really wanna help me, Mel?" he whispered.

"Yes." She'd never seen anyone so desperate before. She just wanted to put an end to all of this. She had hated Keith from the beginning. Now she felt sorry for him. Obviously, his actions weren't really his fault. He was very, very sick. Too sick to realize the things he did. Melody actually felt guilty for how she'd treated him. He needed help. He hadn't needed her hatred.

"Why would you wanna help me, Melody? You know damn well you hate me." He chuckled.

"I…I hate the things you do, Keith." She kept her eyes on the blade. "But I don't think I hate you. I realize now that it's not your fault you do the things you do. I mean, you think you need to stay in control or else you feel like you'll lose everything, right?" He nodded slowly. "I understand that, Keith. I don't blame you for feeling that way. We all want to keep control and have the happiest life we can."

"If you understand it now, how come you couldn't all this time?" He looked at her with fire in his eyes. "Am I supposed to believe you want to help me, now? No, you just want to save your ass. Well, it won't work, Melody! I came here to kill you! Sarah left me because of you! I'm losing everything! Even Lucas has doubts! You're not gonna destroy me! I've worked too hard!" He swung the knife at her face. Melody screamed. The blade missed her mouth by less than an inch.

"Keith, please!" He chased her out of the bedroom. Keith grabbed her on the stairs. She pushed him off before he could stab her.

"Melody!"

"Stop, Keith, please!" She stood against the couch. "Please, don't do this. You don't know what you're doing!"

"I do know. I'm gonna eliminate the problem and the problem is you!" He rushed toward her.

"For Sarah?" she shrieked. "You think killing me will bring her back to you?"

"I don't know. All I know is that I cannot be happy with you in my life one more minute! Ah!" He sliced the knife through the air. Melody ducked. She fell on the floor. She begged for mercy. Keith cornered her against the front door. He stood over her with the knife held high.

"Keith, please!" She cried. "Please don't do this!" He raised his arm.

"No...no...no!" Melody shielded her face with her

hands. Someone knocked on the door. Keith froze. Lucas's voice rang from outside. "Lucas!" Melody tried to open the door. Keith swung the knife to stop her.

"Don't you dare open that door," Keith growled. "I'm gonna finish this, Melody! I gotta finish this because I won't have any peace with you around me! I have to kill you."

"Keith, please don't!" Melody cried.

"I have to kill you," he whispered. "I got to or I won't be able to breathe! You haunt everything I do! I can't get peace of mind with you around! I can't live like this, Melody!"

Melody didn't know what shocked her the most. Keith wanting to kill her or that he felt she ruined his life. All this time she had hated him and wanted him gone. She had no idea that Keith felt the same way. She loathed him for being with Sarah. He loathed her for standing in his way. No other revelation could feel so amazing. She stared at Keith's hard face. They both wanted the same things for different reasons.

They both hated each other. Obviously, Keith hated Melody far more than she could ever hate him. He wanted to kill her. What else was there to think about?

"Melody!" Lucas pounded on the door. "Keith, I know you're in there! I see your car! Don't you dare hurt her!"

"Lucas, I…" Keith rubbed his face. "Right now, this is none of your business! I know you think you love her, but you don't know what she is. She's evil, man! I don't want her to drag you down. She'll try to ruin your life like she ruined mine!"

"You did that all on your own, Keith!" Lucas shouted. Melody whimpered against the door. She tried to stand. Keith's expression warned her against it. "Keith, what has happened to you, man? Is this because of Sarah?" Lucas twisted the doorknob.

"No, it's because of Melody!" Keith pounded the door. "Go away, Lucas! I'm doing this for all of us! Don't you see? We'd all be happy if Melody were dead! She's like some disease! She just gets into your life and tears things apart until you have nothing!" He shook the knife.

"Keith, please," Lucas whispered through the door. "I love you, man. We've been friends for years! You can't do this. You want to go to prison for murder? Keith, I love her. Think about Sarah, man! Think of how she'd feel if you killed Melody. Keith, you can't do this," Lucas begged. "Please, open the door. You're not in your right mind. Sarah and I care about you. We'll get you the help that you need."

"I don't need any help, Lucas! Once this is over you'll see how much better things will be!" He waved the knife. He struck Melody in the shoulder.

"Ahhh! Lucas!" She placed her hand to stop the blood. "Lucas, please help me! He's gonna kill me!"

"Keith, stop!" Lucas pounded the door.

"I raped her, Lucas! I know she told you! Don't pretend you care about me after all of this!" Keith bellowed.

"Wh...what?" Lucas fell against the door. "This can't be true," he whispered. "This can't be true, Keith!" Lucas beat the door.

Keith stared at Melody. "It is! And you know what, Luke? I don't regret it at all!" Keith brought the knife across Melody's chest. Her T-shirt slightly ripped down the middle. He missed her chest by an inch. He swung again.

"Oh, oh, oh!" Melody screamed. "Lucas! Lucas, he's gonna kill me!" She shut her eyes. "Lucas, help me, please!" Lucas noticed a cop car coming down the street. He ran off the porch to flag them down.

"Bitch!" Keith pulled her close. He jabbed the knife into her stomach. The sudden pain prevented her from screaming. She held her stomach. Blood covered her hand, yet she didn't know how deep she'd been cut.

"Oh..." She slipped onto the floor, weak and helpless. She rested her bloody hand beside her face. She hadn't the strength to fight anymore, just like their last meeting. Keith stood beside her. He'd won that night too. She couldn't gather any strength to fight him now. She never thought of what death would feel like.

She eased her eyes closed. Keith would finish her off. She didn't know how she'd gotten into this mess. Would this be how she'd die? At the hands of her enemy? Keith claimed he always kept control. He only needed to stab her one more time to prove it.

The front door popped open. "Freeze!" An officer

aimed his gun at Keith. Another one rushed onto the porch. Keith shifted back and forth. He dropped the knife on the floor. The cops rushed to apprehend him. Lucas ran inside.

"Melody!" He snatched her up. Her eyes opened instantly. "Oh shit!" He saw her stomach and shoulder. "That motherfucker!" he cried. "Melody, are you all right?"

"I'm…I'm losing blood, Lucas. It's getting hard to breathe and I can't feel…"

"We need an ambulance, please!" he shouted to the officers. One called the ambulance. The other escorted Keith outside. Lucas cradled Melody against his chest. "It's over now, Melody. Baby, it's all over now."

She raised her bloody hand to Lucas's face. "I love you." She drifted into unconsciousness.

"Hi, Steve." Brianna stood at their adjoined desks the next morning. He rubbed the collar of his crisp, dark-green shirt. She hadn't meant to hurt him. Hadn't he realized she had no choice? He should have been happy that the nightmare had finally ended. He flipped through some papers. He hadn't spoken to her a few minutes ago in Jersey's office, either. She didn't know why she expected him to be different now.

She scooted on top of his desk. He slightly turned away. She couldn't help grinning at his effort to ignore her. "Steven, I'm sorry if I hurt you, okay? But I was trying to do what I needed to do. Anyway, when he showed up at my house a month ago, I didn't know he wasn't you! Steven, is the way you're treating me fair? There's a bigger picture here."

He stood. "Really?"

She walled her eyes. "You know what? Forget you, Steven." She moved from the desk. Cunningham and a few other officers gazed from their seats. "I don't know why I'm apologizing to your ungrateful ass! Look, I put my life on the line for you! I went way beyond the call of duty because you asked me to. I let the man who tried to rape me into my home. Steven, I sat up day and night trying to figure out ways to help you. And this is how you treat me? You should be apologizing to *me*!"

She scoffed. "You just run off for a month and you don't contact me? You were so selfish that you didn't care that I was worried!" She sighed. "Then you have the nerve to act shitty with me? If it hadn't been for me being bait, your ass may still be a suspect!" He looked at her. "Do you realize that?" She stood close to him. "I refuse to let you make me feel guilty…" He pulled her into a mesmerizing kiss. She floated from his arms afterward. She had to shake her head to snap from the trance. She touched her lips.

"Remember this kiss and how it made you feel, Bree." He rubbed her hair. "I doubt that next time you'll get confused again."

"Wow." Cunningham gaped at Brianna. She nearly fainted. She regained control when she noticed everyone staring.

"You mad that I kissed you?" Steven whispered. Those blue eyes seemed to search every ounce of her thoughts.

"No." She smiled. "And you're right. Next time I won't be confused."

"So, are you two back together?" Cunningham grinned. They didn't answer. Parsons walked up. He switched his cigarette back and forth in his mouth.

"Oh yes." Steven sucked his lip. "Now this is what I've been waiting for, Bree."

She touched his chest to hold him back. "Now, Steve, you just got out of jail. I don't think killing Parsons would be wise. Even if he is an asshole." Brianna glared at Parsons.

"Well." Parsons stood in front of them. "Nice shade of lipstick, Kemp." Steven wiped Brianna's lipstick from his mouth. "I was just at the commissioner's office. They're all abuzz down there, I tell you. I have a feeling the news stations will be heading your way, Kemp. I just wanted to say…"

"No, I got something to say."

"Steve."

"Be quiet, Bree, I've been waiting for this." He cracked his knuckles. "Parsons, I've been waiting to say this ever since you wormed your way into my life. You're the saddest, most pathetic, pitiful…"

"Hold on, okay." Parsons held up his hand. "I wanted to say I was sorry, Detective." Steven looked at Brianna. "I know I came down a little rough on you."

"A little rough?" Steven guffawed. "Parsons you could have cut my balls off, and I wouldn't have thought it was any worse than the way you treated me!"

"I guess I deserve that. I was talking it over with the commissioner as well as my boss at Internal Affairs. You'll receive a full written retraction and formal apology from all of us." Steven gaped. "I really am sorry. But I had a good reason for coming down on you the way I did. I just wanted to find the rapist."

"Parsons, that's the whole damn point. You didn't trust a fellow officer of the law long enough to let me do my job. You didn't even give me the chance you would have given a criminal off the street! How do you think that made me feel?"

"Terrible." He put his hand in his pockets. "Distrusting of the department, I guess. I can only apologize, Kemp. I can't take it back." He held out his hand. "From now on I'll keep it in mind that we're on the same side." Steven hesitated before shaking Parsons' hand. "Maybe we can be friends."

"Oh, hold on, okay." Steven sat at his desk. "I don't love your ass. I just wanted the apology."

Parsons grinned. "So I guess you're all glad to not be seeing me here anymore."

"Ha!" Steven laughed. "You ain't never lied, did you?"

"I really am sorry."

"I think he sees that, Parsons. But you were an asshole." Brianna sat at her desk.

He smirked. "Well, before I go, I'd like to ask you something, Morris."

"And what in the world could you possibly want to ask me?" She crossed her feet on her desk.

He shrugged. "Since this is all over, I figure there's no need for hard feelings. It just so happens that there is this live performance being played over at that jazz club on Fifth." Steven raised an eyebrow. Parsons grinned. "Figured maybe you'd want to go with me tonight."

"Huh?" Steven glared.

Brianna smirked. "Parsons, you can't be serious."

"Why not?"

She laughed. "Parsons, if you were the last man on earth and I had to date you to stay alive, I'd commit suicide." The detectives laughed.

"Good one." Parsons grinned. "But could you give me a real reason why you wouldn't want to go out with me?"

"Goodness!" Brianna laughed. "I can probably think of a million! You accused my partner of rape. You're a downright nasty person. You accused me of breaking the law and busting Steven out of jail. You searched my home and threatened to arrest me. Need another reason?"

Parsons straightened the collar of his blazer. "See, that's what's wrong with chicks. Women always hanging on to the past."

She grinned. "Get lost, Parsons. If I see Jesus before you, then it will still be too soon."

"Okay fine." He moved from the desk. "I guess I have to find another young lady who'd like to see Brian McKnight live, at the VIP table."

"Hold on!" Brianna sprung from her desk like a root. "Did you say Brian McKnight?" Parsons nodded. "Uh, you can pick me up at seven. You already know the address."

"Bree!" Steven stood. "You're actually gonna go out with *Parsons*?"

"Steven, I'd go with the Grand Dragon of the Ku Klux Klan if he had Brian McKnight tickets!"

"I don't believe this." Steven looked at Brianna. "You're gonna go out with the man that nearly ruined my life and my career, Bree? This is certainly turning out to be one hell of a weird day."

"I'll be at your place on the dot, Brianna." Parsons winked.

"Oh, just a minute, what's your first name?" she asked.

"Wilbur." He smiled.

"*Wilbur*?" all the detectives shouted in unison.

"Lord, have mercy." Brianna walled her eyes. "What's your middle name then?"

"Rupert."

"*Rupert!*" the detectives shouted.

"Wait. Your name is Wilbur Rupert Parsons?" Steven grimaced.

"Yes." Parsons looked around. "Something wrong with that?"

"Uh, maybe you should think of officially changing your name to 'Agent.'" Brianna sighed. Parsons left.

"I can't believe you're going out with him, Bree."

"Oh, Steven, please. It is definitely nothing romantic. I'd go out with a cockroach to see Brian McKnight." She laughed. "By the way, when you left for a month, where in the hell did you go?"

He cleared his throat. "Oh, uh, I was taking care of business. I had to lay low to sniff the guy out."

A short, bald detective walked up. He patted Steven on the back. "Hey, Steve! Heard you racked up a fortune in Vegas, man! Way to go!" He walked off.

Brianna blinked. "What did he say?"

"Nothing." Steven rummaged through papers.

"Wait a minute. I know he didn't say your ass was in Vegas."

"Well, I had to find a place to lay low and..."

"Steve! I don't believe you!"

"What?" He grinned.

"You had the nerve to go gambling in Vegas when all hell broke loose down here?"

"I had to get my hands on some extra money. You just be glad I came back when I did. I saved your life, Bree."

"I cannot believe you, Steven. *Vegas*?" Jersey walked out with a file. "Captain, Steve had the nerve to go to Vegas while we were trying to save his ass from prison! Aren't you shocked?"

Jersey guffawed. "I would be if I could stop laughing!" The other officers joined in on the fun.

"It isn't funny at all!" Brianna looked at her peers.

Jersey held her stomach. "The hell it's not!"

Everyone laughed.

Cheyenne Wilson walked up. "Excuse me."

"Miss Wilson." Steven looked at Brianna. "Didn't expect to see you down here. Is everything all right?"

She shrugged. "I heard that you caught the rapist. I guess I wanted to make sure for myself that it was the truth."

"Yes." Brianna nodded. "He's in the holding cell now. Uh, we would have called you to let you know any details."

Cheyenne looked at Steven. "No, I didn't come here just for that. I wanted to apologize to Detective Kemp."

He stood. "Cheyenne, you don't have to do that."

"Yes, I do, Detective. I treated you horribly. I saw everything you went through, and it was because of me."

"No." He smiled. "It was because of the rapist. It wasn't your fault I looked just like him. *I* didn't even know I did." He chuckled. "I don't want you to feel you did anything wrong. You're the victim in this, not me."

"So?" She looked at her purse. "He won't get off, will he?"

"No way. Especially after coming after a cop." Brianna smiled. "And we're gonna do all we can, personally, to make sure he pays."

"As long as we have you and the other victims to come forward and do their part." Steven rubbed Cheyenne's arm.

"I will, don't worry. He's ruined all of our lives, the least I can do is make sure he suffers for it." Cheyenne glanced around the station. "How come I get the strange feeling it's not over?"

Brianna walked toward her. "It'll feel like that to you for a while, Cheyenne. But in time, things will become clear again. And you'll be able to live a normal life. You'll be able to let go of what happened to you."

"And we'll be here if you need us." Steven smiled.

A Week Later

Melody had become addicted to sitting on the porch in the afternoons after work. Sarah constantly teased her, claiming Melody had become an old lady before her eyes. Melody sipped the spicy tea. She loved her new rocking chair. She loved looking into the street. She hadn't realized how beautiful her own neighborhood could be. Hell, Sarah always talked about going to Paris.

Melody grinned. She promised she'd take Melody there soon. Paris didn't have anything on this. Melody couldn't remember the last time she felt so carefree. Well, at least not since Keith Taylor entered her life.

Keith. She stopped rocking. Her mind drifted to that dark planet she tried so hard to escape from. Who could blame her? It would definitely take some time to let go. Sarah had been so strong. She spent her time consoling

Melody. Yet she knew Sarah was dying inside. Melody wished Sarah could finally find a happy ending.

She often wondered what Keith felt. She knew he probably thought about Sarah constantly in jail. Did he ever think about what he'd done to Melody? Melody wished she could see a sign that he had some remorse. Maybe then she could move on.

She rubbed her shoulder and stomach. Stitches were a small price to pay if it meant that Keith finally got what he deserved. She rocked again. Funny, she still felt sorry for him.

She and Sarah would have to deal with him again once the trial began. Melody would take things one day at a time. Unlike Keith, she believed in letting destiny run its course.

The front door opened. Sarah relaxed beside the house in jeans and a flimsy T-shirt. Melody grinned. Sarah displayed a more comfortable style of dress these days. Her thick blonde ponytail blew across her face. She flicked it back with a simple nod. Her green eyes stared in midair. Melody often tried to guess what Sarah thought about these days. They never talked about Keith. They felt it was the only way to move on.

"So, when's Aileen leaving?" Sarah slipped her hands in her pockets.

"Next Monday." Melody rocked. "I can't believe it. My best friend is moving to Dallas."

"Well, you can't blame her. I mean, Jonovan got that

job as supervisor of the headquarters down there." Sarah whistled. "Shit, that's sweet, man." Melody nodded. "I mean, after driving those trucks all this time, now he'll be in charge of the people who drive them." They grinned.

"Yep." Melody sipped. "It'll be good for Aileen, too. I keep teasing her, saying she'll be bored as hell without friends. I know it's not true. Aileen could make friends anywhere. She adjusts quickly."

"How's she doing? You know, since the rape?"

Melody drifted to her own rape for a second. She shook the memory away. "She's doing better. She seems so much like her old self sometimes I gotta wonder if she's just pretending, you know?"

Sarah sat beside her on the upside-down flowerpot.

"And do *you* pretend, Mel?" Sarah looked at the yard. "I want you to know that you don't ever have to hide how you're feeling from me." She took Melody's hand. "I'm always here for you. I always will be. Nothing will change that."

"Funny. I think I worry more about you, Sarah, than you ever could about me."

She stood. She stretched. "Nonsense. Nothing happened to me. It all happened to you."

"No, it happened to both of us, Sarah." Melody shook her head. "Maybe you need to face it and stop feeling guilty." Sarah sighed. "I know you don't want to talk about it, but it won't bother me if that's what you're thinking. Sarah, I love you. I don't hold what happened against you. You only loved Keith. You didn't make him do the things he did."

"I don't know how you can be so understanding with me, after the shit I put you through, Melody. You were right all along and I didn't stand by you. I'll never forgive myself for that." She leaned against the house. "I'm giving up men. It'll be a long time before I even look at one again."

"You?" Melody grinned.

"I'm serious."

"Oh please!" Melody stood. She laughed so hard she nearly dropped her cup. "You couldn't give up men for a month, Sarah."

"Yes, I could!" She chuckled. "I'm not this needy thing, if that's what you think. What's a man, anyway, but a big fat liar? And after that mess we just went through... how could I trust someone new?"

"Being alone isn't the answer, Sarah." Melody took her hand. "I almost lost Lucas because I pushed him away. Then I realized how happy he made me. I realized that in order to get through this, I needed him. I *wanted* him." Sarah nodded. "Sarah, when you're in love for real, it's gonna be so different from anything you've ever experienced. You just need to stop looking and let it find *you*."

"I can't believe this. *You're* giving *me* advice about men?" Sarah shook her head. "Must be a full moon coming tonight!" Melody laughed. They hugged. A red sports car with tinted windows drove up. "Who's that?" Sarah couldn't make out the driver.

"Jeff," Melody whispered. He got out looking as handsome as ever. His eyes immediately found Sarah's. He straightened the end of his navy-blue T-shirt. Soft, indigo jeans hugged his muscular bottom. He stopped before reaching the porch. He watched Sarah as if she were the only woman in the world.

"Hey, Mel." He waved. She smiled. "Hi, Sarah."

"Jeff." She nodded.

"Hi. Uh, Melody, I came for that file that Mr. Lawson asked you to look over. I want to check over it before tomorrow."

"Oh yeah!" She snapped her fingers. She set the tea on the rocking chair. "I'll be right back." She ran into the house.

Jeff moved closer to the porch. "She seems to be doing well. I'm glad things are getting better for her."

"Yeah." Sarah looked at the front door. She turned from his gaze. "Did you really come all the way over here for that file? You could have called. Melody would have gone to work extra early if you needed her to."

"Yeah, I know," he exhaled. "I wanted to see how you were doing. I know this has been very hard on you. Uh, I wanted to let you know that I've seen Keith in jail."

She rubbed her face. "He wanted me to tell you he loves you."

"Well, I don't want to hear it. And I would appreciate

it if you wouldn't come over here with little messages from Keith."

"Sarah, that's not why I came. I just wanted you to know that someone is here for you." She looked at him. "If Melody isn't there or your friends, then you can always come to me. I want to help you in any way I can."

"Jeff, I know that you have feelings for me, right?" He shrugged. "But I'm not ready to even think of being with a man right now. It will be a long time before I trust another man again."

"Sarah, I completely understand." He smiled. "I want to be your friend, though. And I'm not doing it for any other reason than to just be there."

"I appreciate that." She smiled.

Melody walked out with the file. "Here you go, Jeff."

"Thanks." Jeff slid it under his arm. "Sarah, remember what I said, okay? And there's still some good men left in the world. I'd like to think I'm one of them. Just don't let Keith make you think otherwise, okay?" She nodded. "See you, Melody."

"Bye, Jeff." She waved. He looked at Sarah for the longest time, and drove off seconds later. "What was that about?" Melody asked Sarah.

Sarah grinned. "It's about *me*...finally being the one in control." She put her arms around Melody's shoulders.

Melody smiled.

THE END

About the Author

Stacy-Deanne (pronounced Dee-Anne) was born and raised in Houston, Texas. She began writing professionally at nineteen years old. She is the author of the bestselling compilation biography, *Divas of the New Millennium* and the novel *Everlasting*, published by Strebor Books/Simon & Schuster. She was profiled in the 2006 book, *Literary Divas: The Top 100+ Most Admired African-American Women in Writing*. She is a member of the Author's Guild. She resides in Houston, Texas. You can visit her web sites at www.stacy-deanne.net and www.myspace.com/stacydeanne; email her at stacydeanne1@aol.com; or find her on Facebook.